HORIZON

VOLUME 01 REPRISAL

HORIZON CREATED BY
BRANDON THOMAS AND **JUAN GEDEON**

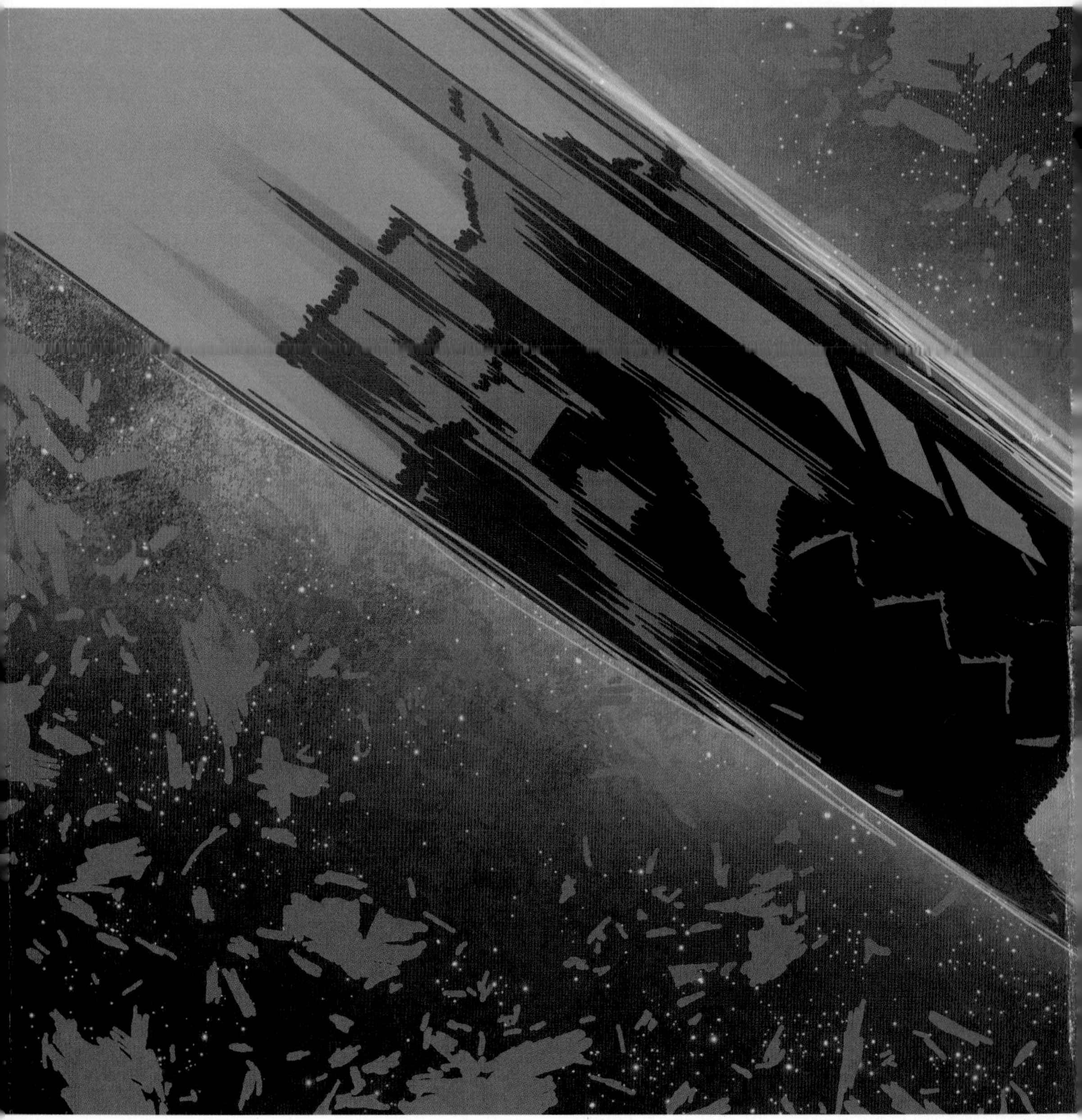

FOR SKYBOUND ENTERTAINMENT

ROBERT KIRKMAN *CHAIRMAN* // **DAVID ALPERT** *CEO* // **SEAN MACKIEWICZ** *EDITORIAL DIRECTOR* // **SHAWN KIRKHAM** *DIRECTOR OF BUSINESS DEVELOPMENT* // **BRIAN HUNTINGTON** *ONLINE EDITORIAL DIRECTOR* // **JUNE ALIAN** *PUBLICITY DIRECTOR* // **JON MOISAN** *EDITOR* // **ARIELLE BASICH** *ASSISTANT EDITOR* // **ANDRES JUAREZ** *GRAPHIC DESIGNER* // **PAUL SHIN** *BUSINESS DEVELOPMENT ASSISTANT* // **JOHNNY O'DELL** *ONLINE EDITORIAL ASSISTANT* // **DAN PETERSEN** *OPERATIONS MANAGER* // **NICK PALMER** *OPERATIONS COORDINATOR*

INTERNATIONAL INQUIRIES: AG@SEQUENTIALRIGHTS.COM
LICENSING INQUIRIES: CONTACT@SKYBOUND.COM

WWW.SKYBOUND.COM

IMAGE COMICS, INC.

ROBERT KIRKMAN *CHIEF OPERATING OFFICER* // **ERIK LARSEN** *CHIEF FINANCIAL OFFICER* // **TODD MCFARLANE** *PRESIDENT* // **MARC SILVESTRI** *CHIEF EXECUTIVE OFFICER* // **JIM VALENTINO** *VICE-PRESIDENT* // **ERIC STEPHENSON** *PUBLISHER* // **COREY MURPHY** *DIRECTOR OF SALES* // **JEFF BOISON** *DIRECTOR OF PUBLISHING PLANNING & BOOK TRADE SALES* // **CHRIS ROSS** *DIRECTOR OF DIGITAL SALES* // **KAT SALAZAR** *DIRECTOR OF PR & MARKETING* // **BRANWYN BIGGLESTONE** *CONTROLLER* // **SUSAN KORPELA** *ACCOUNTS MANAGER* // **DREW GILL** *ART DIRECTOR* // **BRETT WARNOCK** *PRODUCTION MANAGER* // **MEREDITH WALLACE** *PRINT MANAGER* // **BRIAH SKELLY** *PUBLICIST* // **SASHA HEAD** *SALES & MARKETING PRODUCTION DESIGNER* // **DAVID BROTHERS** *BRANDING MANAGER* // **MELISSA GIFFORD** *CONTENT MANAGER* // **ADDISON DUKE** *PRODUCTION ARTIST* // **ERIKA SCHNATZ** *PRODUCTION ARTIST* // **TRICIA RAMOS** *PRODUCTION ARTIST* // **JEFF STANG** *DIRECT MARKET SALES REPRESENTATIVE* // **EMILIO BAUTISTA** *DIGITAL SALES ASSOCIATE* // **LEANNA CAUNTER** *ACCOUNTING ASSISTANT* // **CHLOE RAMOS-PETERSON** *LIBRARY MARKET SALES REPRESENTATIVE*

WWW.IMAGECOMICS.COM

BRANDON THOMAS
WRITER

JUAN GEDEON
ARTIST

FRANK MARTIN
COLORIST

RUS WOOTON
LETTERER

SEAN MACKIEWICZ
EDITOR

ARIELLE BASICH
ASSISTANT EDITOR

JASON HOWARD
COVER

HORIZON VOLUME 1: REPRISAL. FIRST PRINTING. ISBN: 978-1-5343-0047-7. PUBLISHED BY IMAGE COMICS, INC. OFFICE OF PUBLICATION: 2701 NW VAUGHN ST., STE. 780, PORTLAND, OR 97210. COPYRIGHT
© 2017 SKYBOUND, LLC. ALL RIGHTS RESERVED. ORIGINALLY PUBLISHED IN SINGLE MAGAZINE FORM AS HORIZON #1-6. HORIZON™ (INCLUDING ALL PROMINENT CHARACTERS FEATURED HEREIN), ITS LOGO AND
ALL CHARACTER LIKENESSES ARE TRADEMARKS OF SKYBOUND, LLC, UNLESS OTHERWISE NOTED. IMAGE COMICS® AND ITS LOGOS ARE REGISTERED TRADEMARKS AND COPYRIGHTS OF IMAGE COMICS, INC. ALL RIGHTS
RESERVED. NO PART OF THIS PUBLICATION MAY BE REPRODUCED OR TRANSMITTED IN ANY FORM OR BY ANY MEANS (EXCEPT FOR SHORT EXCERPTS FOR REVIEW PURPOSES) WITHOUT THE EXPRESS WRITTEN PERMISSION
OF IMAGE COMICS, INC. ALL NAMES, CHARACTERS, EVENTS AND LOCALES IN THIS PUBLICATION ARE ENTIRELY FICTIONAL. ANY RESEMBLANCE TO ACTUAL PERSONS (LIVING OR DEAD), EVENTS OR PLACES,
WITHOUT SATIRIC INTENT, IS COINCIDENTAL. PRINTED IN THE U.S.A. FOR INFORMATION REGARDING THE CPSIA ON THIS PRINTED MATERIAL CALL: 203-595-3636 AND PROVIDE REFERENCE # RICH - 719466.

LANGUAGE KEY

NATIVE VALIAN   EARTH ENGLISH

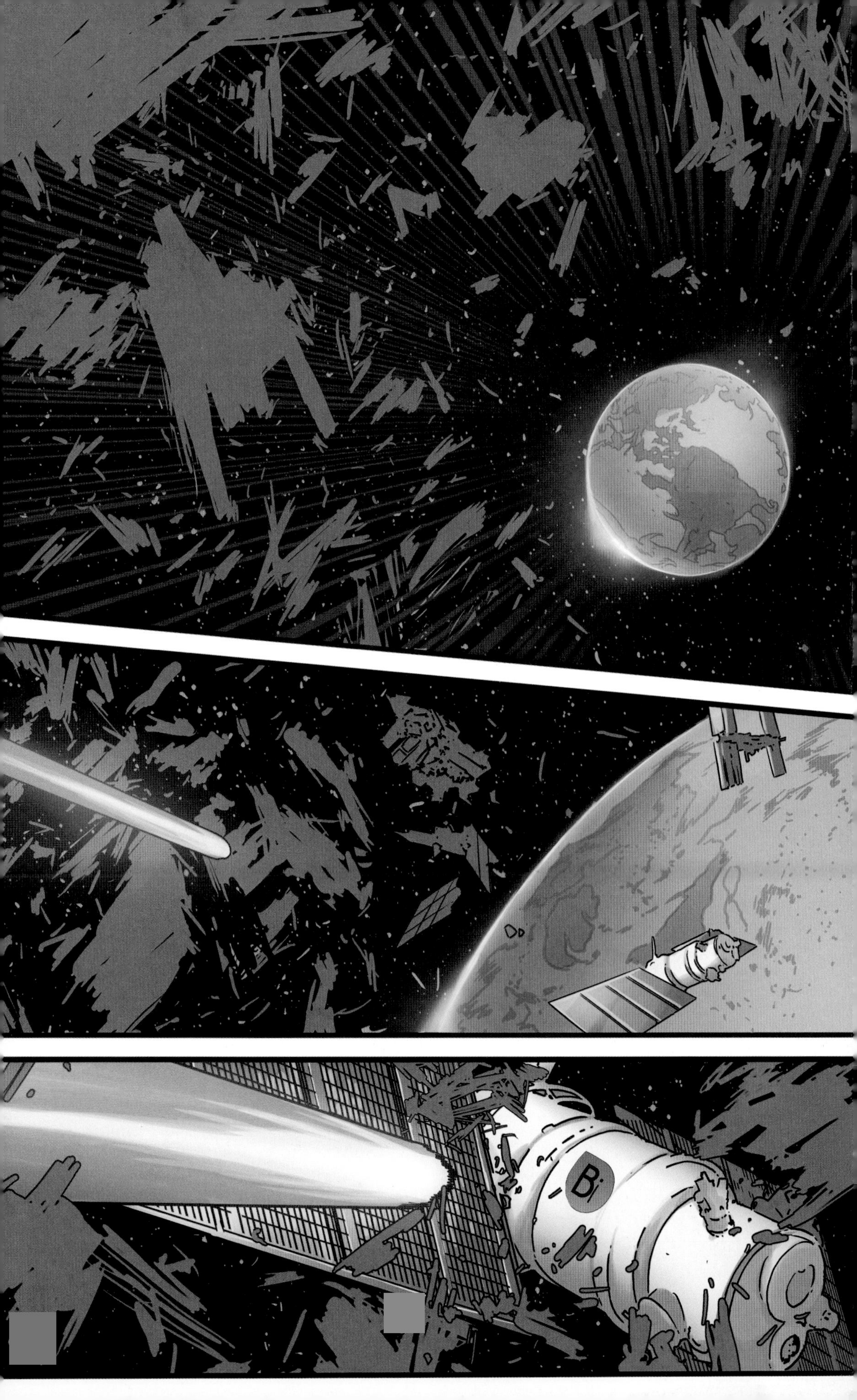
Bi

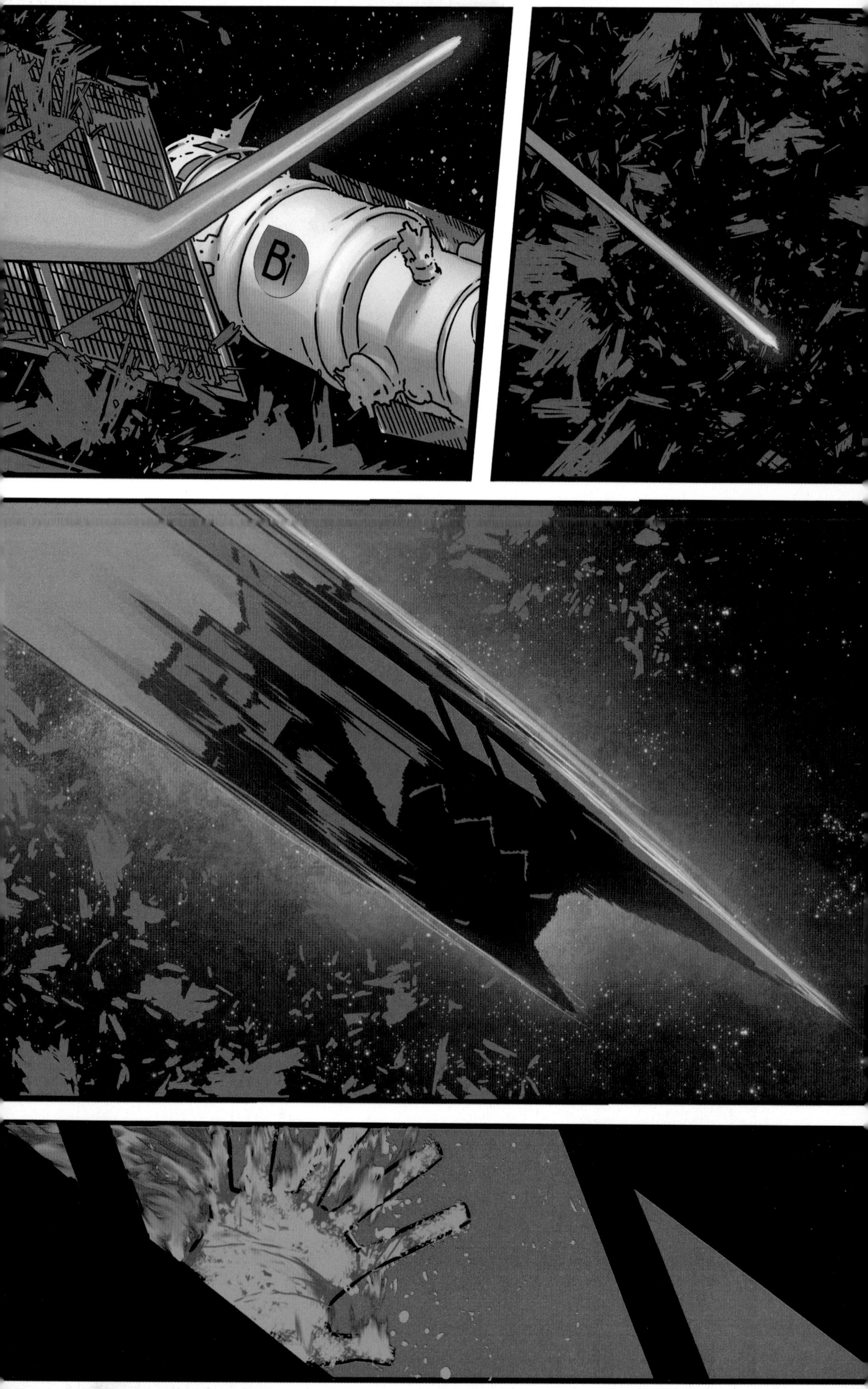
Bi

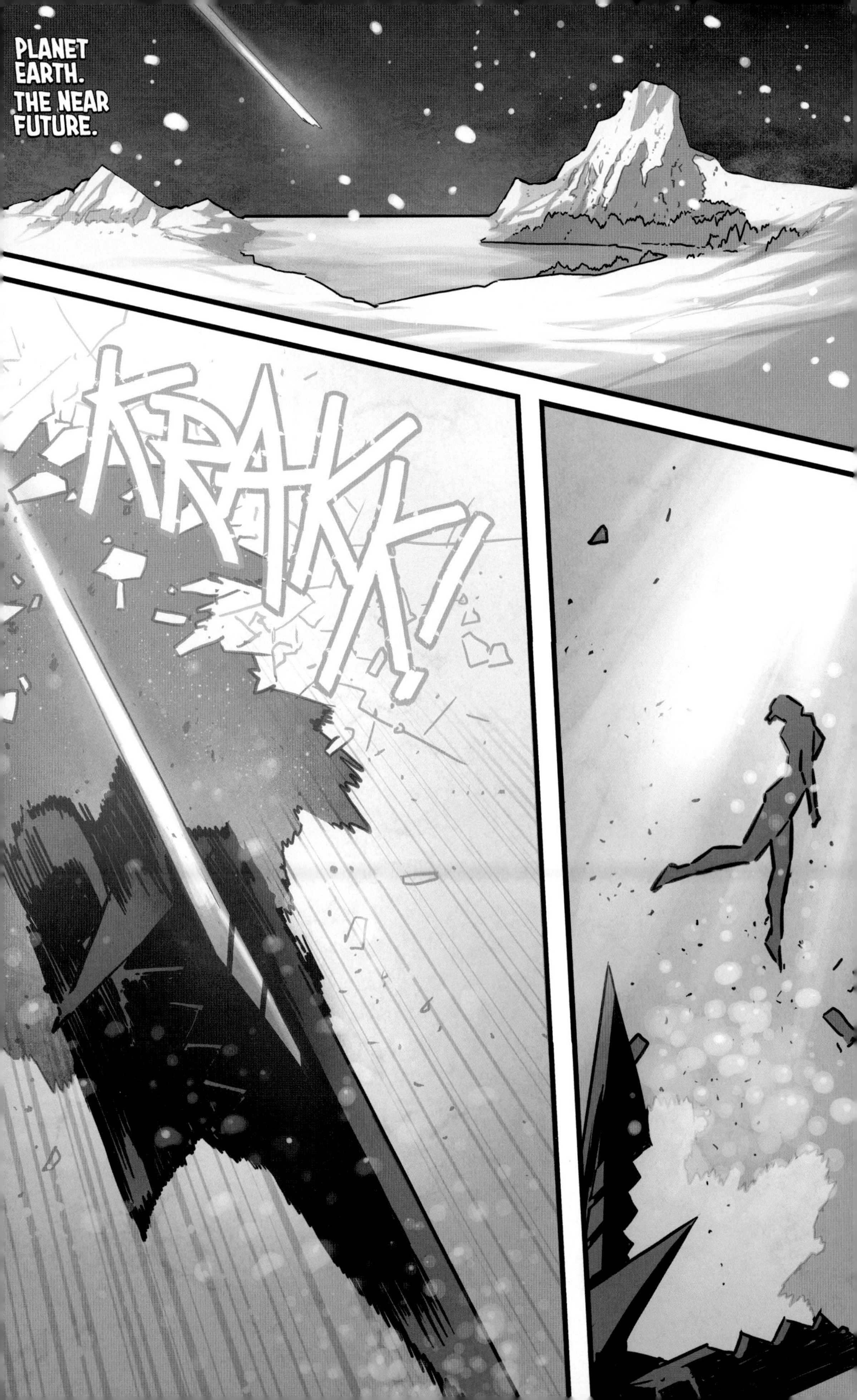
PLANET EARTH.
THE NEAR FUTURE.
KRAKK!

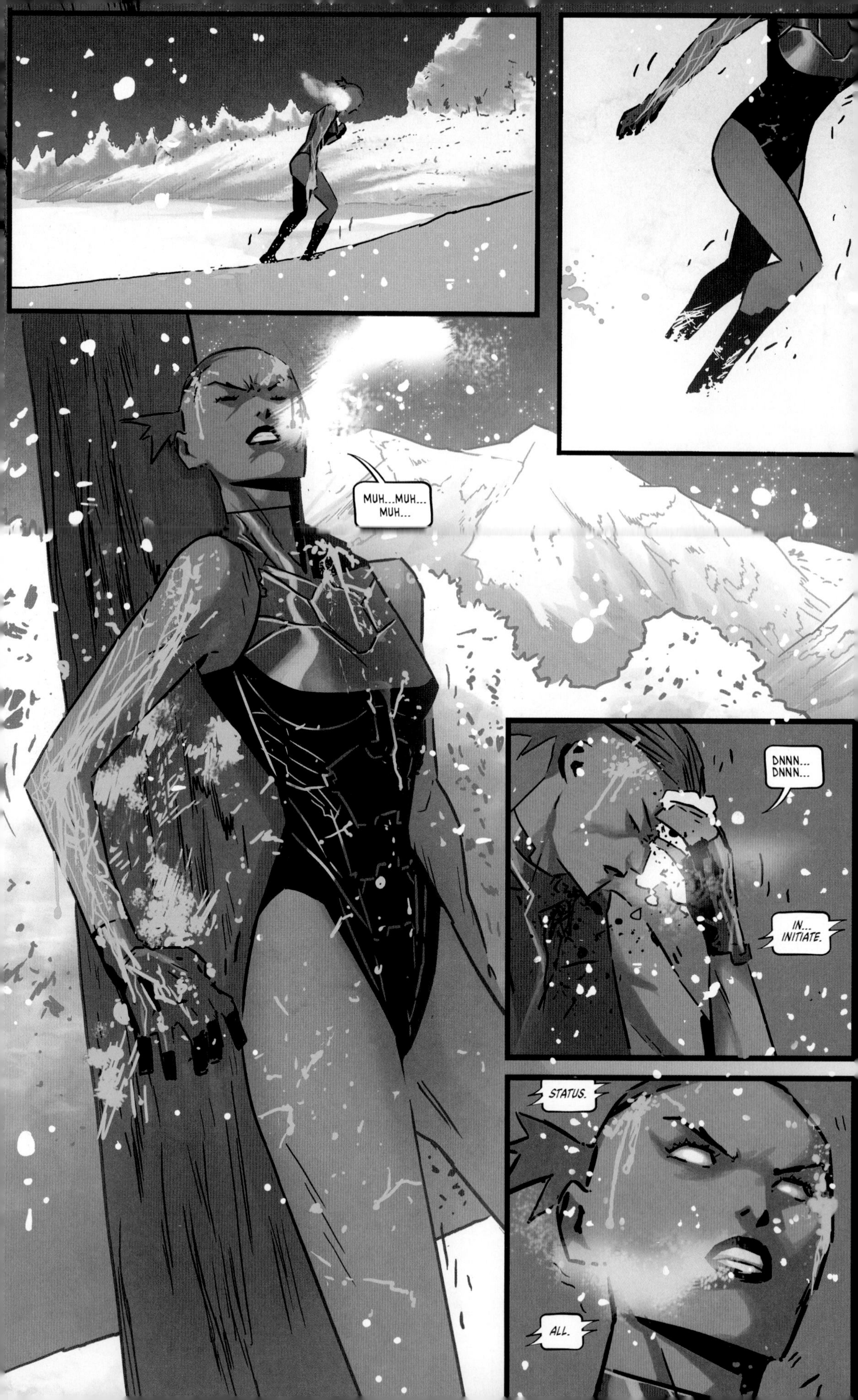
MUH...MUH...
MUH...
DNNN...
DNNN...
IN...
INITIATE.
STATUS.
ALL.

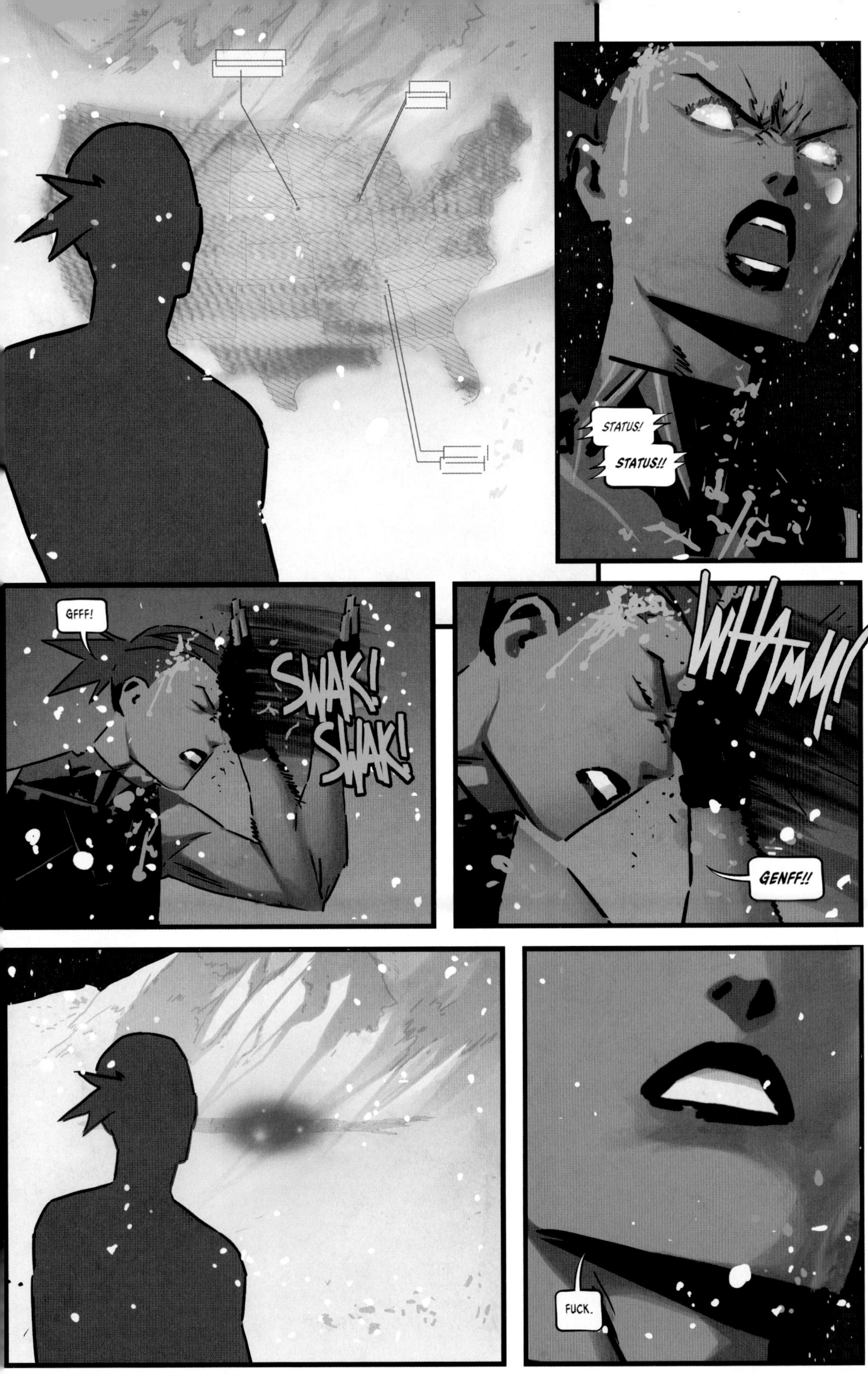
STATUS!
STATUS!!
GFFF!
SWAK!
SWAK!
GENFF!!
FUCK.

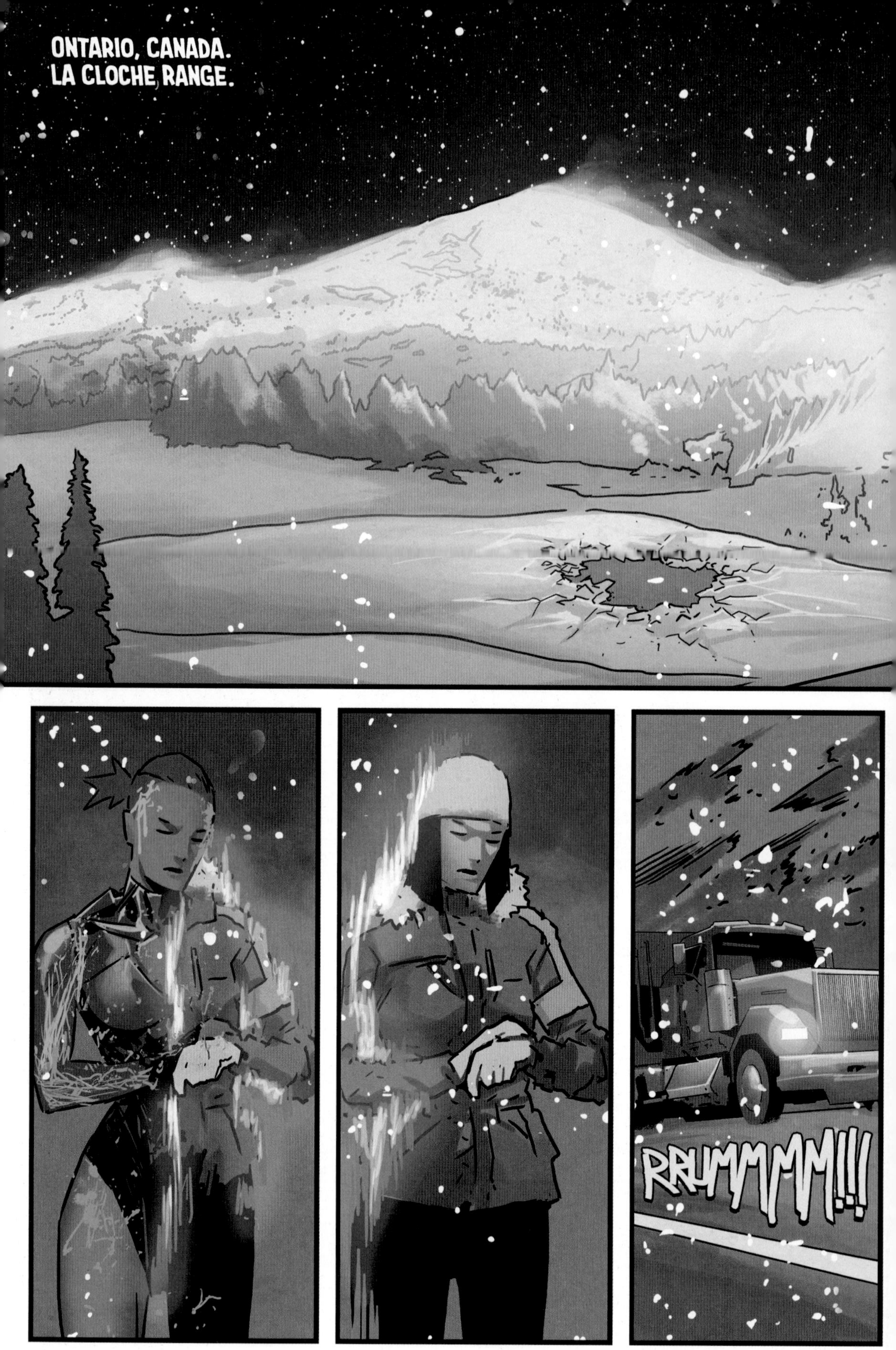
ONTARIO, CANADA.
LA CLOCHE RANGE.
RRUMMMM!!!

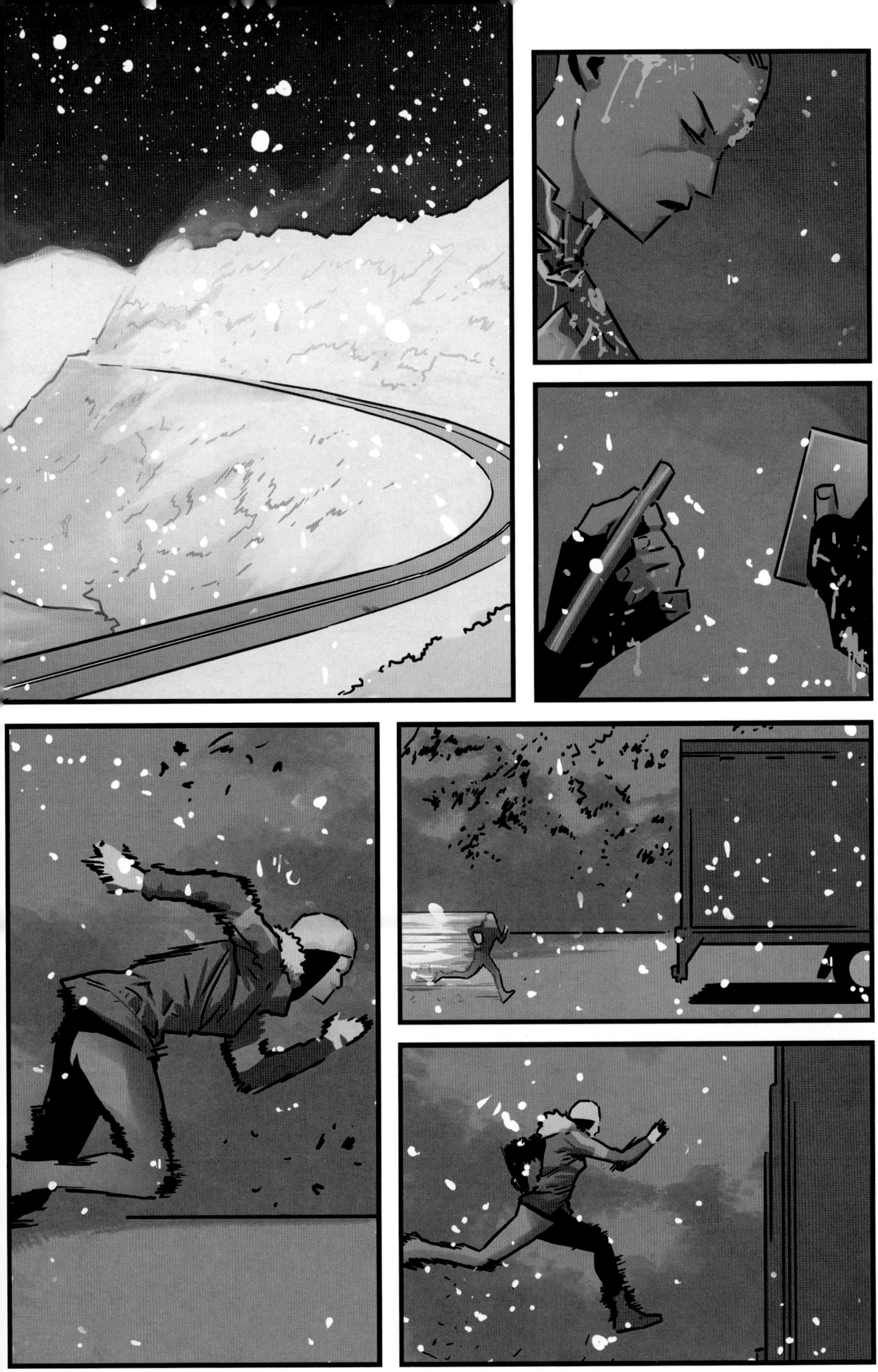

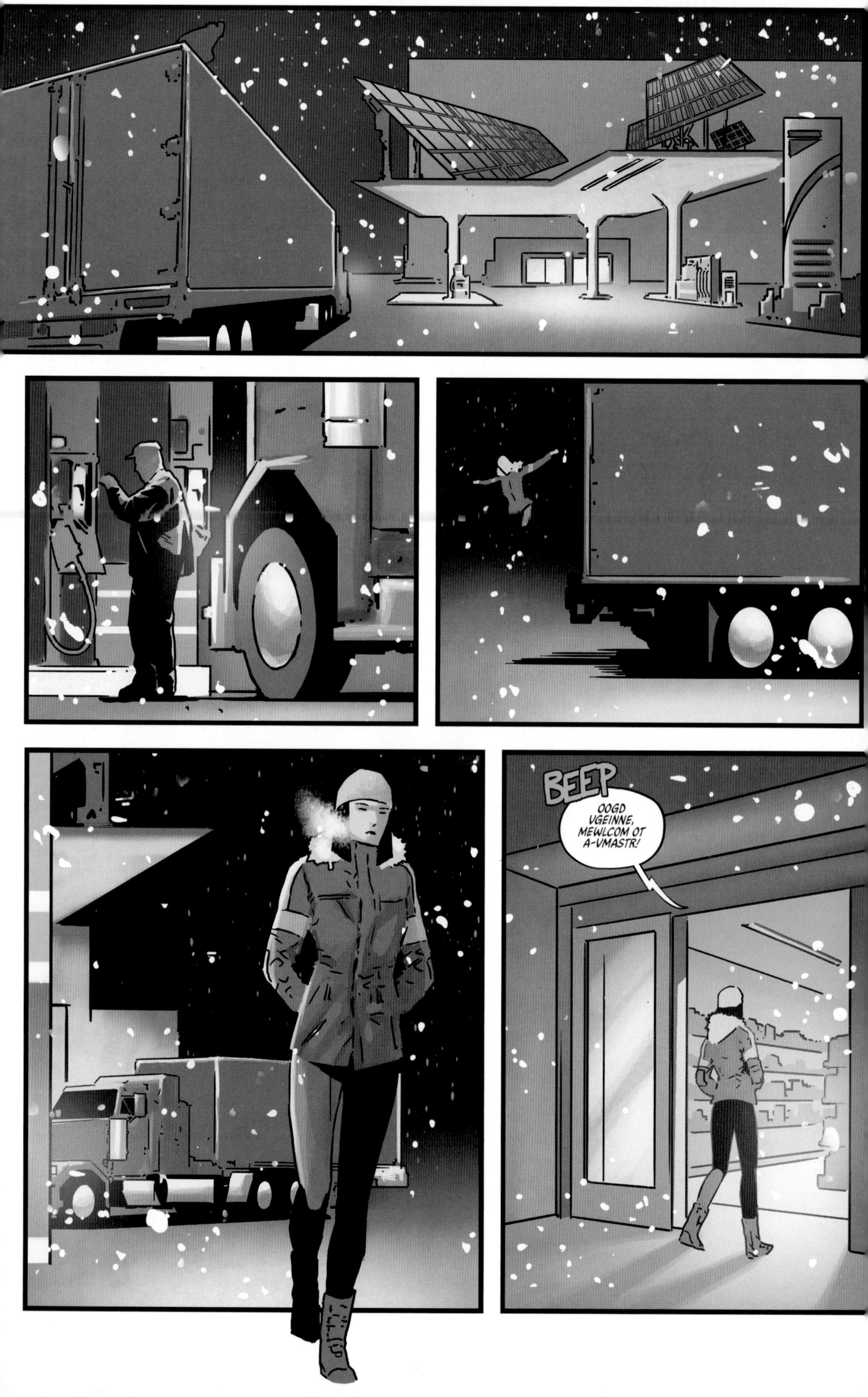
BEEP
OOGD VGEINNE, MEWLCOM OT A-VMASTR!

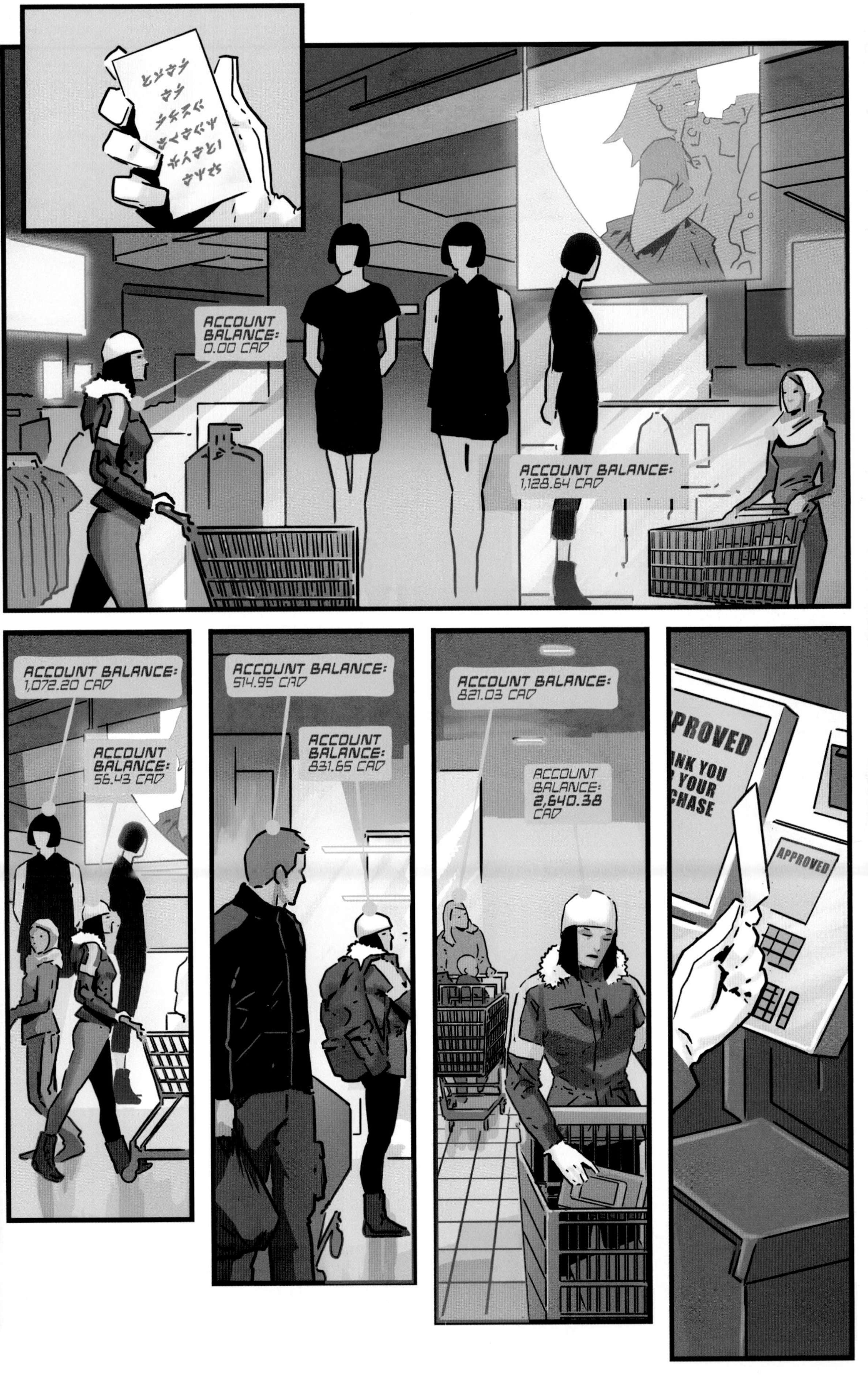

ACCOUNT BALANCE: 0.00 CAD
ACCOUNT BALANCE: 1,128.64 CAD
ACCOUNT BALANCE: 1,072.20 CAD
ACCOUNT BALANCE: 56.43 CAD
ACCOUNT BALANCE: 514.95 CAD
ACCOUNT BALANCE: 831.65 CAD
ACCOUNT BALANCE: 821.03 CAD
ACCOUNT BALANCE: 2,640.38 CAD
PROVED
NK YOU
YOUR
CHASE
APPROVED

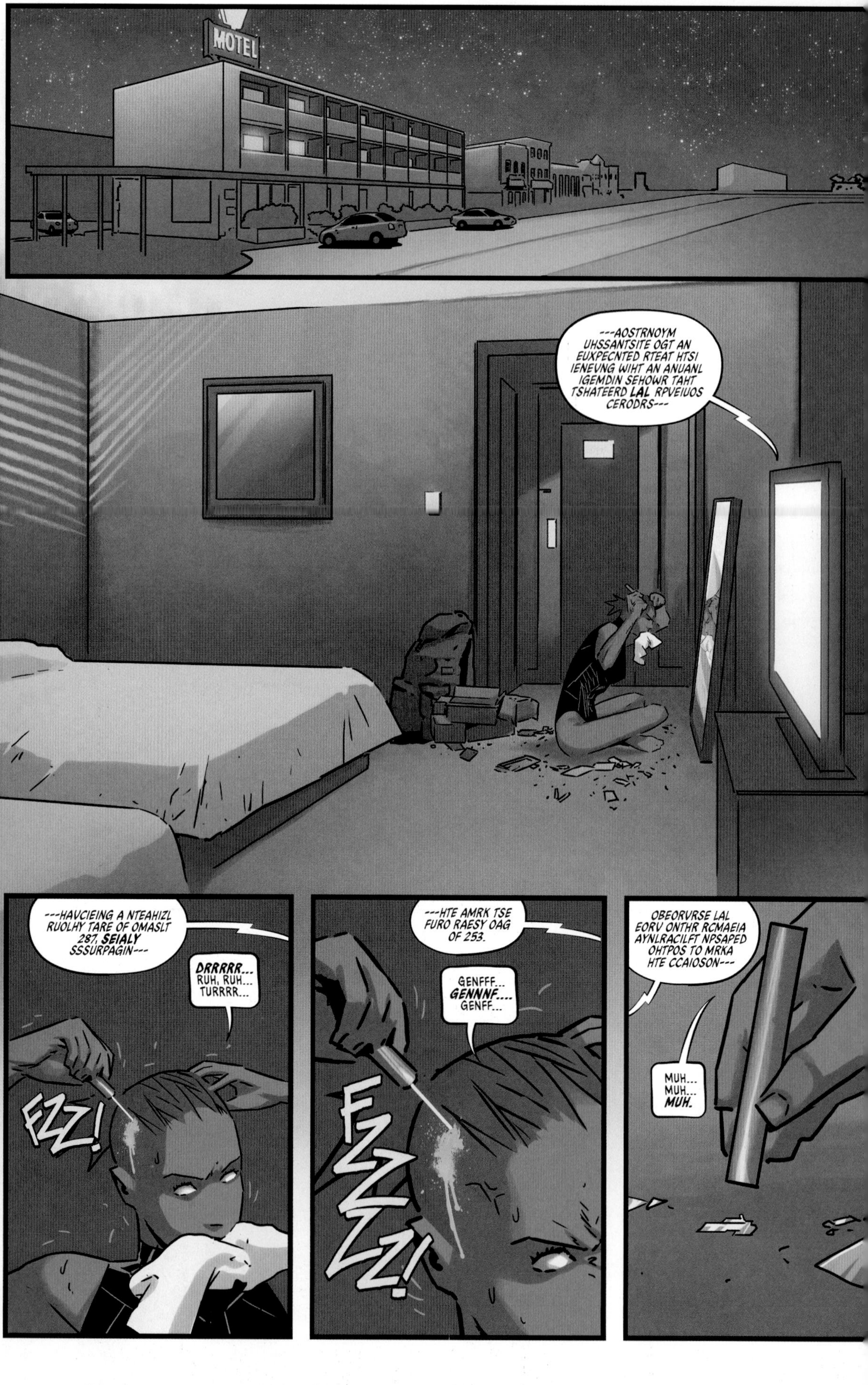
MOTEL
---AOSTRNOYM UHSSANTSITE OGT AN EUXPECNTED RTEAT HTSI IENEVNG WIHT AN ANUANL IGEMDIN SEHOWR TAHT TSHATEERD **LAL** RPVEIUOS CERODRS---
---HAVCIEING A NTEAHIZL RUOLHY TARE OF OMASLT 287, **SEIALY** SSSURPAGIN---
DRRRRR... RUH, RUH... TURRRR...
FZZ!
---HTE AMRK TSE FURO RAESY OAG OF 253.
GENFFF... **GENNNF....** GENFF...
FZZZZ!
OBEORVRSE LAL EORV ONTHR RCMAEIA AYNLRACILFT NPSAPED OHTPOS TO MRKA HTE CCAIOSON---
MUH... MUH... **MUH.**

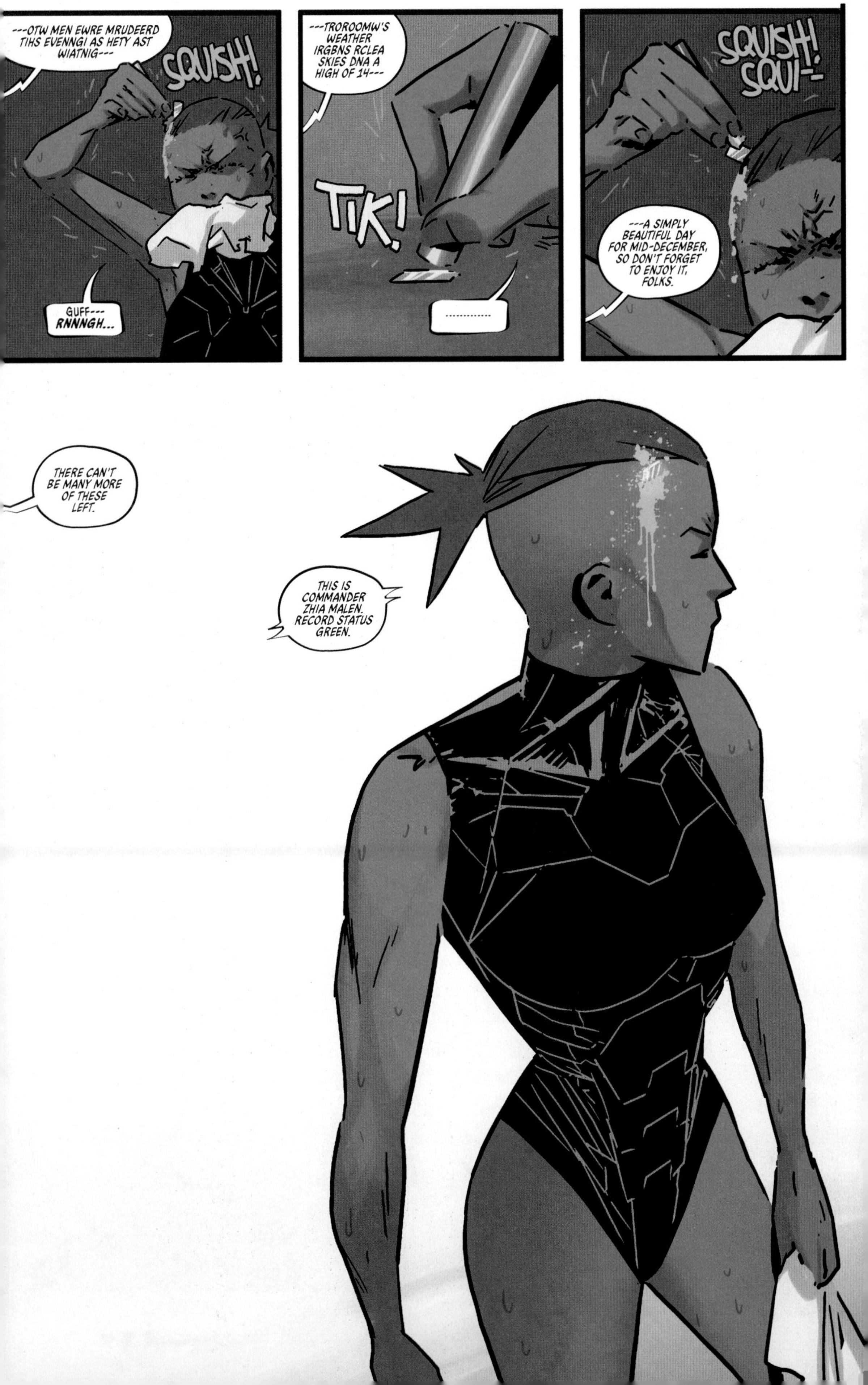
---OTW MEN EWRE MRUDEERD TIHS EVENNGI AS HETY AST WIATNIG---
SQUISH!
GUFF--- RNNNGH...
---TROROOMW'S WEATHER IRGBNS RCLEA SKIES DNA A HIGH OF 14---
TIK!
....
SQUISH! SQUI-
---A SIMPLY BEAUTIFUL DAY FOR MID-DECEMBER, SO DON'T FORGET TO ENJOY IT, FOLKS.
THERE CAN'T BE MANY MORE OF THESE LEFT.
THIS IS COMMANDER ZHIA MALEN. RECORD STATUS GREEN.

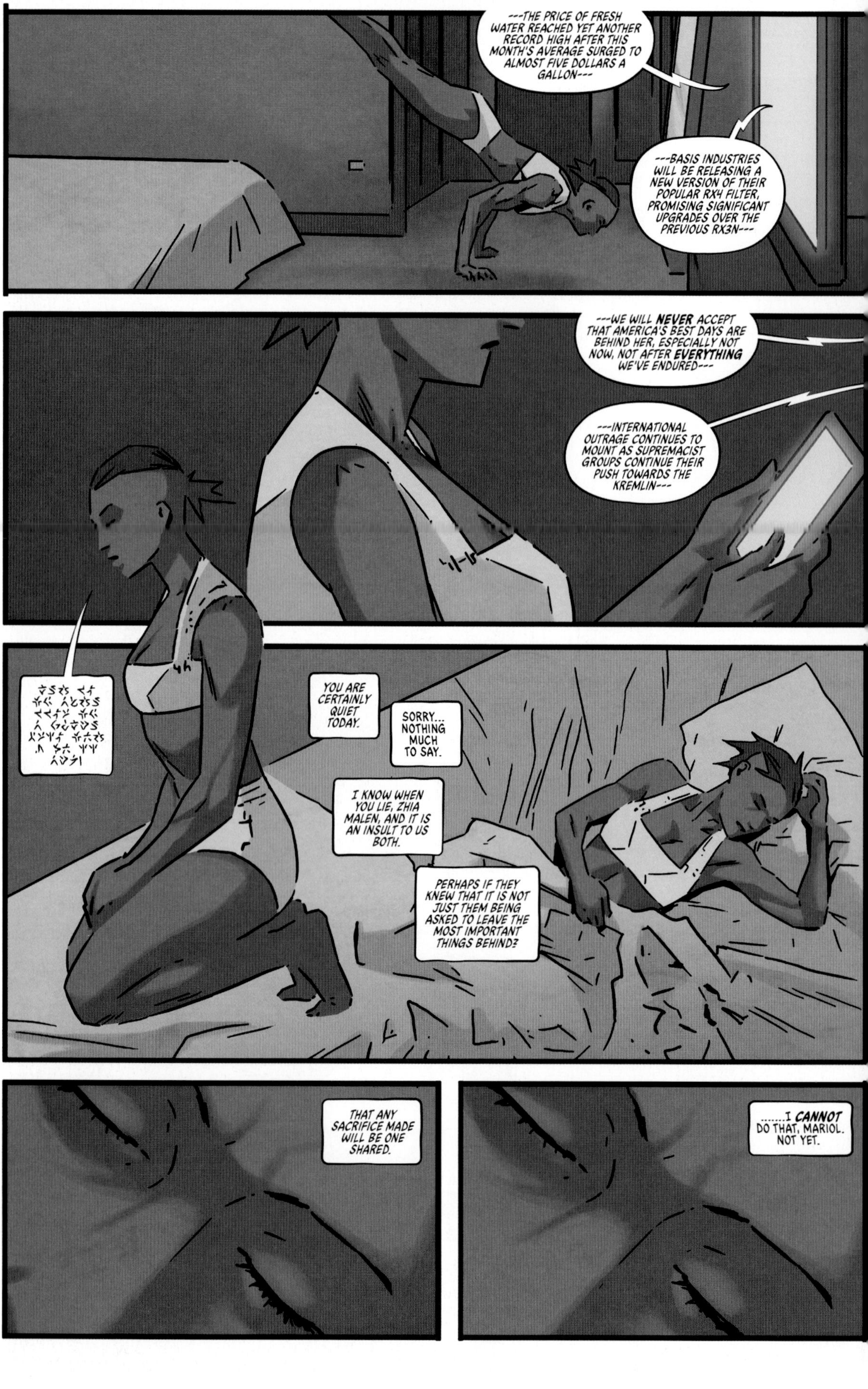

---THE PRICE OF FRESH WATER REACHED YET ANOTHER RECORD HIGH AFTER THIS MONTH'S AVERAGE SURGED TO ALMOST FIVE DOLLARS A GALLON---
---BASIS INDUSTRIES WILL BE RELEASING A NEW VERSION OF THEIR POPULAR RX4 FILTER, PROMISING SIGNIFICANT UPGRADES OVER THE PREVIOUS RX3N---
---WE WILL NEVER ACCEPT THAT AMERICA'S BEST DAYS ARE BEHIND HER, ESPECIALLY NOT NOW, NOT AFTER EVERYTHING WE'VE ENDURED---
---INTERNATIONAL OUTRAGE CONTINUES TO MOUNT AS SUPREMACIST GROUPS CONTINUE THEIR PUSH TOWARDS THE KREMLIN---
YOU ARE CERTAINLY QUIET TODAY.
SORRY... NOTHING MUCH TO SAY.
I KNOW WHEN YOU LIE, ZHIA MALEN, AND IT IS AN INSULT TO US BOTH.
PERHAPS IF THEY KNEW THAT IT IS NOT JUST THEM BEING ASKED TO LEAVE THE MOST IMPORTANT THINGS BEHIND?
THAT ANY SACRIFICE MADE WILL BE ONE SHARED.
.......I CANNOT DO THAT, MARIOL. NOT YET.

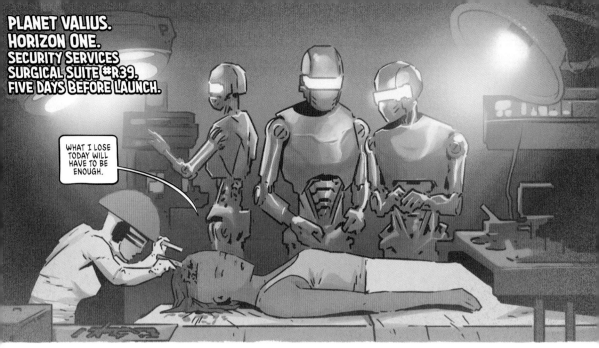

PLANET VALIUS.
HORIZON ONE.
SECURITY SERVICES
SURGICAL SUITE #R39.
FIVE DAYS BEFORE LAUNCH.

WHAT I LOSE TODAY WILL HAVE TO BE ENOUGH.

THIRTY YEARS FROM YOUR LIFE, ZHIA---AND ANY MANNER OF *IRREVERSIBLE* NEUROLOGICAL DAMAGE. ARE YOU TRULY PREPARED TO PAY THAT COST?

IF IT MEANS THAT VALIUS LIVES ON, *YES,* AND IF---

IF YOU WILL HOLD MY HAND.

UNIT 2, HOLD HER, PLEASE.

UNIT 1, EXECUTE PROCEDURE ZVCFT, SIXTH MANEUVER.

I WILL NOT THINK *ANY* LESS OF YOU. I DO ONLY WANT THE VERY BEST FOR YOU.

BUT I STILL DO NOT *DESERVE* IT, MADAME COZA.

BEGIN, DOCTOR.

SKKREEE--WHHINNEEE!

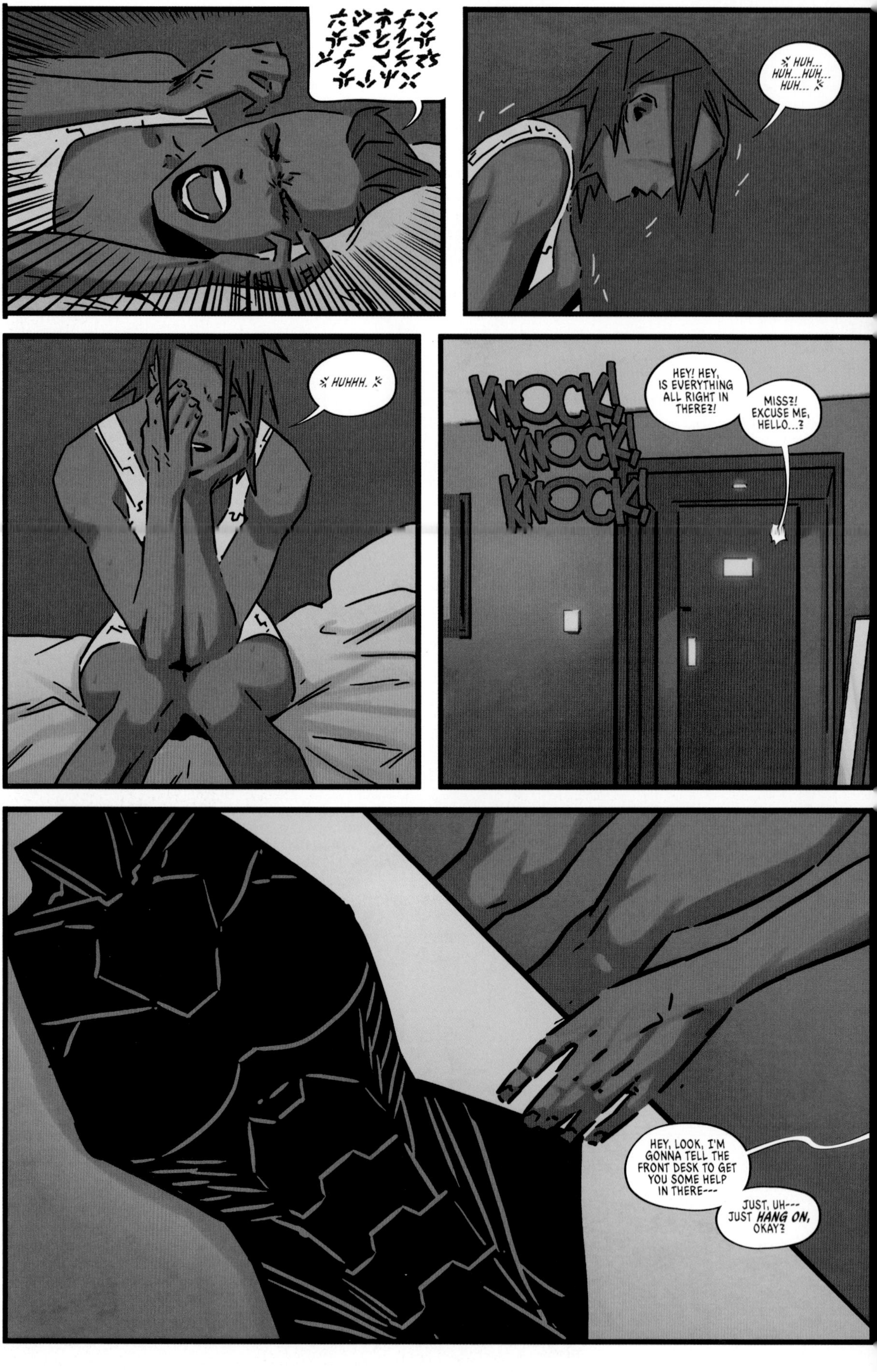
HUH... HUH...HUH... HUH...
HUHHH.
KNOCK! KNOCK! KNOCK!
HEY! HEY, IS EVERYTHING ALL RIGHT IN THERE?!
MISS?! EXCUSE ME, HELLO...?
HEY, LOOK, I'M GONNA TELL THE FRONT DESK TO GET YOU SOME HELP IN THERE---
JUST, UH--- JUST HANG ON, OKAY?

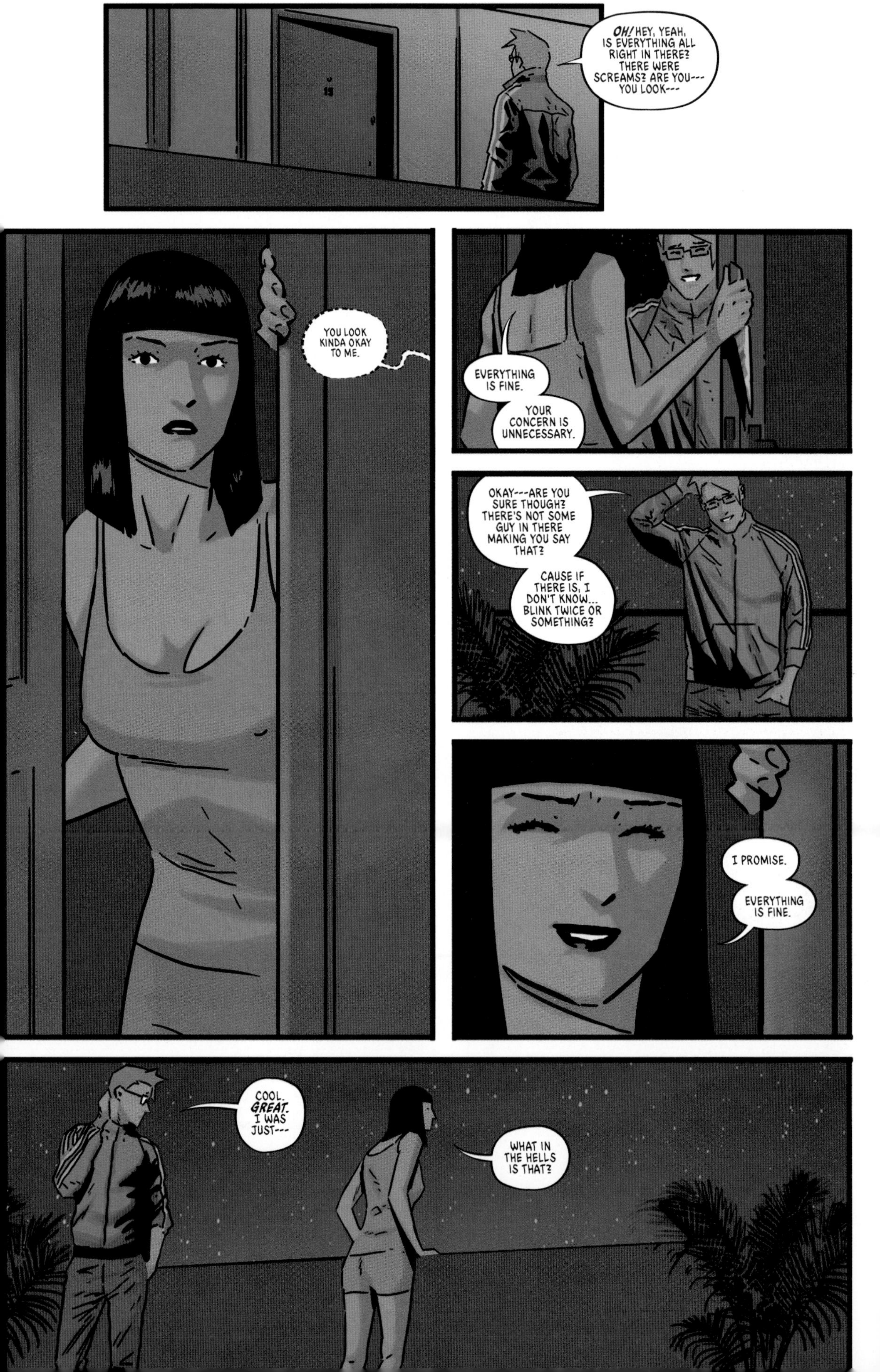
OH! HEY, YEAH, IS EVERYTHING ALL RIGHT IN THERE? THERE WERE SCREAMS? ARE YOU--- YOU LOOK---
YOU LOOK KINDA OKAY TO ME.
EVERYTHING IS FINE.
YOUR CONCERN IS UNNECESSARY.
OKAY---ARE YOU SURE THOUGH? THERE'S NOT SOME GUY IN THERE MAKING YOU SAY THAT?
CAUSE IF THERE IS, I DON'T KNOW... BLINK TWICE OR SOMETHING?
I PROMISE.
EVERYTHING IS FINE.
COOL. GREAT. I WAS JUST---
WHAT IN THE HELLS IS THAT?

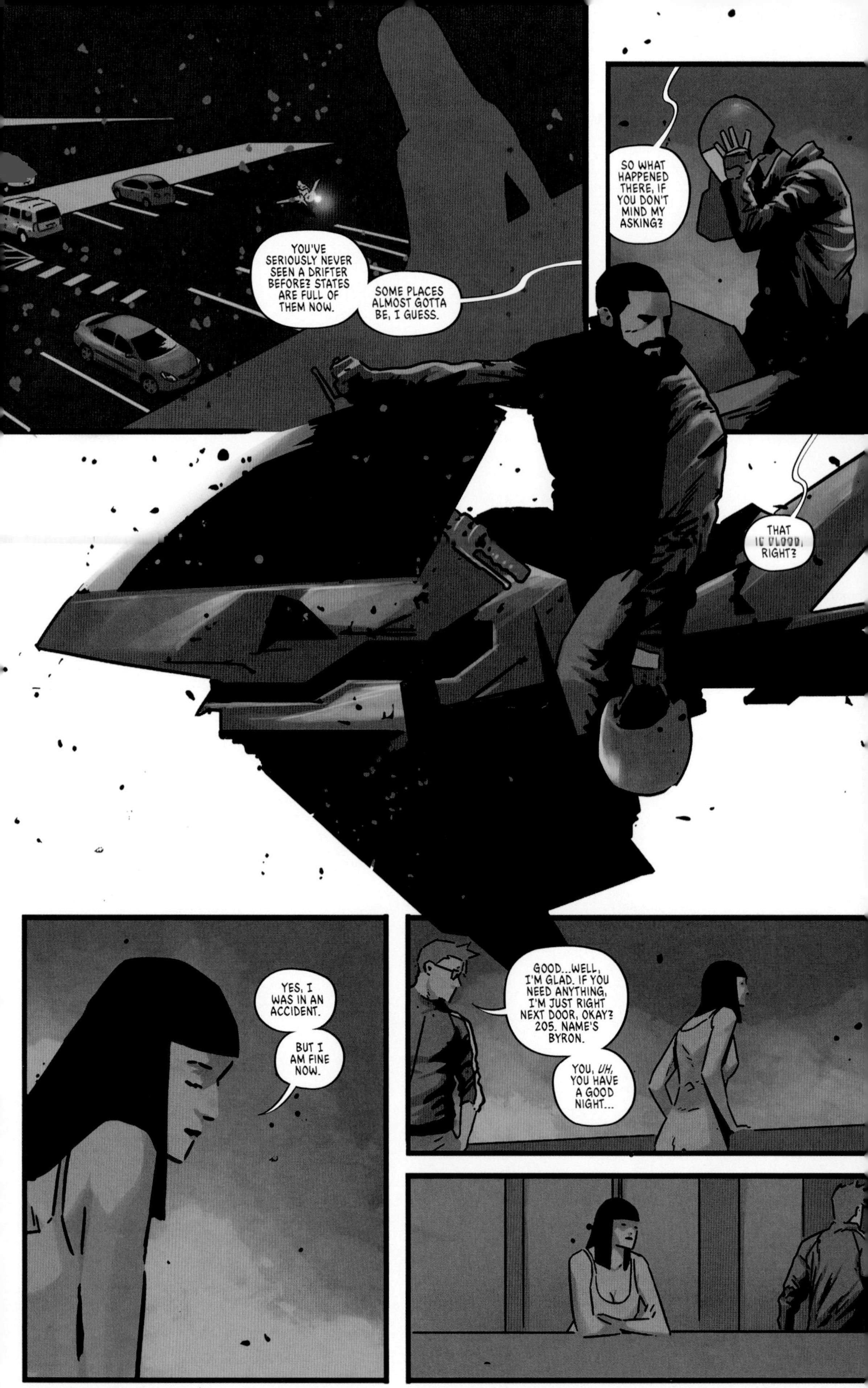

YOU'VE SERIOUSLY NEVER SEEN A DRIFTER BEFORE? STATES ARE FULL OF THEM NOW.
SOME PLACES ALMOST GOTTA BE, I GUESS.
SO WHAT HAPPENED THERE, IF YOU DON'T MIND MY ASKING?
THAT IS BLOOD, RIGHT?
YES, I WAS IN AN ACCIDENT.
BUT I AM FINE NOW.
GOOD...WELL, I'M GLAD. IF YOU NEED ANYTHING, I'M JUST RIGHT NEXT DOOR, OKAY? 205. NAME'S BYRON.
YOU, *UH*, YOU HAVE A GOOD NIGHT...

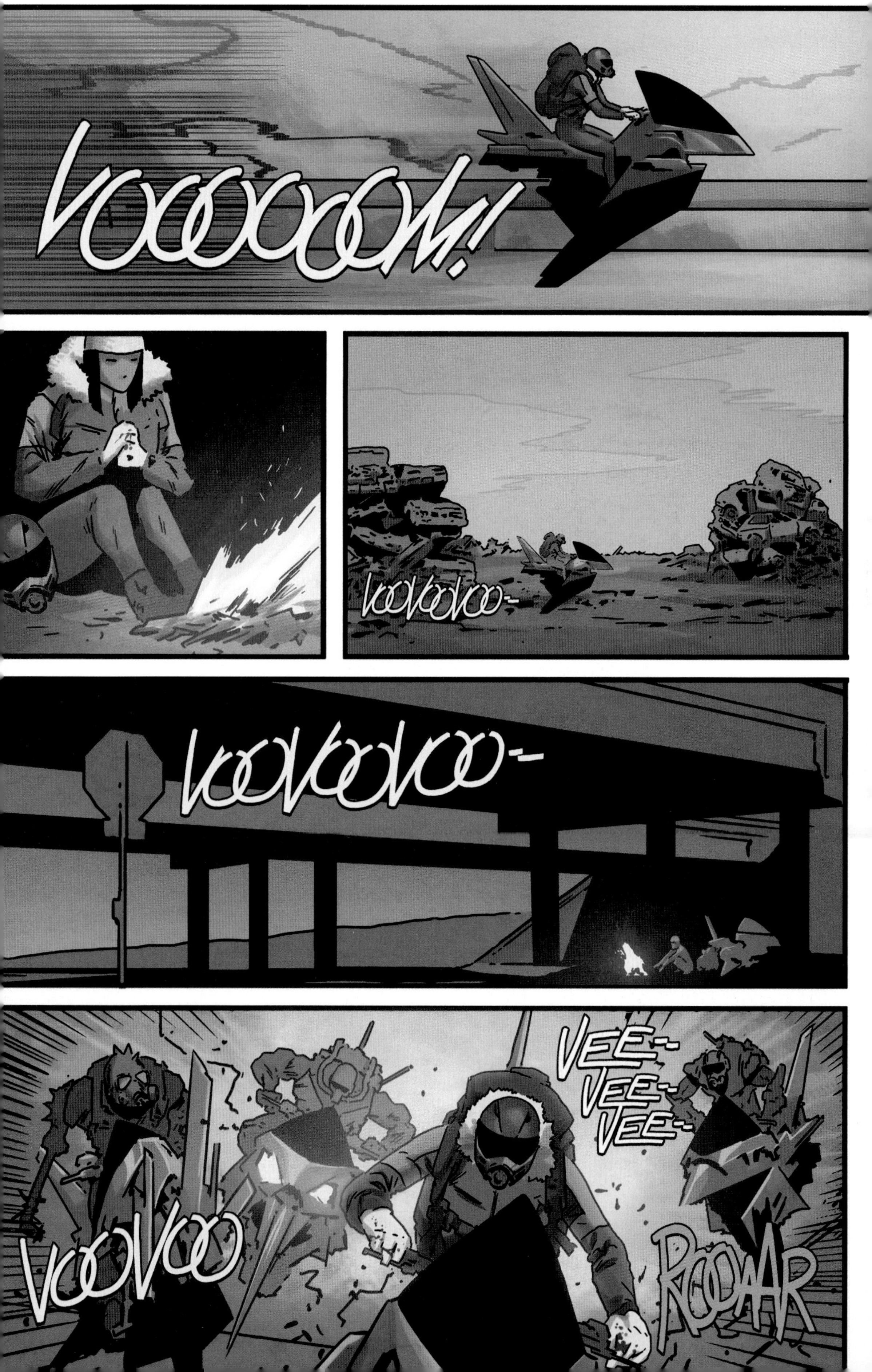
VOOOOOOM!
VOOVOOVOO~
VOOVOOVOO~
VEE~
VEE~
VEE~
VOOVOO
ROOAAR

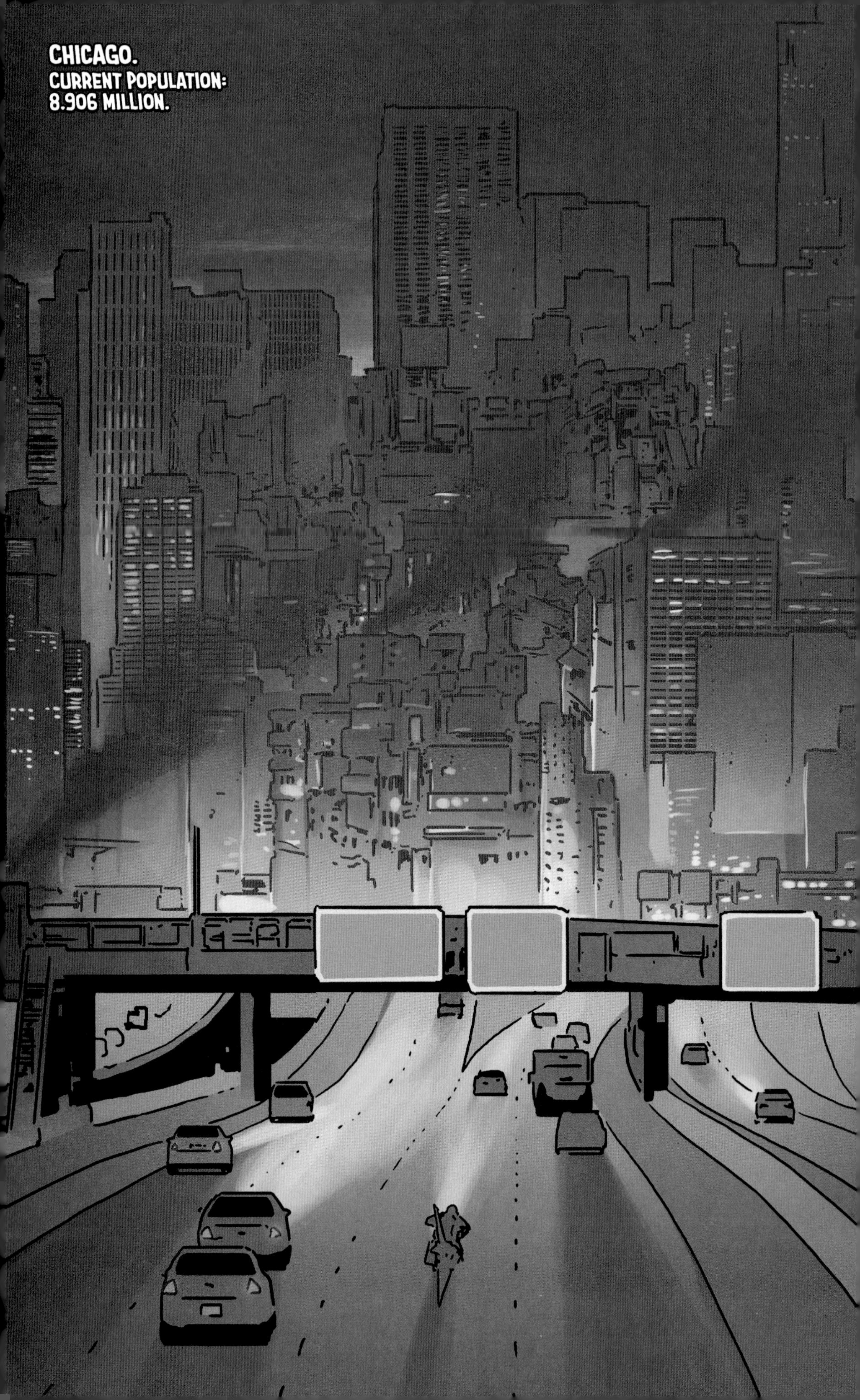
CHICAGO.
CURRENT POPULATION:
8.906 MILLION.

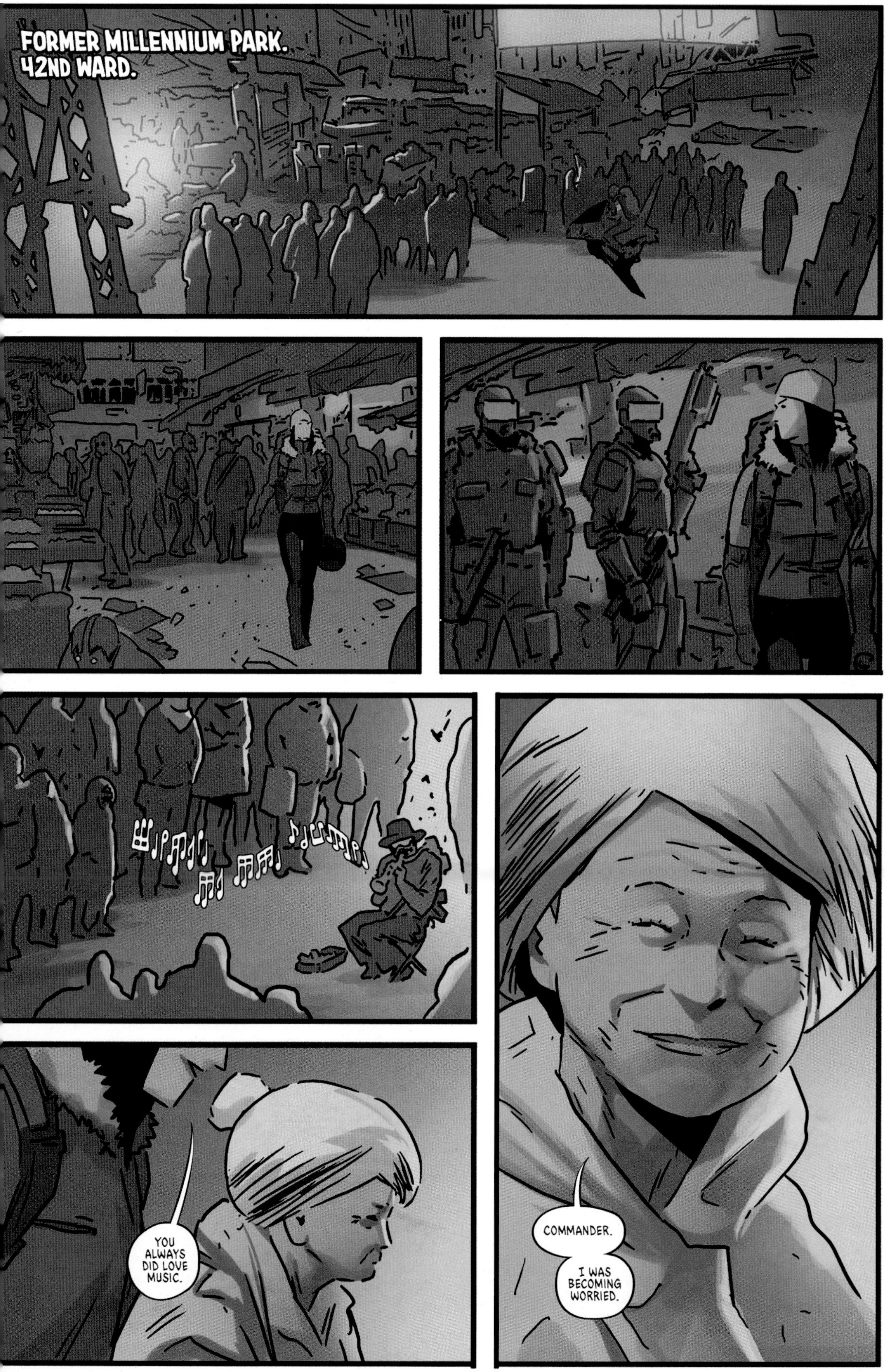
FORMER MILLENNIUM PARK.
42ND WARD.
YOU ALWAYS DID LOVE MUSIC.
COMMANDER.
I WAS BECOMING WORRIED.

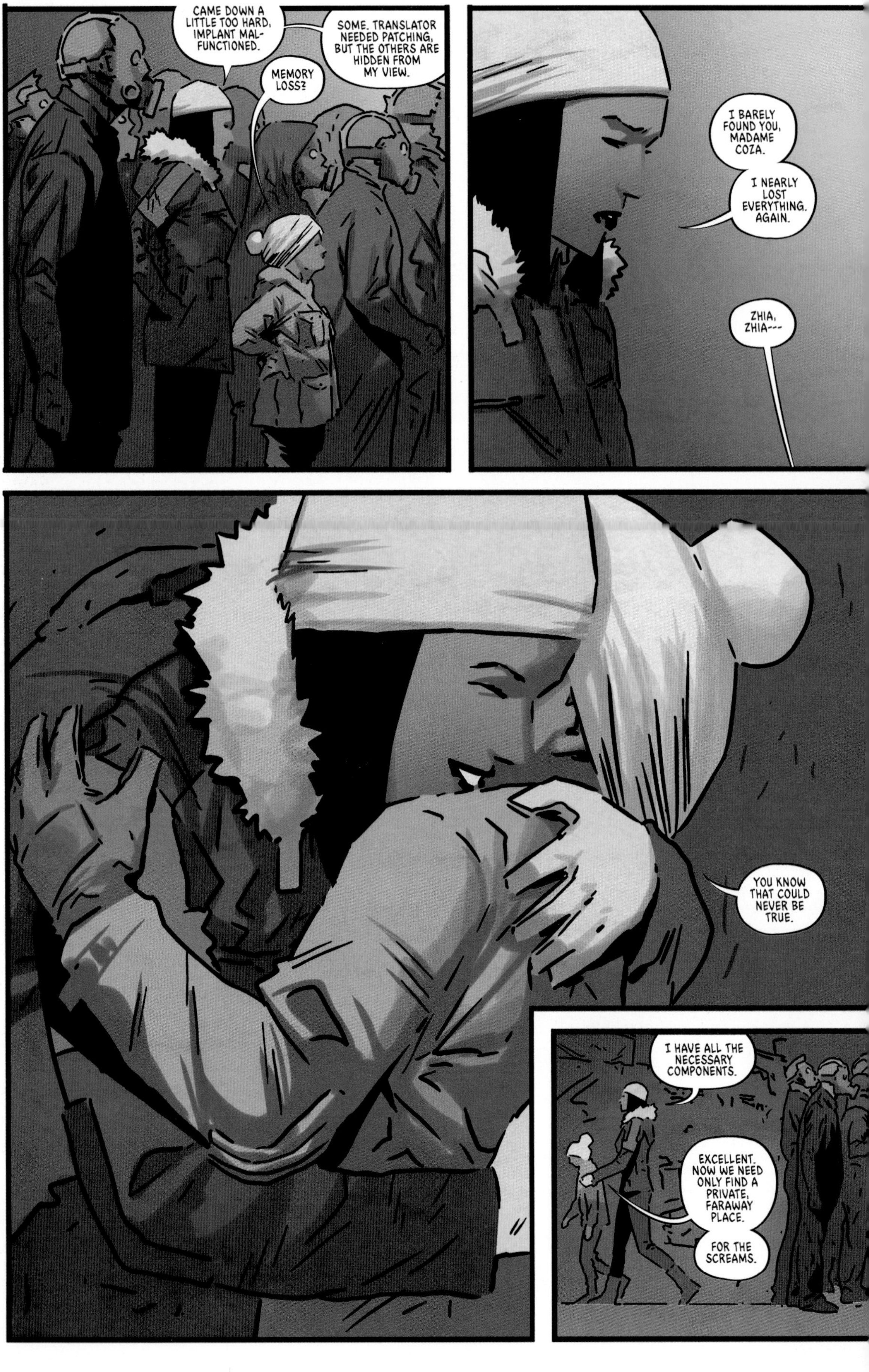
CAME DOWN A LITTLE TOO HARD, IMPLANT MAL-FUNCTIONED.
MEMORY LOSS?
SOME. TRANSLATOR NEEDED PATCHING, BUT THE OTHERS ARE HIDDEN FROM MY VIEW.
I BARELY FOUND YOU, MADAME COZA.
I NEARLY LOST EVERYTHING. AGAIN.
ZHIA, ZHIA---
YOU KNOW THAT COULD NEVER BE TRUE.
I HAVE ALL THE NECESSARY COMPONENTS.
EXCELLENT. NOW WE NEED ONLY FIND A PRIVATE, FARAWAY PLACE.
FOR THE SCREAMS.

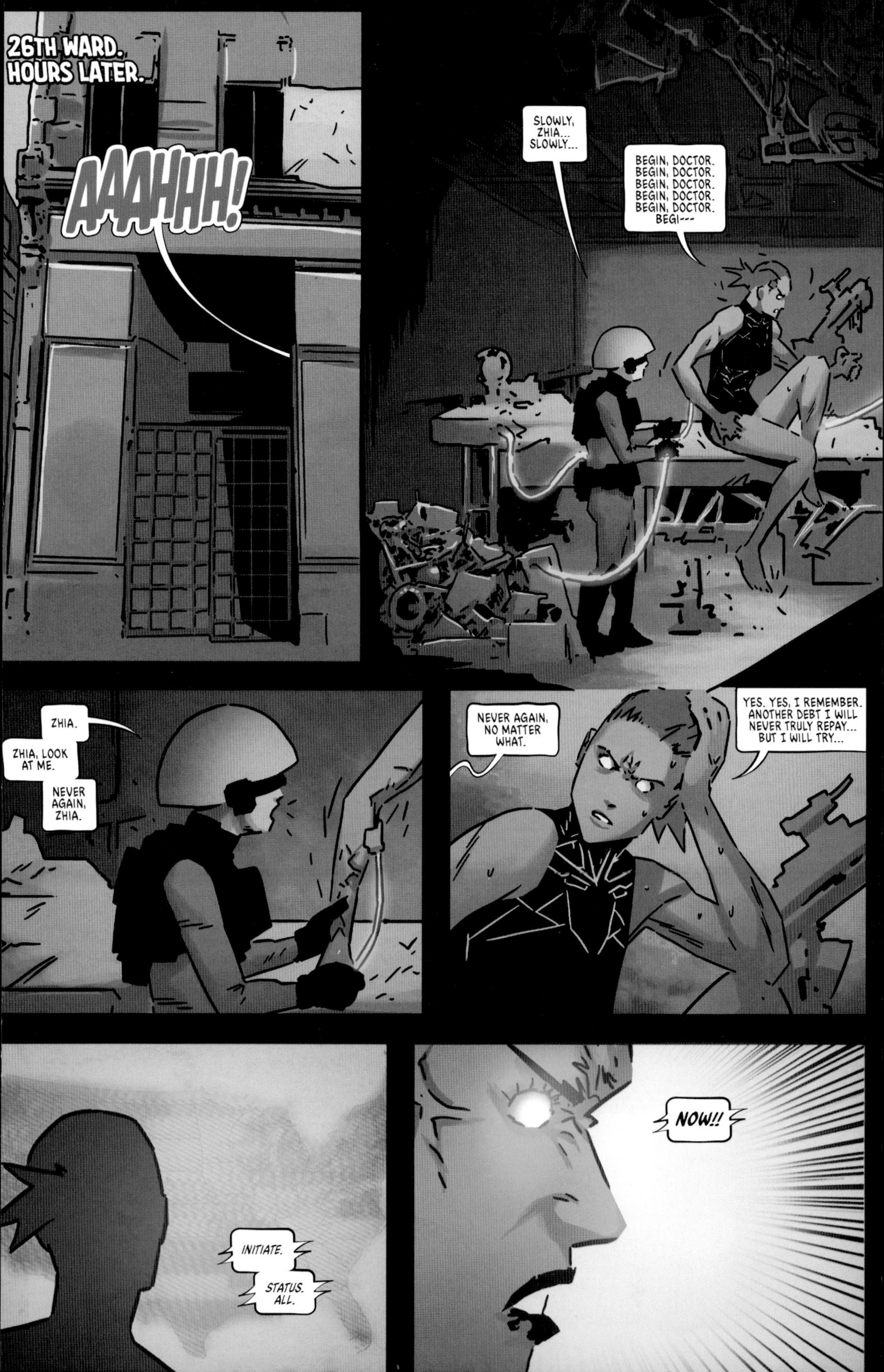
26TH WARD.
HOURS LATER.
AAAHHH!
SLOWLY, ZHIA... SLOWLY...
BEGIN, DOCTOR. BEGIN, DOCTOR. BEGIN, DOCTOR. BEGIN, DOCTOR. BEGIN, DOCTOR. BEGI---
ZHIA.
ZHIA, LOOK AT ME.
NEVER AGAIN, ZHIA.
NEVER AGAIN, NO MATTER WHAT.
YES. YES, I REMEMBER. ANOTHER DEBT I WILL NEVER TRULY REPAY... BUT I WILL TRY...
INITIATE.
STATUS. ALL.
NOW!!

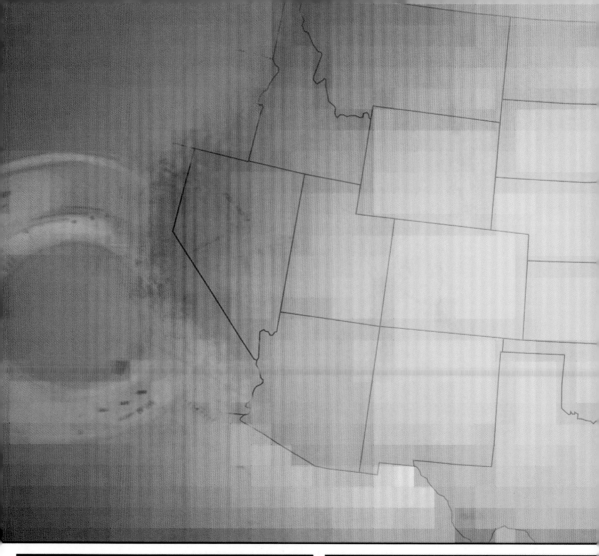

AGENT DAVIX IS STATUS GREEN AND HEADED TOWARDS US. FINN IS---

FINN IS *RED.*

YOUR ORDERS, COMMANDER?

THEY WANT OFF THIS DYING ROCK, MARIOL.

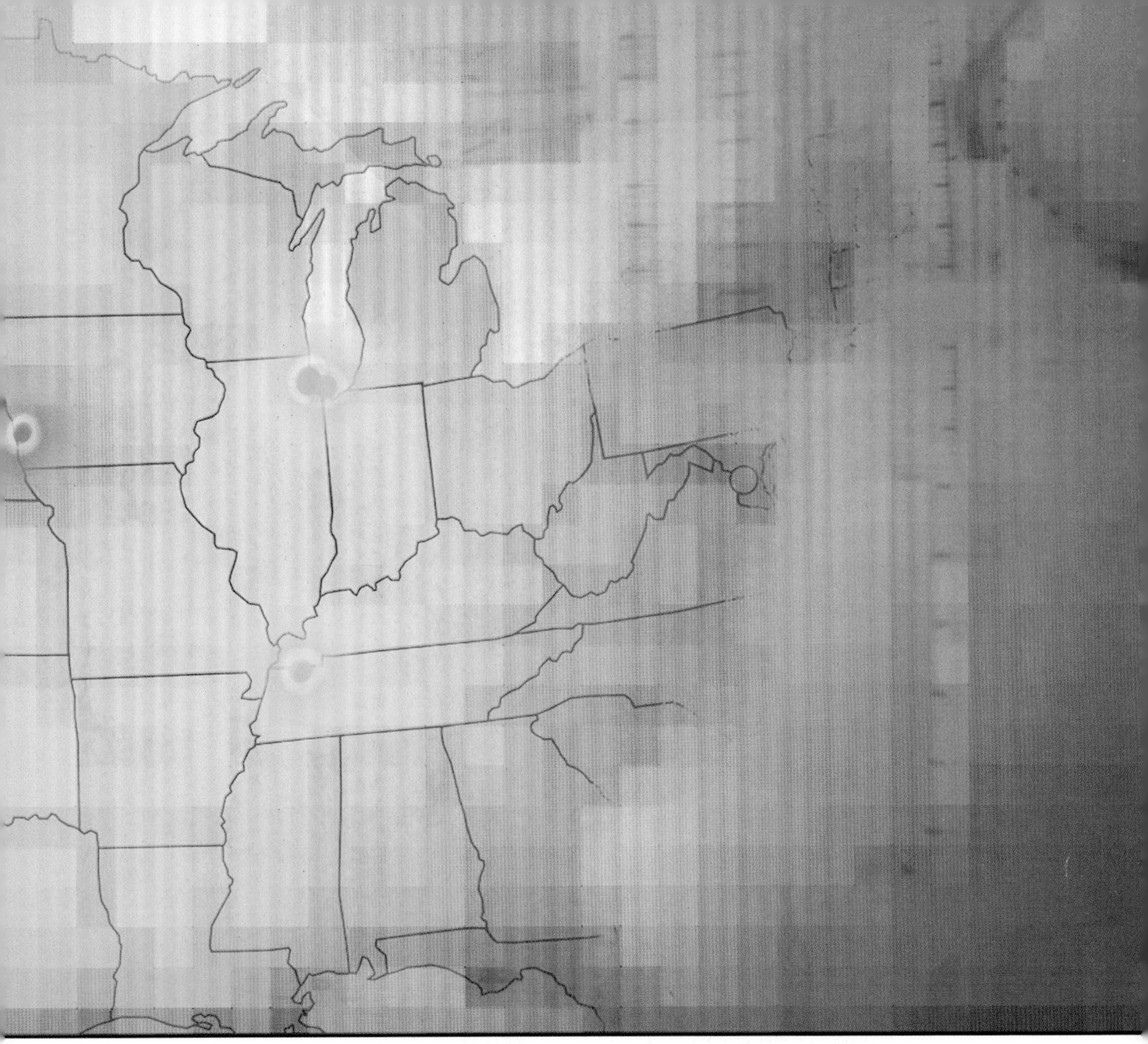

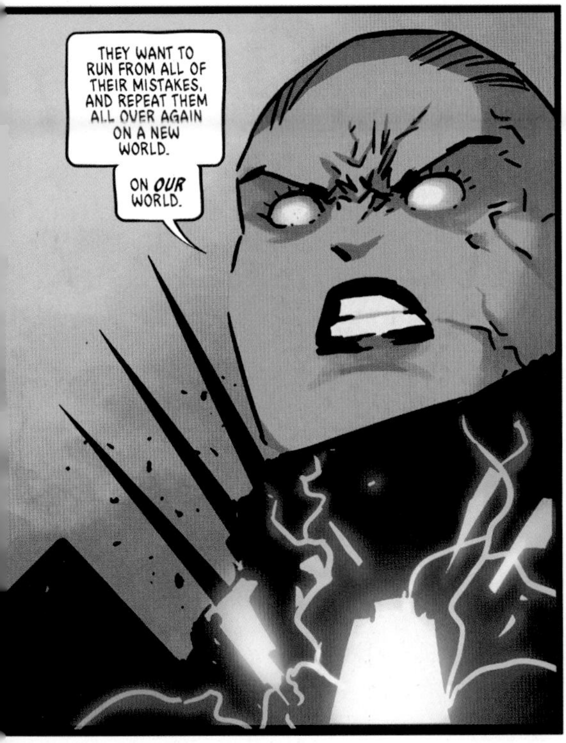

THEY WANT TO RUN FROM ALL OF THEIR MISTAKES, AND REPEAT THEM ALL OVER AGAIN ON A NEW WORLD.
ON *OUR* WORLD.

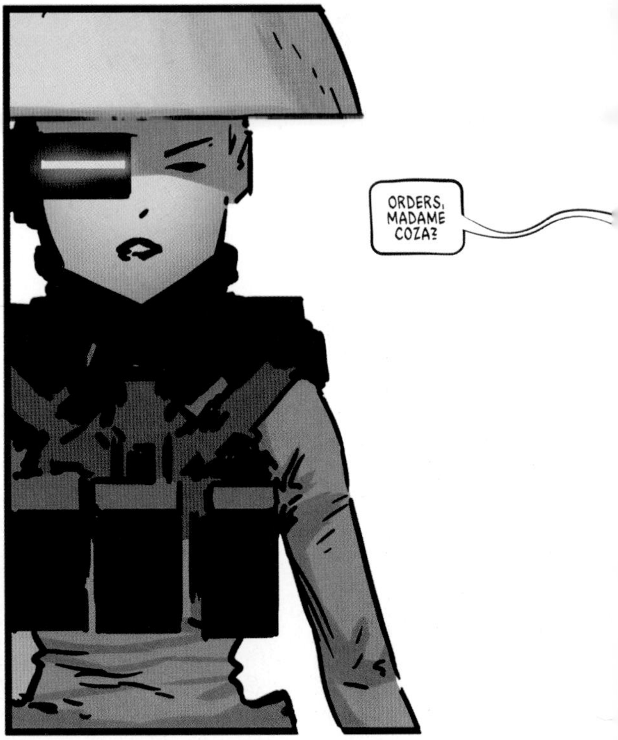

ORDERS, MADAME COZA?

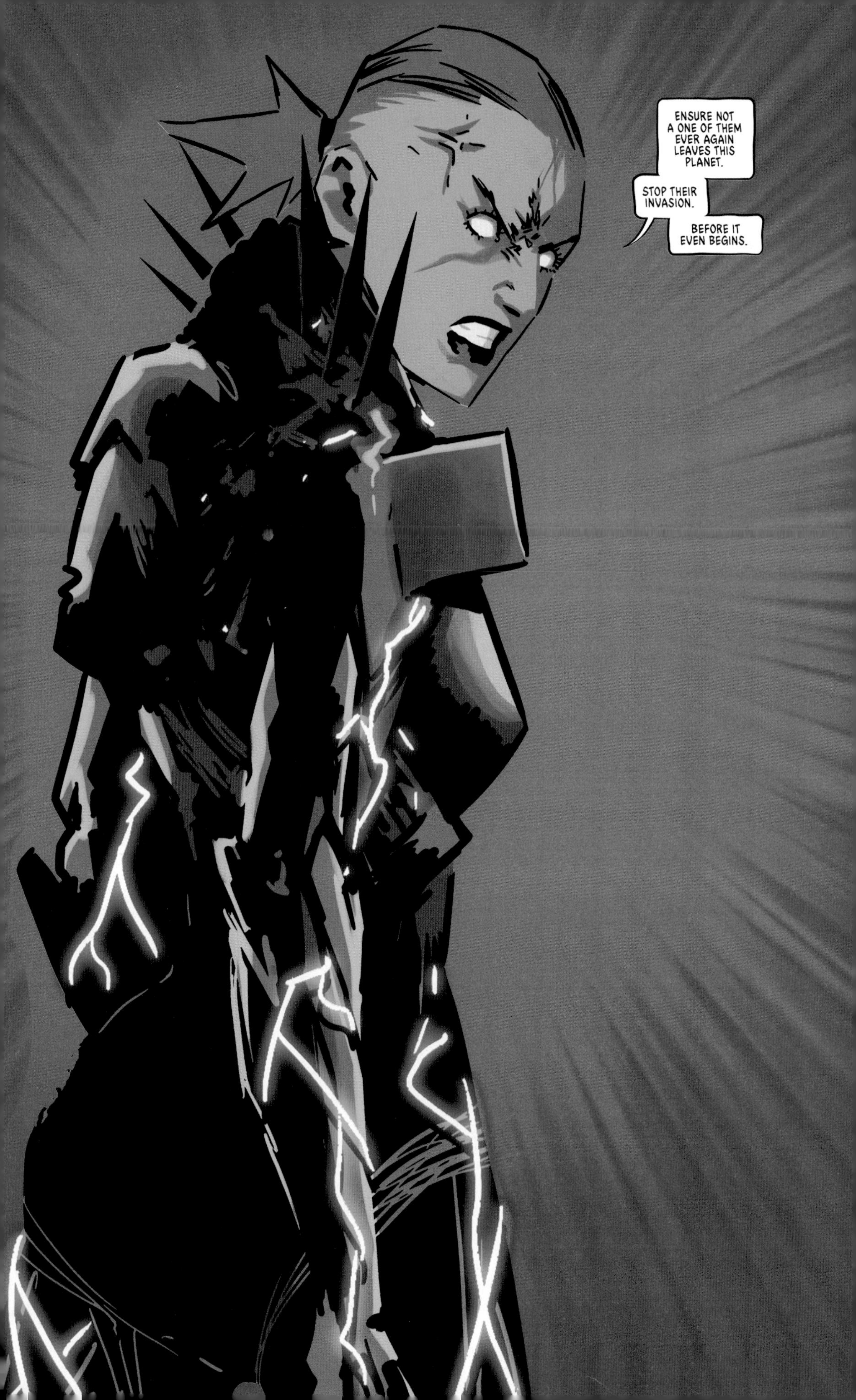
ENSURE NOT A ONE OF THEM EVER AGAIN LEAVES THIS PLANET.
STOP THEIR INVASION.
BEFORE IT EVEN BEGINS.

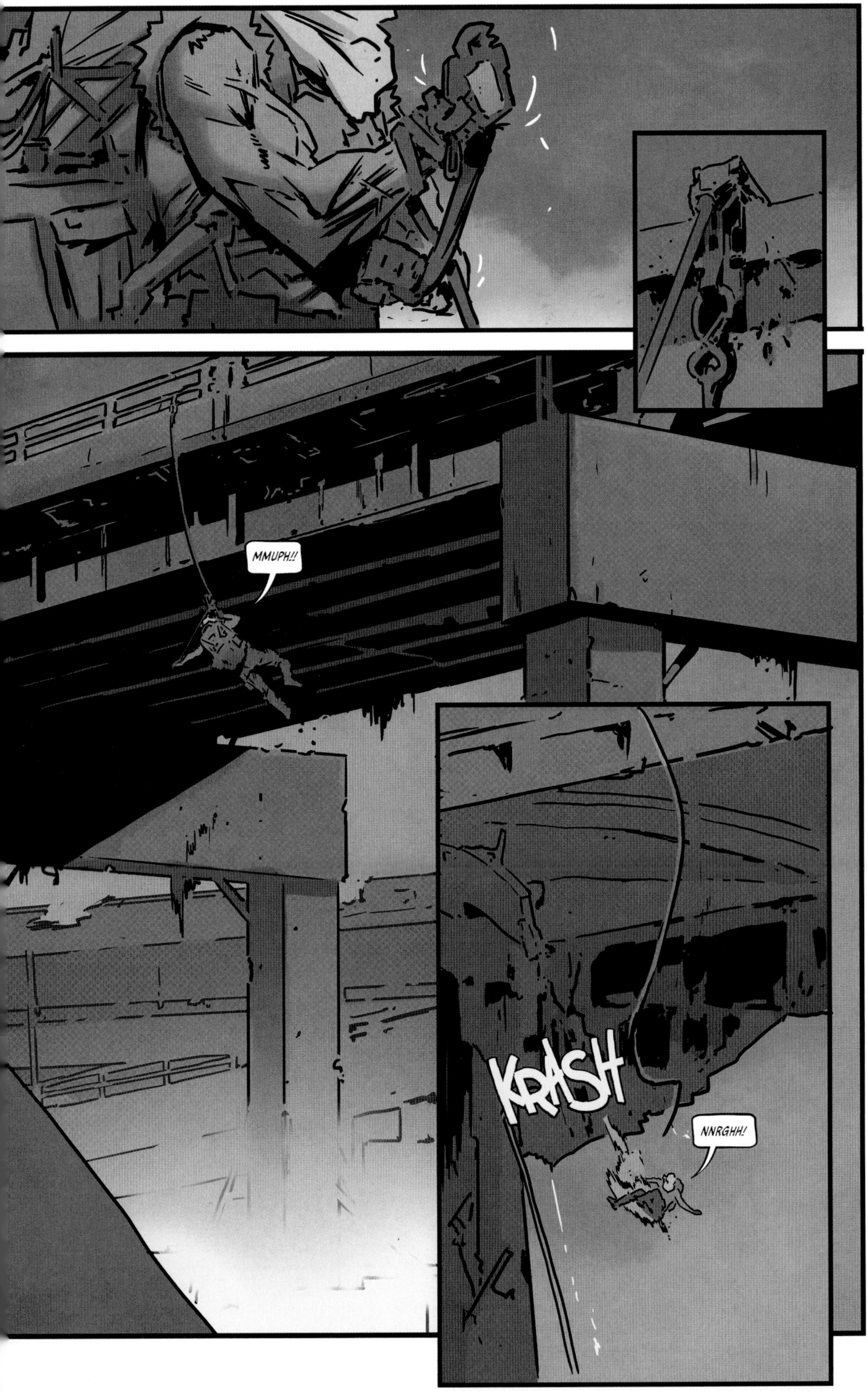
MMUPH!!
KRASH
NNRGHH!

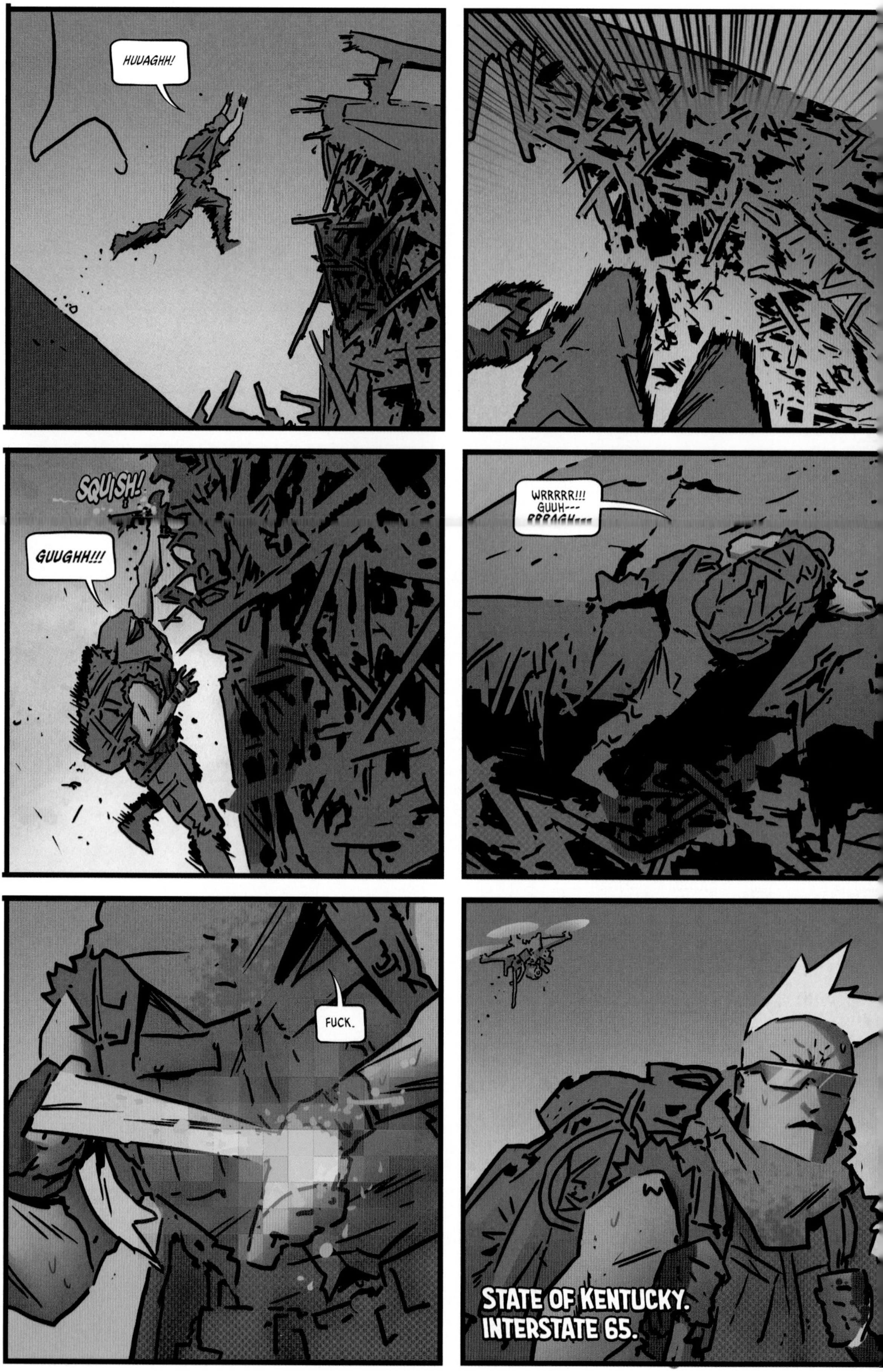
HUUAGHH!
SQUISH!
GUUGHH!!!
WRRRRR!!!
GUUH---
RRRAGH---
FUCK.
STATE OF KENTUCKY.
INTERSTATE 65.

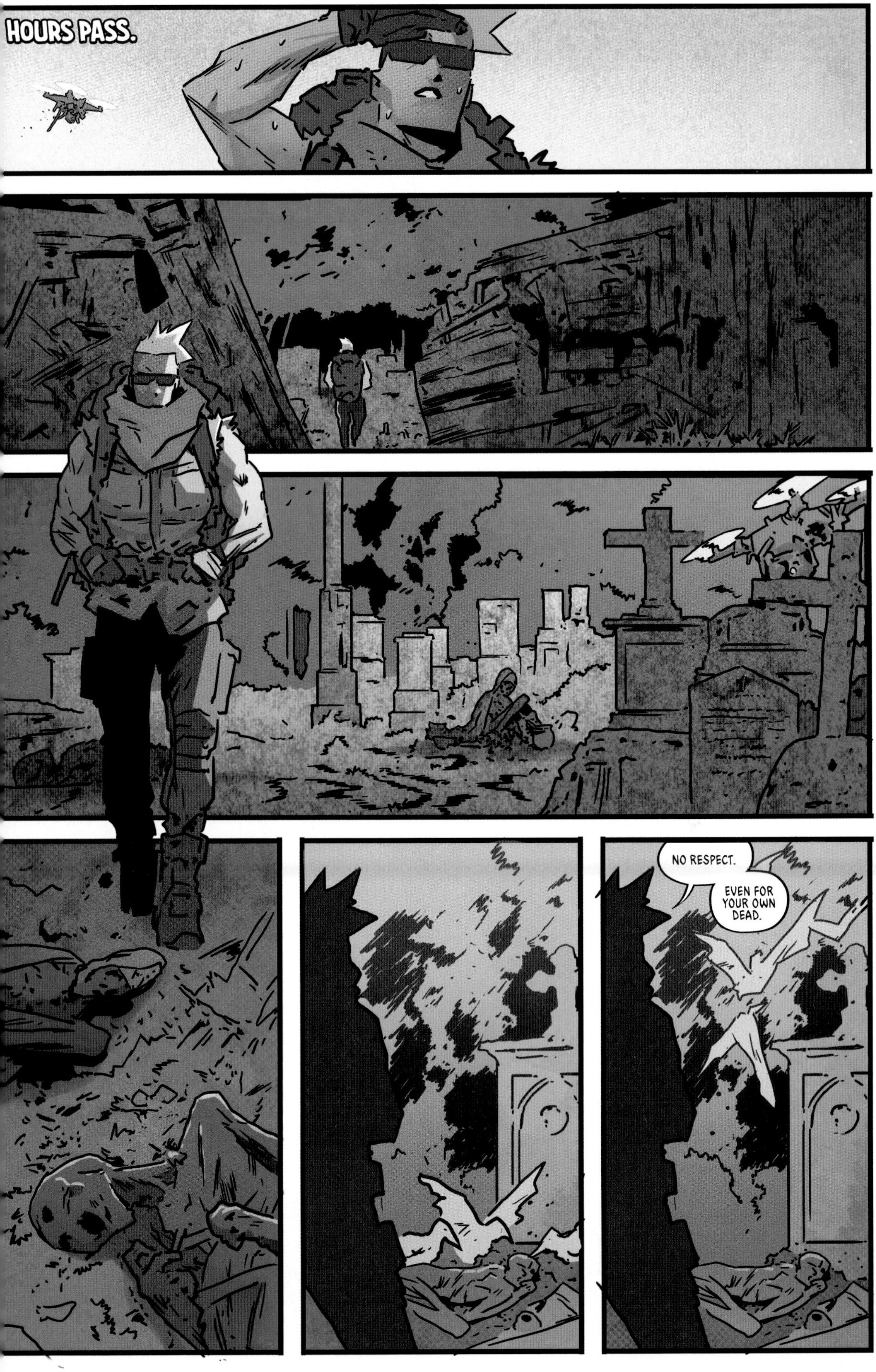
HOURS PASS.
NO RESPECT.
EVEN FOR YOUR OWN DEAD.

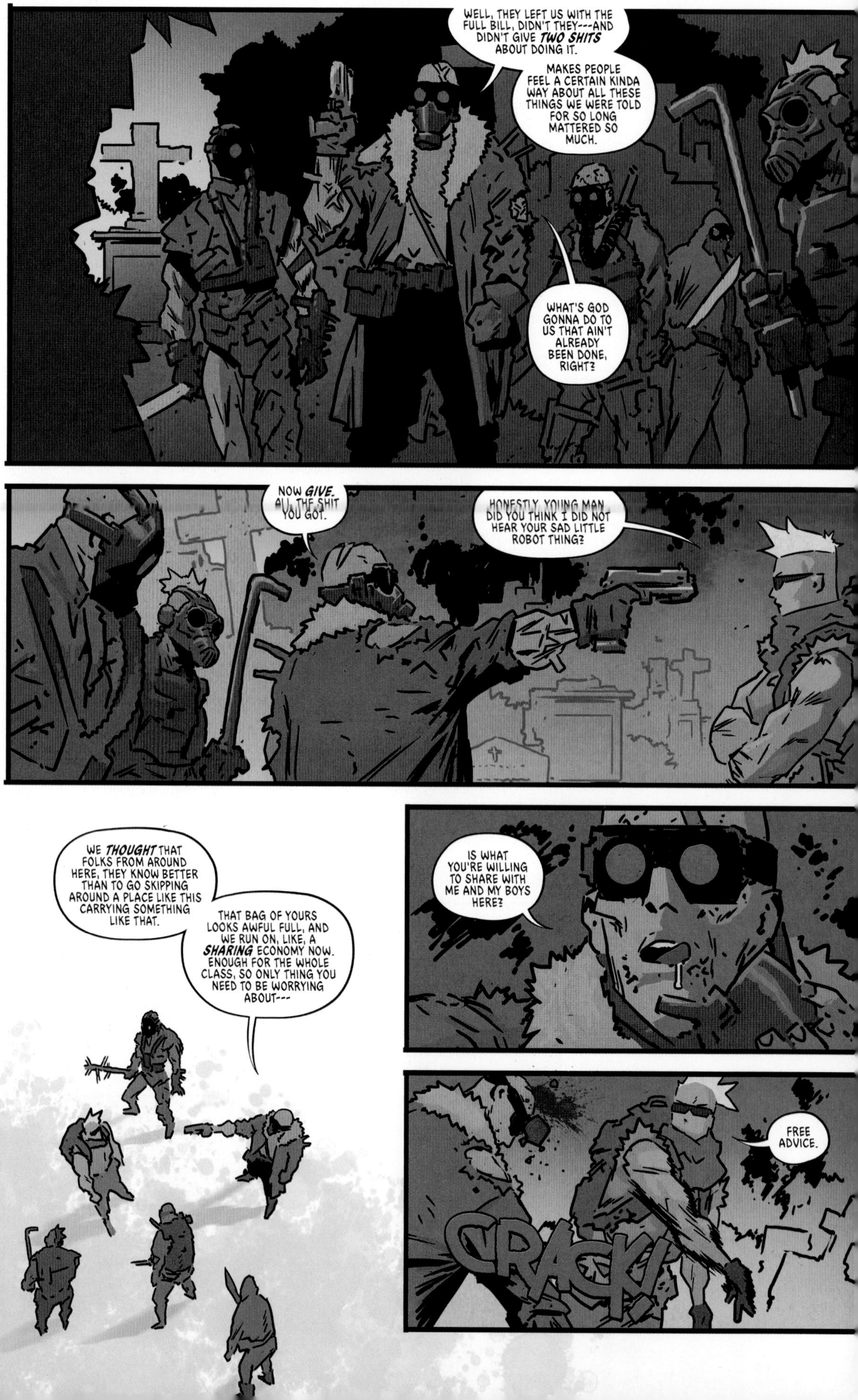

WELL, THEY LEFT US WITH THE FULL BILL, DIDN'T THEY---AND DIDN'T GIVE *TWO SHITS* ABOUT DOING IT.
MAKES PEOPLE FEEL A CERTAIN KINDA WAY ABOUT ALL THESE THINGS WE WERE TOLD FOR SO LONG MATTERED SO MUCH.
WHAT'S GOD GONNA DO TO US THAT AIN'T ALREADY BEEN DONE, RIGHT?
NOW *GIVE*. ALL THE SHIT YOU GOT.
HONESTLY YOUNG MAN DID YOU THINK I DID NOT HEAR YOUR SAD LITTLE ROBOT THING?
WE *THOUGHT* THAT FOLKS FROM AROUND HERE, THEY KNOW BETTER THAN TO GO SKIPPING AROUND A PLACE LIKE THIS CARRYING SOMETHING LIKE THAT.
THAT BAG OF YOURS LOOKS AWFUL FULL, AND WE RUN ON, LIKE, A *SHARING* ECONOMY NOW. ENOUGH FOR THE WHOLE CLASS, SO ONLY THING YOU NEED TO BE WORRYING ABOUT---
IS WHAT YOU'RE WILLING TO SHARE WITH ME AND MY BOYS HERE?
FREE ADVICE.
CRACK!

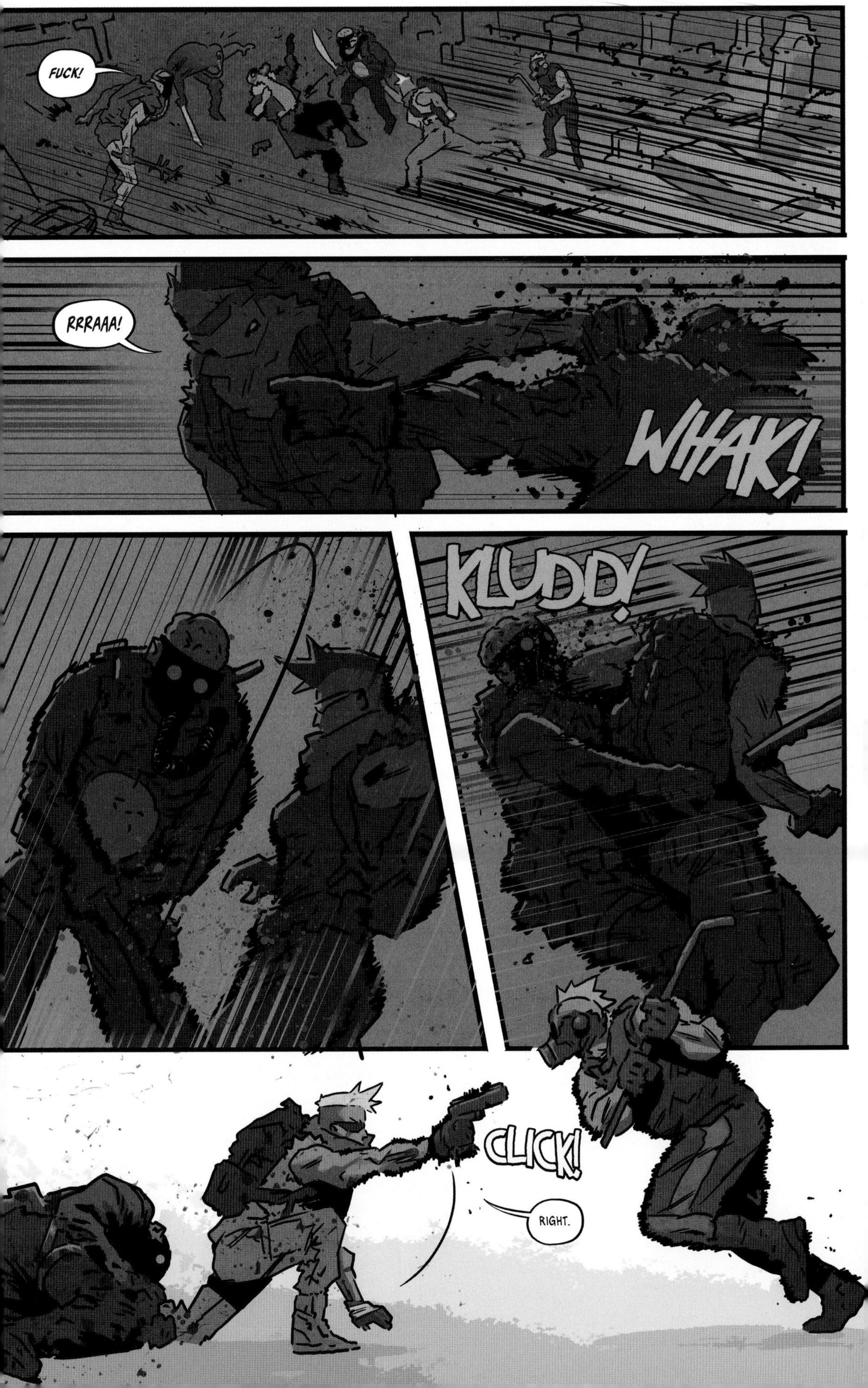
FUCK!
RRRAAA!
WHAK!
KLUDD!
CLICK!
RIGHT.

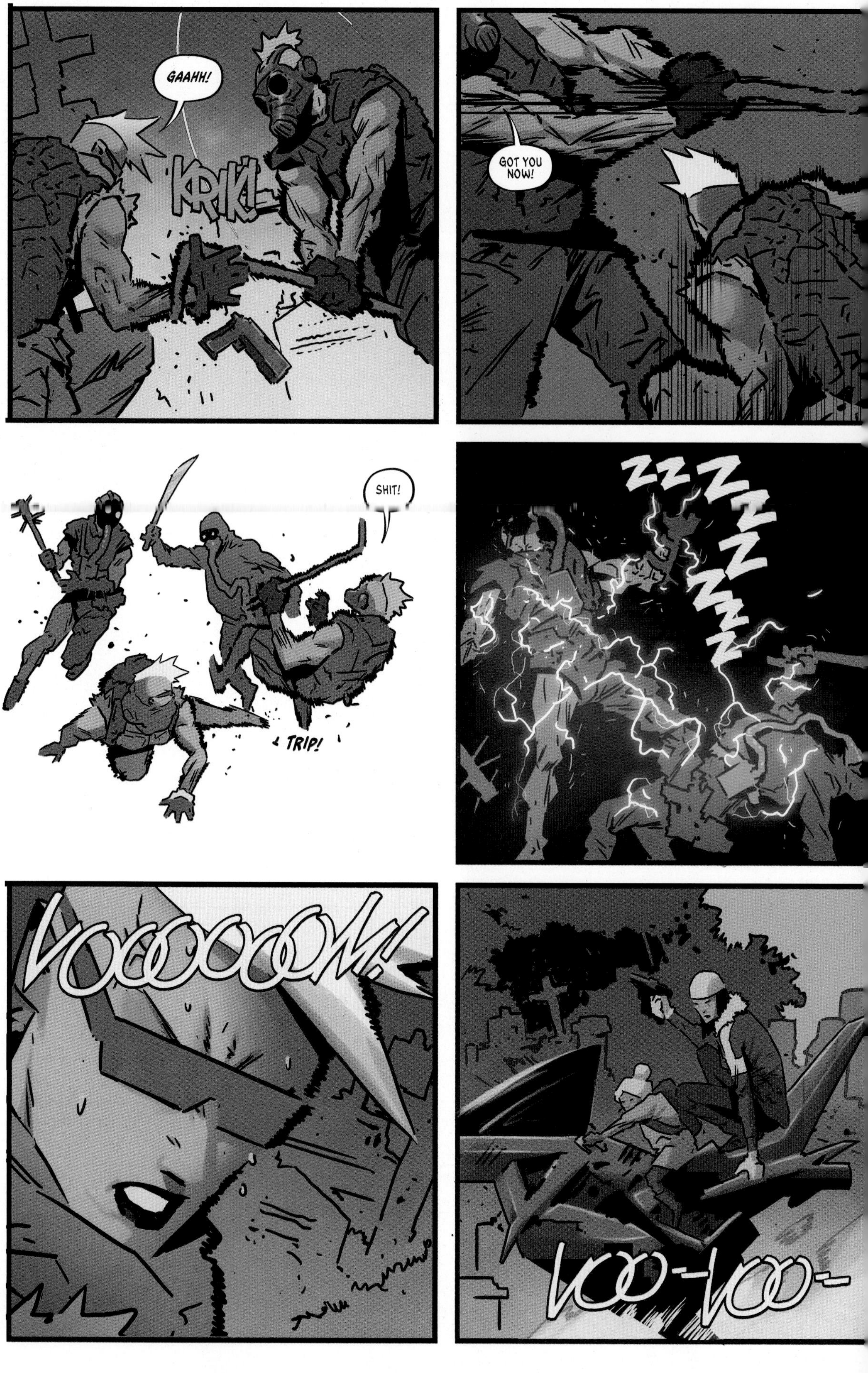
GAAHH!
KRIK!
GOT YOU NOW!
SHIT!
TRIP!
ZZZZZZZZZZ
VOOOOOOM!
VOO-VOO-

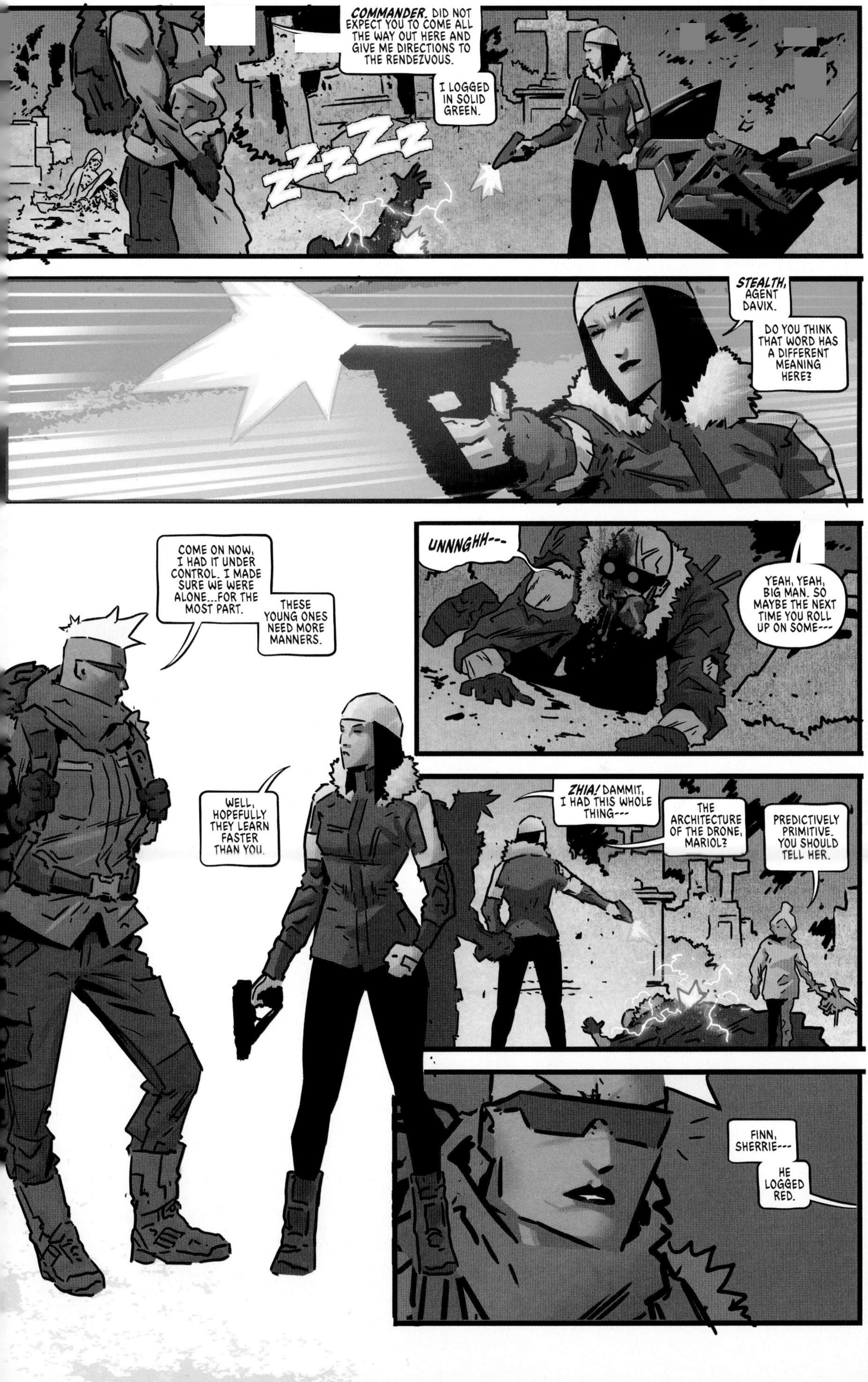

COMMANDER. DID NOT EXPECT YOU TO COME ALL THE WAY OUT HERE AND GIVE ME DIRECTIONS TO THE RENDEZVOUS.
I LOGGED IN SOLID GREEN.
ZZZZZ
STEALTH, AGENT DAVIX.
DO YOU THINK THAT WORD HAS A DIFFERENT MEANING HERE?
UNNNGHH---
YEAH, YEAH, BIG MAN. SO MAYBE THE NEXT TIME YOU ROLL UP ON SOME---
ZHIA! DAMMIT, I HAD THIS WHOLE THING---
THE ARCHITECTURE OF THE DRONE, MARIOL?
PREDICTIVELY PRIMITIVE. YOU SHOULD TELL HER.
COME ON NOW, I HAD IT UNDER CONTROL. I MADE SURE WE WERE ALONE...FOR THE MOST PART.
THESE YOUNG ONES NEED MORE MANNERS.
WELL, HOPEFULLY THEY LEARN FASTER THAN YOU.
FINN, SHERRIE---
HE LOGGED RED.

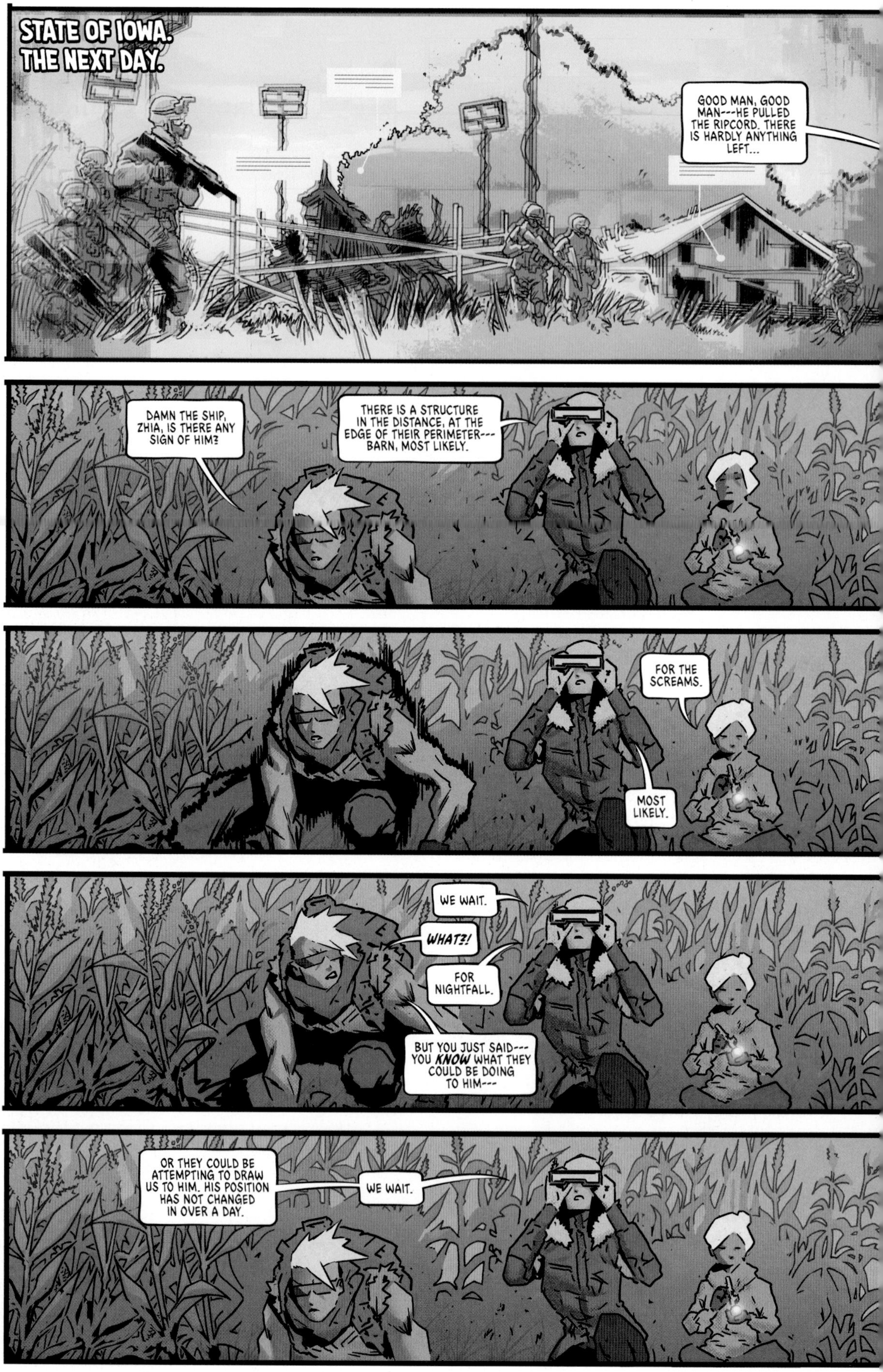
STATE OF IOWA.
THE NEXT DAY.
GOOD MAN, GOOD MAN---HE PULLED THE RIPCORD. THERE IS HARDLY ANYTHING LEFT...
DAMN THE SHIP, ZHIA, IS THERE ANY SIGN OF HIM?
THERE IS A STRUCTURE IN THE DISTANCE, AT THE EDGE OF THEIR PERIMETER---BARN, MOST LIKELY.
MOST LIKELY.
FOR THE SCREAMS.
WE WAIT.
WHAT?!
FOR NIGHTFALL.
BUT YOU JUST SAID---YOU KNOW WHAT THEY COULD BE DOING TO HIM---
OR THEY COULD BE ATTEMPTING TO DRAW US TO HIM. HIS POSITION HAS NOT CHANGED IN OVER A DAY.
WE WAIT.

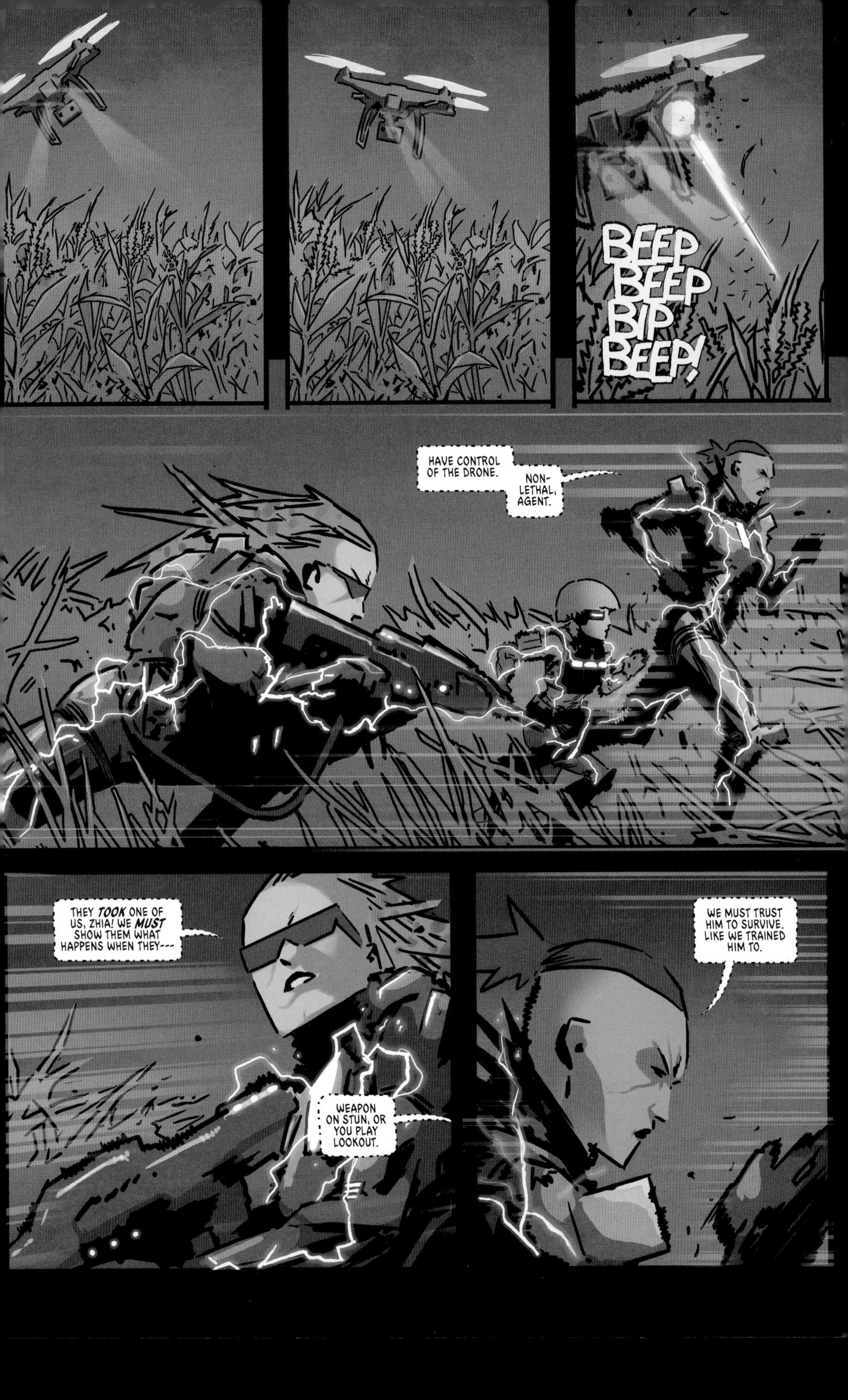
BEEP BEEP BIP BEEP!
HAVE CONTROL OF THE DRONE.
NON-LETHAL, AGENT.
THEY *TOOK* ONE OF US, ZHIA! WE *MUST* SHOW THEM WHAT HAPPENS WHEN THEY---
WEAPON ON STUN, OR YOU PLAY LOOKOUT.
WE MUST TRUST HIM TO SURVIVE. LIKE WE TRAINED HIM TO.

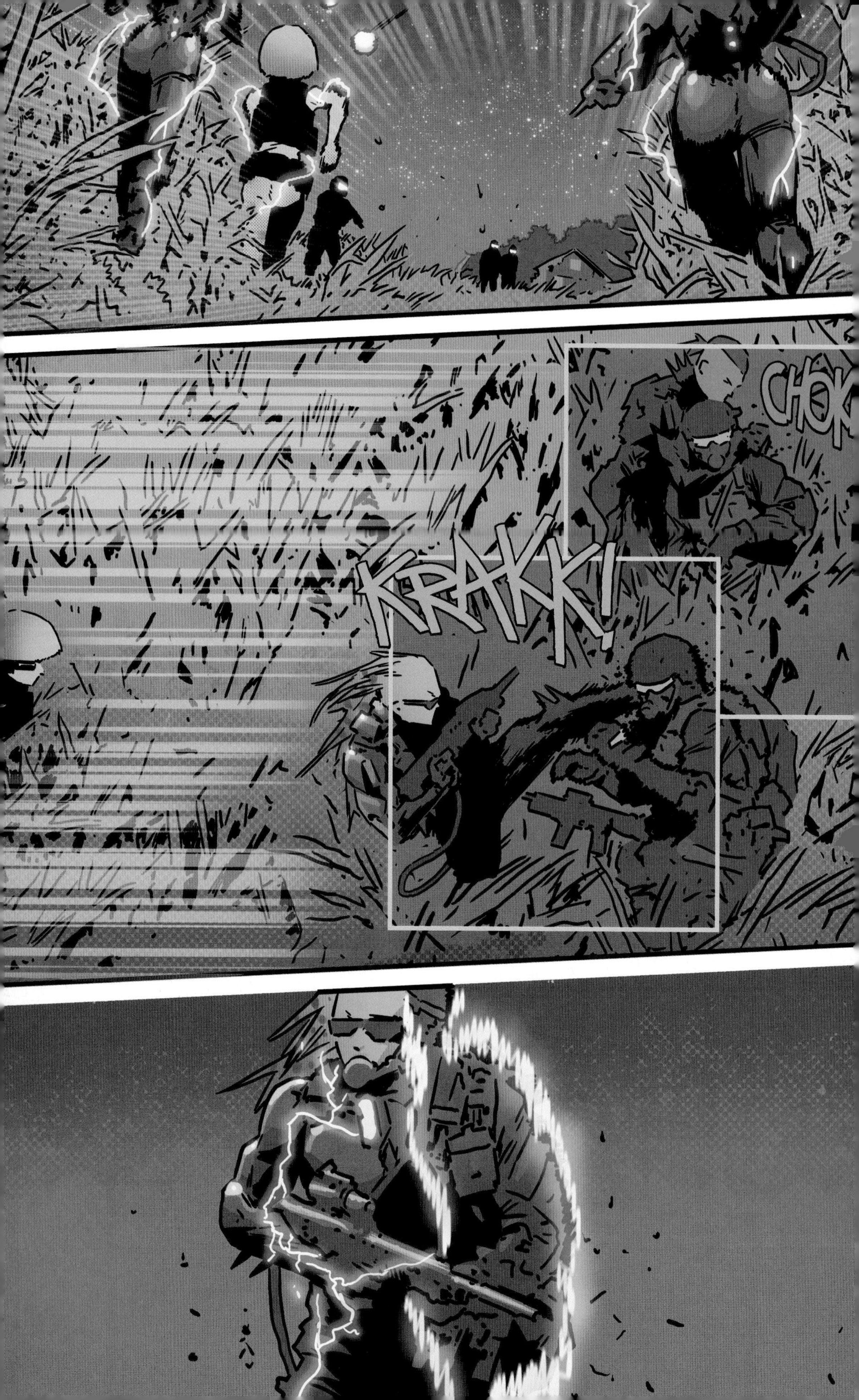
CHOK
KRAKK!

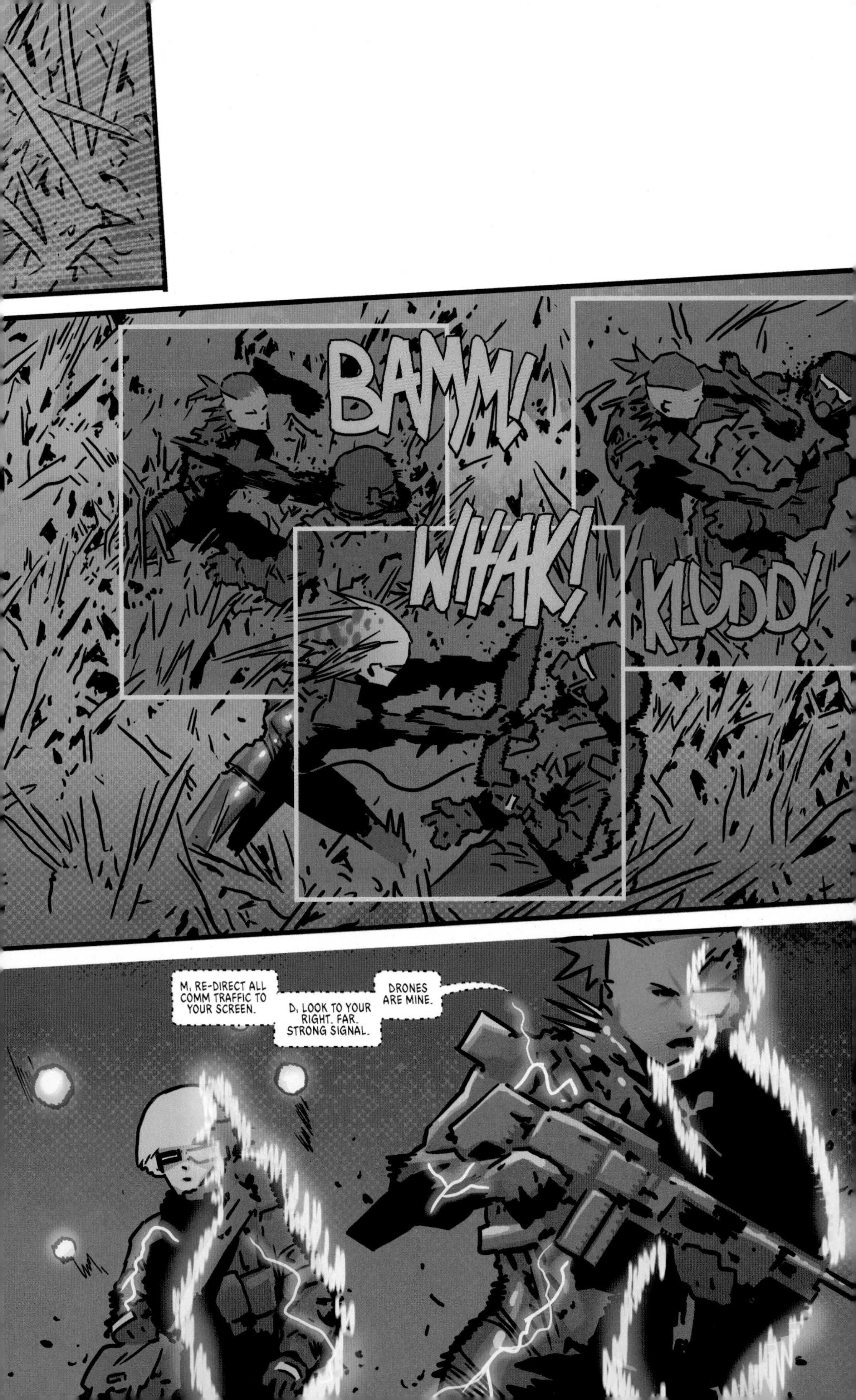
BAMM!
WHAK!
KLUDD!
M, RE-DIRECT ALL COMM TRAFFIC TO YOUR SCREEN.
D, LOOK TO YOUR RIGHT. FAR. STRONG SIGNAL.
DRONES ARE MINE.

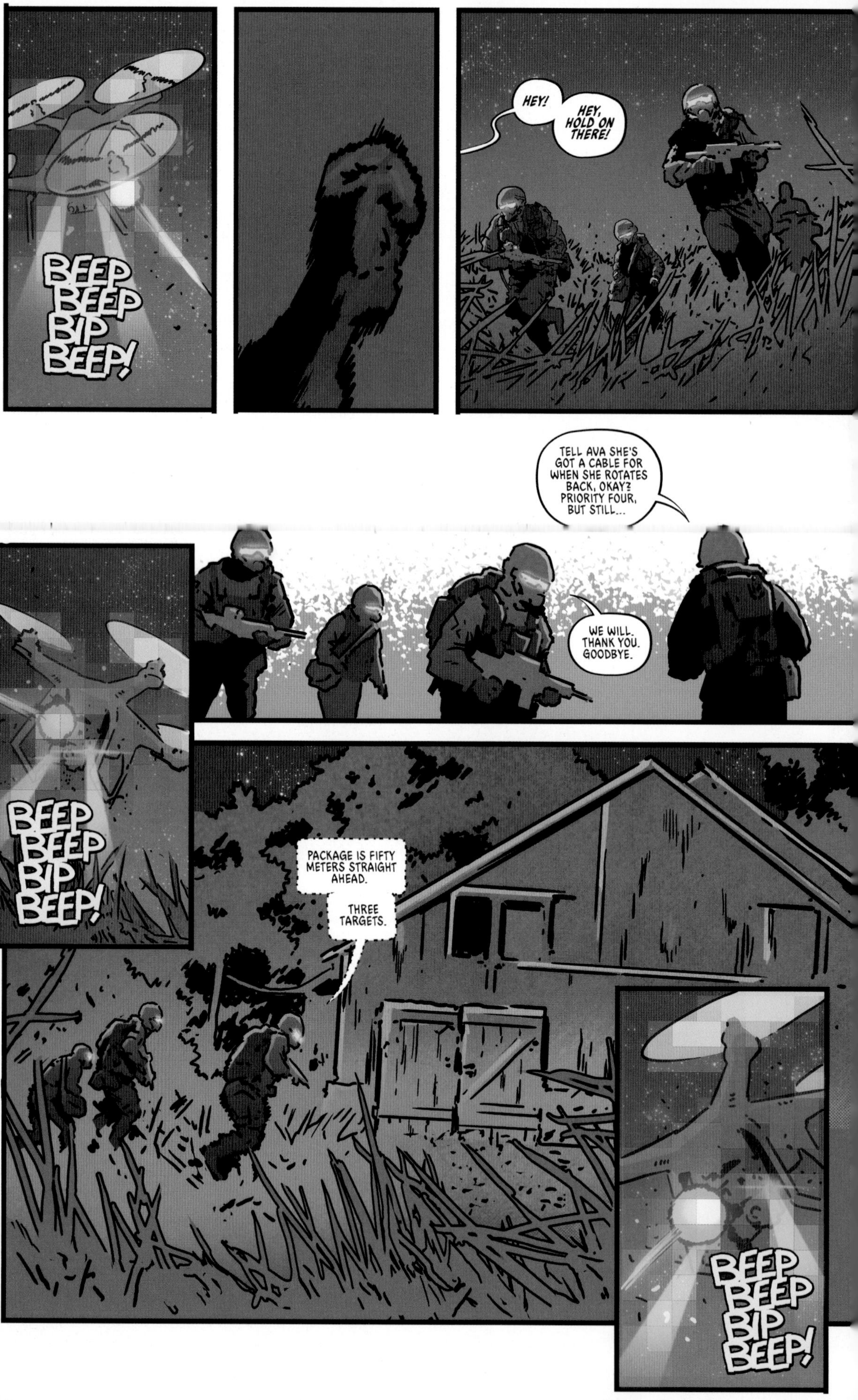
BEEP BEEP BIP BEEP!
HEY!
HEY, HOLD ON THERE!
TELL AVA SHE'S GOT A CABLE FOR WHEN SHE ROTATES BACK, OKAY? PRIORITY FOUR, BUT STILL...
WE WILL. THANK YOU. GOODBYE.
BEEP BEEP BIP BEEP!
PACKAGE IS FIFTY METERS STRAIGHT AHEAD.
THREE TARGETS.
BEEP BEEP BIP BEEP!

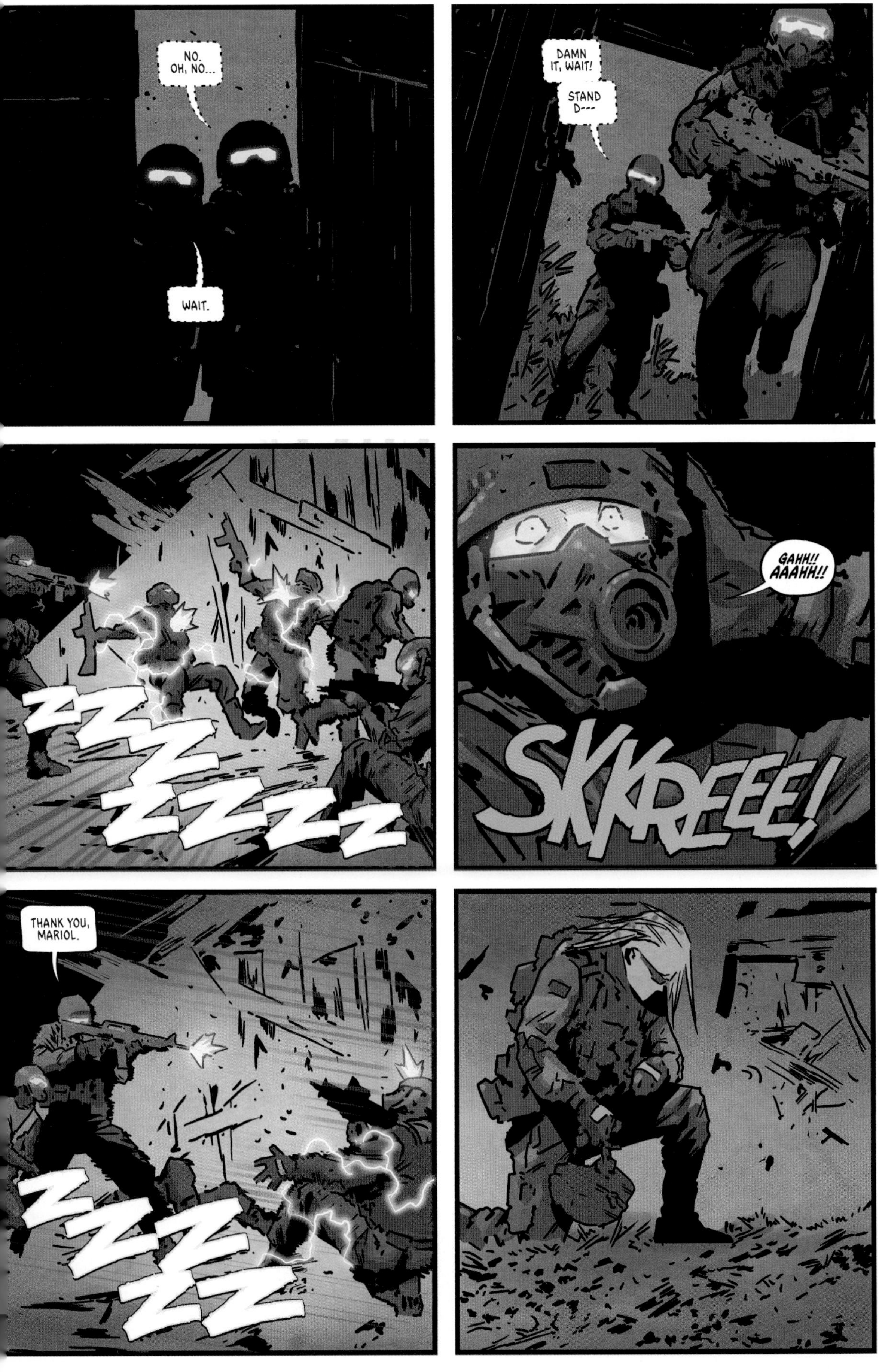
NO.
OH, NO...
WAIT.
DAMN IT, WAIT!
STAND D---
ZZZZZZZZ
GAHH!! AAAHH!!
SKKREEE!
THANK YOU, MARIOL.
ZZZZZZ

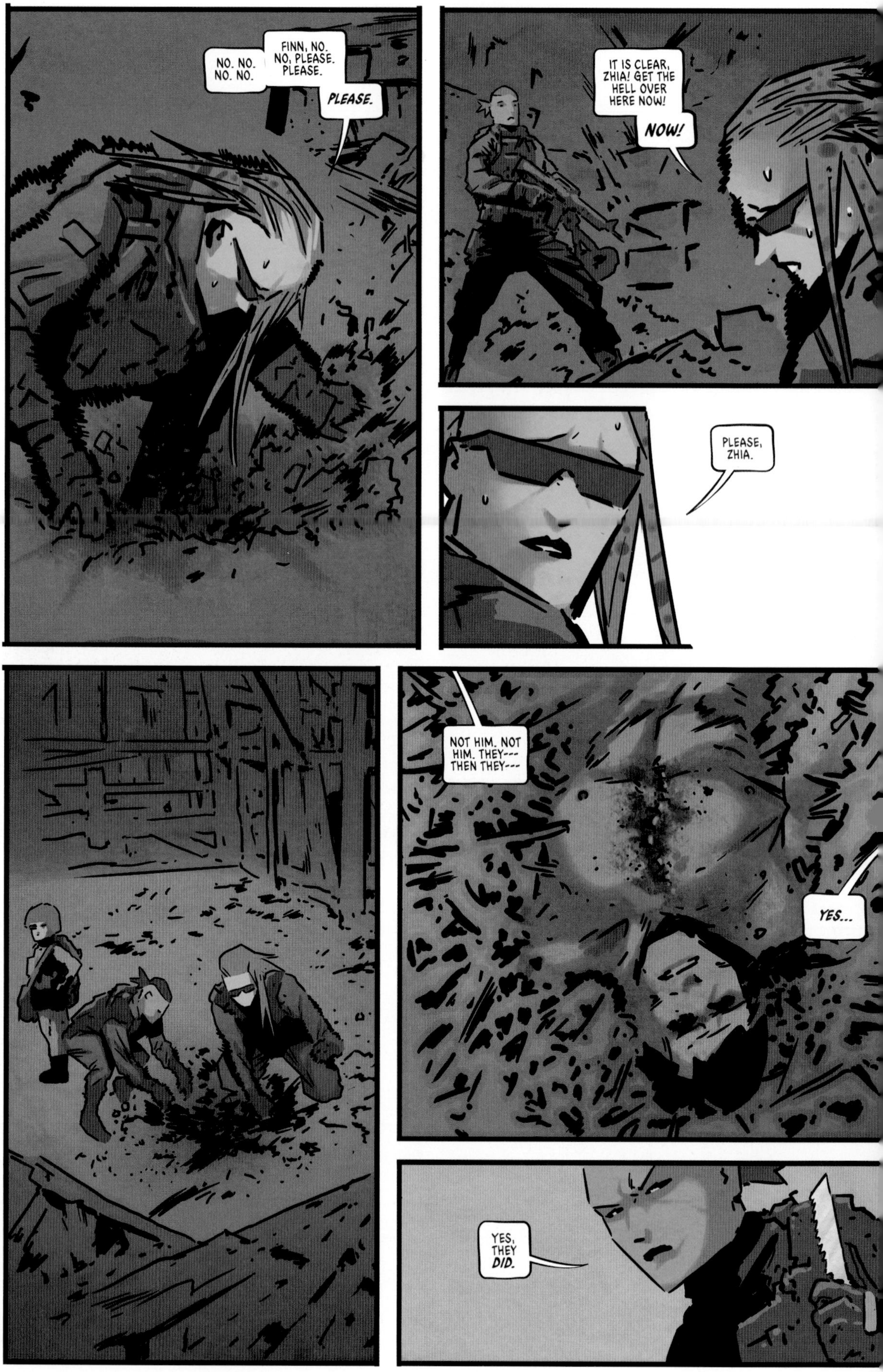
NO. NO. NO. NO.
FINN, NO. NO, PLEASE. PLEASE.
PLEASE.
IT IS CLEAR, ZHIA! GET THE HELL OVER HERE NOW!
NOW!
PLEASE, ZHIA.
NOT HIM. NOT HIM. THEY--- THEN THEY---
YES...
YES, THEY DID.

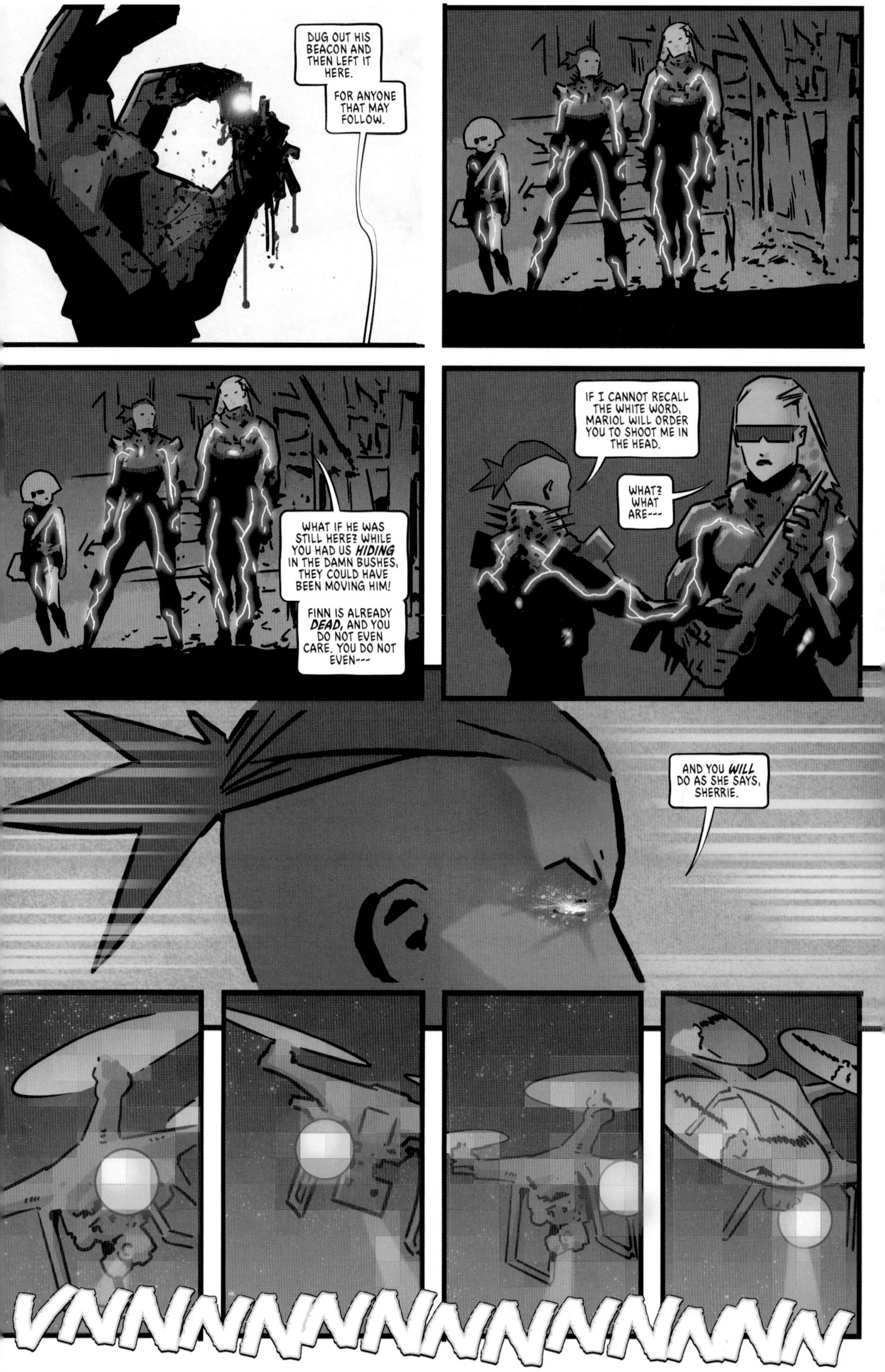
DUG OUT HIS BEACON AND THEN LEFT IT HERE.
FOR ANYONE THAT MAY FOLLOW.
WHAT IF HE WAS STILL HERE? WHILE YOU HAD US HIDING IN THE DAMN BUSHES, THEY COULD HAVE BEEN MOVING HIM!
FINN IS ALREADY DEAD, AND YOU DO NOT EVEN CARE. YOU DO NOT EVEN---
IF I CANNOT RECALL THE WHITE WORD, MARIOL WILL ORDER YOU TO SHOOT ME IN THE HEAD.
WHAT? WHAT ARE---
AND YOU WILL DO AS SHE SAYS, SHERRIE.
VNNNNNNNNNNNNNNN

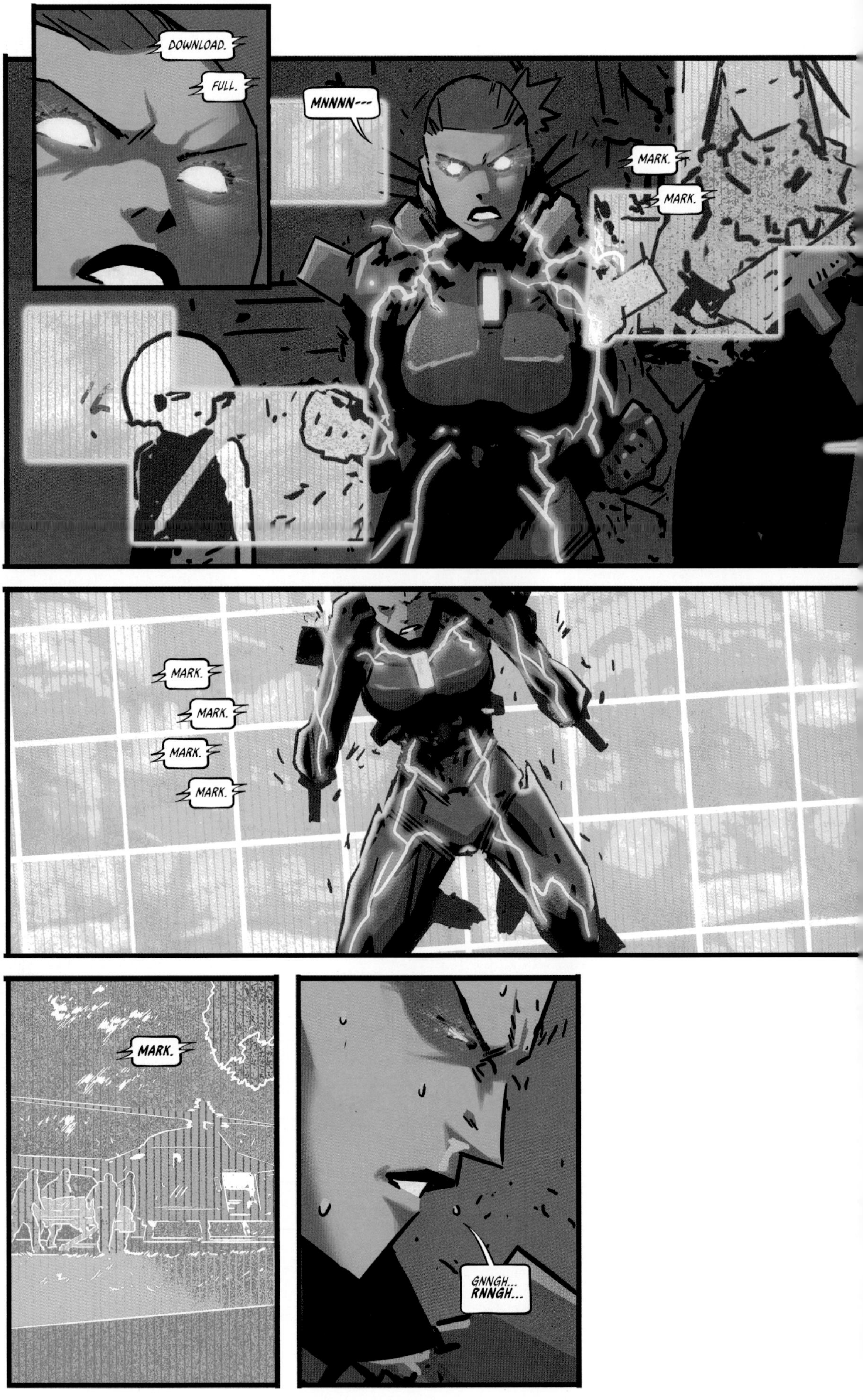
DOWNLOAD.
FULL.
MNNNN---
MARK.
MARK.
MARK.
MARK.
MARK.
MARK.
MARK.
GNNGH...
RNNGH...

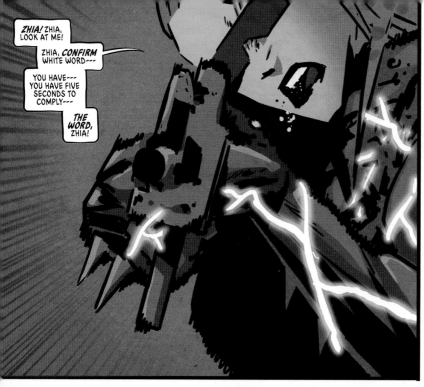

ZHIA! ZHIA, LOOK AT ME!

ZHIA, *CONFIRM* WHITE WORD---

YOU HAVE--- YOU HAVE FIVE SECONDS TO COMPLY---

THE WORD, ZHIA!

JACELL.

THAT IS CORRECT.

A FLYING MACHINE LEFT HERE YESTERDAY WITH FINN ONBOARD, AND IT LEFT A TRAIL.

WE *WILL* FIND HIM.

....

THANK YOU, COMMANDER.

NOT YET.

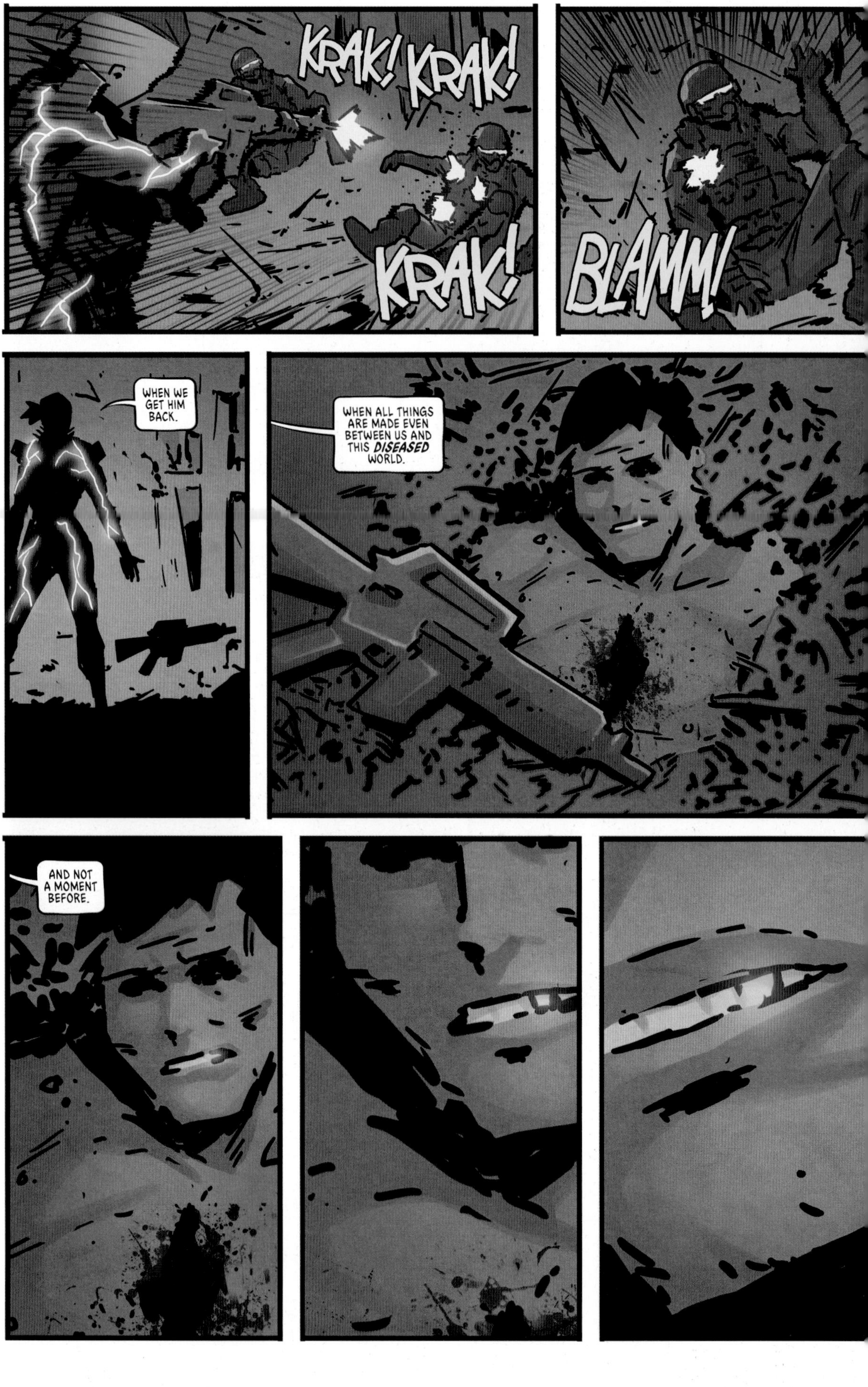
KRAK! KRAK!
KRAK!
BLAMM!
WHEN WE GET HIM BACK.
WHEN ALL THINGS ARE MADE EVEN BETWEEN US AND THIS *DISEASED* WORLD.
AND NOT A MOMENT BEFORE.

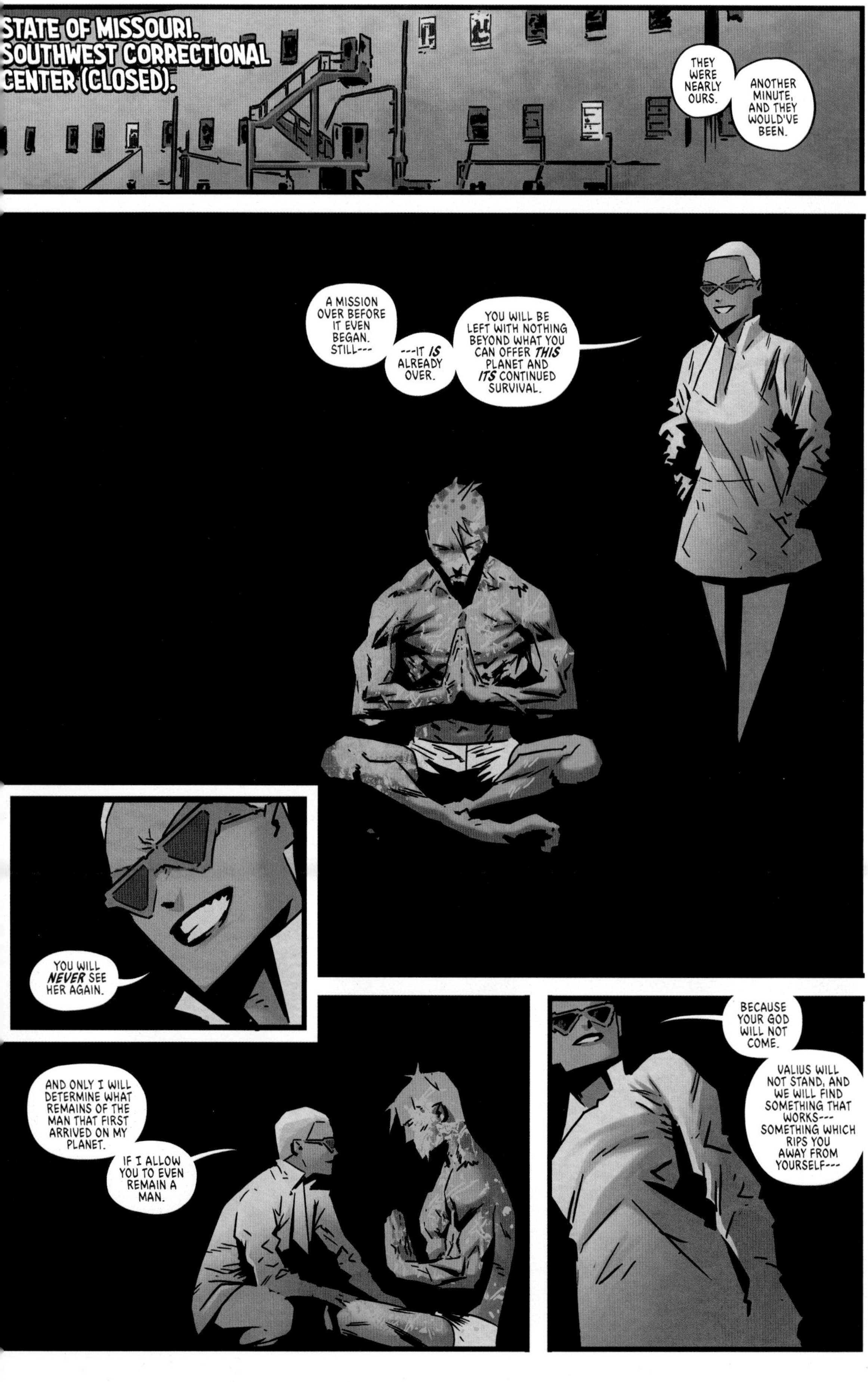
STATE OF MISSOURI. SOUTHWEST CORRECTIONAL CENTER (CLOSED).
THEY WERE NEARLY OURS.
ANOTHER MINUTE, AND THEY WOULD'VE BEEN.
A MISSION OVER BEFORE IT EVEN BEGAN. STILL---
---IT *IS* ALREADY OVER.
YOU WILL BE LEFT WITH NOTHING BEYOND WHAT YOU CAN OFFER *THIS* PLANET AND *ITS* CONTINUED SURVIVAL.
YOU WILL *NEVER* SEE HER AGAIN.
AND ONLY I WILL DETERMINE WHAT REMAINS OF THE MAN THAT FIRST ARRIVED ON MY PLANET.
IF I ALLOW YOU TO EVEN REMAIN A MAN.
BECAUSE YOUR GOD WILL NOT COME.
VALIUS WILL NOT STAND, AND WE WILL FIND SOMETHING THAT WORKS---
SOMETHING WHICH RIPS YOU AWAY FROM YOURSELF---

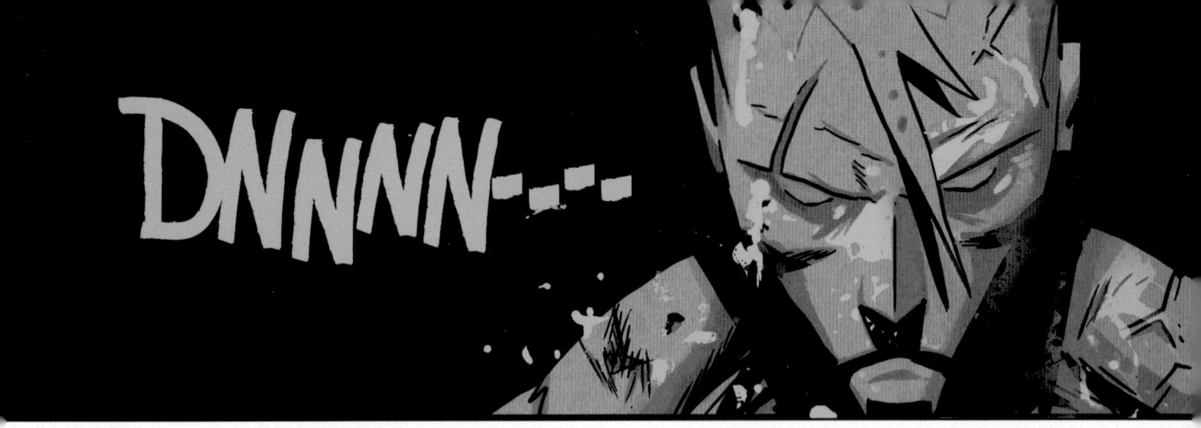
DNNNN-----

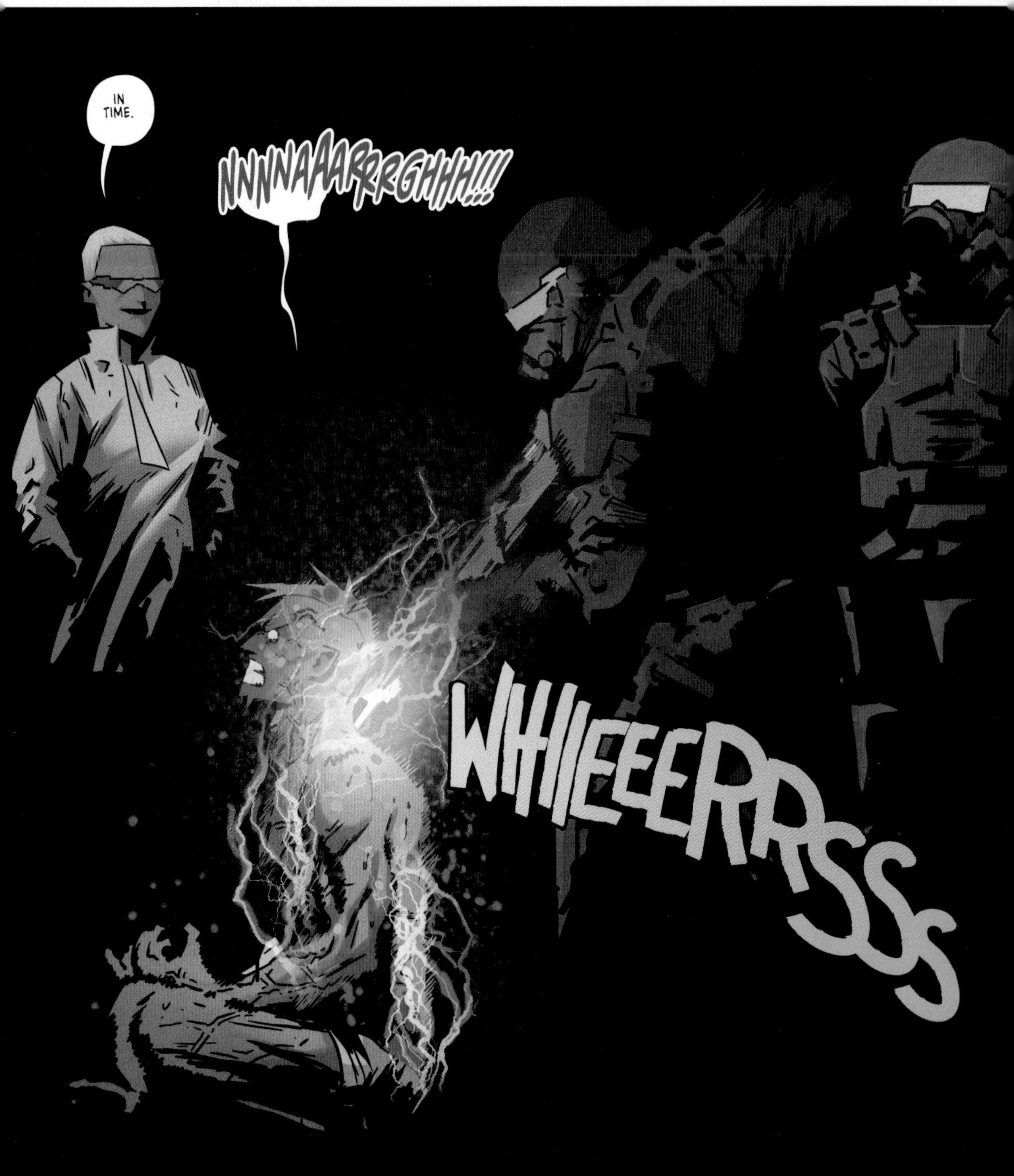
IN TIME.
NNNNAAARRRGHHH!!!
WHIIEEERRSSS

EARTH DAYS IN CAPTIVITY: THREE.

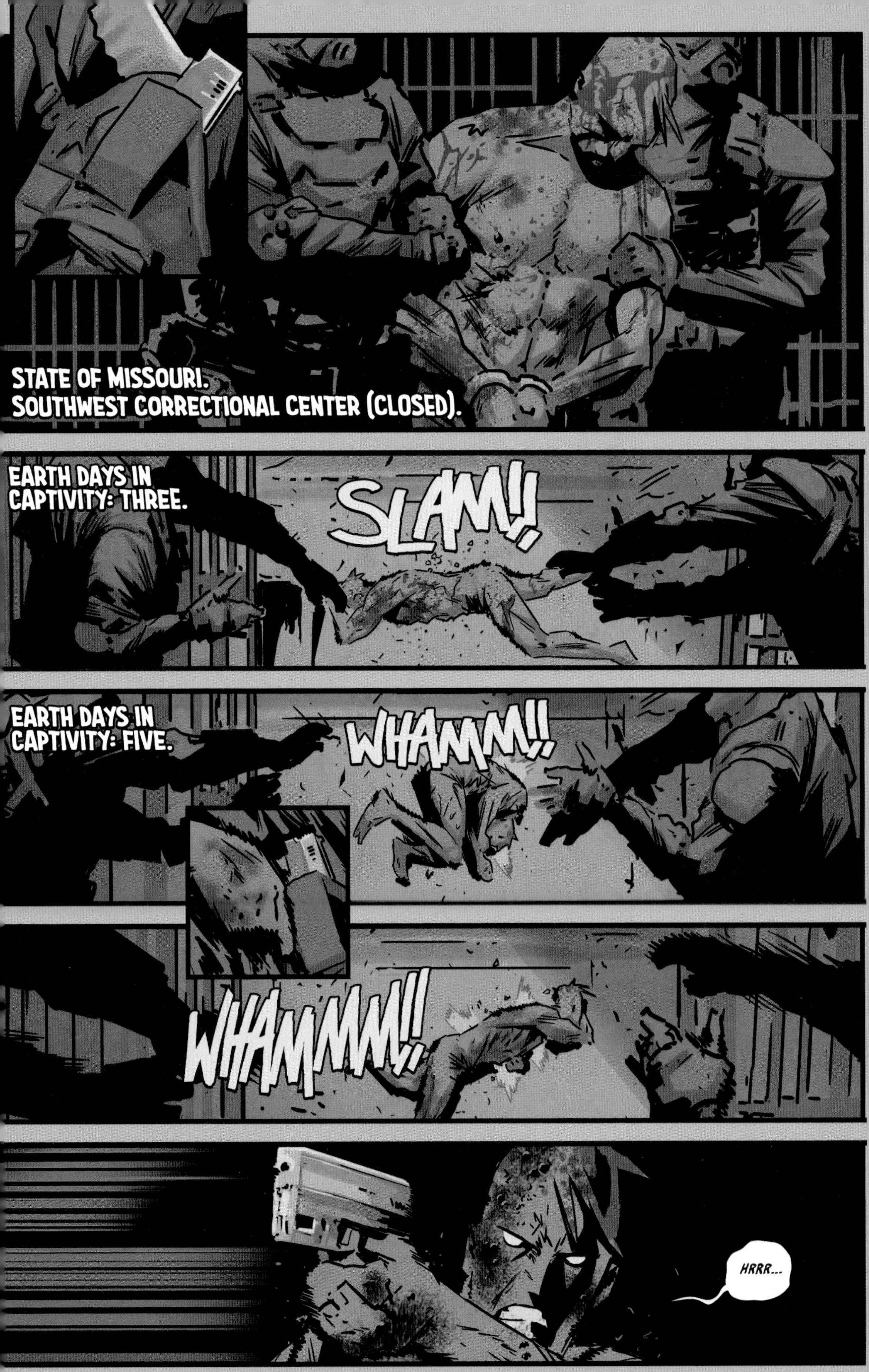
STATE OF MISSOURI.
SOUTHWEST CORRECTIONAL CENTER (CLOSED).
EARTH DAYS IN CAPTIVITY: THREE.
SLAM!!
EARTH DAYS IN CAPTIVITY: FIVE.
WHAMM!!
WHAMMM!!
HRRR...

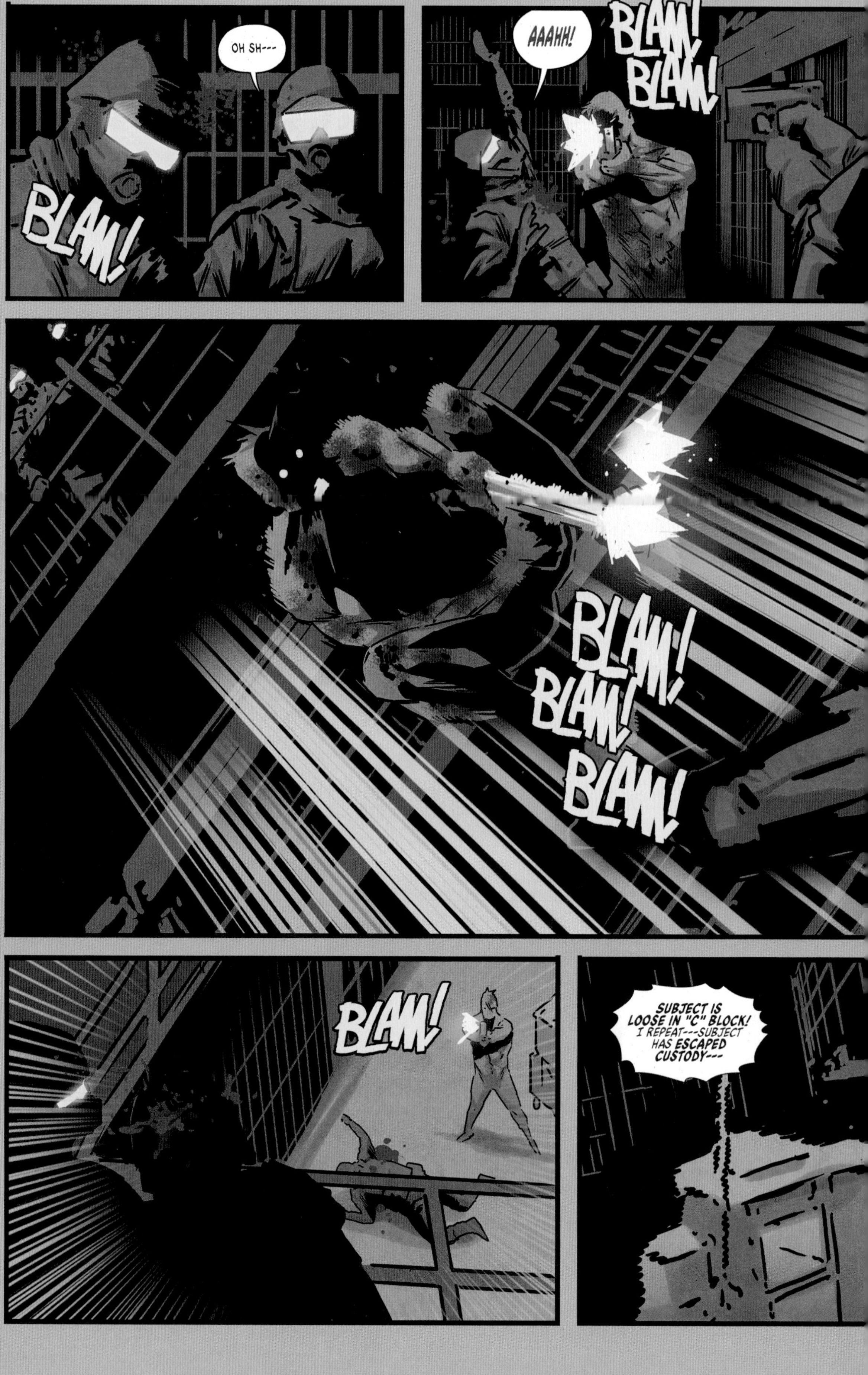
OH SH---
BLAM!
AAAHH!
BLAM! BLAM!
BLAM! BLAM! BLAM!
BLAM!
SUBJECT IS LOOSE IN "C" BLOCK! I REPEAT---SUBJECT HAS ESCAPED CUSTODY---

BLAM!

GUUH--

GUK! GUK! GUUKK---

CRUNNNCH!!!

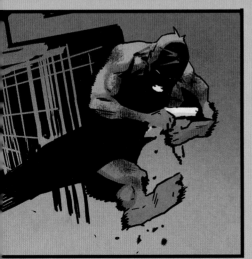

E.B.E. IS ARMED AND EXTREMELY DANGEROUS!

MINUTES LATER.
"E" BLOCK.

UNN---
UNNGH---

THANK YOU.

SEE, THE REST OF THEM...THEY DIDN'T THINK THIS WOULD HAPPEN SO SOON.

BUT *ME*...?

MAN, I *BELIEVED* IN YOU.

LIKE I KNOW YOU CAN UNDERSTAND OUR QUESTIONS JUST FINE...THAT ALIEN GIBBERISH SHIT YOU'VE BEEN FEEDING US IS A *NICE* TOUCH. REALLY.

CAN'T BLAME YOU FOR HOLDING ONTO A FEW CARDS.

PUSH!

FIRST RULE OF FIRST CONTACT IS *ALWAYS* GONNA BE, NO MATTER FUCKIN' WHAT---

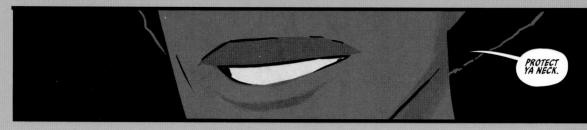

PROTECT YA NECK.

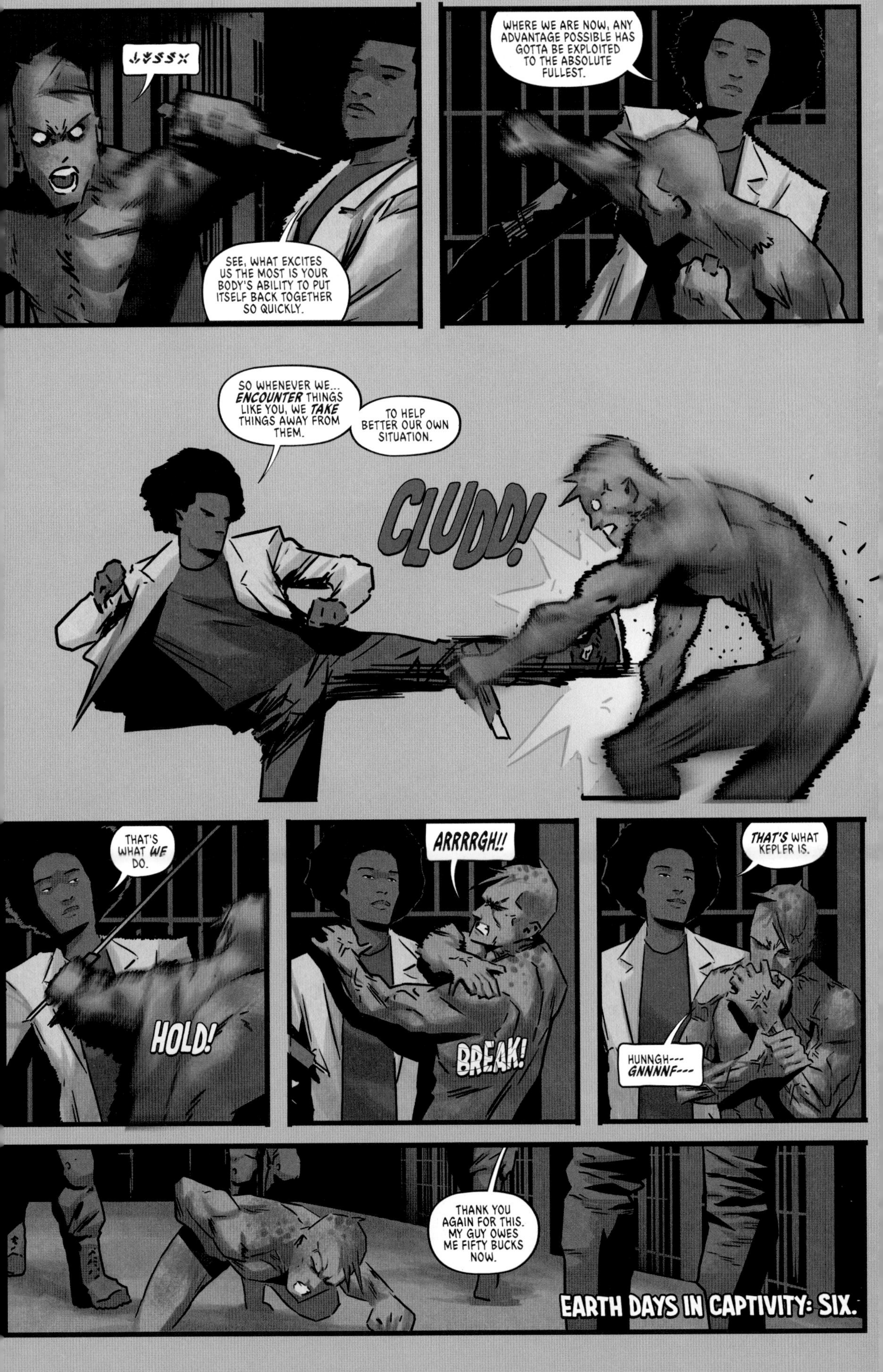
SEE, WHAT EXCITES US THE MOST IS YOUR BODY'S ABILITY TO PUT ITSELF BACK TOGETHER SO QUICKLY.
WHERE WE ARE NOW, ANY ADVANTAGE POSSIBLE HAS GOTTA BE EXPLOITED TO THE ABSOLUTE FULLEST.
SO WHENEVER WE... ENCOUNTER THINGS LIKE YOU, WE TAKE THINGS AWAY FROM THEM.
TO HELP BETTER OUR OWN SITUATION.
CLUDD!
THAT'S WHAT WE DO.
HOLD!
ARRRRGH!!
BREAK!
THAT'S WHAT KEPLER IS.
HUNNGH--- GNNNNF---
THANK YOU AGAIN FOR THIS. MY GUY OWES ME FIFTY BUCKS NOW.
EARTH DAYS IN CAPTIVITY: SIX.

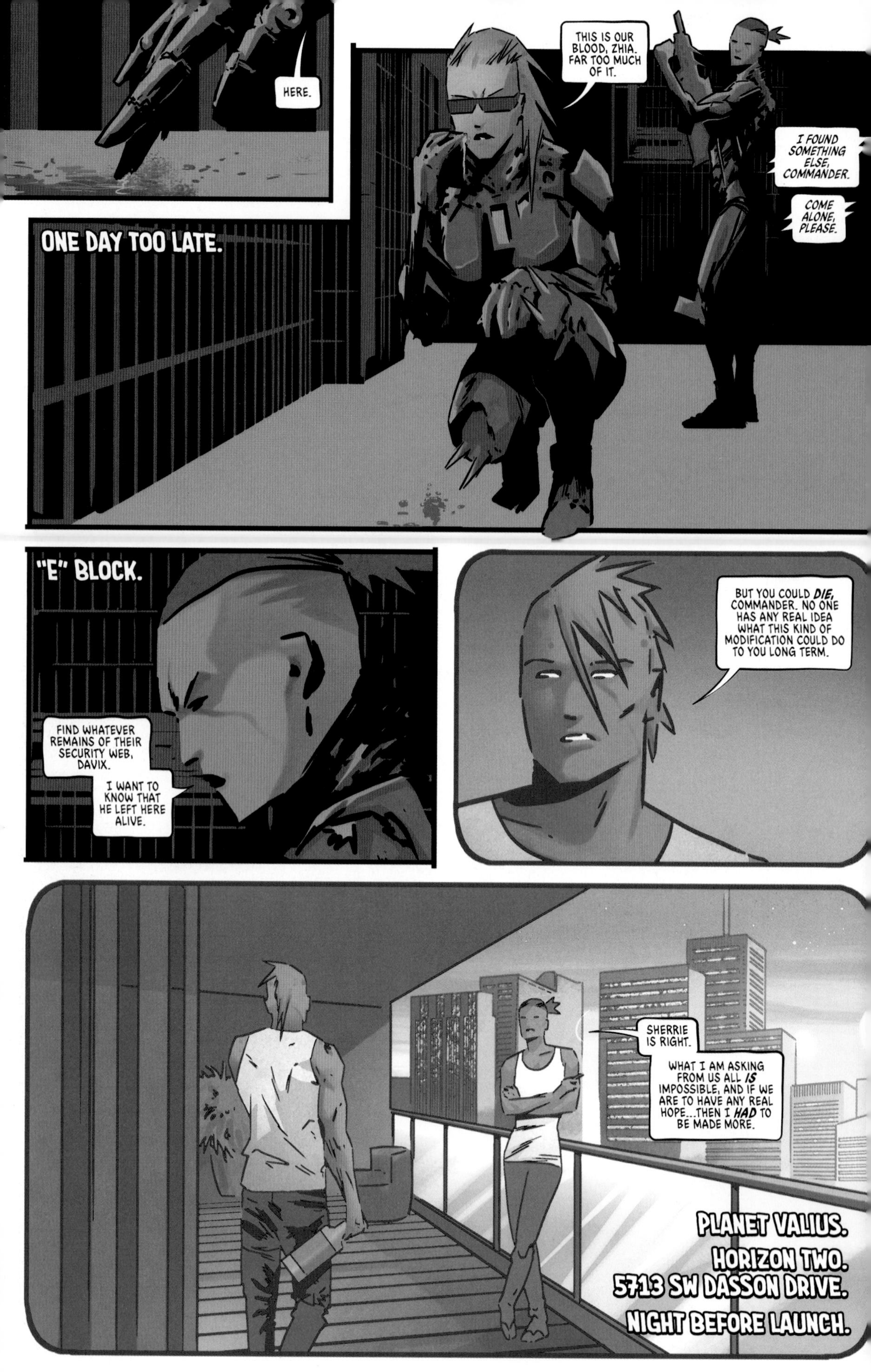
HERE.
ONE DAY TOO LATE.
THIS IS OUR BLOOD, ZHIA. FAR TOO MUCH OF IT.
I FOUND SOMETHING ELSE, COMMANDER.
COME ALONE, PLEASE.
"E" BLOCK.
FIND WHATEVER REMAINS OF THEIR SECURITY WEB, DAVIX.
I WANT TO KNOW THAT HE LEFT HERE ALIVE.
BUT YOU COULD DIE, COMMANDER. NO ONE HAS ANY REAL IDEA WHAT THIS KIND OF MODIFICATION COULD DO TO YOU LONG TERM.
SHERRIE IS RIGHT.
WHAT I AM ASKING FROM US ALL IS IMPOSSIBLE, AND IF WE ARE TO HAVE ANY REAL HOPE...THEN I HAD TO BE MADE MORE.
PLANET VALIUS.
HORIZON TWO.
5713 SW DASSON DRIVE.
NIGHT BEFORE LAUNCH.

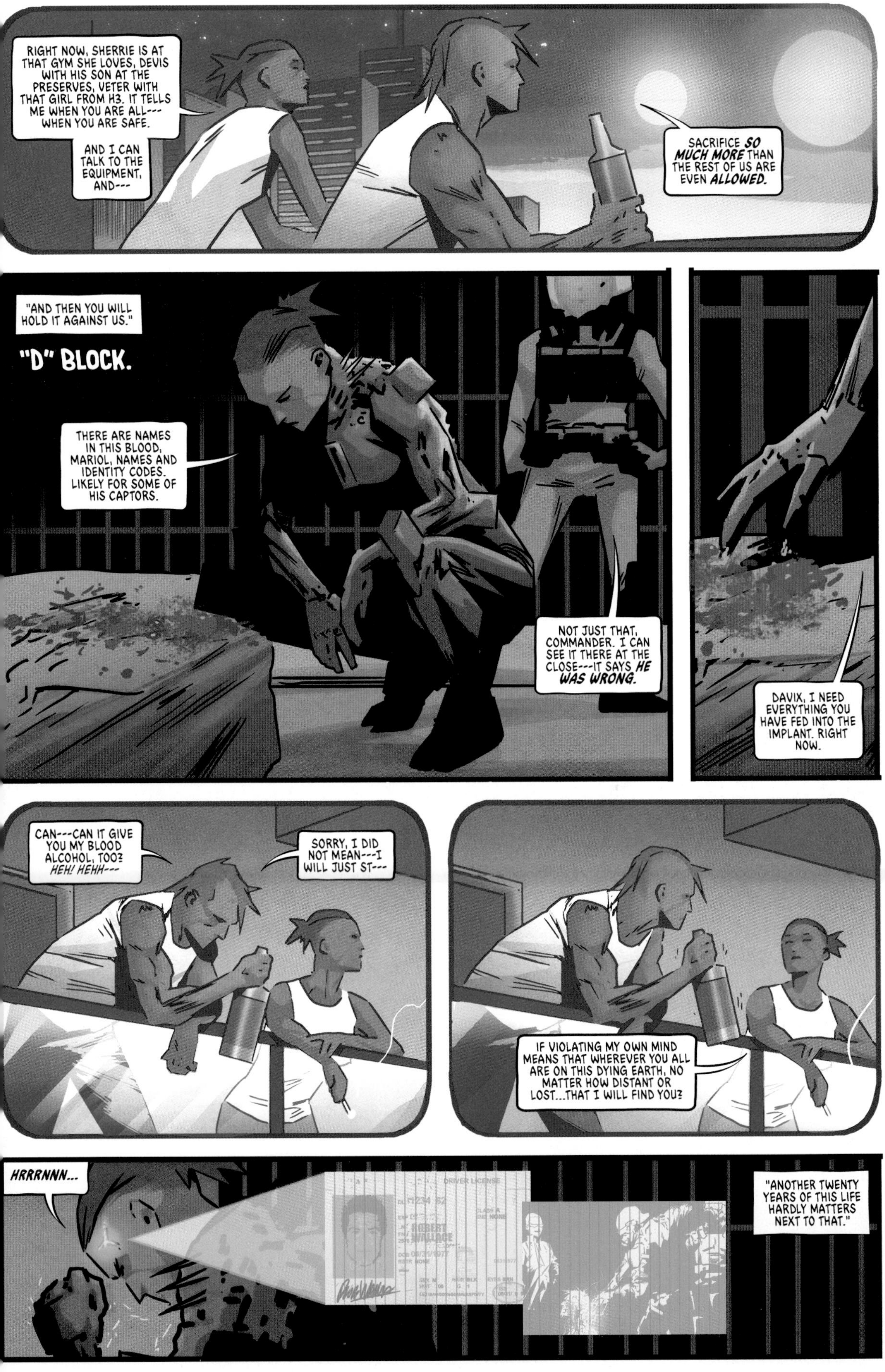
RIGHT NOW, SHERRIE IS AT THAT GYM SHE LOVES, DEVIS WITH HIS SON AT THE PRESERVES, VETER WITH THAT GIRL FROM H3. IT TELLS ME WHEN YOU ARE ALL---WHEN YOU ARE SAFE.
AND I CAN TALK TO THE EQUIPMENT, AND---
SACRIFICE SO MUCH MORE THAN THE REST OF US ARE EVEN ALLOWED.
"AND THEN YOU WILL HOLD IT AGAINST US."
"D" BLOCK.
THERE ARE NAMES IN THIS BLOOD, MARIOL, NAMES AND IDENTITY CODES. LIKELY FOR SOME OF HIS CAPTORS.
NOT JUST THAT, COMMANDER. I CAN SEE IT THERE AT THE CLOSE---IT SAYS HE WAS WRONG.
DAVIX, I NEED EVERYTHING YOU HAVE FED INTO THE IMPLANT. RIGHT NOW.
CAN---CAN IT GIVE YOU MY BLOOD ALCOHOL, TOO? HEH! HEHH---
SORRY, I DID NOT MEAN---I WILL JUST ST---
IF VIOLATING MY OWN MIND MEANS THAT WHEREVER YOU ALL ARE ON THIS DYING EARTH, NO MATTER HOW DISTANT OR LOST...THAT I WILL FIND YOU?
HRRRNNN...
DRIVER LICENSE
"ANOTHER TWENTY YEARS OF THIS LIFE HARDLY MATTERS NEXT TO THAT."

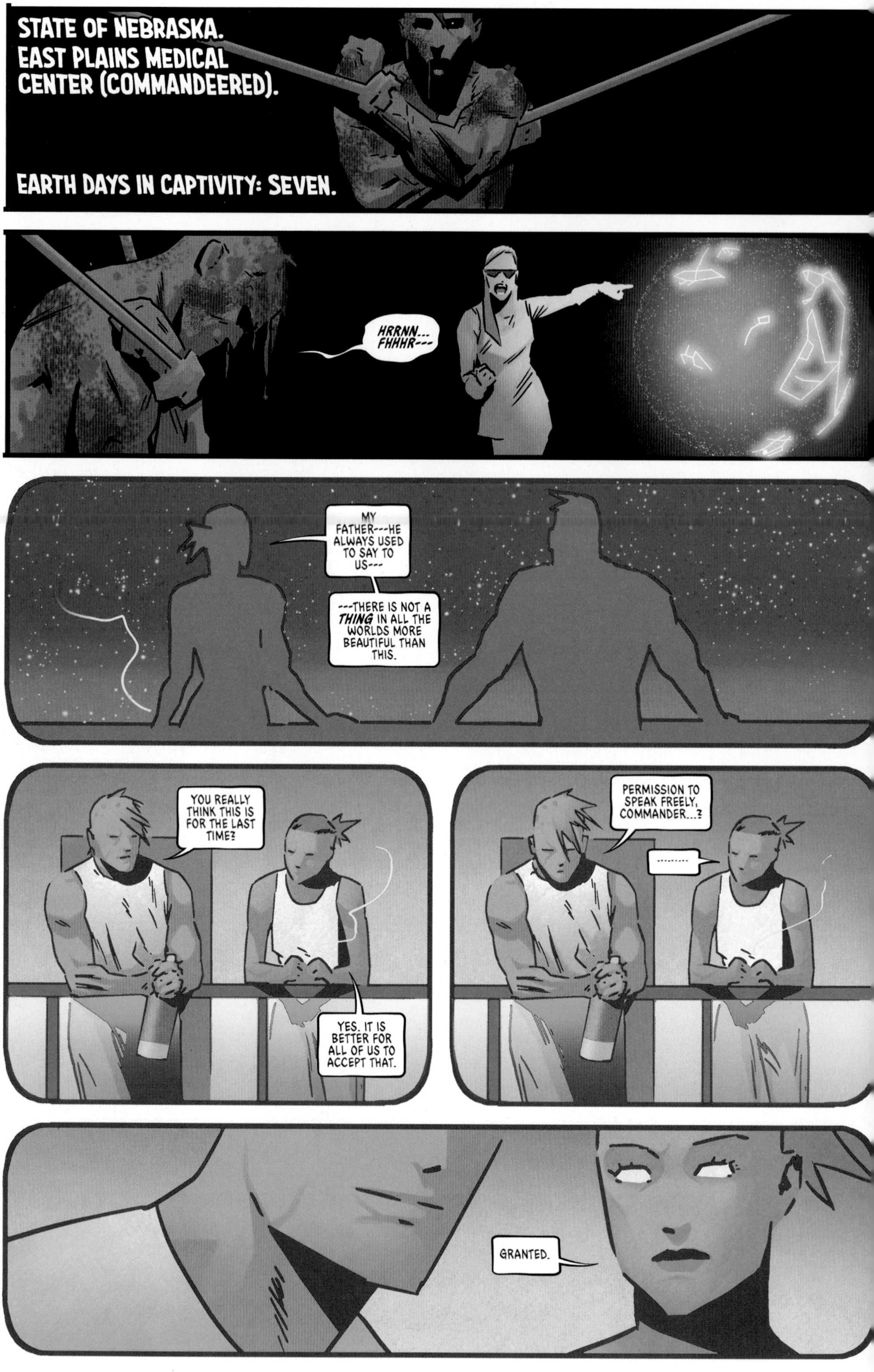
STATE OF NEBRASKA.
EAST PLAINS MEDICAL CENTER (COMMANDEERED).
EARTH DAYS IN CAPTIVITY: SEVEN.
HRRNN... FHHHR---
MY FATHER---HE ALWAYS USED TO SAY TO US---
---THERE IS NOT A THING IN ALL THE WORLDS MORE BEAUTIFUL THAN THIS.
YOU REALLY THINK THIS IS FOR THE LAST TIME?
YES. IT IS BETTER FOR ALL OF US TO ACCEPT THAT.
PERMISSION TO SPEAK FREELY, COMMANDER...?
....
GRANTED.

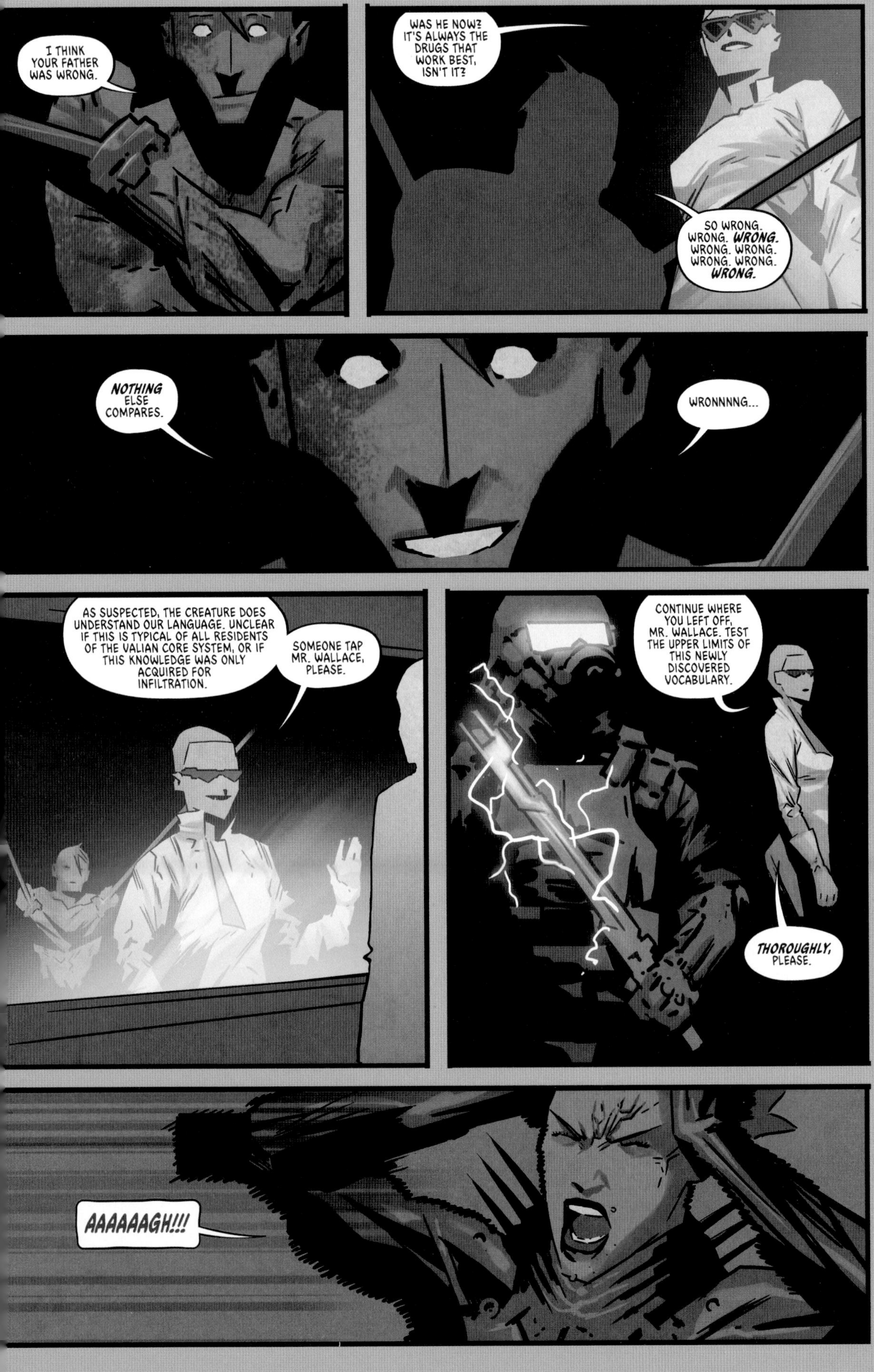
I THINK YOUR FATHER WAS WRONG.
WAS HE NOW? IT'S ALWAYS THE DRUGS THAT WORK BEST, ISN'T IT?
SO WRONG. WRONG. **WRONG.** WRONG. WRONG. WRONG. WRONG. **WRONG.**
NOTHING ELSE COMPARES.
WRONNNNG...
AS SUSPECTED, THE CREATURE DOES UNDERSTAND OUR LANGUAGE. UNCLEAR IF THIS IS TYPICAL OF ALL RESIDENTS OF THE VALIAN CORE SYSTEM, OR IF THIS KNOWLEDGE WAS ONLY ACQUIRED FOR INFILTRATION.
SOMEONE TAP MR. WALLACE, PLEASE.
CONTINUE WHERE YOU LEFT OFF, MR. WALLACE. TEST THE UPPER LIMITS OF THIS NEWLY DISCOVERED VOCABULARY.
THOROUGHLY, PLEASE.
AAAAAAGH!!!

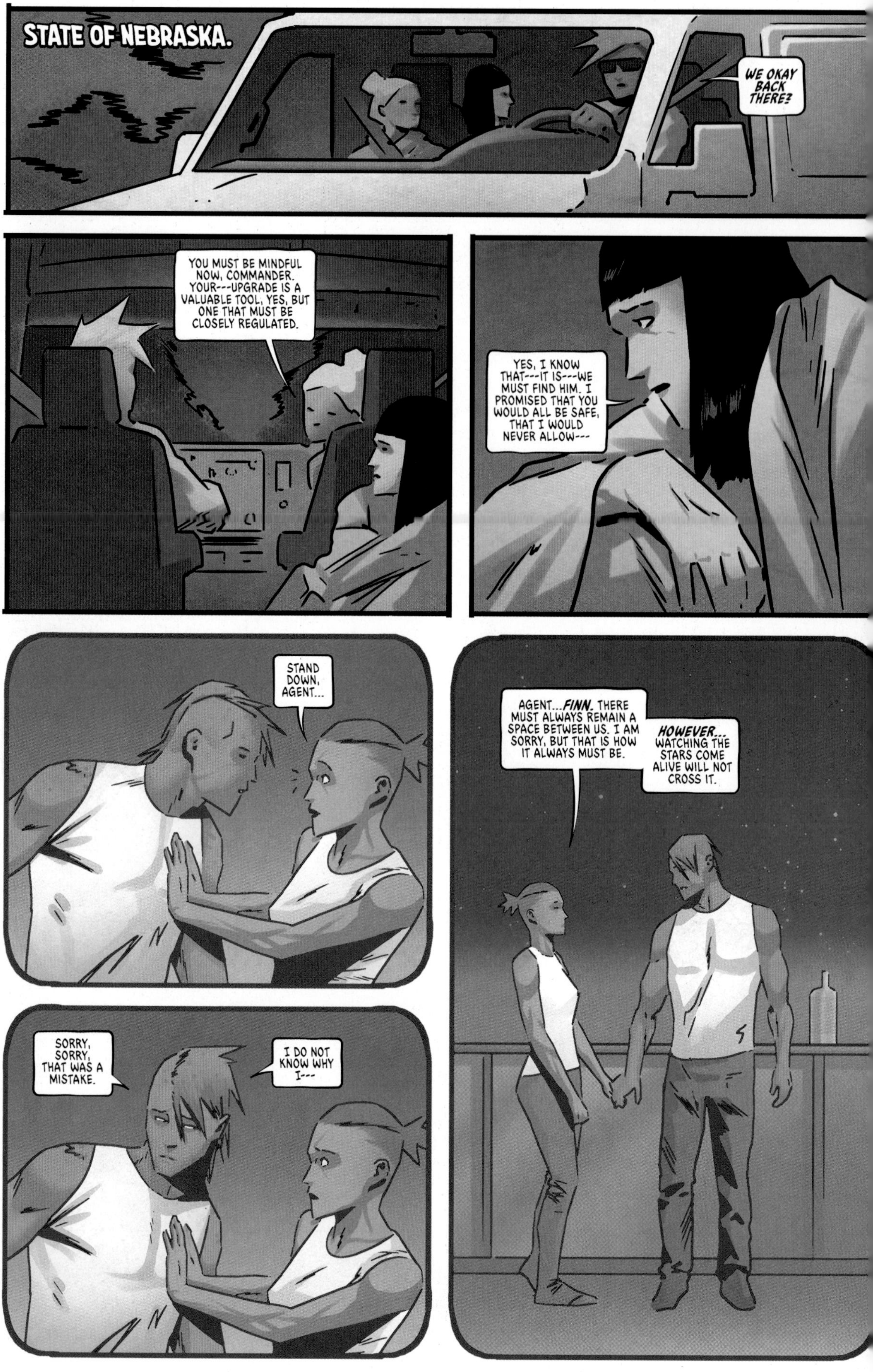
STATE OF NEBRASKA.
WE OKAY BACK THERE?
YOU MUST BE MINDFUL NOW, COMMANDER. YOUR---UPGRADE IS A VALUABLE TOOL, YES, BUT ONE THAT MUST BE CLOSELY REGULATED.
YES, I KNOW THAT---IT IS---WE MUST FIND HIM. I PROMISED THAT YOU WOULD ALL BE SAFE, THAT I WOULD NEVER ALLOW---
STAND DOWN, AGENT...
SORRY, SORRY, THAT WAS A MISTAKE.
I DO NOT KNOW WHY I---
AGENT...FINN. THERE MUST ALWAYS REMAIN A SPACE BETWEEN US. I AM SORRY, BUT THAT IS HOW IT ALWAYS MUST BE.
HOWEVER... WATCHING THE STARS COME ALIVE WILL NOT CROSS IT.

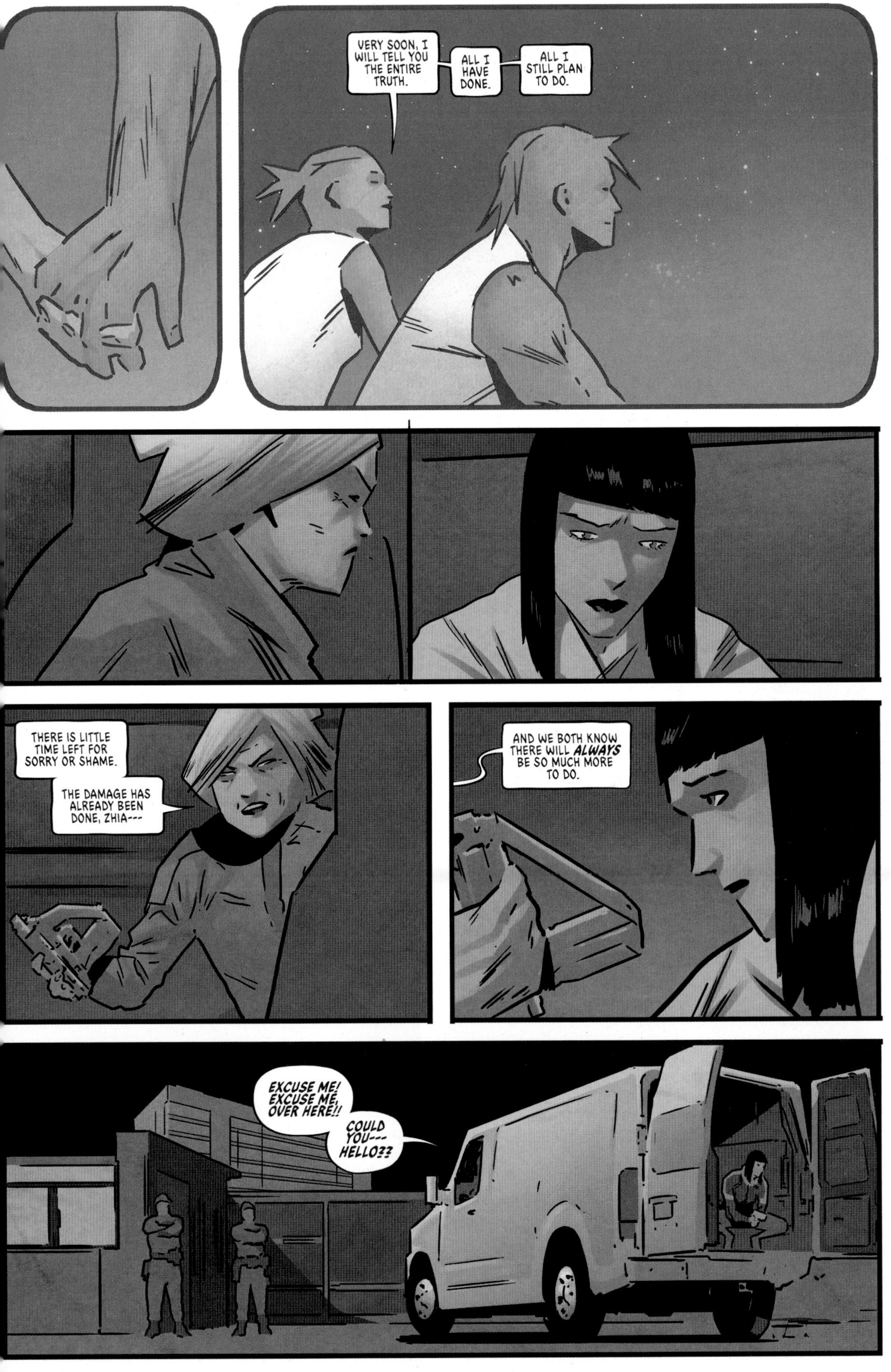
VERY SOON, I WILL TELL YOU THE ENTIRE TRUTH.
ALL I HAVE DONE.
ALL I STILL PLAN TO DO.
THERE IS LITTLE TIME LEFT FOR SORRY OR SHAME.
THE DAMAGE HAS ALREADY BEEN DONE, ZHIA---
AND WE BOTH KNOW THERE WILL *ALWAYS* BE SO MUCH MORE TO DO.
EXCUSE ME! EXCUSE ME, OVER HERE!!
COULD YOU--- HELLO??

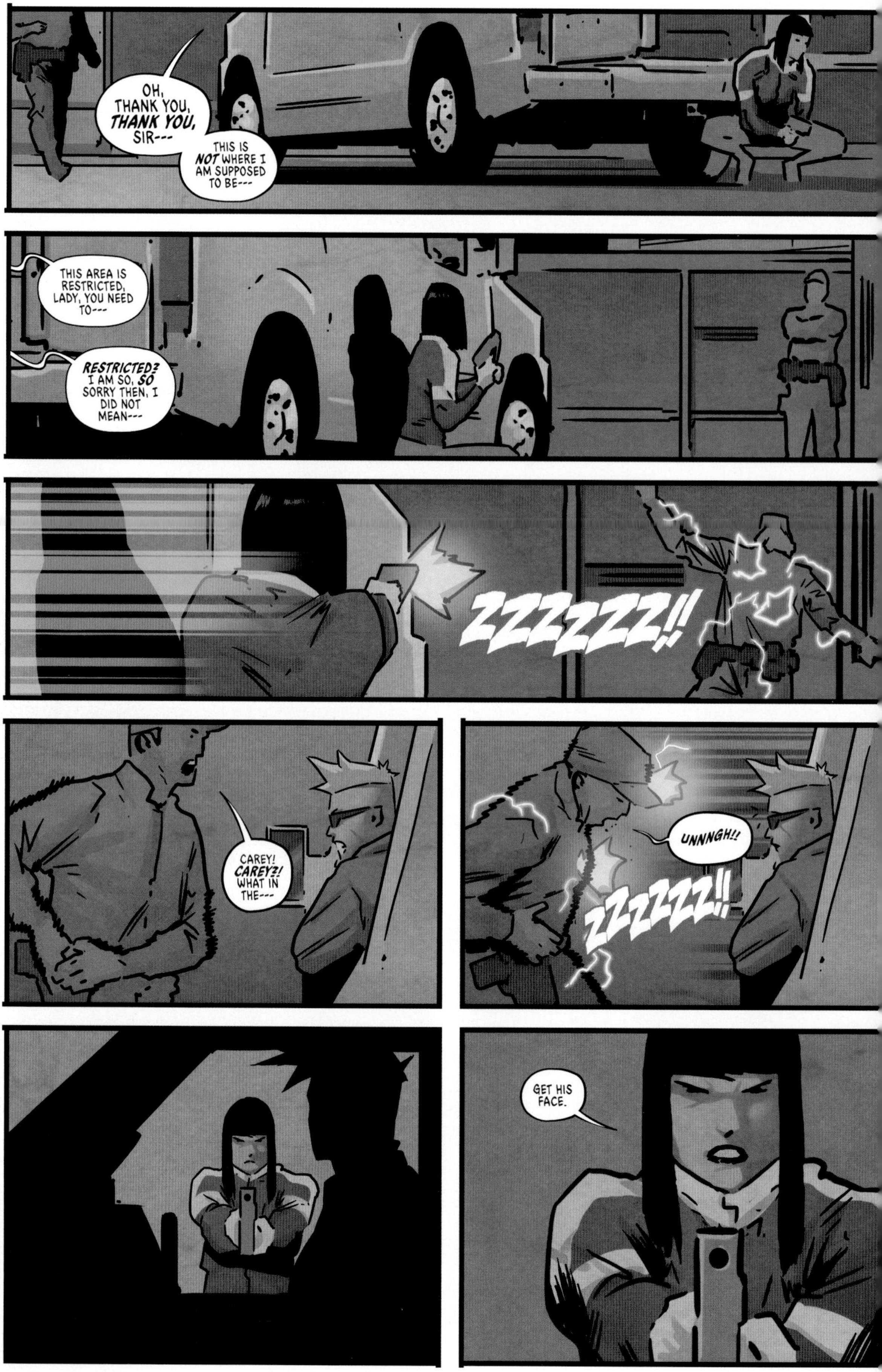
OH, THANK YOU, THANK YOU, SIR---
THIS IS NOT WHERE I AM SUPPOSED TO BE---
THIS AREA IS RESTRICTED, LADY, YOU NEED TO---
RESTRICTED? I AM SO, SO SORRY THEN, I DID NOT MEAN---
ZZZZZZZ!!
CAREY! CAREY?! WHAT IN THE---
UNNNGH!!
ZZZZZZ!!
GET HIS FACE.

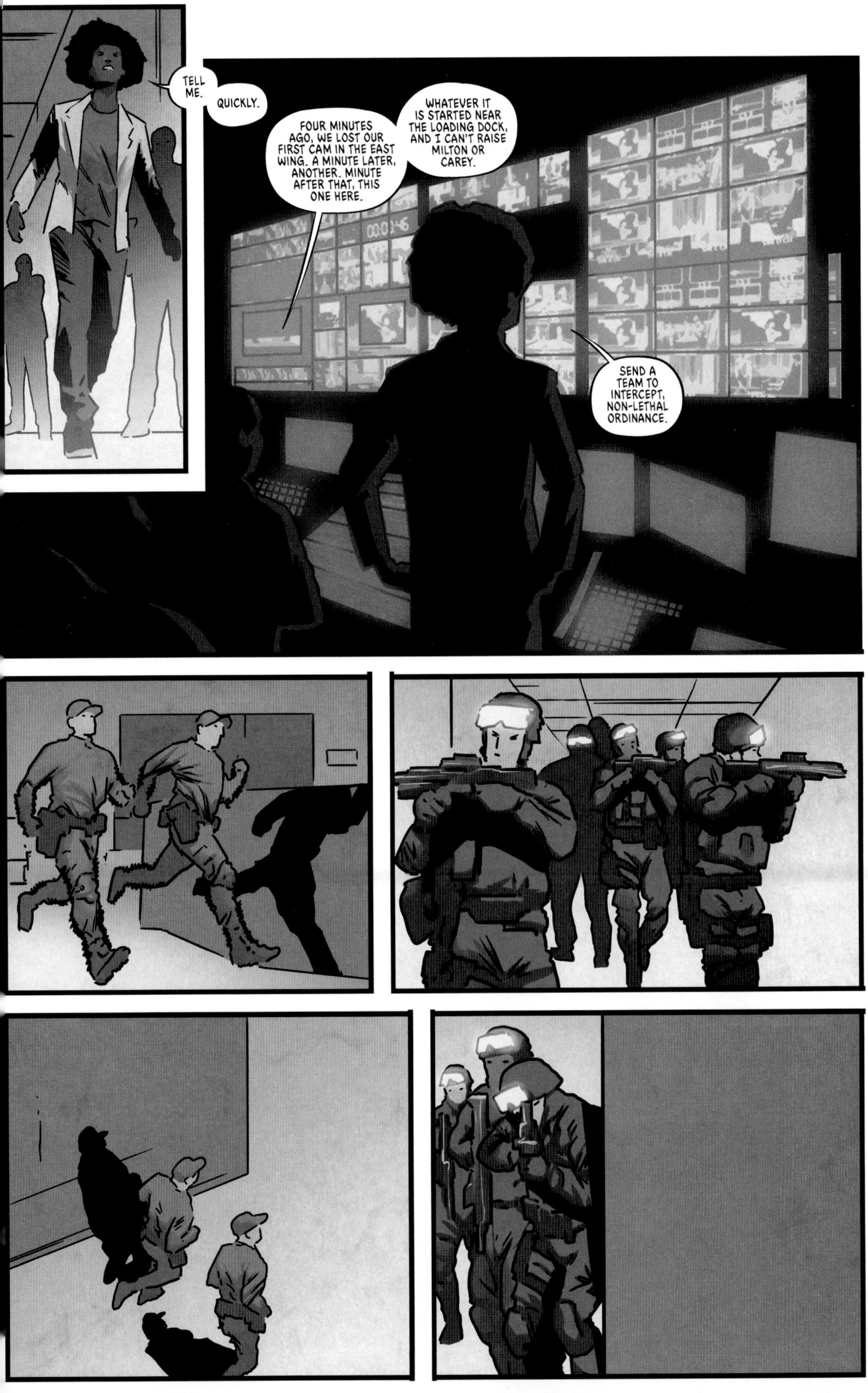
TELL ME.
QUICKLY.
FOUR MINUTES AGO, WE LOST OUR FIRST CAM IN THE EAST WING. A MINUTE LATER, ANOTHER. MINUTE AFTER THAT, THIS ONE HERE.
WHATEVER IT IS STARTED NEAR THE LOADING DOCK, AND I CAN'T RAISE MILTON OR CAREY.
SEND A TEAM TO INTERCEPT, NON-LETHAL ORDINANCE.

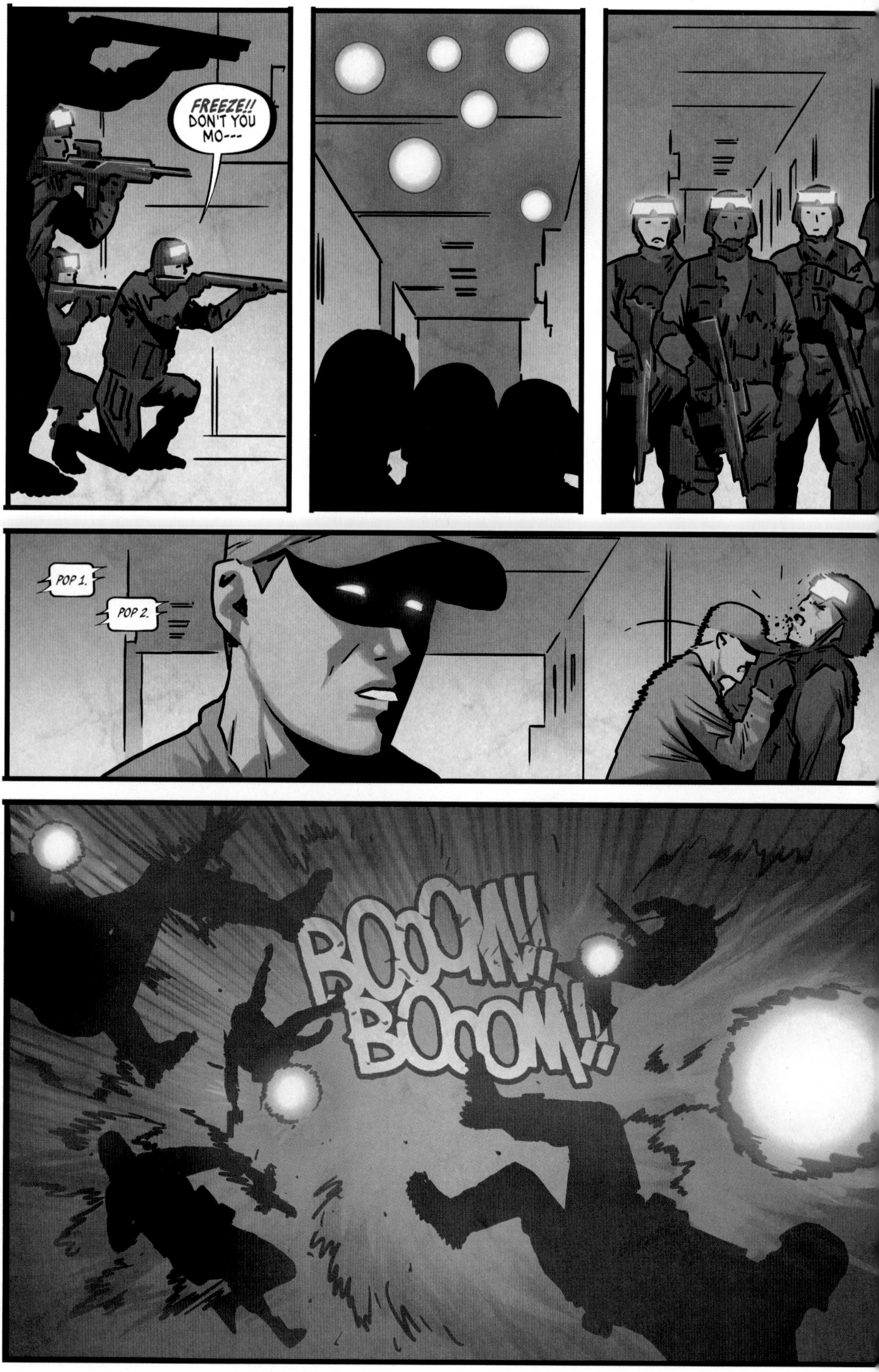
FREEZE!! DON'T YOU MO---
POP 1.
POP 2.
BOOOM!!
BOOOM!!

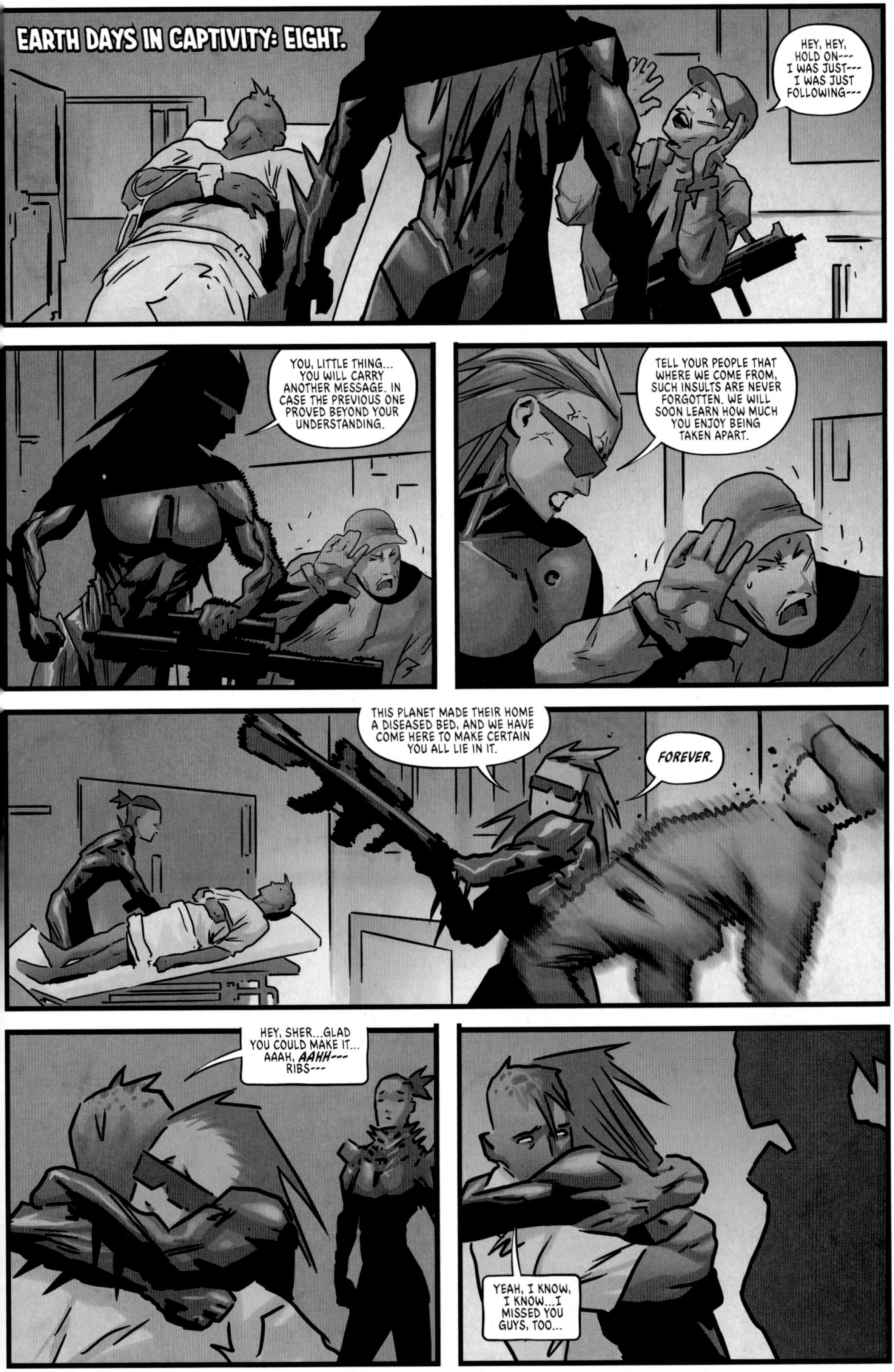
EARTH DAYS IN CAPTIVITY: EIGHT.
HEY, HEY, HOLD ON--- I WAS JUST--- I WAS JUST FOLLOWING---
YOU, LITTLE THING... YOU WILL CARRY ANOTHER MESSAGE. IN CASE THE PREVIOUS ONE PROVED BEYOND YOUR UNDERSTANDING.
TELL YOUR PEOPLE THAT WHERE WE COME FROM, SUCH INSULTS ARE NEVER FORGOTTEN. WE WILL SOON LEARN HOW MUCH YOU ENJOY BEING TAKEN APART.
THIS PLANET MADE THEIR HOME A DISEASED BED, AND WE HAVE COME HERE TO MAKE CERTAIN YOU ALL LIE IN IT.
FOREVER.
HEY, SHER...GLAD YOU COULD MAKE IT... AAAH, AAHH--- RIBS---
YEAH, I KNOW, I KNOW...I MISSED YOU GUYS, TOO...

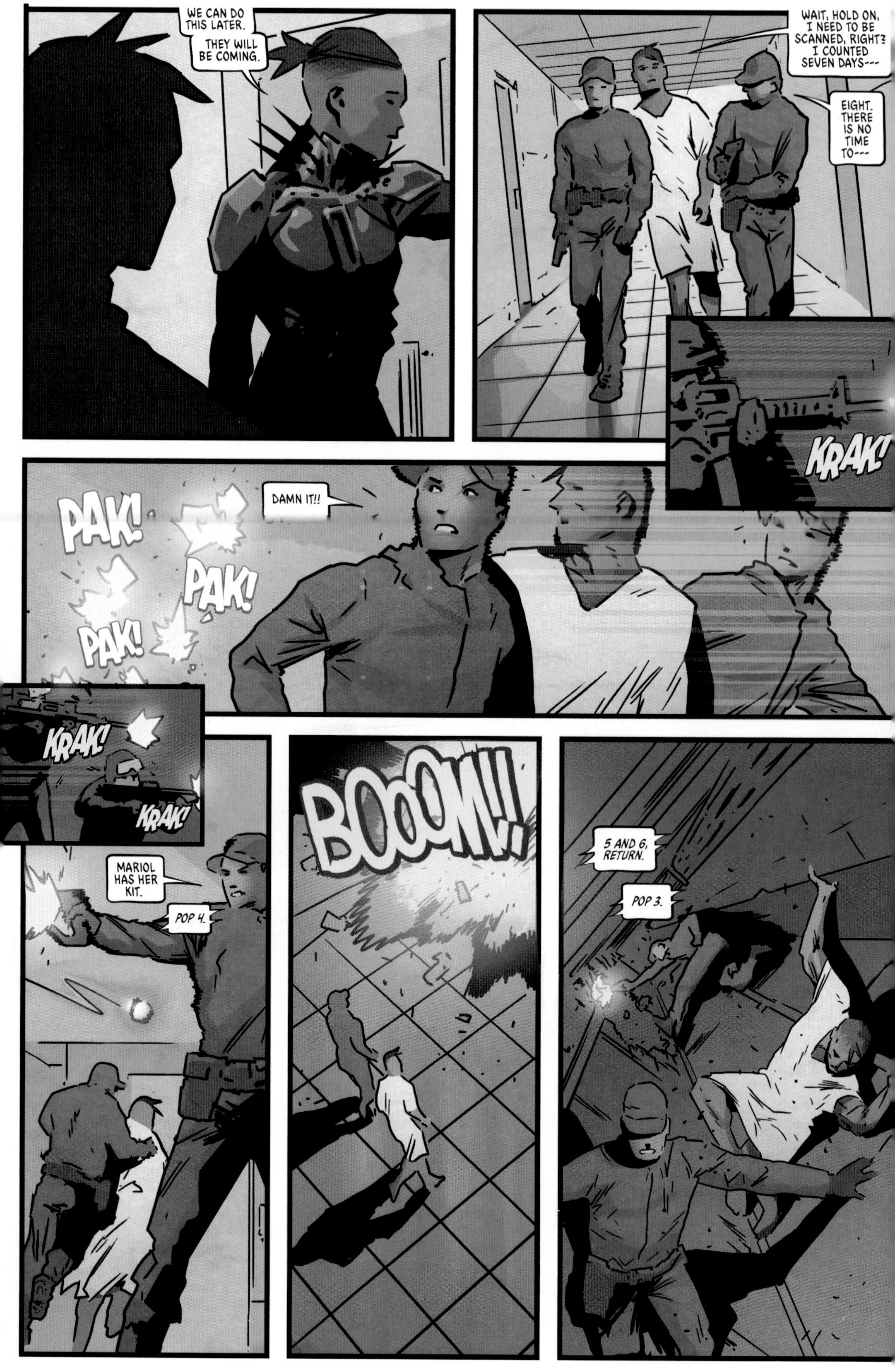
WE CAN DO THIS LATER.
THEY WILL BE COMING.
WAIT, HOLD ON, I NEED TO BE SCANNED, RIGHT? I COUNTED SEVEN DAYS---
EIGHT. THERE IS NO TIME TO---
KRAK!
PAK!
PAK!
PAK!
DAMN IT!!
KRAK!
KRAK!
MARIOL HAS HER KIT.
POP 4.
BOOOM!!
5 AND 6, RETURN.
POP 3.

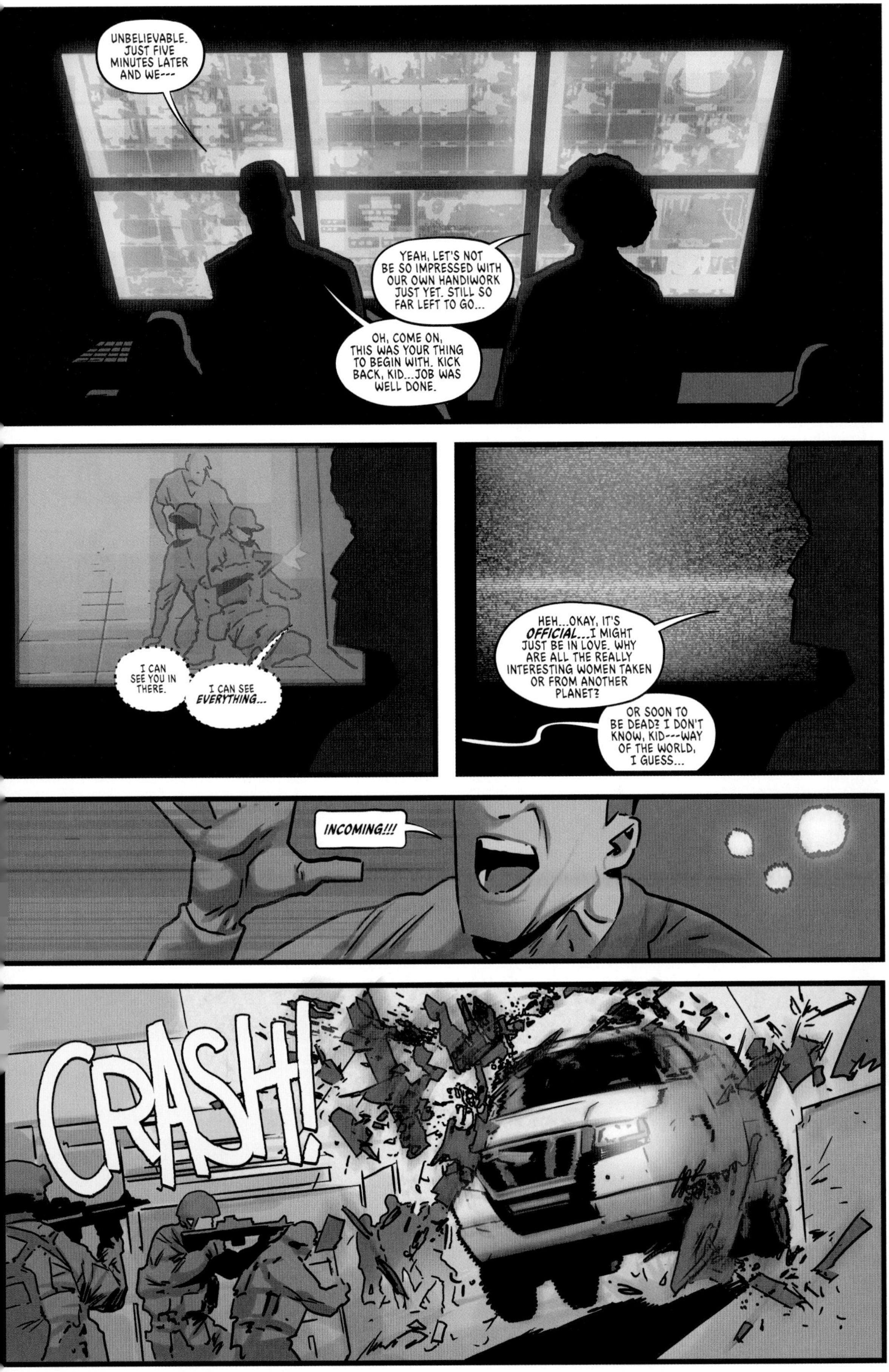
UNBELIEVABLE. JUST FIVE MINUTES LATER AND WE---
YEAH, LET'S NOT BE SO IMPRESSED WITH OUR OWN HANDIWORK JUST YET. STILL SO FAR LEFT TO GO...
OH, COME ON, THIS WAS YOUR THING TO BEGIN WITH. KICK BACK, KID...JOB WAS WELL DONE.
I CAN SEE YOU IN THERE.
I CAN SEE *EVERYTHING...*
HEH...OKAY, IT'S *OFFICIAL*...I MIGHT JUST BE IN LOVE. WHY ARE ALL THE REALLY INTERESTING WOMEN TAKEN OR FROM ANOTHER PLANET?
OR SOON TO BE DEAD? I DON'T KNOW, KID---WAY OF THE WORLD, I GUESS...
INCOMING!!!
CRASH!

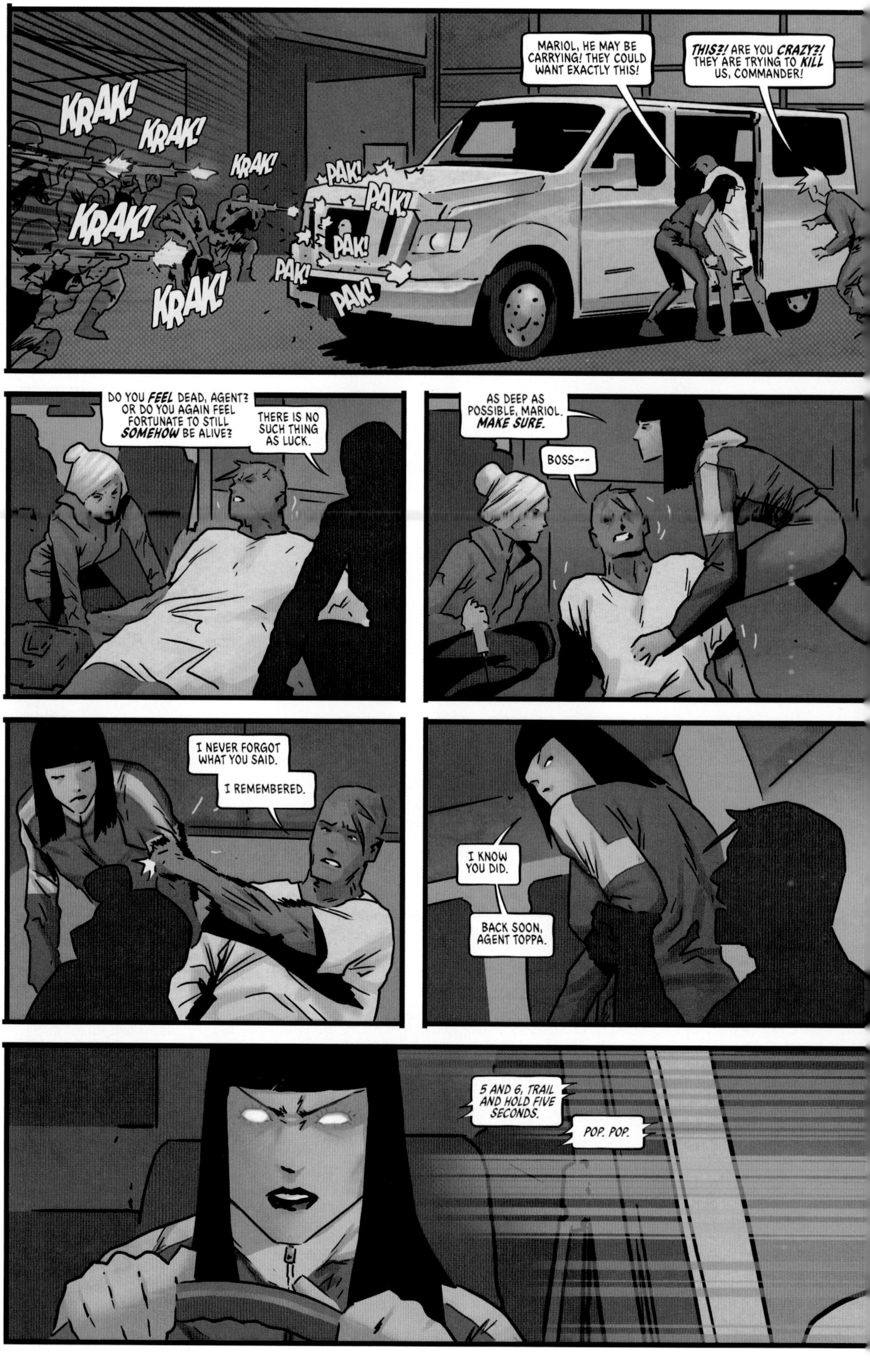
KRAK!
KRAK!
KRAK!
KRAK!
KRAK!
PAK!
PAK!
PAK!
PAK!
PAK!
MARIOL, HE MAY BE CARRYING! THEY COULD WANT EXACTLY THIS!
THIS?! ARE YOU CRAZY?! THEY ARE TRYING TO KILL US, COMMANDER!
DO YOU FEEL DEAD, AGENT? OR DO YOU AGAIN FEEL FORTUNATE TO STILL SOMEHOW BE ALIVE?
THERE IS NO SUCH THING AS LUCK.
AS DEEP AS POSSIBLE, MARIOL. MAKE SURE.
BOSS---
I NEVER FORGOT WHAT YOU SAID.
I REMEMBERED.
I KNOW YOU DID.
BACK SOON, AGENT TOPPA.
5 AND 6, TRAIL AND HOLD FIVE SECONDS.
POP. POP.

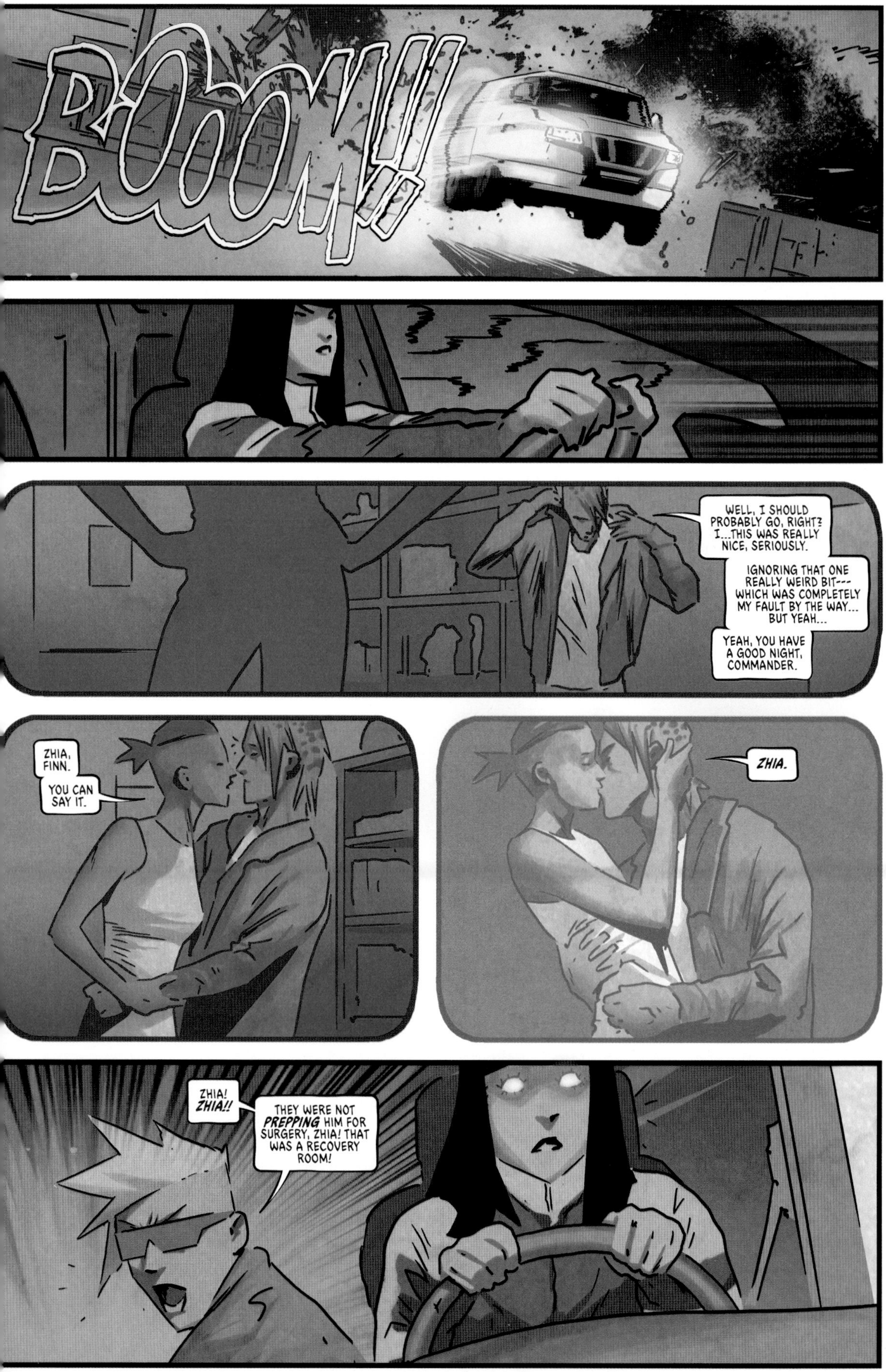
BOOOM!!
WELL, I SHOULD PROBABLY GO, RIGHT? I...THIS WAS REALLY NICE, SERIOUSLY.
IGNORING THAT ONE REALLY WEIRD BIT--- WHICH WAS COMPLETELY MY FAULT BY THE WAY... BUT YEAH...
YEAH, YOU HAVE A GOOD NIGHT, COMMANDER.
ZHIA, FINN.
YOU CAN SAY IT.
ZHIA.
ZHIA! ZHIA!!
THEY WERE NOT PREPPING HIM FOR SURGERY, ZHIA! THAT WAS A RECOVERY ROOM!

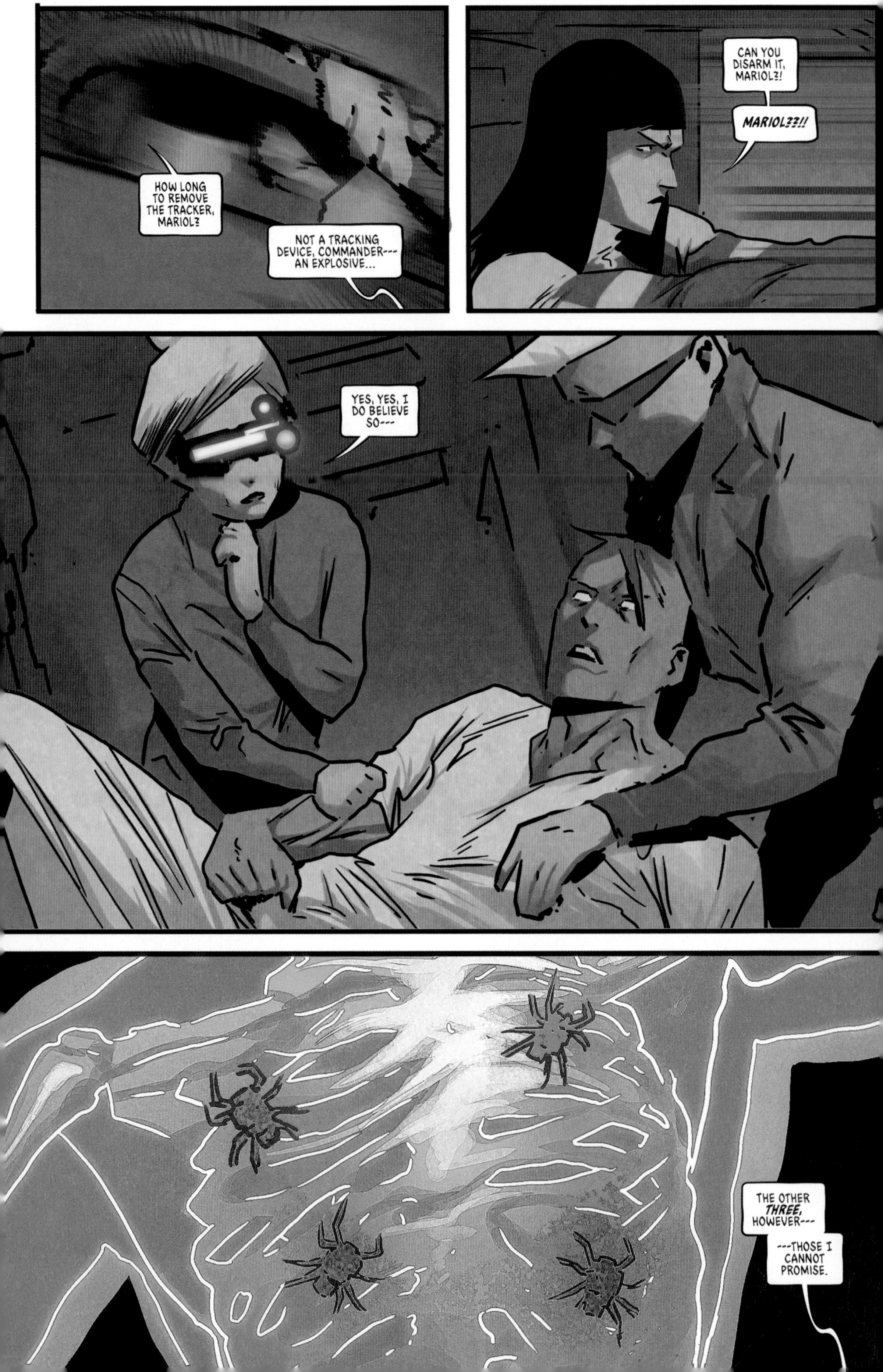

HOW LONG TO REMOVE THE TRACKER, MARIOLZ?
NOT A TRACKING DEVICE, COMMANDER--- AN EXPLOSIVE...
CAN YOU DISARM IT, MARIOLZ?!
MARIOLZ?!!
YES, YES, I DO BELIEVE SO---
THE OTHER THREE, HOWEVER---
---THOSE I CANNOT PROMISE.

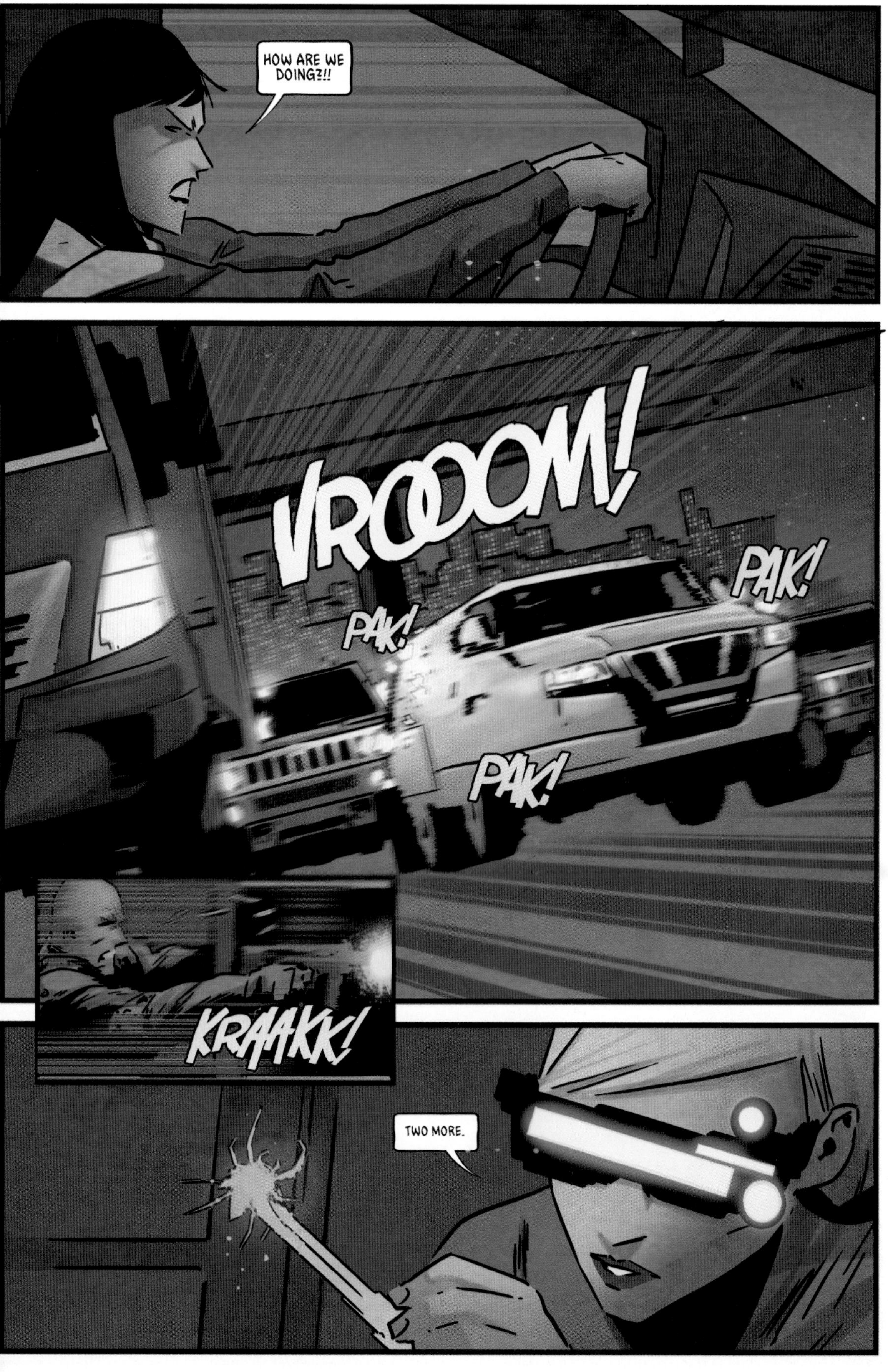
HOW ARE WE DOING?!!
VROOOM!
PAK!
PAK!
PAK!
KRAAKK!
TWO MORE.

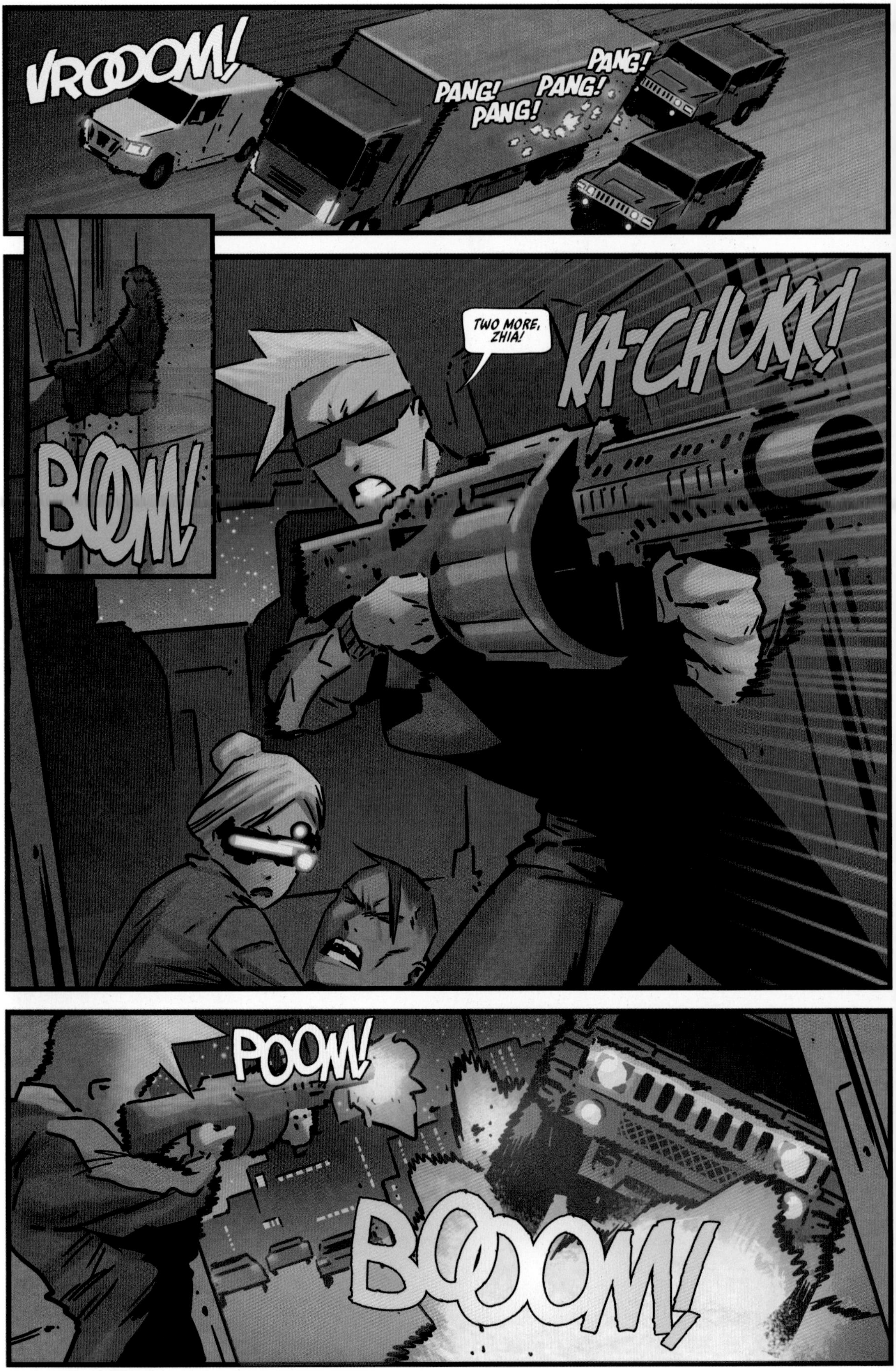
VROOOM!
PANG!
PANG!
PANG!
PANG!
BOOM!
TWO MORE, ZHIA!
KA-CHUKK!
POOM!
BOOOOM!

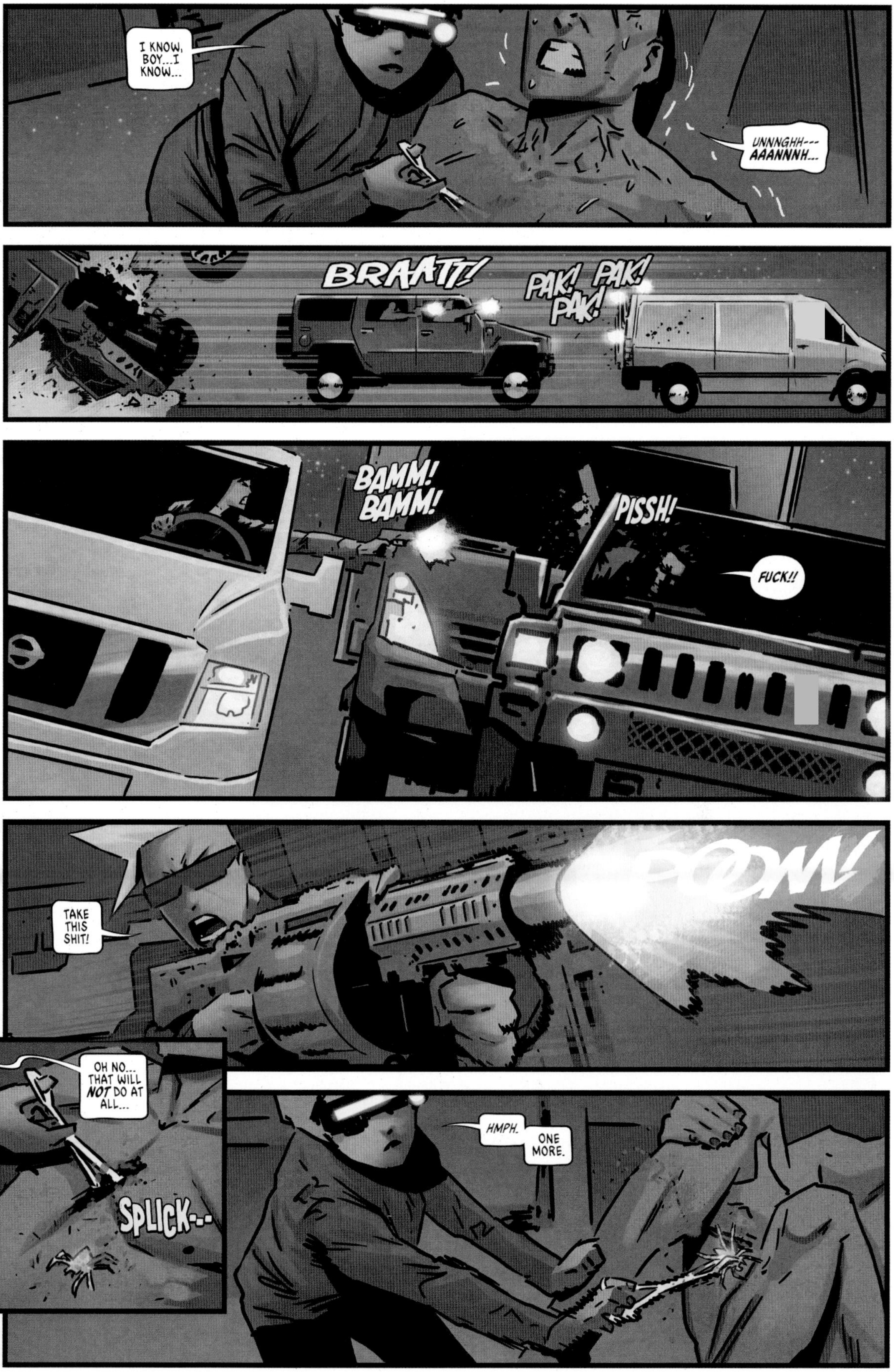
I KNOW, BOY... I KNOW...
UNNNGHH--- AAANNNH...
BRAATT!
PAK! PAK! PAK!
BAMM! BAMM!
PISSH!
FUCK!!
TAKE THIS SHIT!
OH NO... THAT WILL *NOT* DO AT ALL...
SPLICK-..
HMPH.
ONE MORE.

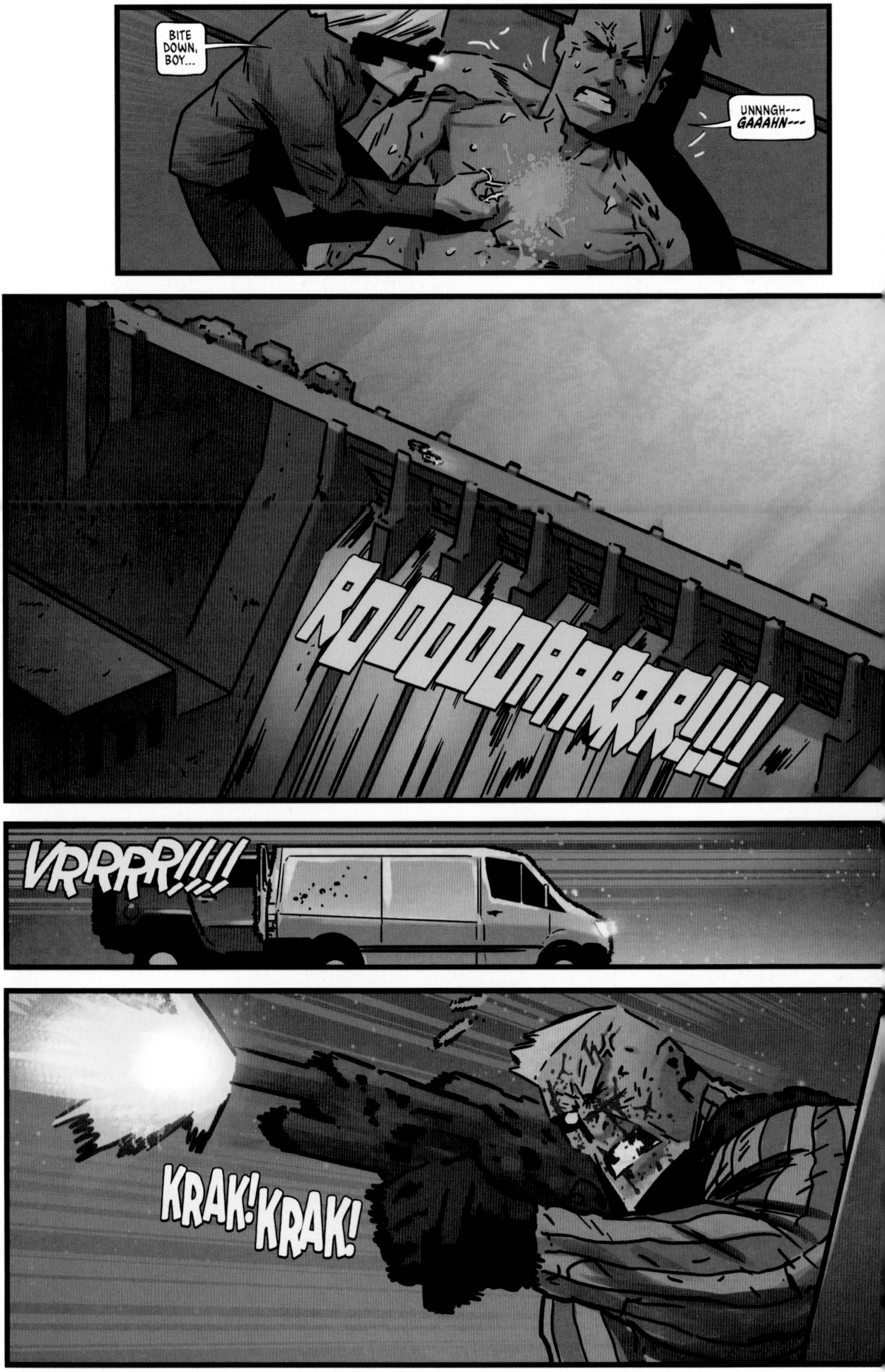
BITE DOWN, BOY...
UNNNGH--- GAAAHN---
ROOOOOAARRR!!!!
VRRRR!!!!
KRAK! KRAK!

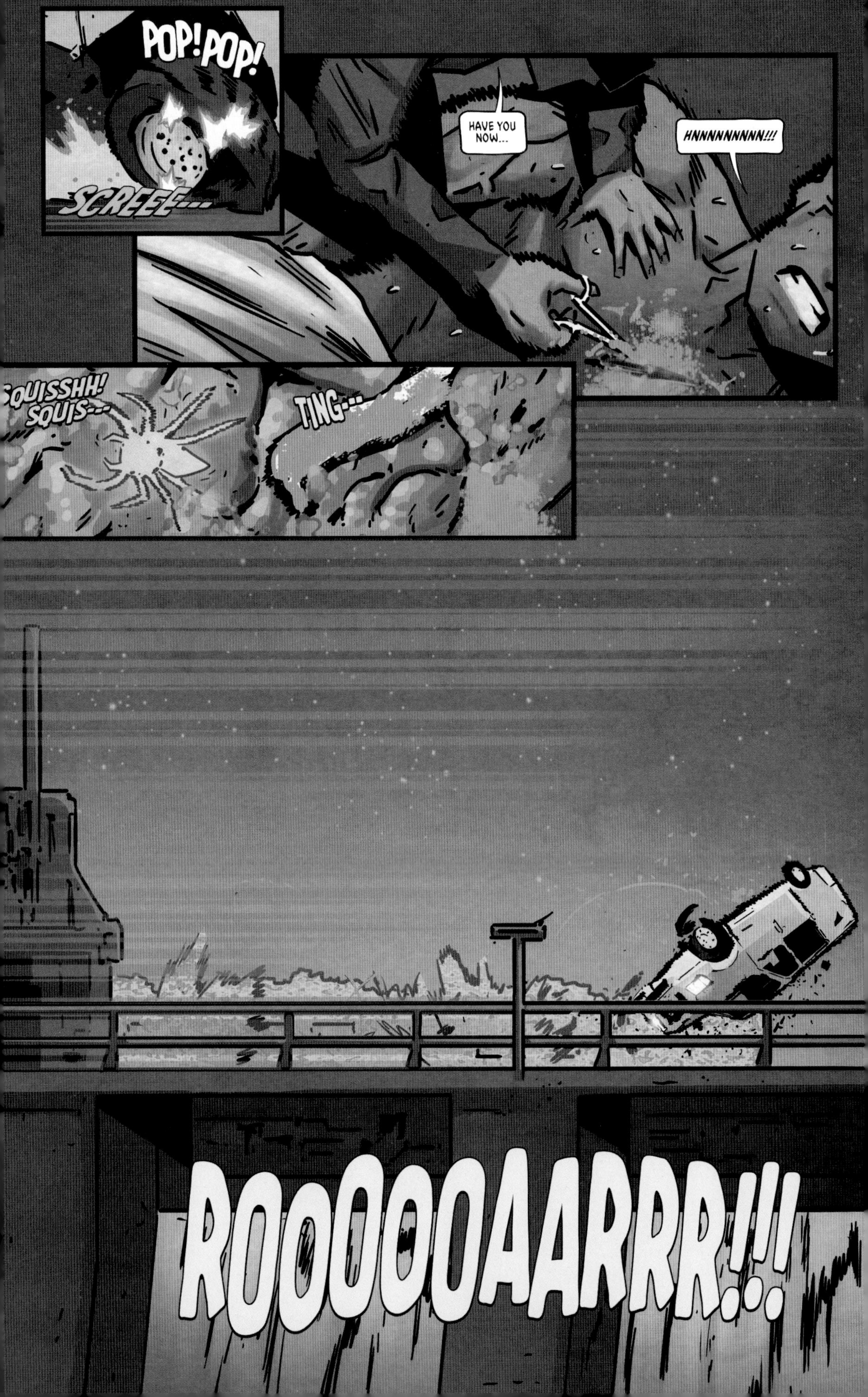
POP! POP!
SCREEE...
HAVE YOU NOW...
HNNNNNNNNN!!!
SQUISSHH! SQUIS--
TING--
ROOOOOAARRR!!!

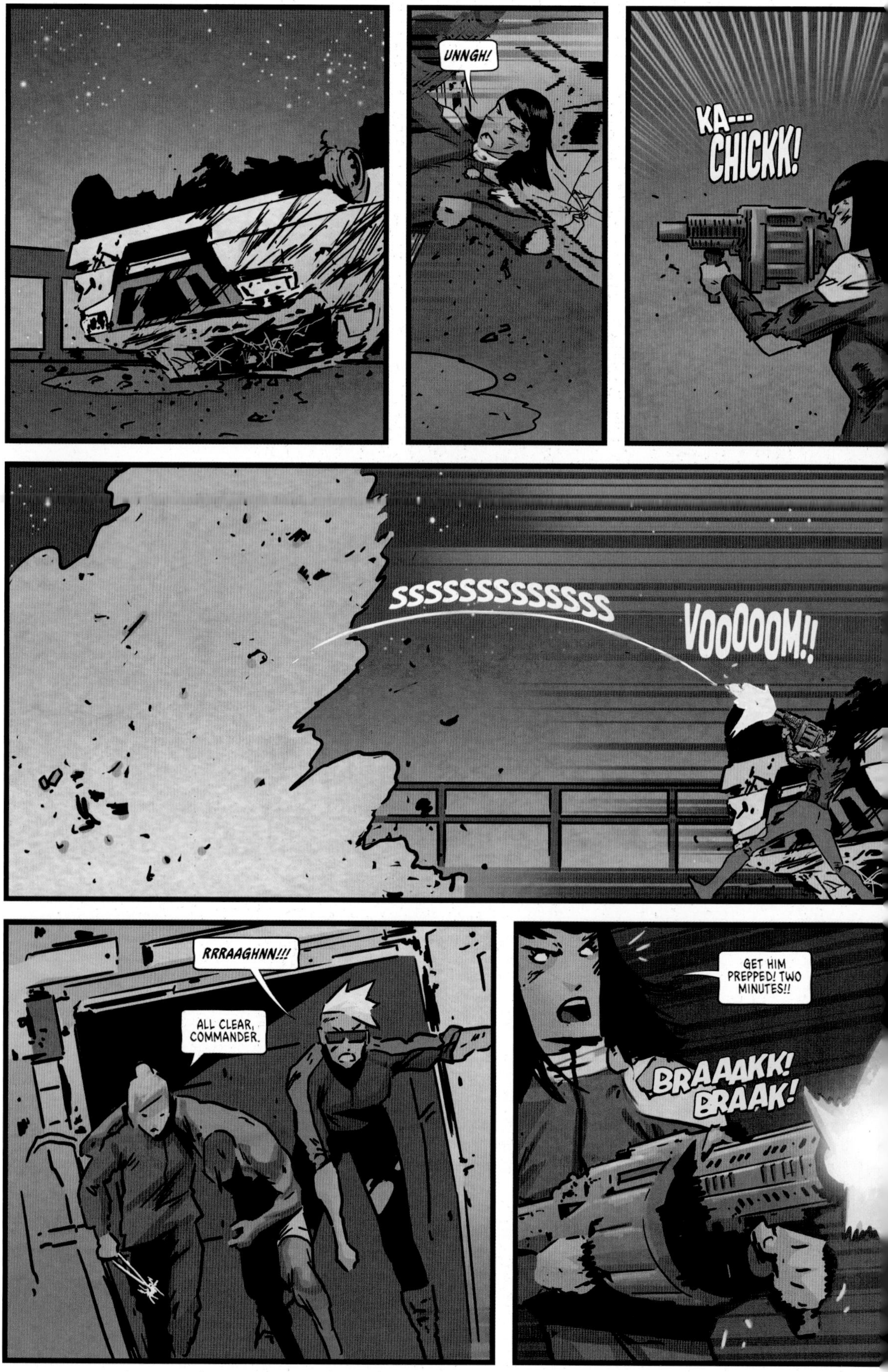
UNNGH!
KA---
CHICKK!
SSSSSSSSSSSSS
VOOOOOM!!
RRRAAGHNN!!!
ALL CLEAR, COMMANDER.
GET HIM PREPPED! TWO MINUTES!!
BRAAAKK!
BRAAK!

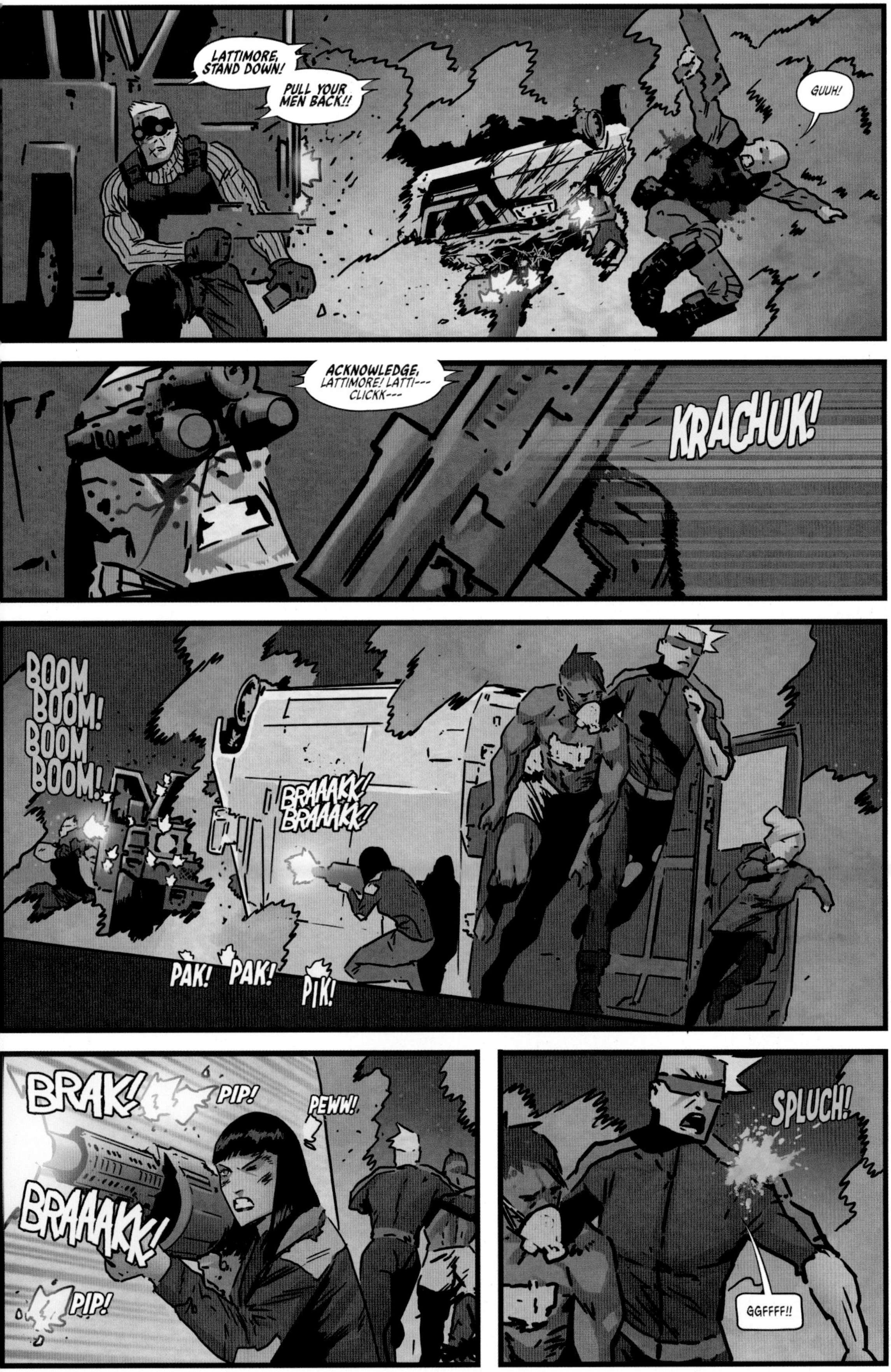
LATTIMORE, STAND DOWN!
PULL YOUR MEN BACK!!
GUUH!
ACKNOWLEDGE, LATTIMORE! LATTI---
CLICKK---
KRACHUK!
BOOM BOOM! BOOM BOOM!
BRAAAKK! BRAAAKK!
PAK! PAK!
PIK!
BRAK!
PIP!
PEWW!
BRAAAKK!
PIP!
SPLUCH!
GGFFFF!!

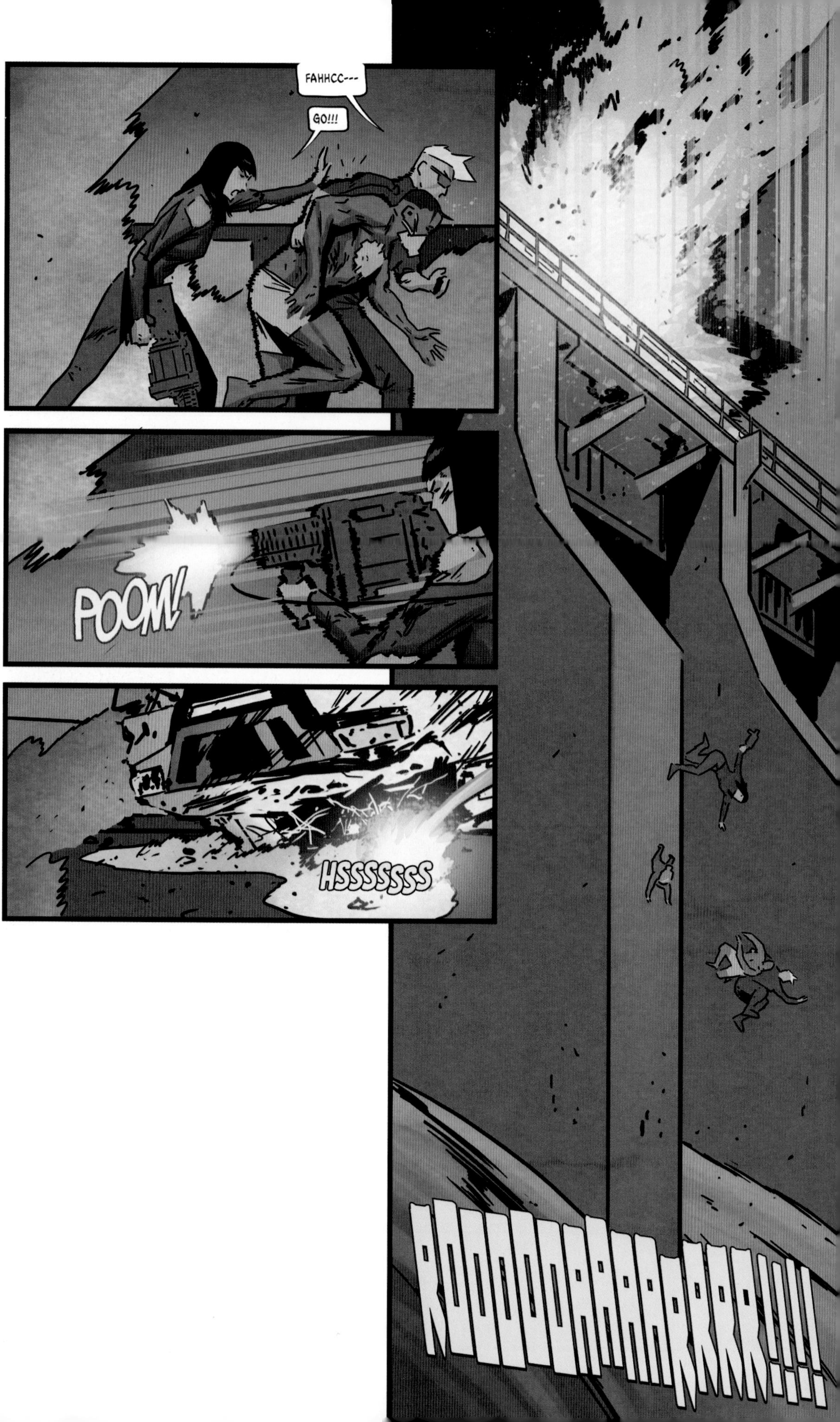
FAHHCC---
GO!!!
POOM!
HSSSSSSS
ROOOOOAAAARRRR!!!!

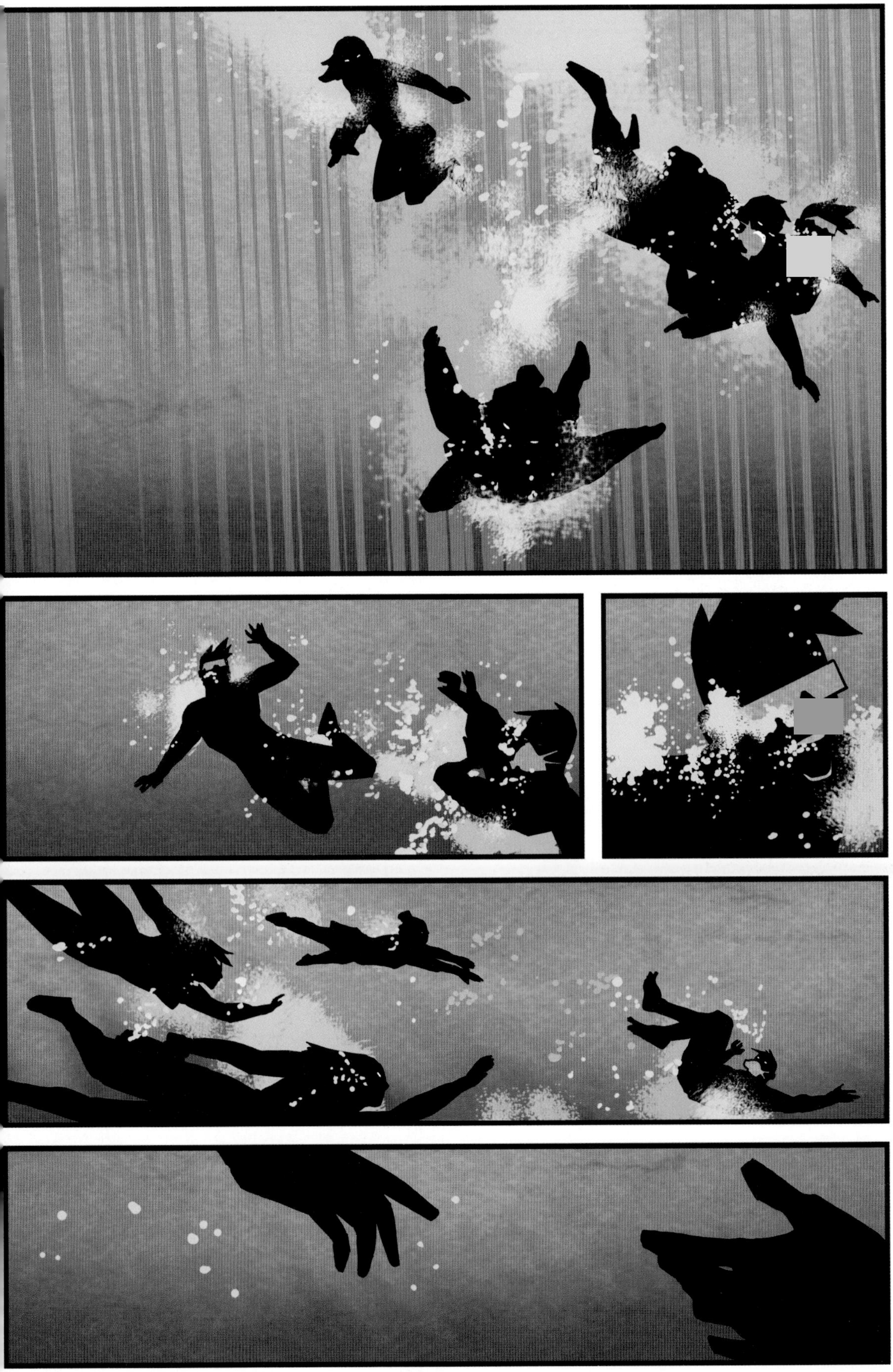

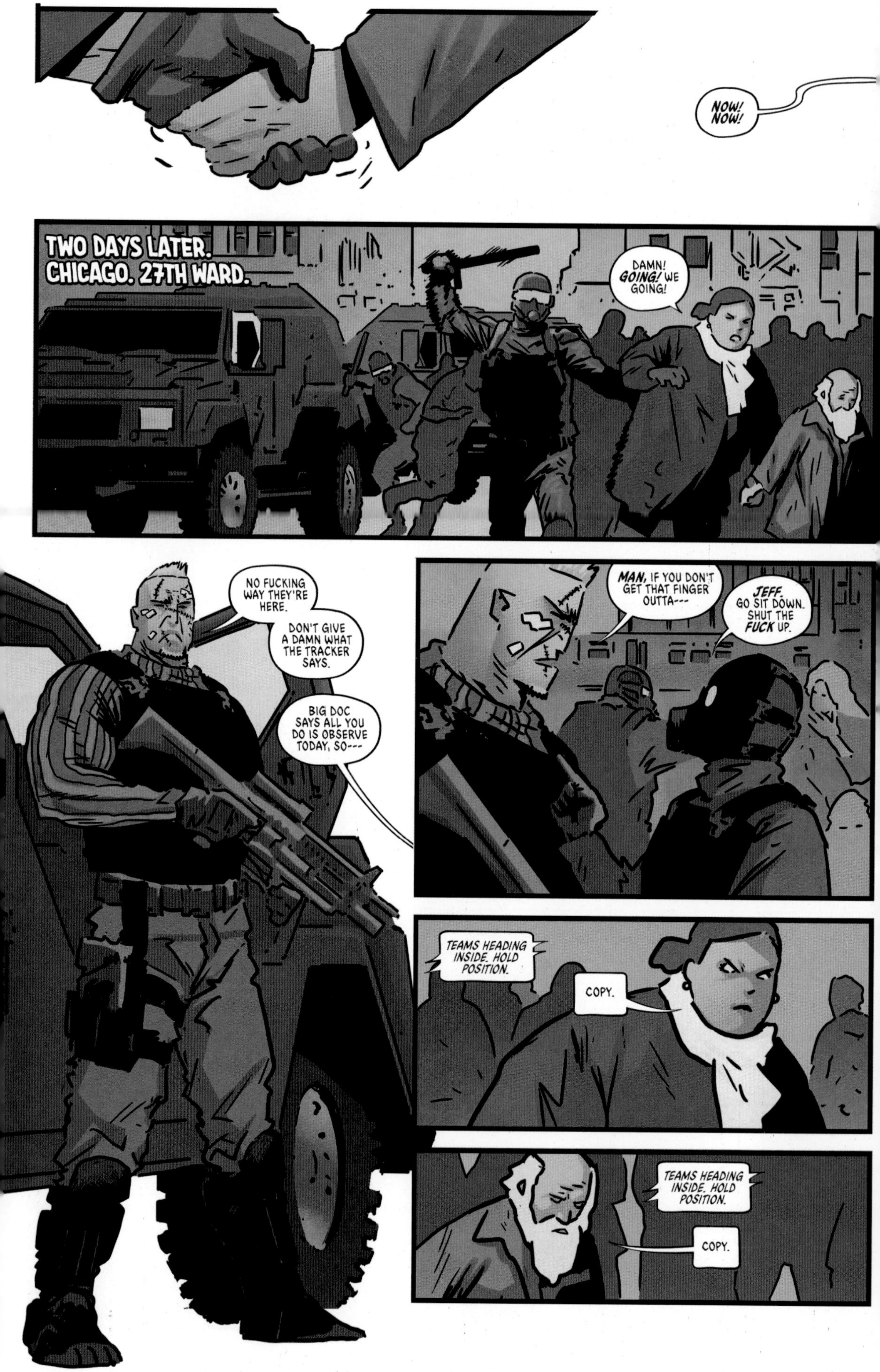
NOW! NOW!
TWO DAYS LATER. CHICAGO. 27TH WARD.
DAMN! GOING! WE GOING!
NO FUCKING WAY THEY'RE HERE.
DON'T GIVE A DAMN WHAT THE TRACKER SAYS.
BIG DOC SAYS ALL YOU DO IS OBSERVE TODAY, SO---
MAN, IF YOU DON'T GET THAT FINGER OUTTA---
JEFF. GO SIT DOWN. SHUT THE FUCK UP.
TEAMS HEADING INSIDE. HOLD POSITION.
COPY.
TEAMS HEADING INSIDE. HOLD POSITION.
COPY.

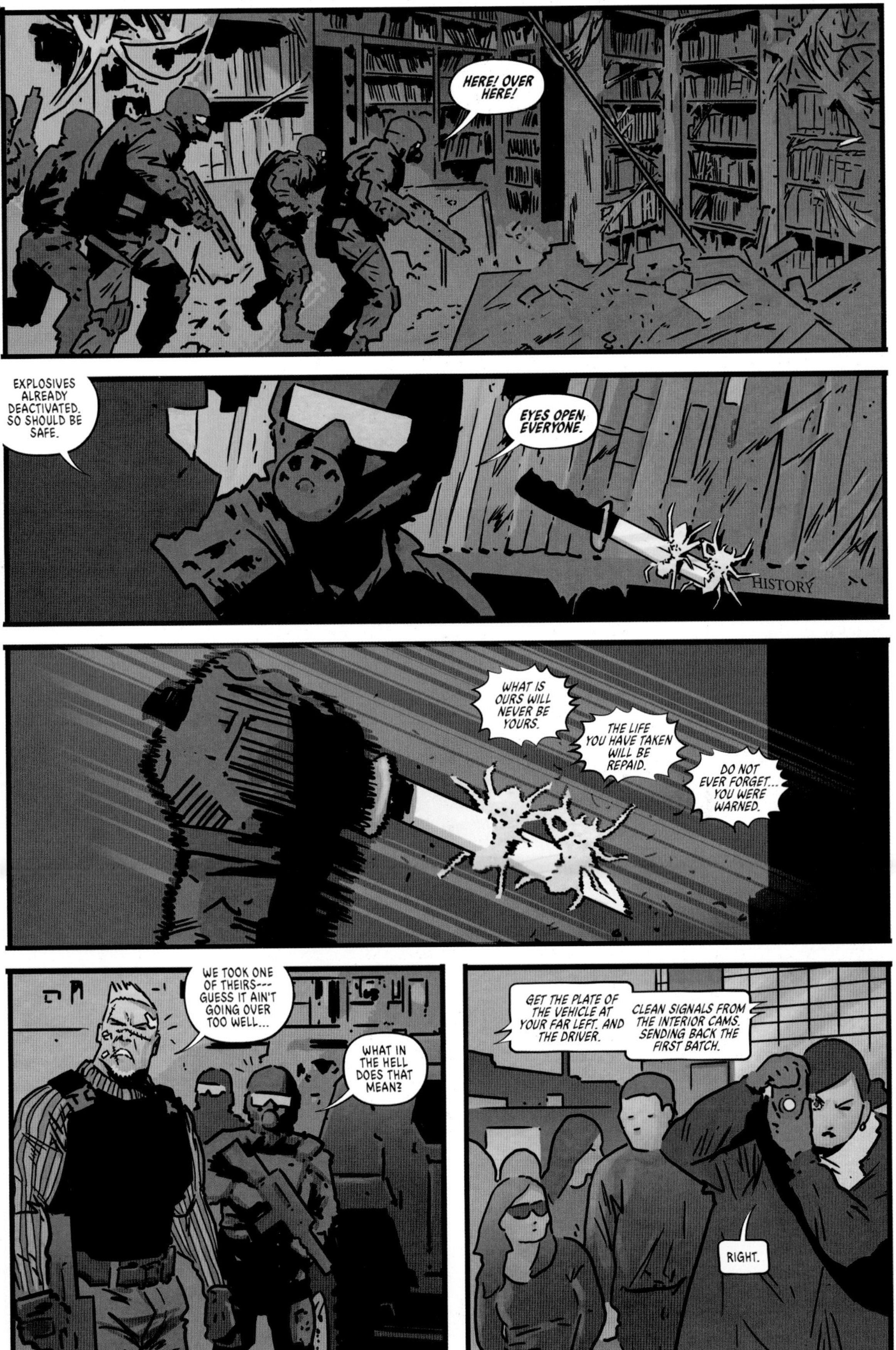
HERE! OVER HERE!
EXPLOSIVES ALREADY DEACTIVATED. SO SHOULD BE SAFE.
EYES OPEN, EVERYONE.
HISTORY
WHAT IS OURS WILL NEVER BE YOURS.
THE LIFE YOU HAVE TAKEN WILL BE REPAID.
DO NOT EVER FORGET... YOU WERE WARNED.
WE TOOK ONE OF THEIRS--- GUESS IT AIN'T GOING OVER TOO WELL...
WHAT IN THE HELL DOES THAT MEAN?
GET THE PLATE OF THE VEHICLE AT YOUR FAR LEFT. AND THE DRIVER.
CLEAN SIGNALS FROM THE INTERIOR CAMS. SENDING BACK THE FIRST BATCH.
RIGHT.

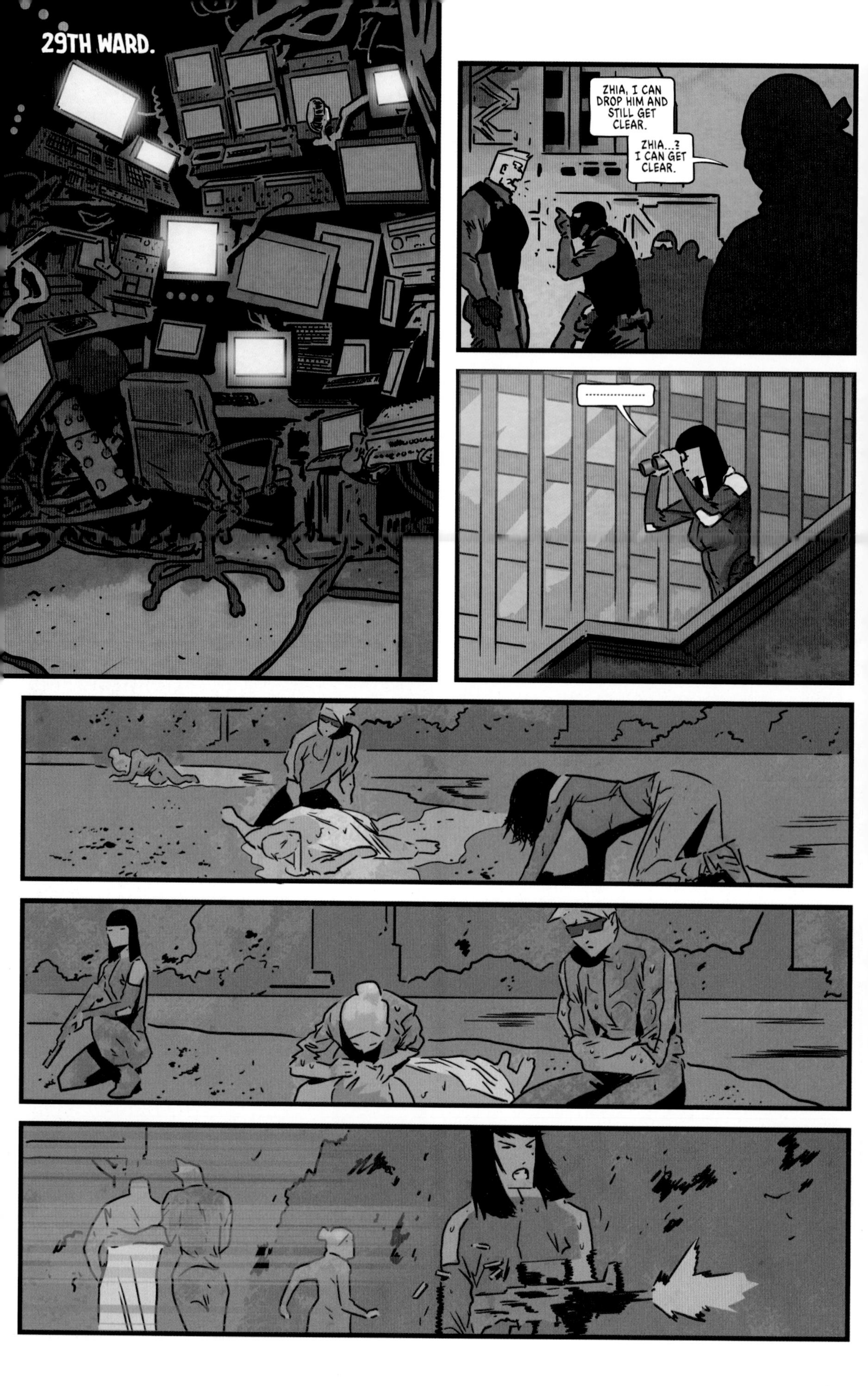
29TH WARD.
ZHIA, I CAN DROP HIM AND STILL GET CLEAR.
ZHIA...? I CAN GET CLEAR.
....

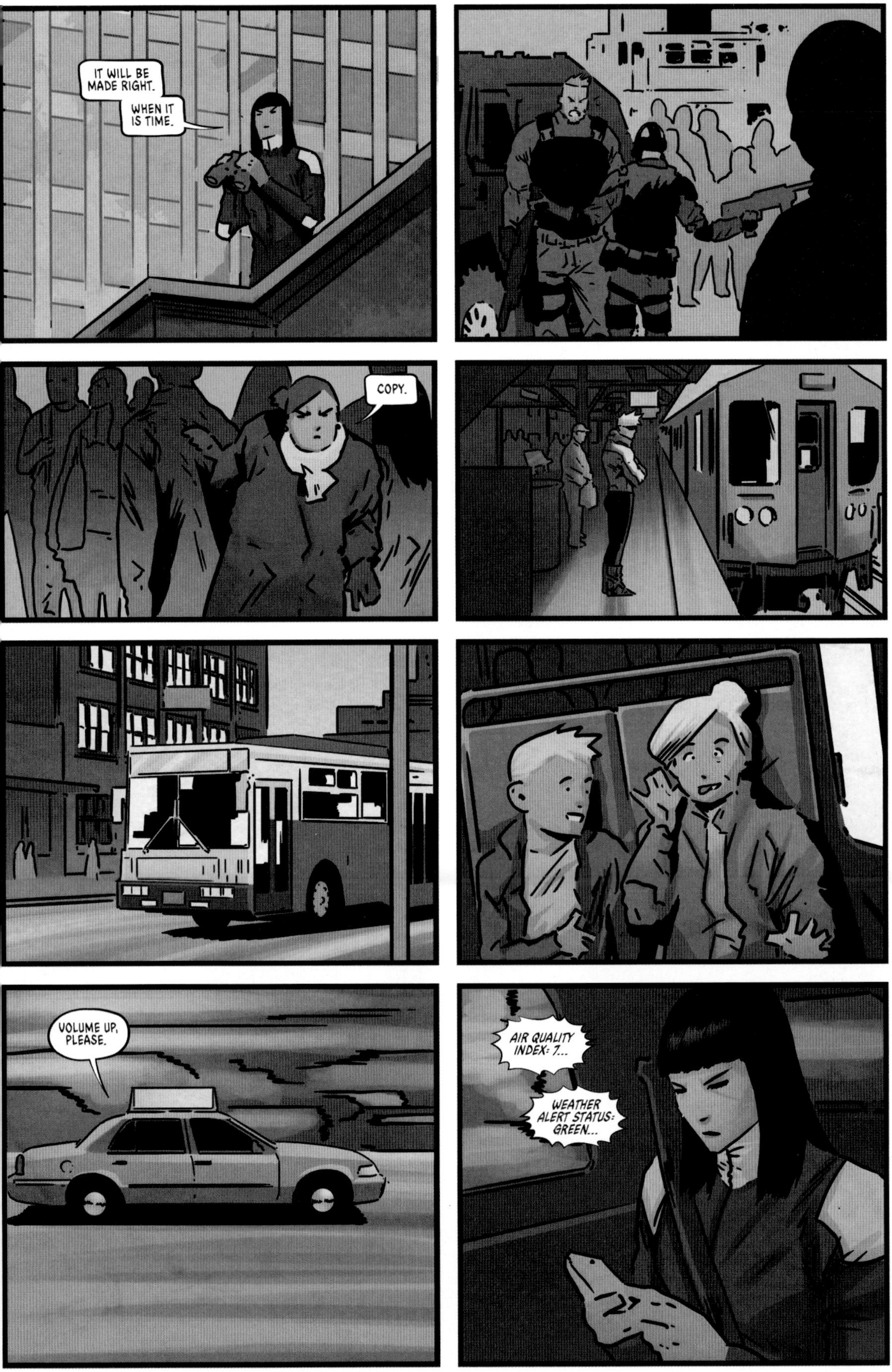
IT WILL BE MADE RIGHT.
WHEN IT IS TIME.
COPY.
VOLUME UP, PLEASE.
AIR QUALITY INDEX: 7...
WEATHER ALERT STATUS: GREEN...

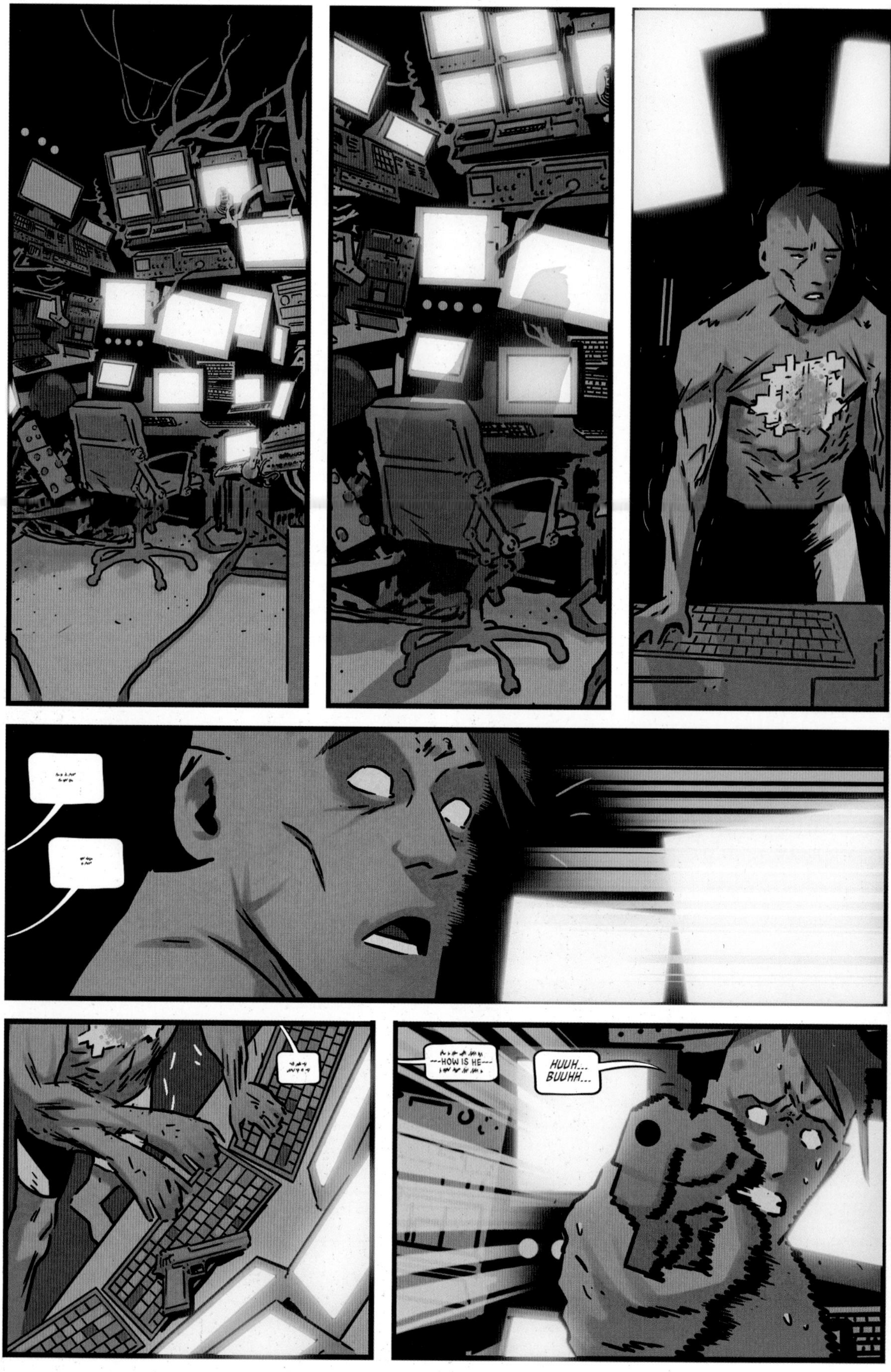
---HOW IS HE---
HUUH... BUUHH...

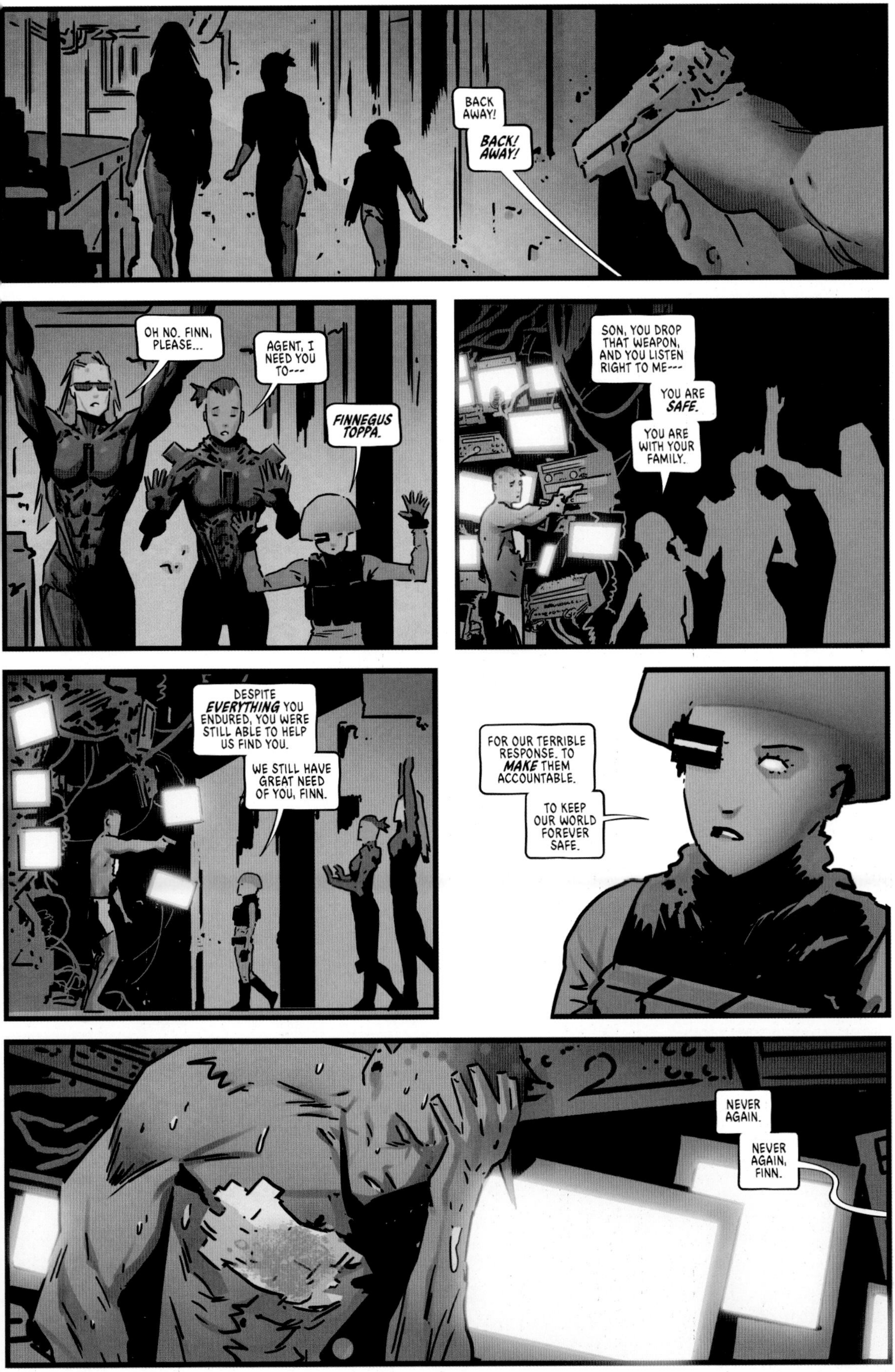
BACK AWAY!
BACK! AWAY!
OH NO. FINN, PLEASE...
AGENT, I NEED YOU TO---
FINNEGUS TOPPA.
SON, YOU DROP THAT WEAPON, AND YOU LISTEN RIGHT TO ME---
YOU ARE SAFE.
YOU ARE WITH YOUR FAMILY.
DESPITE EVERYTHING YOU ENDURED, YOU WERE STILL ABLE TO HELP US FIND YOU.
WE STILL HAVE GREAT NEED OF YOU, FINN.
FOR OUR TERRIBLE RESPONSE. TO MAKE THEM ACCOUNTABLE.
TO KEEP OUR WORLD FOREVER SAFE.
NEVER AGAIN.
NEVER AGAIN, FINN.

NO MATTER WHAT...

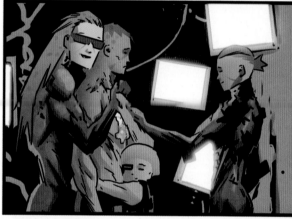

I---I---

I THOUGHT I SAW SOMETHING. SOMEONE. ON THE BOARD.

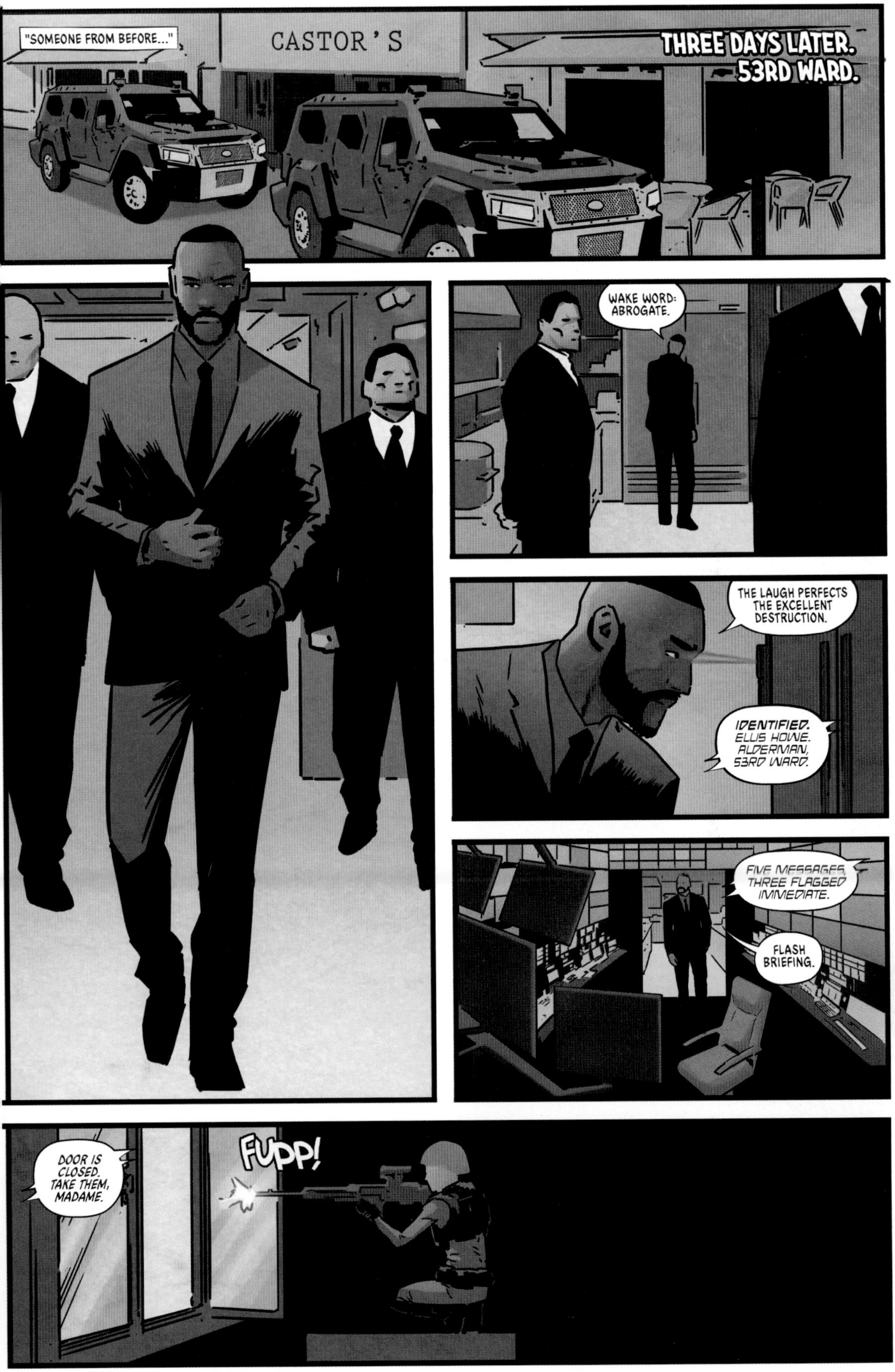
"SOMEONE FROM BEFORE..."
CASTOR'S
THREE DAYS LATER.
53RD WARD.
WAKE WORD:
ABROGATE.
THE LAUGH PERFECTS THE EXCELLENT DESTRUCTION.
IDENTIFIED. ELLIS HOWE. ALDERMAN, 53RD WARD.
FIVE MESSAGES, THREE FLAGGED IMMEDIATE.
FLASH BRIEFING.
DOOR IS CLOSED. TAKE THEM, MADAME.
FUPP!

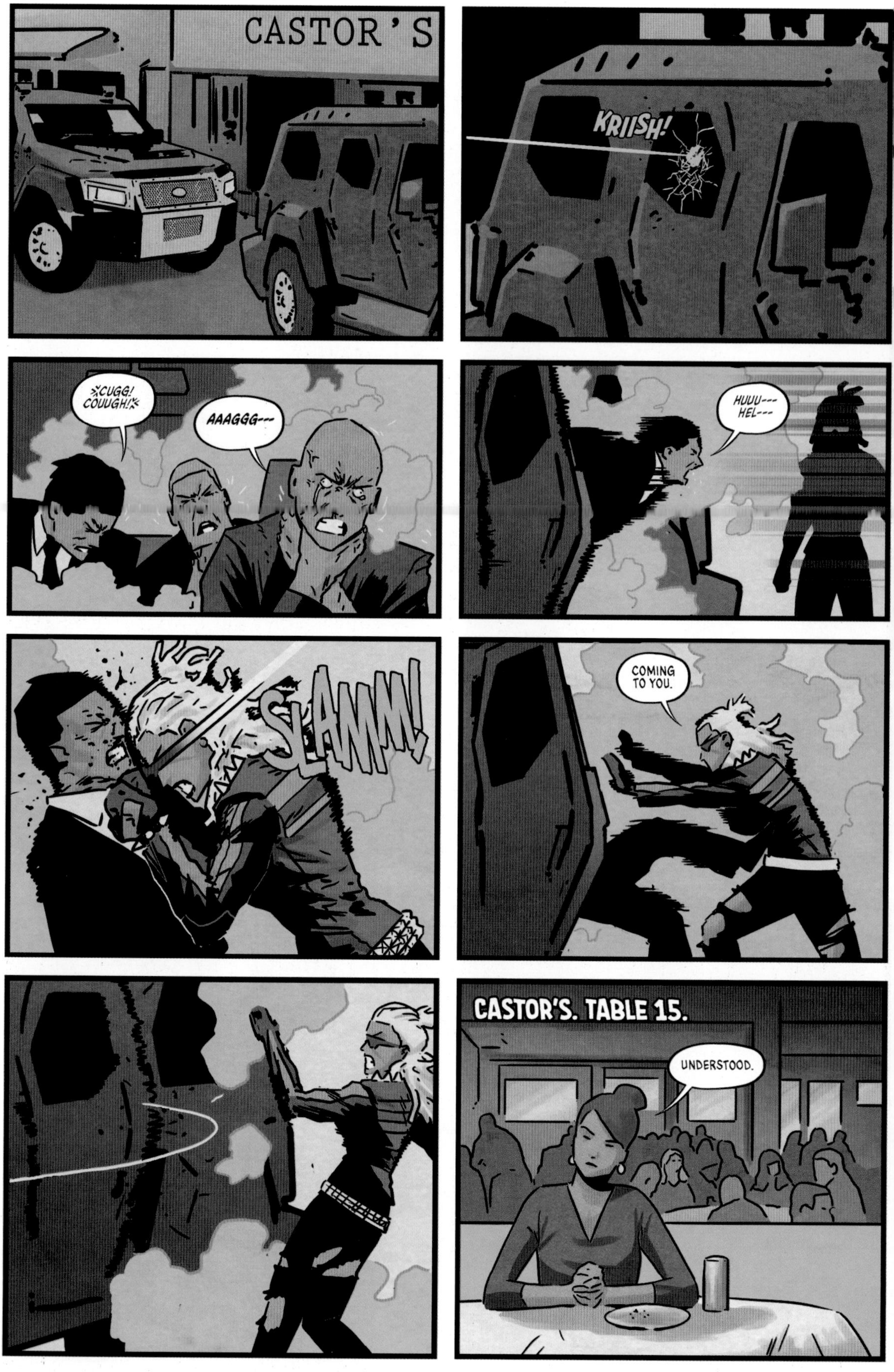
CASTOR'S
KRIISH!
CUGG! COUUGH!
AAAGGG---
HUUU--- HEL---
SLAMM!
COMING TO YOU.
CASTOR'S. TABLE 15.
UNDERSTOOD.

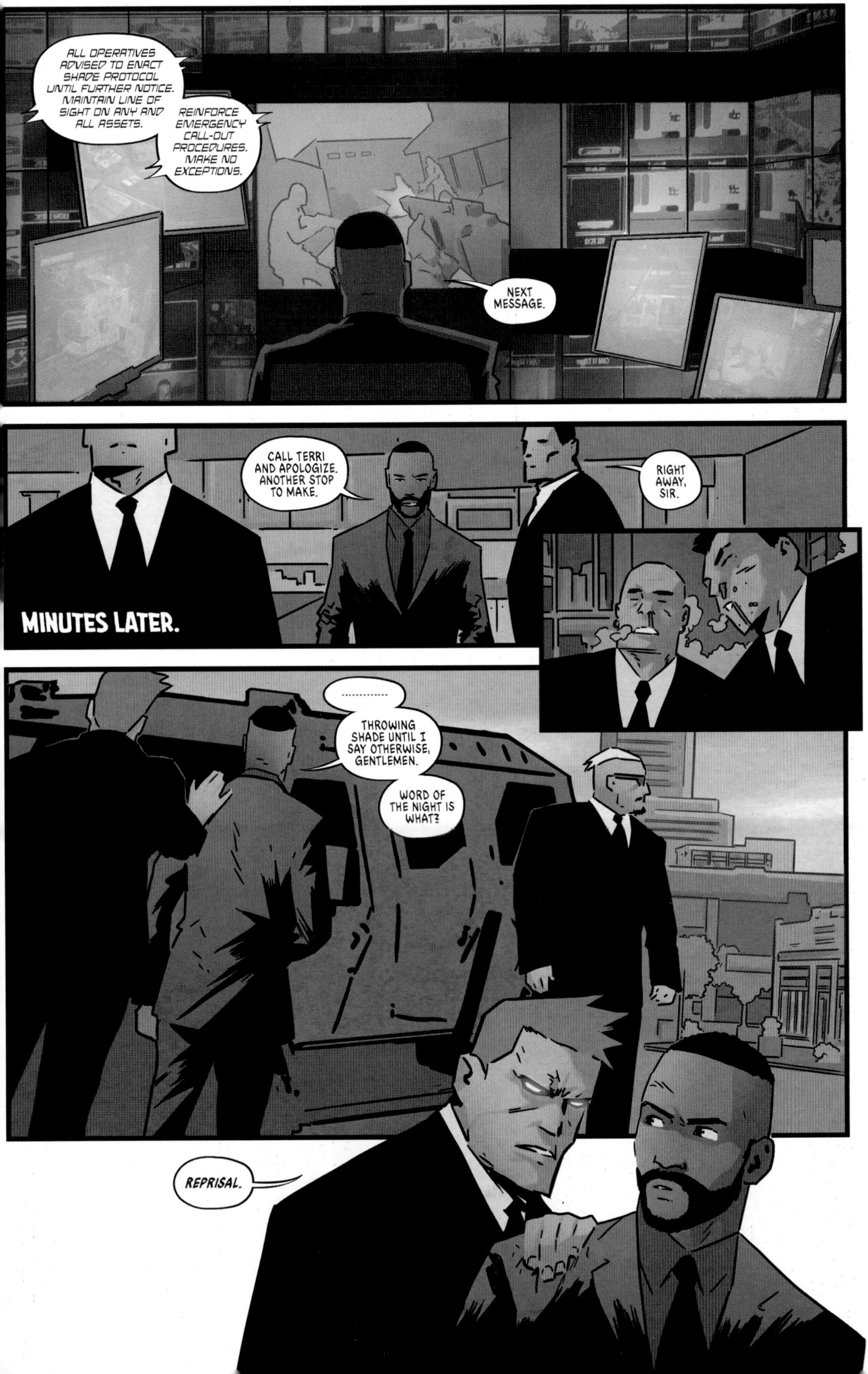
ALL OPERATIVES ADVISED TO ENACT SHADE PROTOCOL UNTIL FURTHER NOTICE. MAINTAIN LINE OF SIGHT ON ANY AND ALL ASSETS.
REINFORCE EMERGENCY CALL-OUT PROCEDURES. MAKE NO EXCEPTIONS.
NEXT MESSAGE.
CALL TERRI AND APOLOGIZE. ANOTHER STOP TO MAKE.
RIGHT AWAY, SIR.
MINUTES LATER.
....
THROWING SHADE UNTIL I SAY OTHERWISE, GENTLEMEN.
WORD OF THE NIGHT IS WHAT?
REPRISAL.

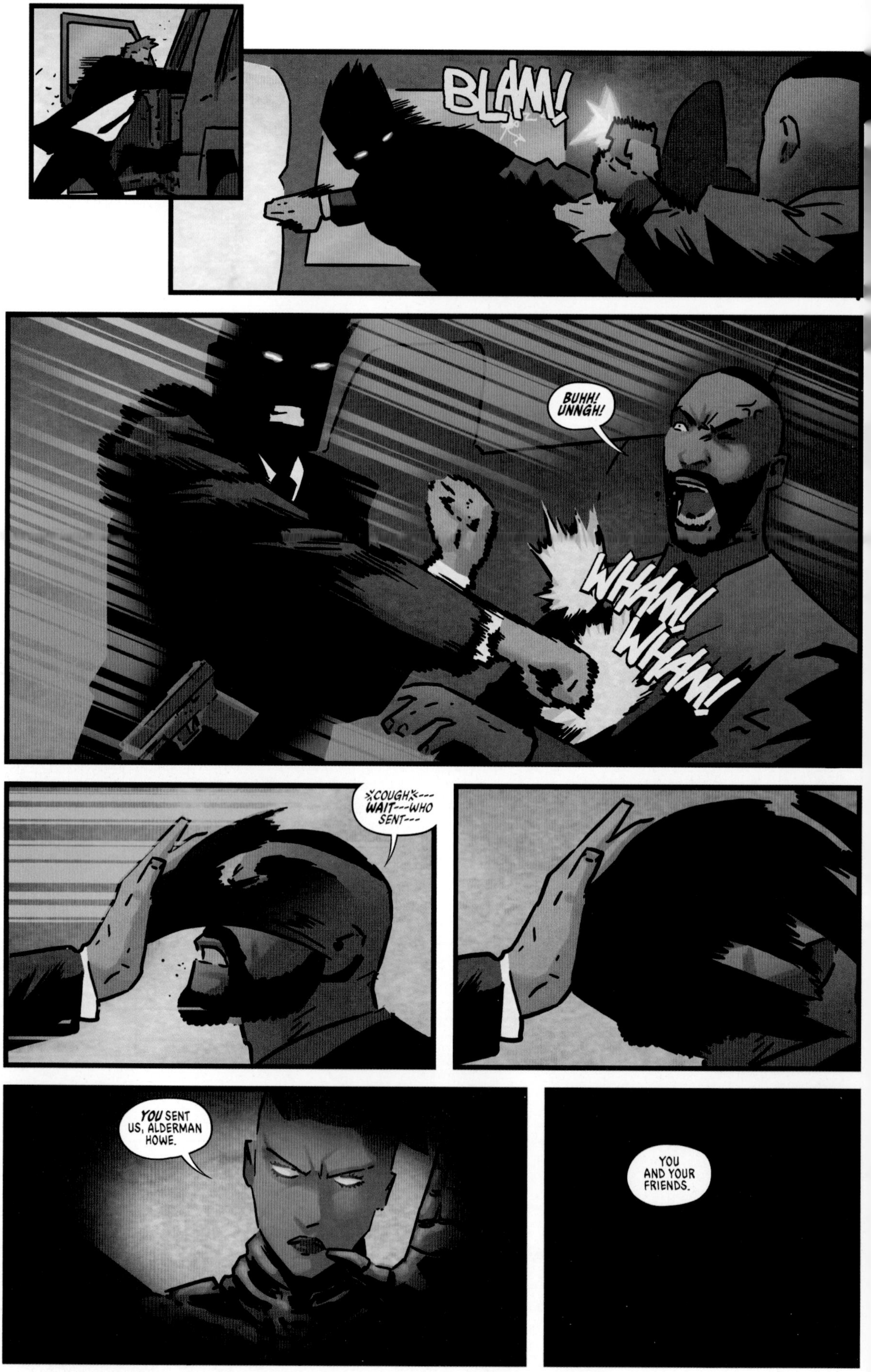
BLAM!
BUHH! UNNGH!
WHAM! WHAM! WHAM!
COUGH---WAIT---WHO SENT---
YOU SENT US, ALDERMAN HOWE.
YOU AND YOUR FRIENDS.

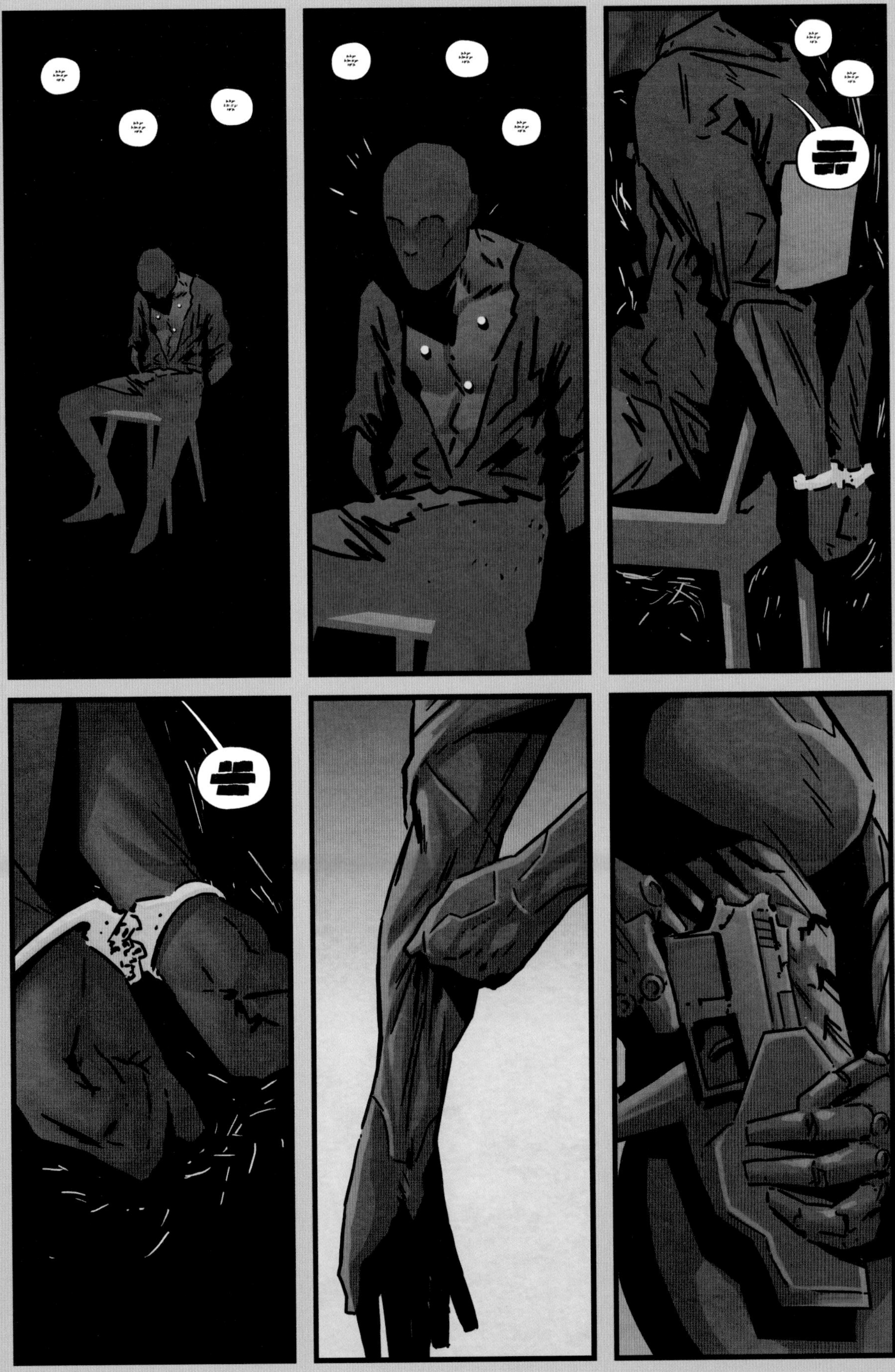

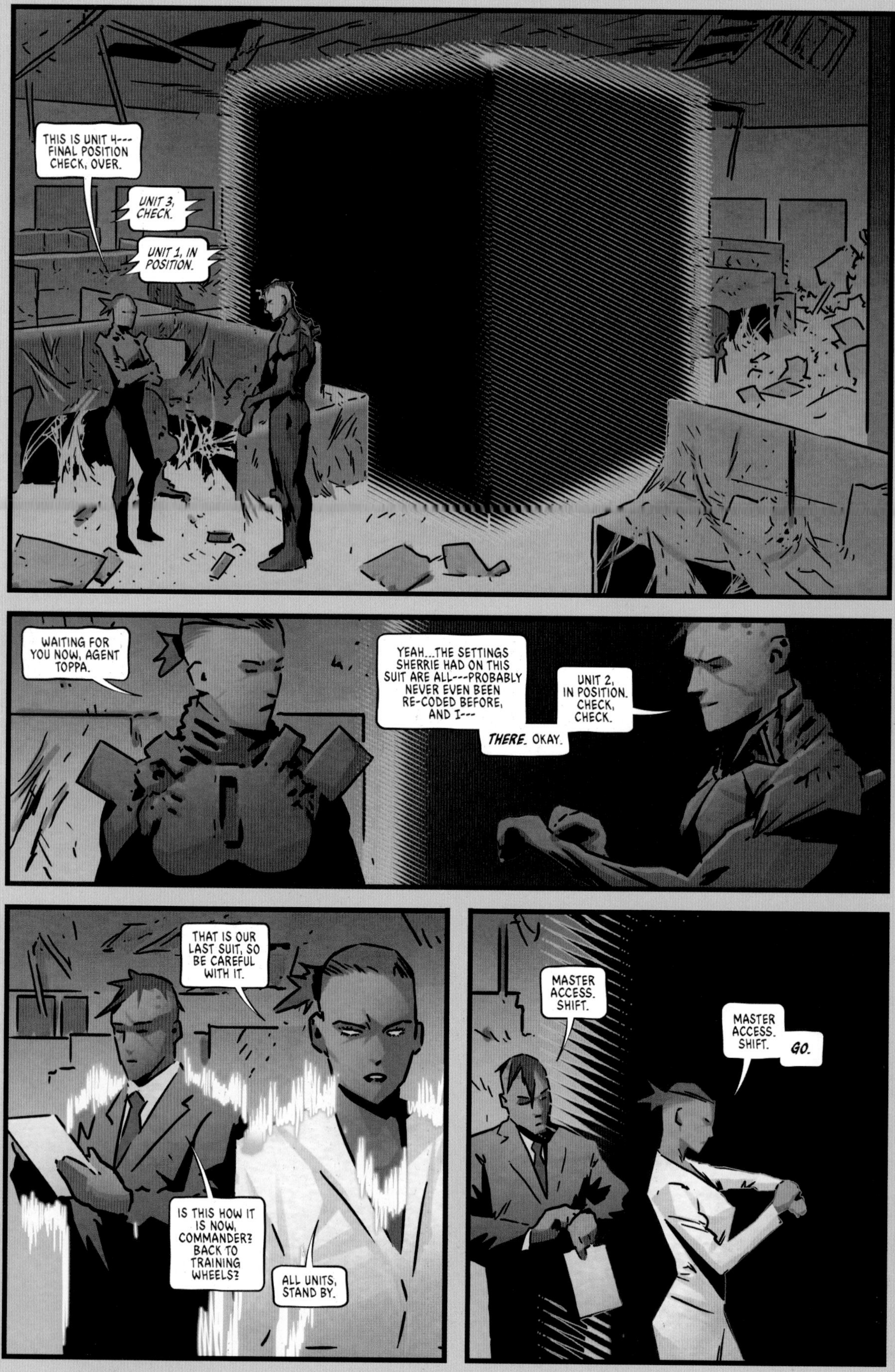
THIS IS UNIT 4---FINAL POSITION CHECK, OVER.
UNIT 3, CHECK.
UNIT 1, IN POSITION.
WAITING FOR YOU NOW, AGENT TOPPA.
YEAH...THE SETTINGS SHERRIE HAD ON THIS SUIT ARE ALL---PROBABLY NEVER EVEN BEEN RE-CODED BEFORE, AND I---
THERE. OKAY.
UNIT 2, IN POSITION. CHECK, CHECK.
THAT IS OUR LAST SUIT, SO BE CAREFUL WITH IT.
IS THIS HOW IT IS NOW, COMMANDER? BACK TO TRAINING WHEELS?
ALL UNITS, STAND BY.
MASTER ACCESS. SHIFT.
MASTER ACCESS. SHIFT.
GO.

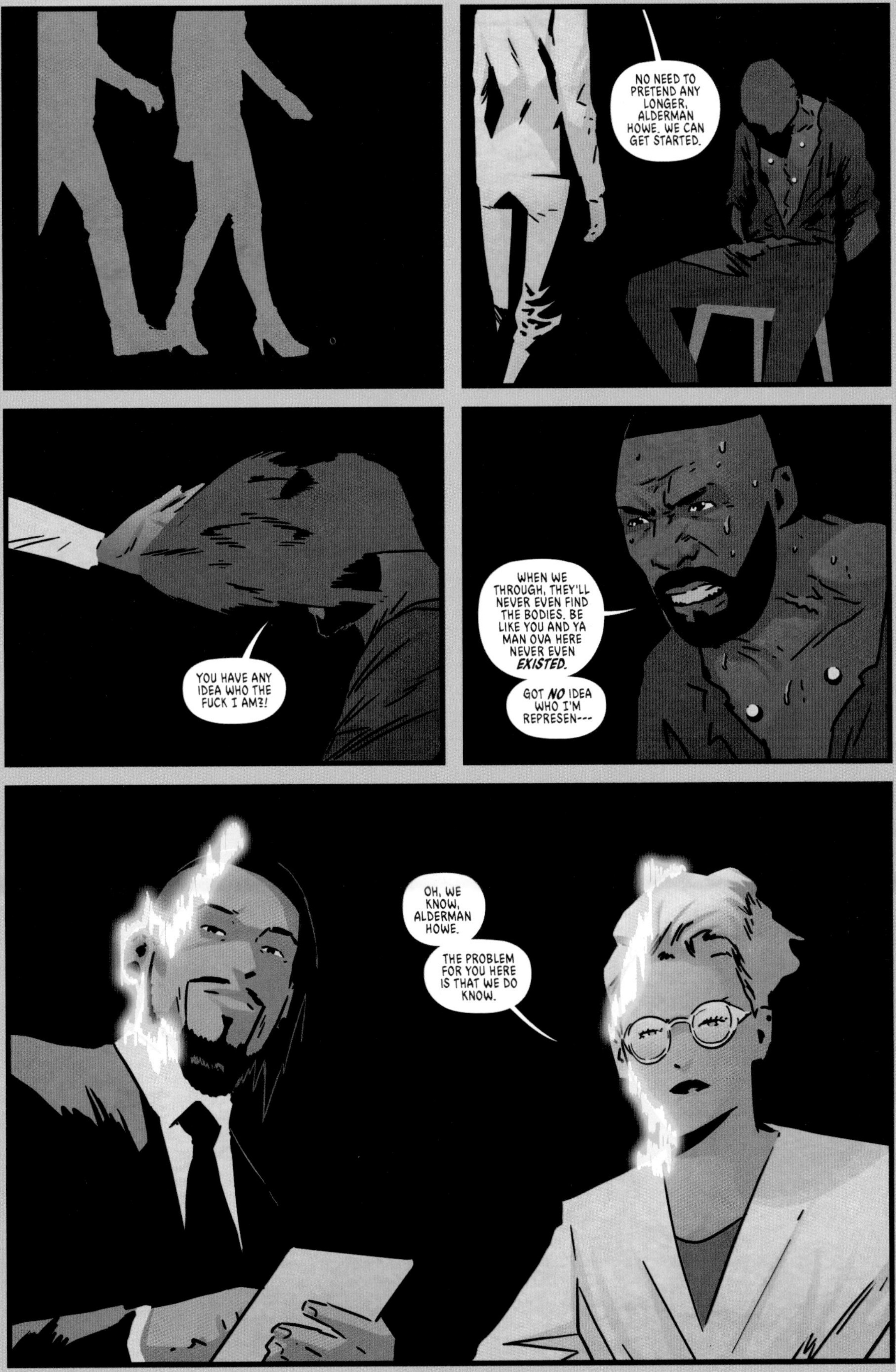
NO NEED TO PRETEND ANY LONGER, ALDERMAN HOWE. WE CAN GET STARTED.
YOU HAVE ANY IDEA WHO THE FUCK I AM?!
WHEN WE THROUGH, THEY'LL NEVER EVEN FIND THE BODIES. BE LIKE YOU AND YA MAN OVA HERE NEVER EVEN EXISTED.
GOT NO IDEA WHO I'M REPRESEN---
OH, WE KNOW, ALDERMAN HOWE.
THE PROBLEM FOR YOU HERE IS THAT WE DO KNOW.

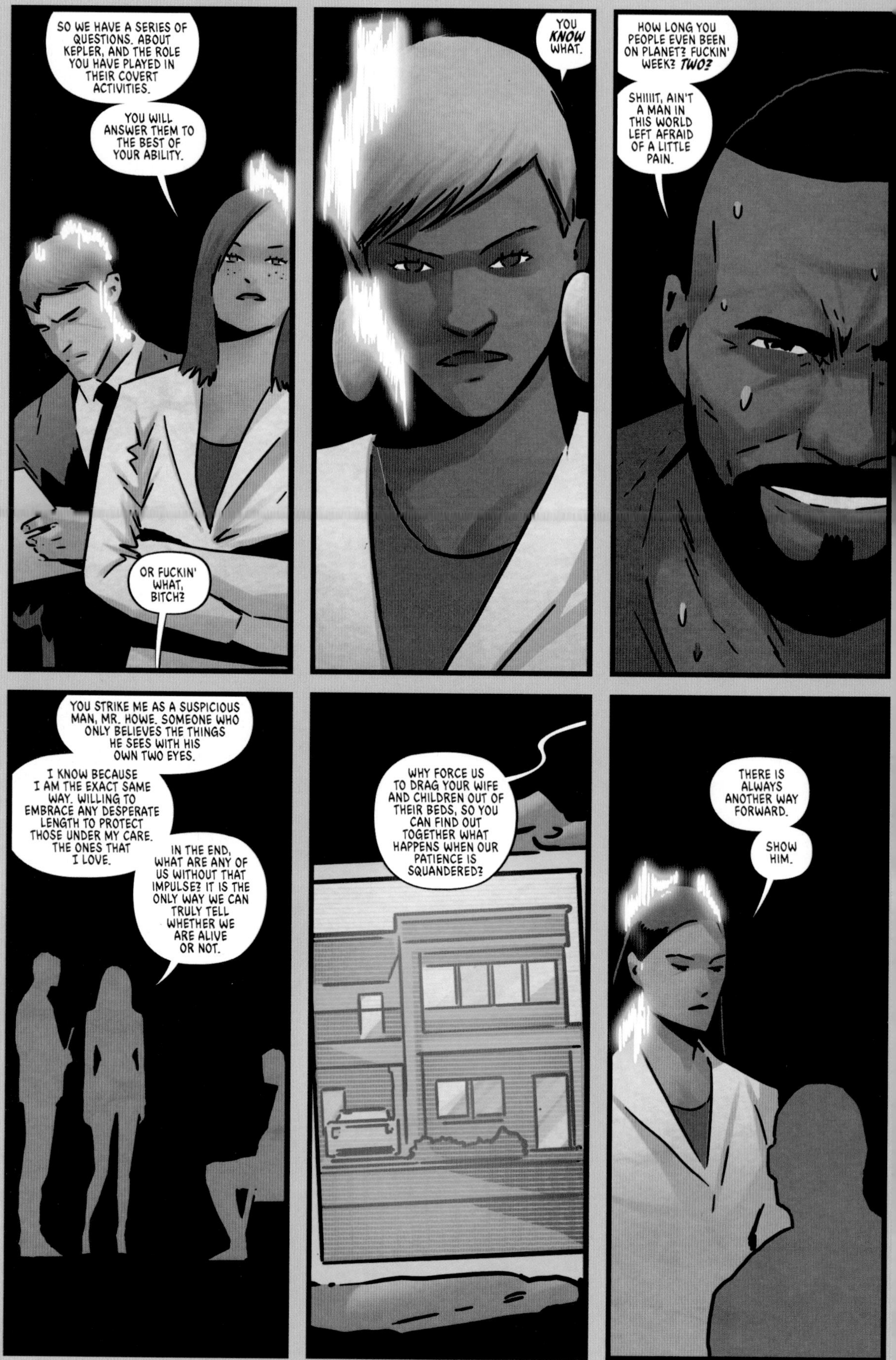
SO WE HAVE A SERIES OF QUESTIONS. ABOUT KEPLER, AND THE ROLE YOU HAVE PLAYED IN THEIR COVERT ACTIVITIES.
YOU WILL ANSWER THEM TO THE BEST OF YOUR ABILITY.
OR FUCKIN' WHAT, BITCH?
YOU *KNOW* WHAT.
HOW LONG YOU PEOPLE EVEN BEEN ON PLANET? FUCKIN' WEEK? *TWO?*
SHIIIIT, AIN'T A MAN IN THIS WORLD LEFT AFRAID OF A LITTLE PAIN.
YOU STRIKE ME AS A SUSPICIOUS MAN, MR. HOWE. SOMEONE WHO ONLY BELIEVES THE THINGS HE SEES WITH HIS OWN TWO EYES.
I KNOW BECAUSE I AM THE EXACT SAME WAY. WILLING TO EMBRACE ANY DESPERATE LENGTH TO PROTECT THOSE UNDER MY CARE. THE ONES THAT I LOVE.
IN THE END, WHAT ARE ANY OF US WITHOUT THAT IMPULSE? IT IS THE ONLY WAY WE CAN TRULY TELL WHETHER WE ARE ALIVE OR NOT.
WHY FORCE US TO DRAG YOUR WIFE AND CHILDREN OUT OF THEIR BEDS, SO YOU CAN FIND OUT TOGETHER WHAT HAPPENS WHEN OUR PATIENCE IS SQUANDERED?
THERE IS ALWAYS ANOTHER WAY FORWARD.
SHOW HIM.

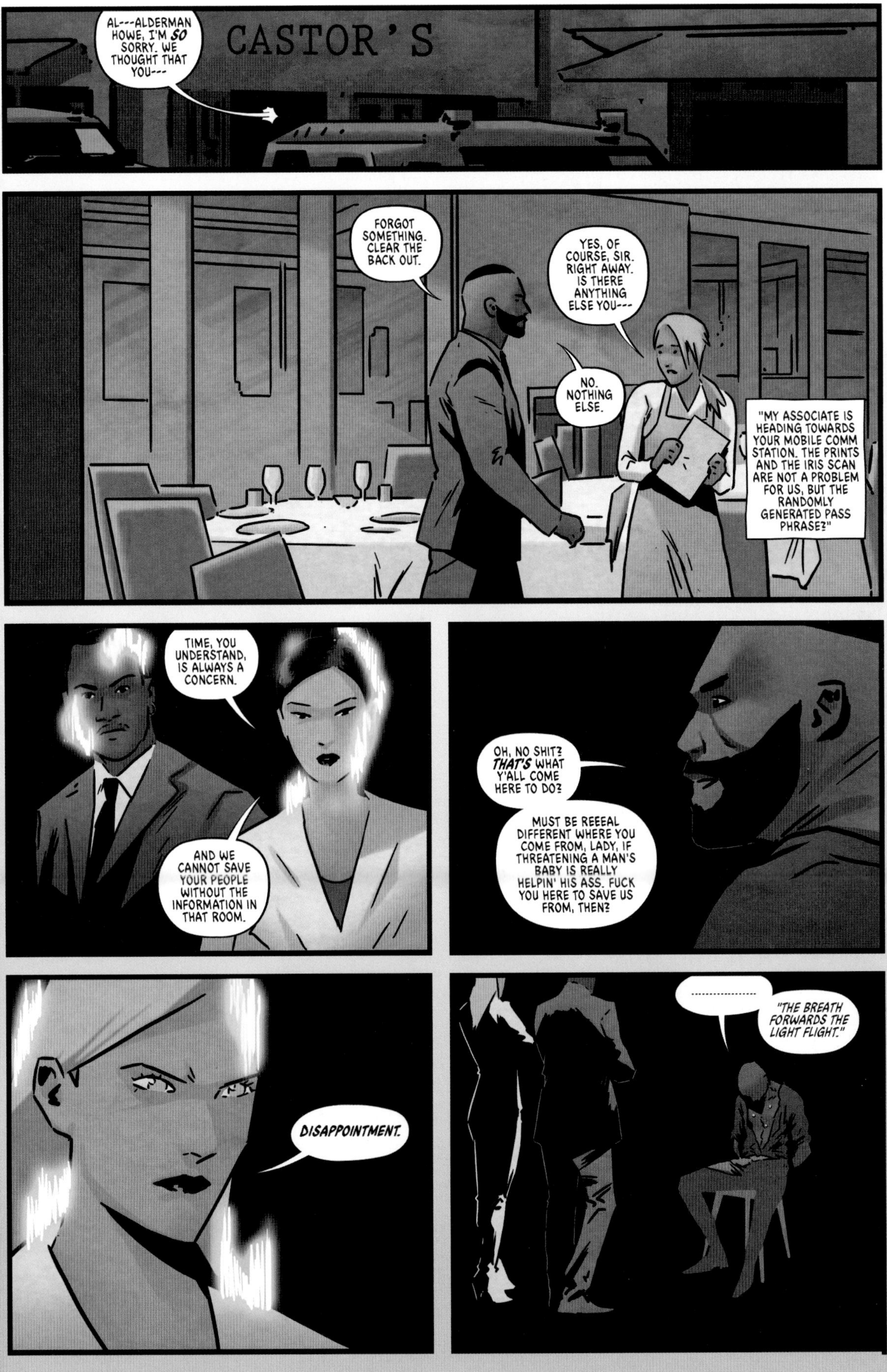
CASTOR'S
AL---ALDERMAN HOWE, I'M SO SORRY. WE THOUGHT THAT YOU---
FORGOT SOMETHING. CLEAR THE BACK OUT.
YES, OF COURSE, SIR. RIGHT AWAY. IS THERE ANYTHING ELSE YOU---
NO. NOTHING ELSE.
"MY ASSOCIATE IS HEADING TOWARDS YOUR MOBILE COMM STATION. THE PRINTS AND THE IRIS SCAN ARE NOT A PROBLEM FOR US, BUT THE RANDOMLY GENERATED PASS PHRASE?"
TIME, YOU UNDERSTAND, IS ALWAYS A CONCERN.
AND WE CANNOT SAVE YOUR PEOPLE WITHOUT THE INFORMATION IN THAT ROOM.
OH, NO SHIT? THAT'S WHAT Y'ALL COME HERE TO DO?
MUST BE REEEAL DIFFERENT WHERE YOU COME FROM, LADY, IF THREATENING A MAN'S BABY IS REALLY HELPIN' HIS ASS. FUCK YOU HERE TO SAVE US FROM, THEN?
DISAPPOINTMENT.
....
"THE BREATH FORWARDS THE LIGHT FLIGHT."

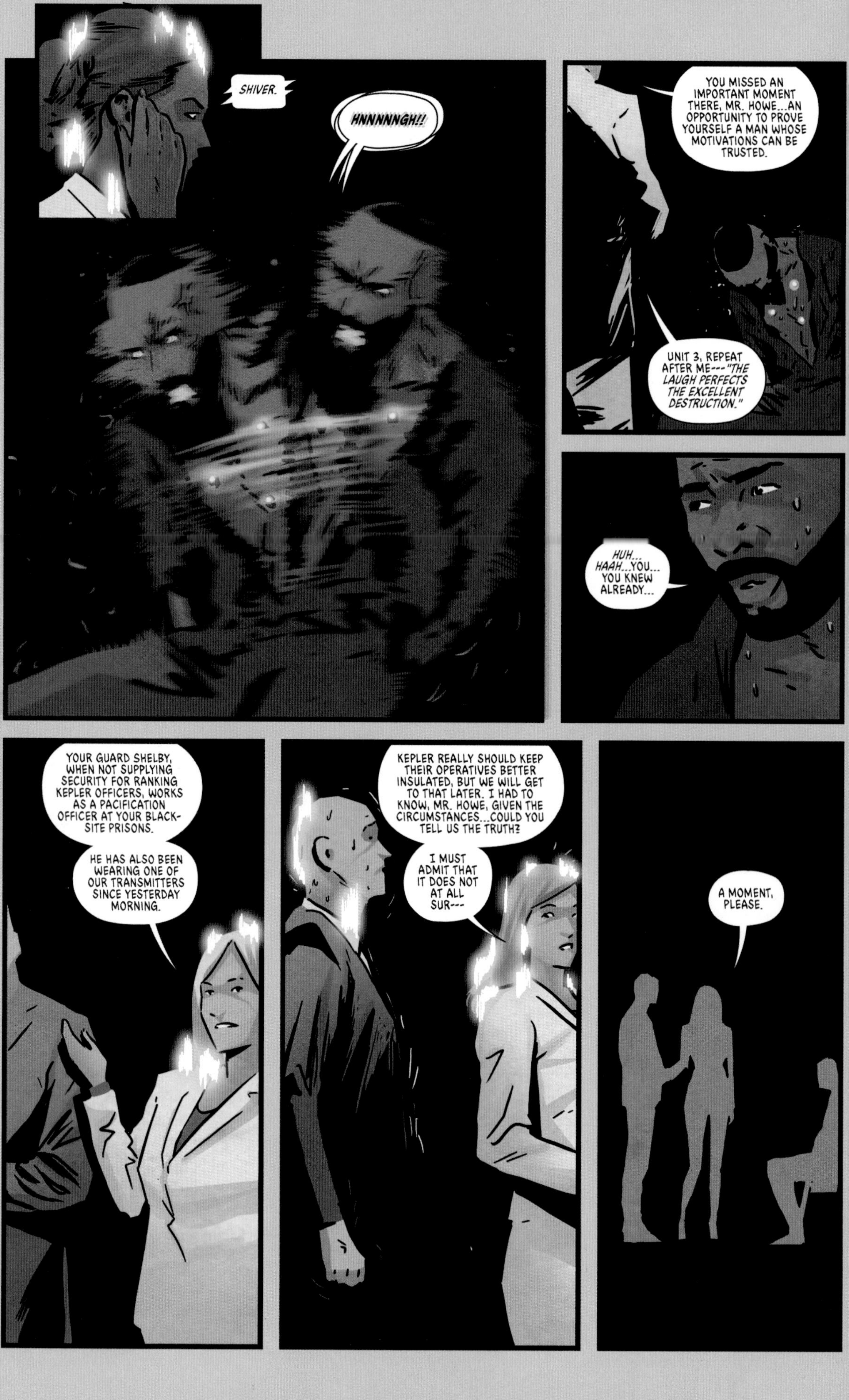
SHIVER.
HNNNNNGH!!
YOU MISSED AN IMPORTANT MOMENT THERE, MR. HOWE...AN OPPORTUNITY TO PROVE YOURSELF A MAN WHOSE MOTIVATIONS CAN BE TRUSTED.
UNIT 3, REPEAT AFTER ME---"THE LAUGH PERFECTS THE EXCELLENT DESTRUCTION."
HUH... HAAH...YOU... YOU KNEW ALREADY...
YOUR GUARD SHELBY, WHEN NOT SUPPLYING SECURITY FOR RANKING KEPLER OFFICERS, WORKS AS A PACIFICATION OFFICER AT YOUR BLACK-SITE PRISONS.
HE HAS ALSO BEEN WEARING ONE OF OUR TRANSMITTERS SINCE YESTERDAY MORNING.
KEPLER REALLY SHOULD KEEP THEIR OPERATIVES BETTER INSULATED, BUT WE WILL GET TO THAT LATER. I HAD TO KNOW, MR. HOWE, GIVEN THE CIRCUMSTANCES...COULD YOU TELL US THE TRUTH?
I MUST ADMIT THAT IT DOES NOT AT ALL SUR---
A MOMENT, PLEASE.

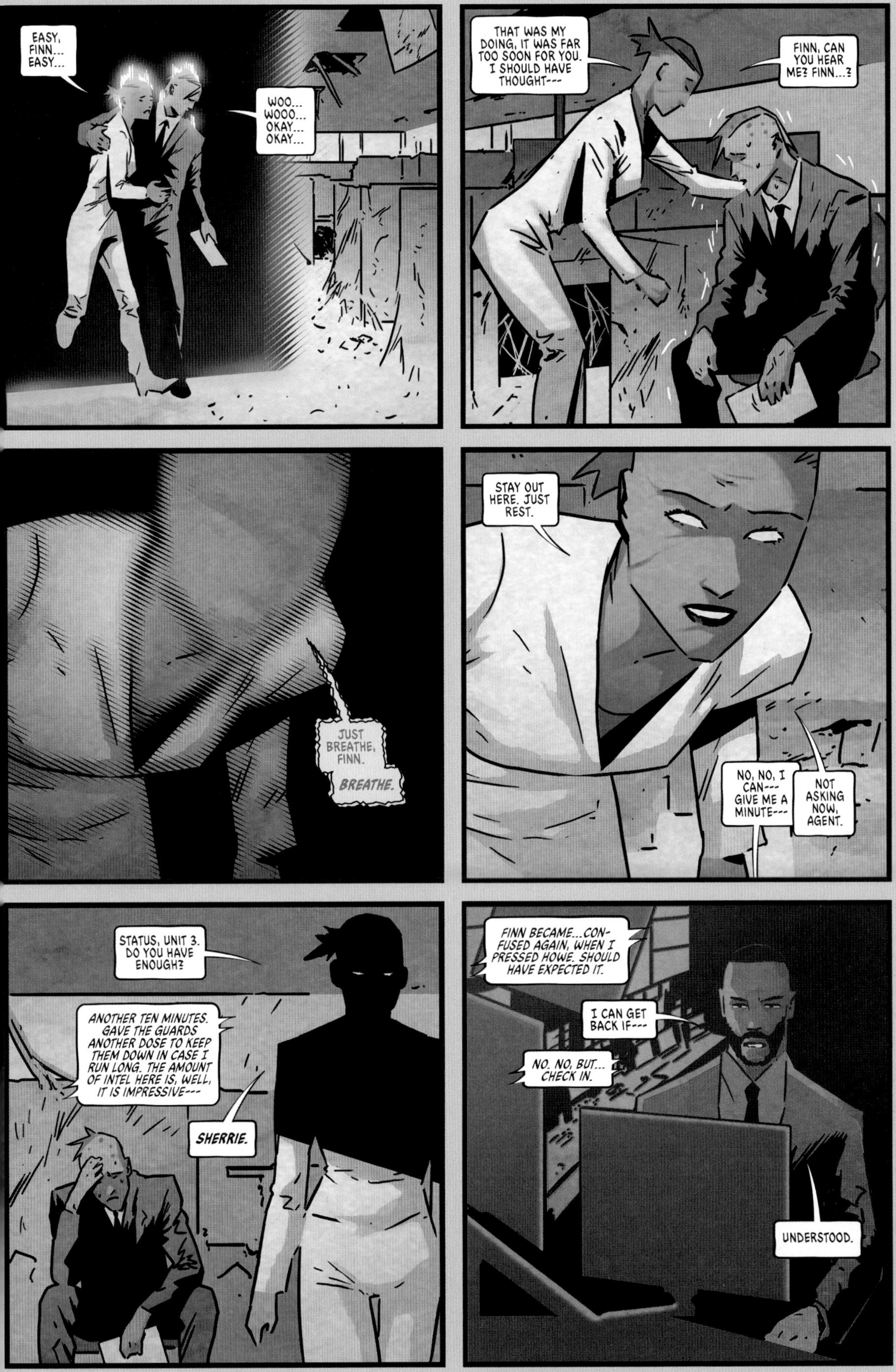
EASY, FINN... EASY...
WOO... WOOO... OKAY... OKAY...
THAT WAS MY DOING, IT WAS FAR TOO SOON FOR YOU. I SHOULD HAVE THOUGHT---
FINN, CAN YOU HEAR ME? FINN...?
JUST BREATHE, FINN.
BREATHE.
STAY OUT HERE. JUST REST.
NO, NO, I CAN--- GIVE ME A MINUTE---
NOT ASKING NOW, AGENT.
STATUS, UNIT 3. DO YOU HAVE ENOUGH?
ANOTHER TEN MINUTES. GAVE THE GUARDS ANOTHER DOSE TO KEEP THEM DOWN IN CASE I RUN LONG. THE AMOUNT OF INTEL HERE IS, WELL, IT IS IMPRESSIVE---
SHERRIE.
FINN BECAME...CON-FUSED AGAIN, WHEN I PRESSED HOWE. SHOULD HAVE EXPECTED IT.
I CAN GET BACK IF---
NO. NO, BUT... CHECK IN.
UNDERSTOOD.

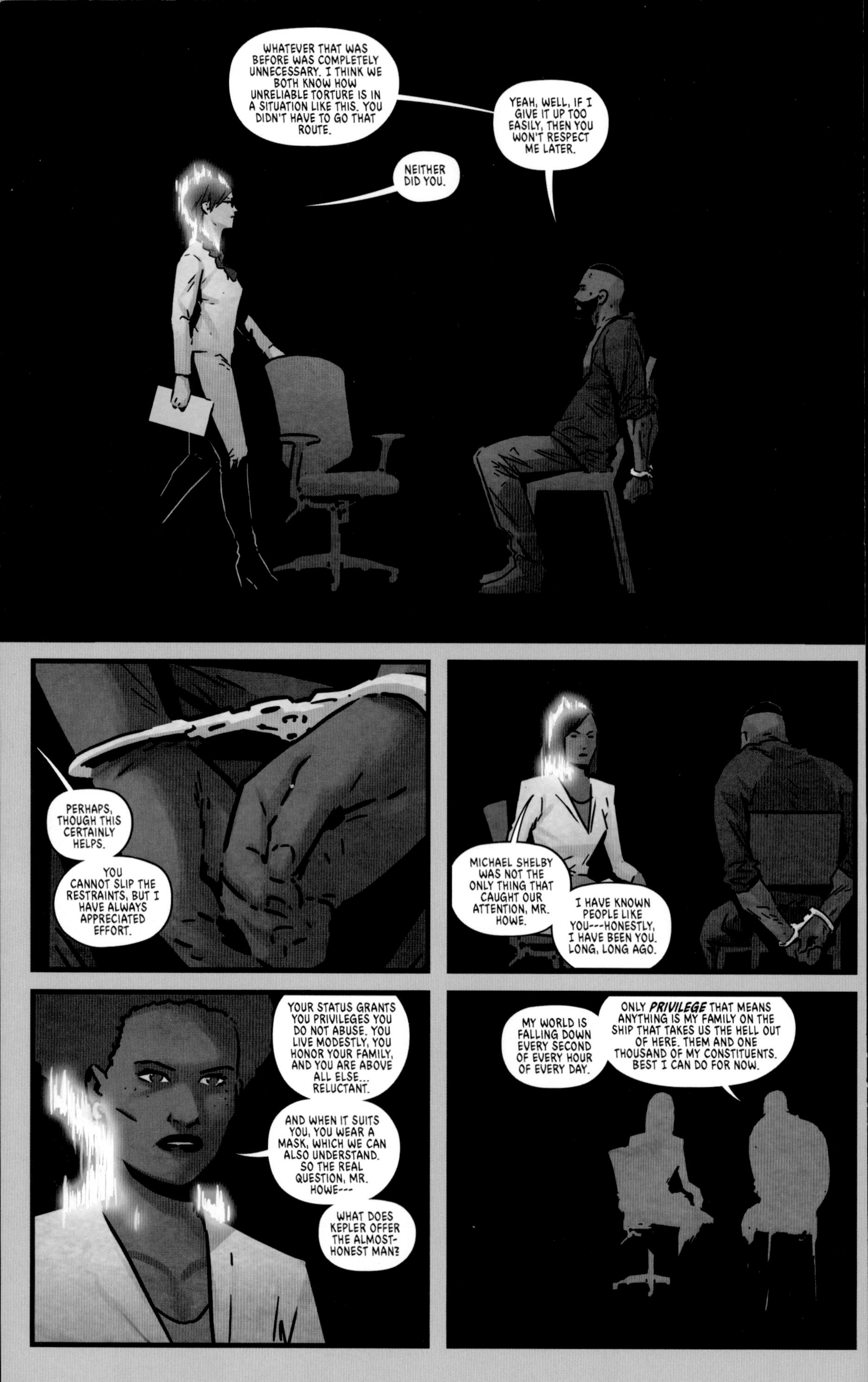
WHATEVER THAT WAS BEFORE WAS COMPLETELY UNNECESSARY. I THINK WE BOTH KNOW HOW UNRELIABLE TORTURE IS IN A SITUATION LIKE THIS. YOU DIDN'T HAVE TO GO THAT ROUTE.
YEAH, WELL, IF I GIVE IT UP TOO EASILY, THEN YOU WON'T RESPECT ME LATER.
NEITHER DID YOU.
PERHAPS, THOUGH THIS CERTAINLY HELPS.
YOU CANNOT SLIP THE RESTRAINTS, BUT I HAVE ALWAYS APPRECIATED EFFORT.
MICHAEL SHELBY WAS NOT THE ONLY THING THAT CAUGHT OUR ATTENTION, MR. HOWE.
I HAVE KNOWN PEOPLE LIKE YOU---HONESTLY, I HAVE BEEN YOU. LONG, LONG AGO.
YOUR STATUS GRANTS YOU PRIVILEGES YOU DO NOT ABUSE. YOU LIVE MODESTLY, YOU HONOR YOUR FAMILY, AND YOU ARE ABOVE ALL ELSE... RELUCTANT.
AND WHEN IT SUITS YOU, YOU WEAR A MASK, WHICH WE CAN ALSO UNDERSTAND. SO THE REAL QUESTION, MR. HOWE---
WHAT DOES KEPLER OFFER THE ALMOST-HONEST MAN?
MY WORLD IS FALLING DOWN EVERY SECOND OF EVERY HOUR OF EVERY DAY.
ONLY ***PRIVILEGE*** THAT MEANS ANYTHING IS MY FAMILY ON THE SHIP THAT TAKES US THE HELL OUT OF HERE. THEM AND ONE THOUSAND OF MY CONSTITUENTS. BEST I CAN DO FOR NOW.

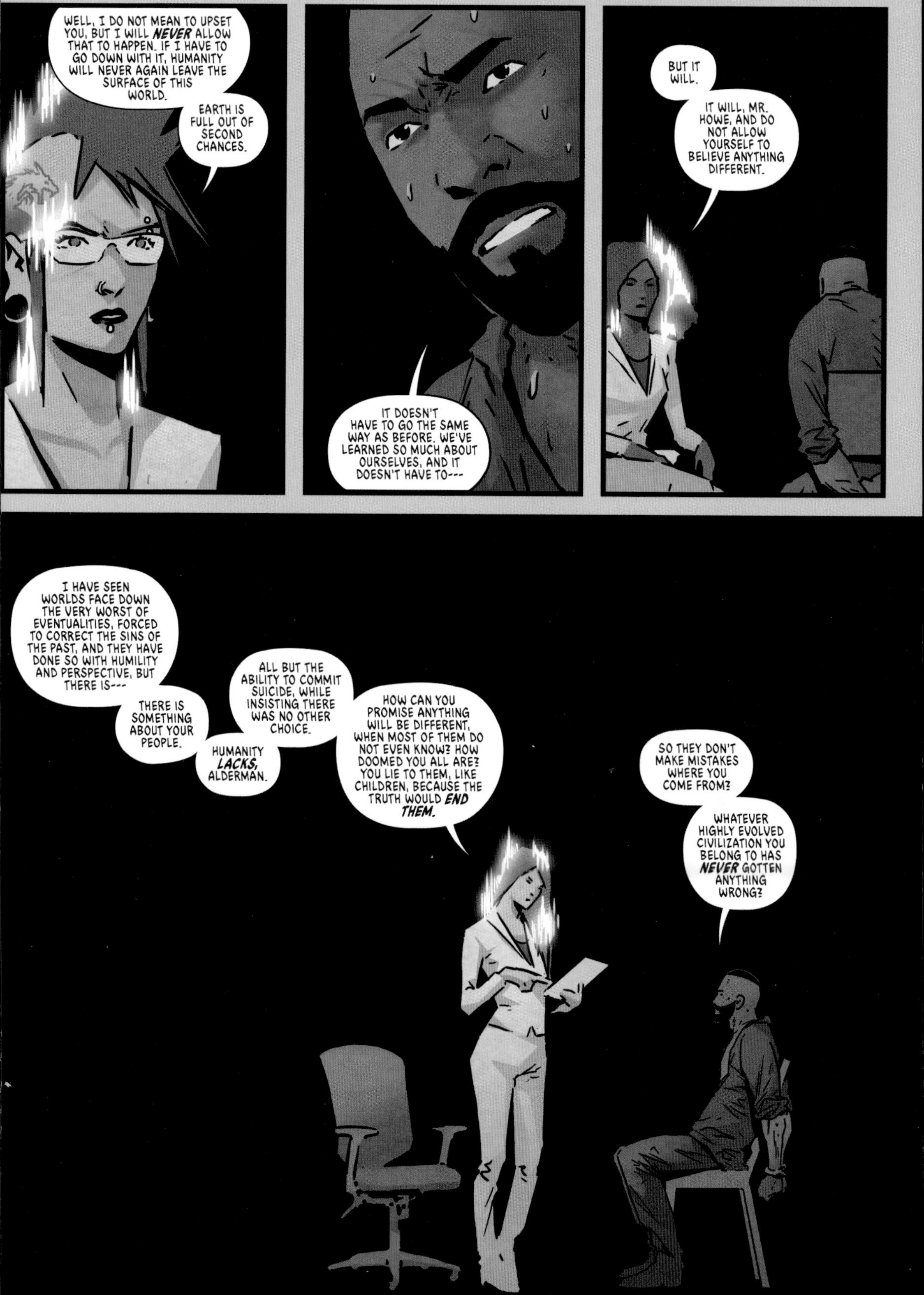
WELL, I DO NOT MEAN TO UPSET YOU, BUT I WILL *NEVER* ALLOW THAT TO HAPPEN. IF I HAVE TO GO DOWN WITH IT, HUMANITY WILL NEVER AGAIN LEAVE THE SURFACE OF THIS WORLD.
EARTH IS FULL OUT OF SECOND CHANCES.
IT DOESN'T HAVE TO GO THE SAME WAY AS BEFORE. WE'VE LEARNED SO MUCH ABOUT OURSELVES, AND IT DOESN'T HAVE TO---
BUT IT WILL.
IT WILL, MR. HOWE, AND DO NOT ALLOW YOURSELF TO BELIEVE ANYTHING DIFFERENT.
I HAVE SEEN WORLDS FACE DOWN THE VERY WORST OF EVENTUALITIES, FORCED TO CORRECT THE SINS OF THE PAST, AND THEY HAVE DONE SO WITH HUMILITY AND PERSPECTIVE, BUT THERE IS---
THERE IS SOMETHING ABOUT YOUR PEOPLE.
HUMANITY *LACKS*, ALDERMAN.
ALL BUT THE ABILITY TO COMMIT SUICIDE, WHILE INSISTING THERE WAS NO OTHER CHOICE.
HOW CAN YOU PROMISE ANYTHING WILL BE DIFFERENT, WHEN MOST OF THEM DO NOT EVEN KNOW? HOW DOOMED YOU ALL ARE? YOU LIE TO THEM, LIKE CHILDREN, BECAUSE THE TRUTH WOULD *END THEM.*
SO THEY DON'T MAKE MISTAKES WHERE YOU COME FROM?
WHATEVER HIGHLY EVOLVED CIVILIZATION YOU BELONG TO HAS *NEVER* GOTTEN ANYTHING WRONG?

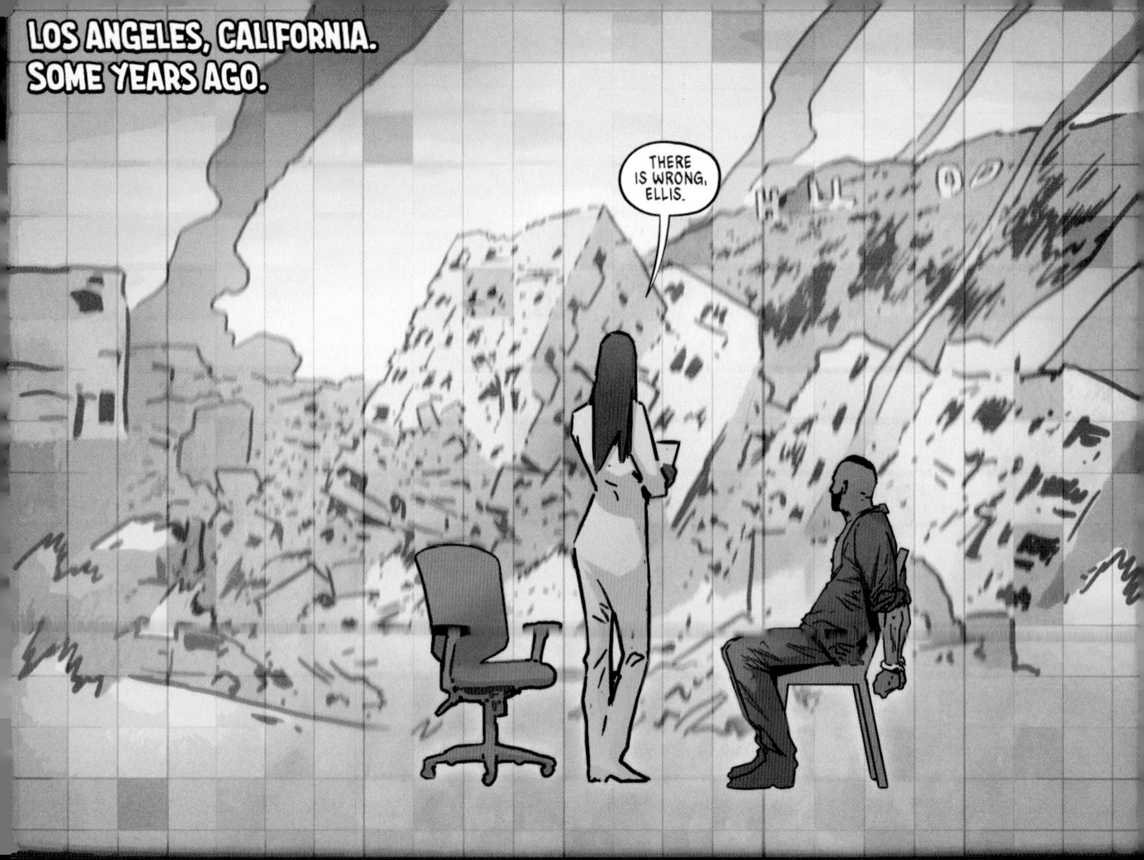
LOS ANGELES, CALIFORNIA.
SOME YEARS AGO.
THERE IS WRONG, ELLIS.
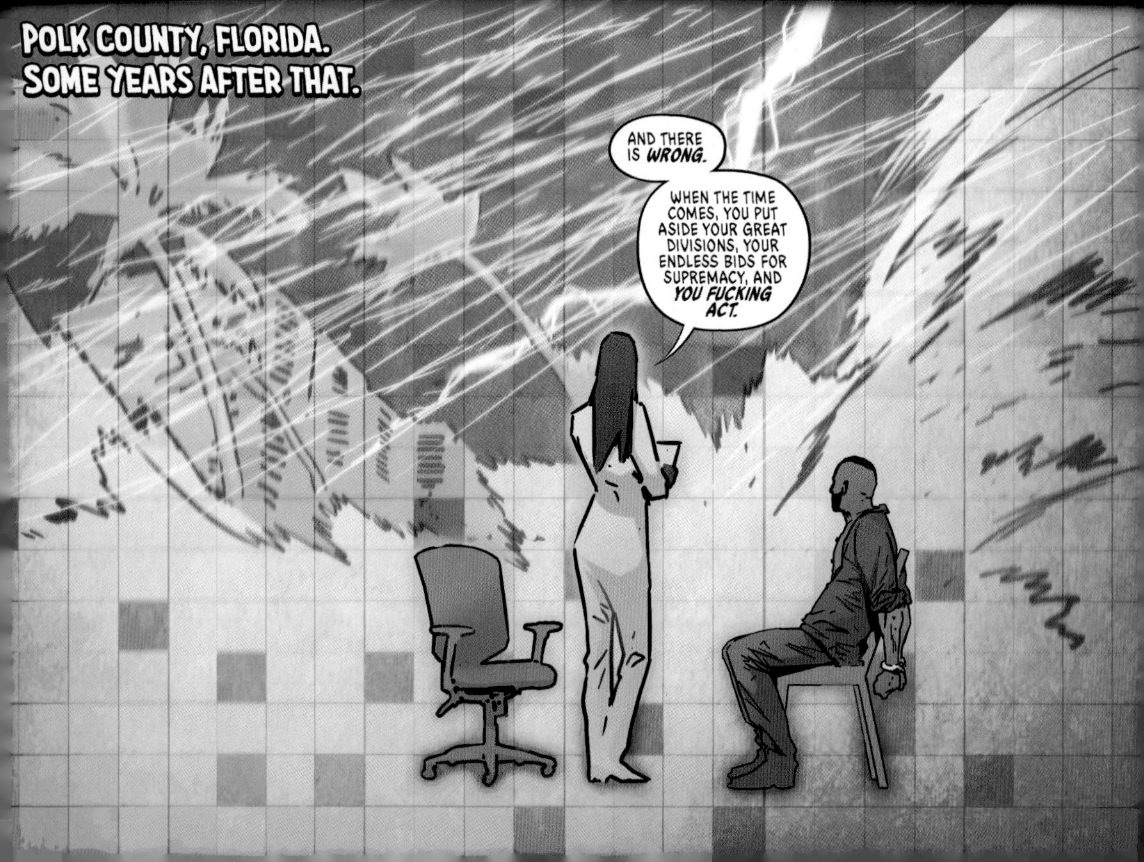
POLK COUNTY, FLORIDA.
SOME YEARS AFTER THAT.
AND THERE IS *WRONG*.
WHEN THE TIME COMES, YOU PUT ASIDE YOUR GREAT DIVISIONS, YOUR ENDLESS BIDS FOR SUPREMACY, AND ***YOU FUCKING ACT.***

YOU HAD THE TECHNOLOGY, THE INTELLECTUAL CAPACITY TO AVERT ALL OF THIS, BUT YOU COULD NOT BE BOTHERED ENOUGH TO EVEN SAVE YOURSELVES.

SO YES, ALDERMAN HOWE, YOU SHOULD *THANK* US FOR SAVING YOU FROM THE INEVITABLE DISAPPOINTMENT OF DESTROYING YET ANOTHER PLANET.

YOU MARCHED YOURSELVES INTO THE DARK WILLINGLY, AND WE HAVE COME HERE TO ENSURE YOU EMBRACE THE EXISTENCE YOU ALL HAVE SO WELL EARNED---

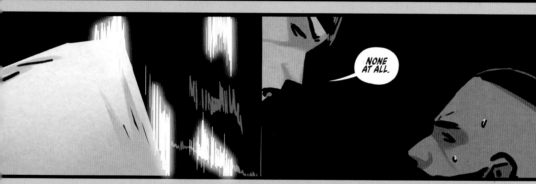

NONE AT ALL.

YOU WERE RIGHT, YOU KNOW...WE SHOULD *NEVER* HAVE COME HERE.

I THOUGHT IT WOULD JUST BE ANOTHER MISSION, BUT...*EVERYTHING* IS DIFFERENT NOW.

SORRY, IS THIS DISTRACTING? SHERRIE? YOU STILL THERE?

SHER...?

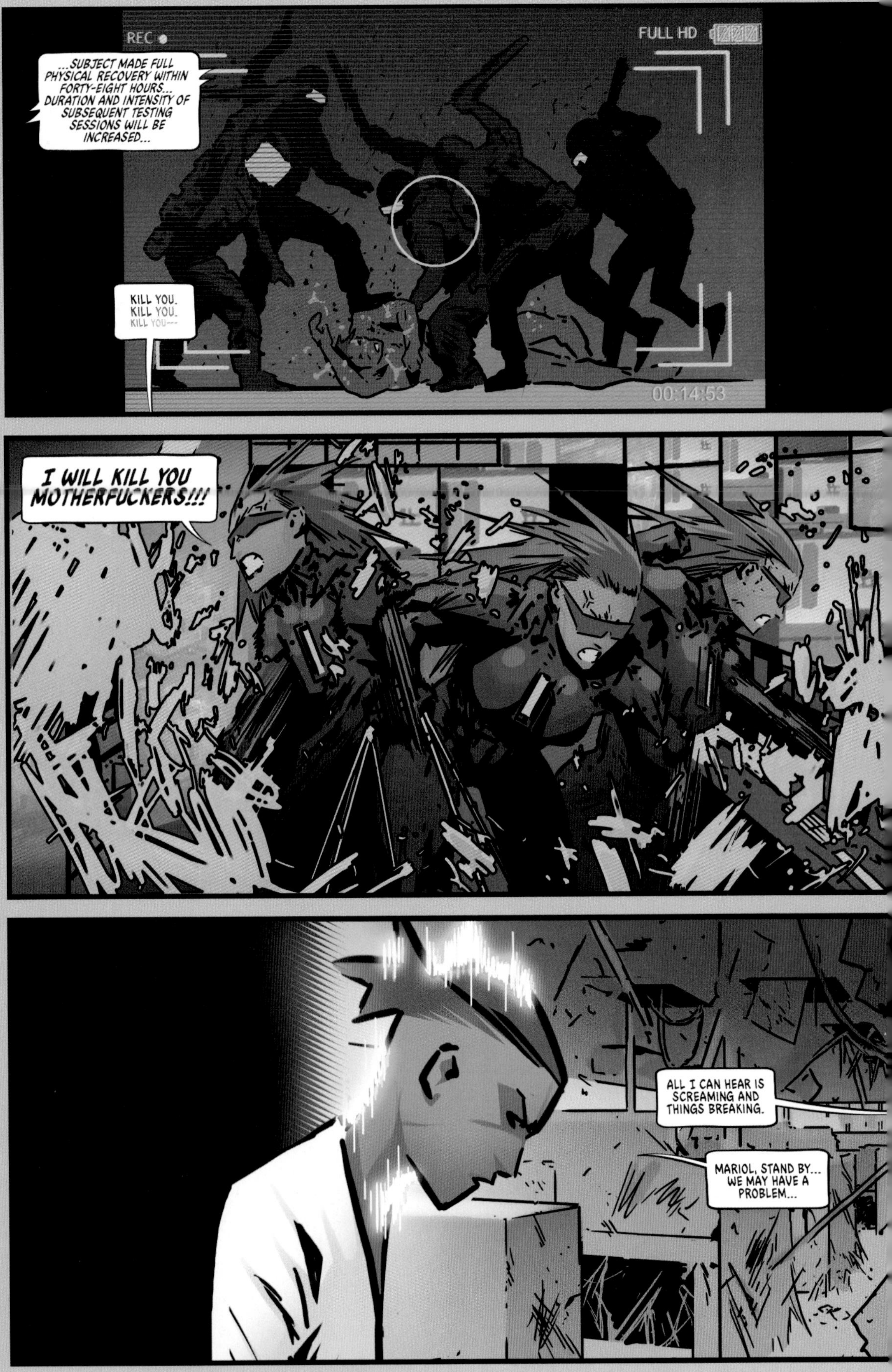
REC
FULL HD
...SUBJECT MADE FULL PHYSICAL RECOVERY WITHIN FORTY-EIGHT HOURS... DURATION AND INTENSITY OF SUBSEQUENT TESTING SESSIONS WILL BE INCREASED...
KILL YOU. KILL YOU. KILL YOU---
00:14:53
I WILL KILL YOU MOTHERFUCKERS!!!
ALL I CAN HEAR IS SCREAMING AND THINGS BREAKING.
MARIOL, STAND BY... WE MAY HAVE A PROBLEM...

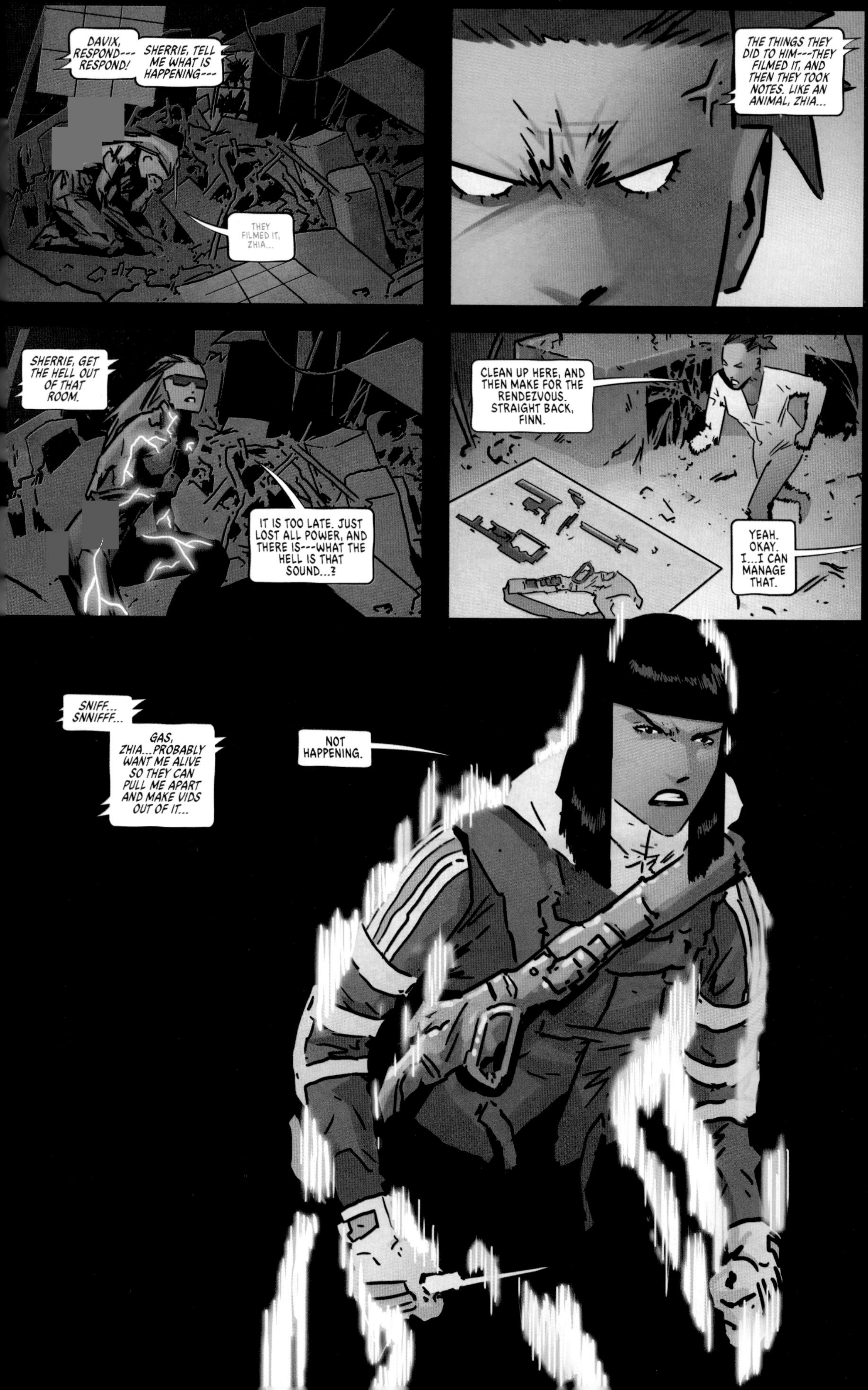
DAVIX, RESPOND--- RESPOND!
SHERRIE, TELL ME WHAT IS HAPPENING---
THEY FILMED IT, ZHIA...
THE THINGS THEY DID TO HIM---THEY FILMED IT, AND THEN THEY TOOK NOTES. LIKE AN ANIMAL, ZHIA...
SHERRIE, GET THE HELL OUT OF THAT ROOM.
IT IS TOO LATE. JUST LOST ALL POWER, AND THERE IS---WHAT THE HELL IS THAT SOUND...?
CLEAN UP HERE, AND THEN MAKE FOR THE RENDEZVOUS. STRAIGHT BACK, FINN.
YEAH. OKAY. I...I CAN MANAGE THAT.
SNIFF... SNNIFFF...
GAS, ZHIA...PROBABLY WANT ME ALIVE SO THEY CAN PULL ME APART AND MAKE VIDS OUT OF IT...
NOT HAPPENING.

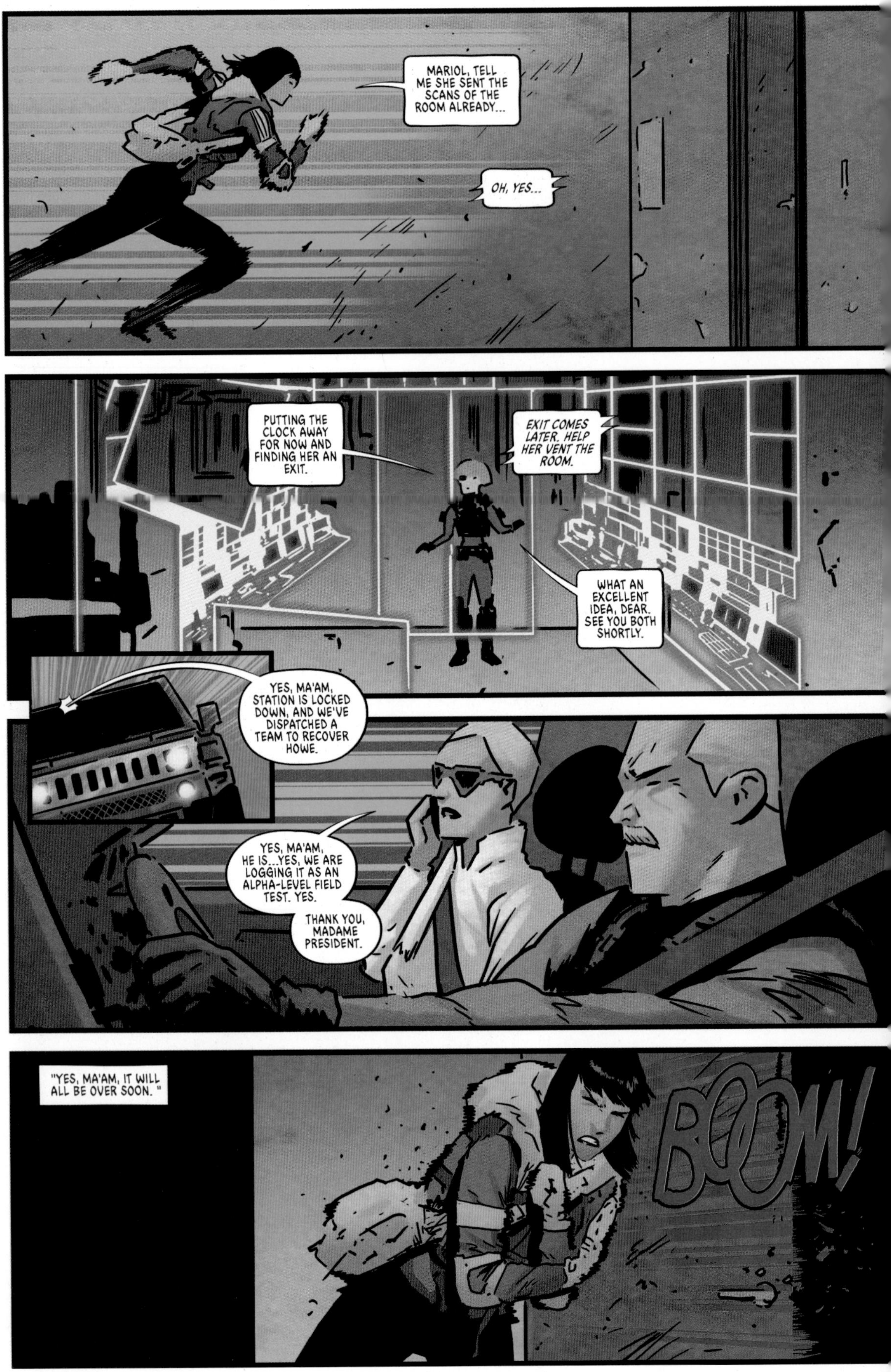
MARIOL, TELL ME SHE SENT THE SCANS OF THE ROOM ALREADY...
OH, YES...
PUTTING THE CLOCK AWAY FOR NOW AND FINDING HER AN EXIT.
EXIT COMES LATER. HELP HER VENT THE ROOM.
WHAT AN EXCELLENT IDEA, DEAR. SEE YOU BOTH SHORTLY.
YES, MA'AM, STATION IS LOCKED DOWN, AND WE'VE DISPATCHED A TEAM TO RECOVER HOWE.
YES, MA'AM, HE IS...YES, WE ARE LOGGING IT AS AN ALPHA-LEVEL FIELD TEST. YES.
THANK YOU, MADAME PRESIDENT.
"YES, MA'AM, IT WILL ALL BE OVER SOON."
BOOM!

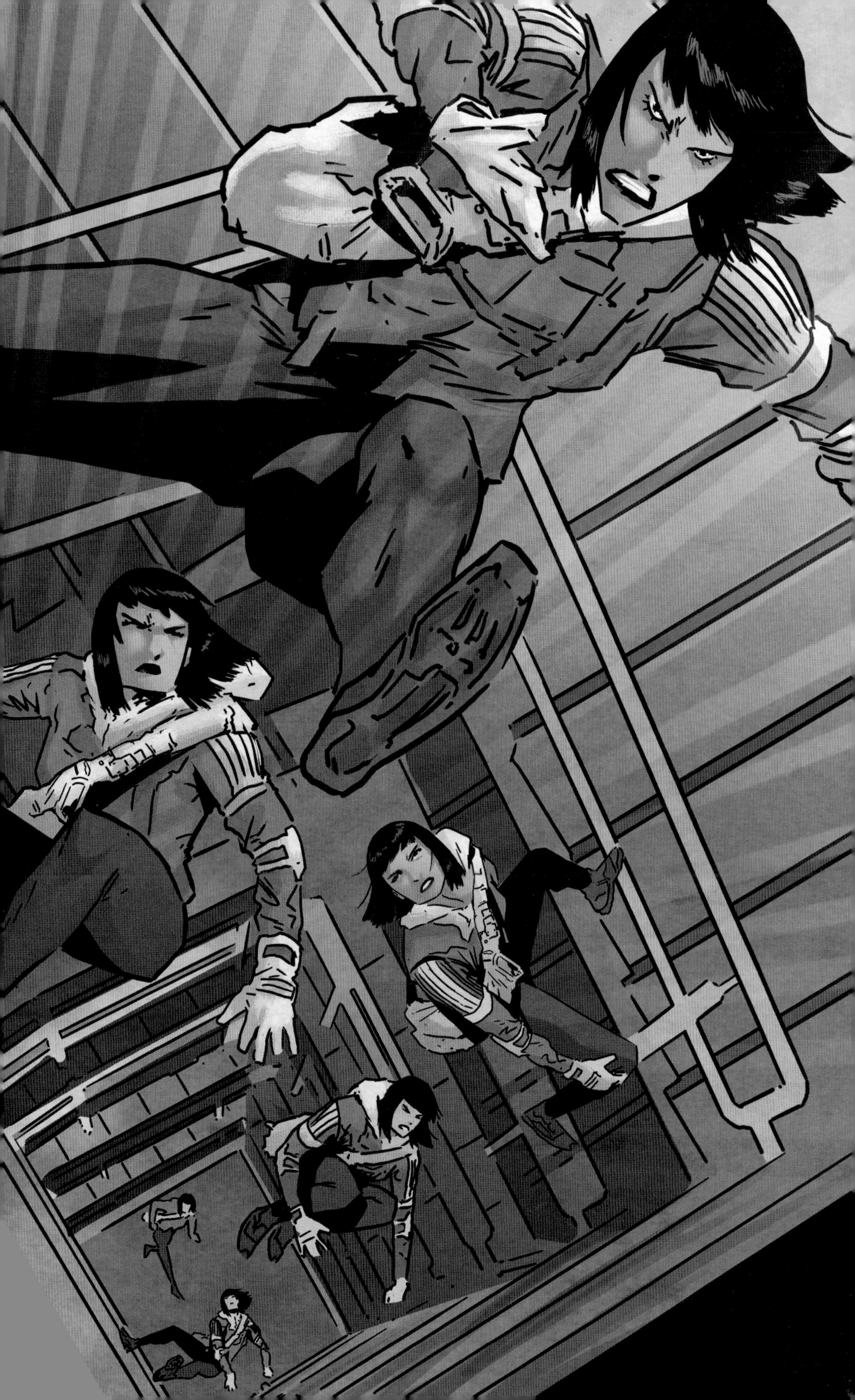

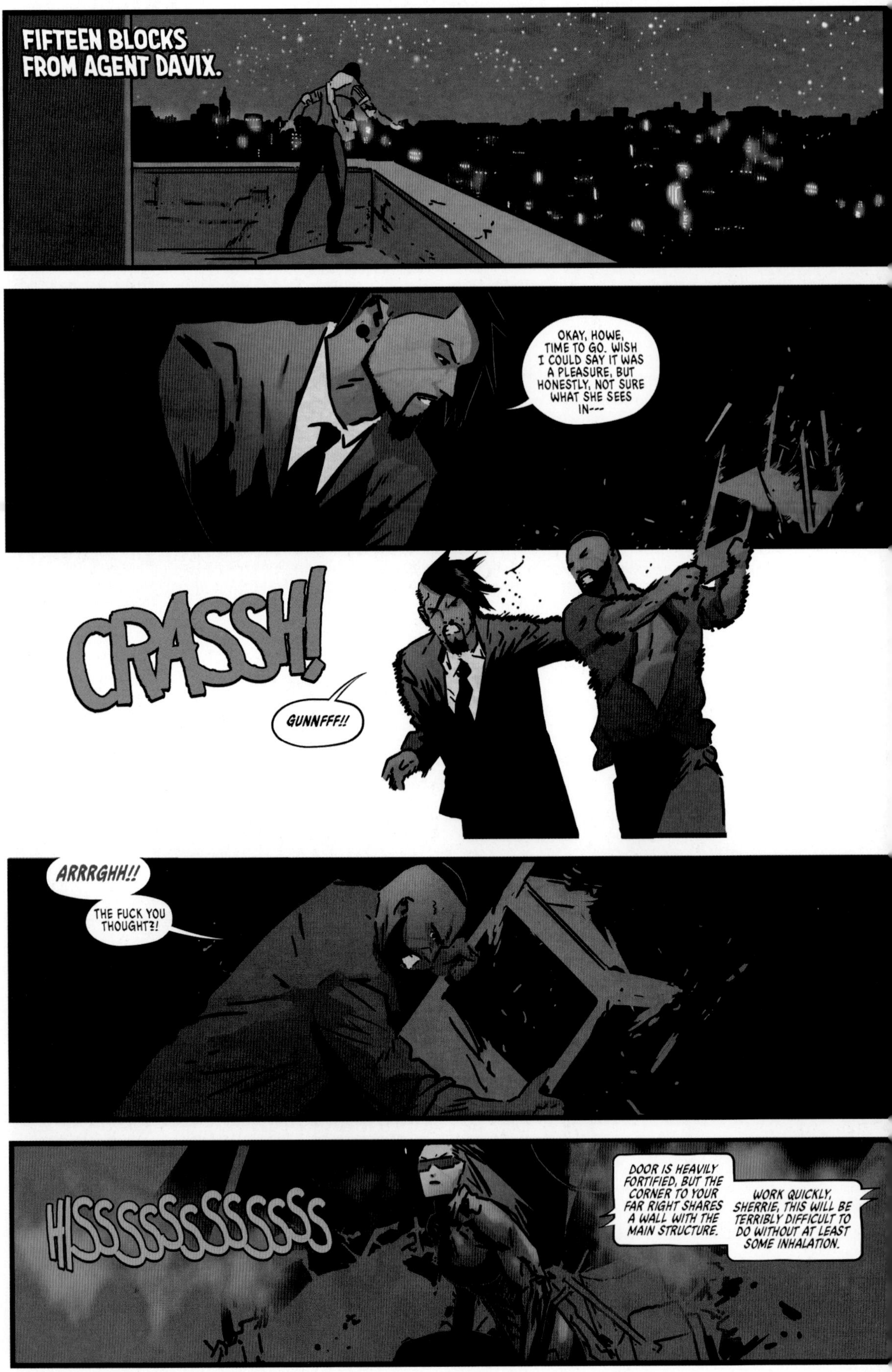
FIFTEEN BLOCKS FROM AGENT DAVIX.
OKAY, HOWE, TIME TO GO. WISH I COULD SAY IT WAS A PLEASURE, BUT HONESTLY, NOT SURE WHAT SHE SEES IN---
CRASSH!
GUNNFFF!!
ARRRGHH!!
THE FUCK YOU THOUGHT?!
HISSSSSSSSSSSS
DOOR IS HEAVILY FORTIFIED, BUT THE CORNER TO YOUR FAR RIGHT SHARES A WALL WITH THE MAIN STRUCTURE.
WORK QUICKLY, SHERRIE, THIS WILL BE TERRIBLY DIFFICULT TO DO WITHOUT AT LEAST SOME INHALATION.

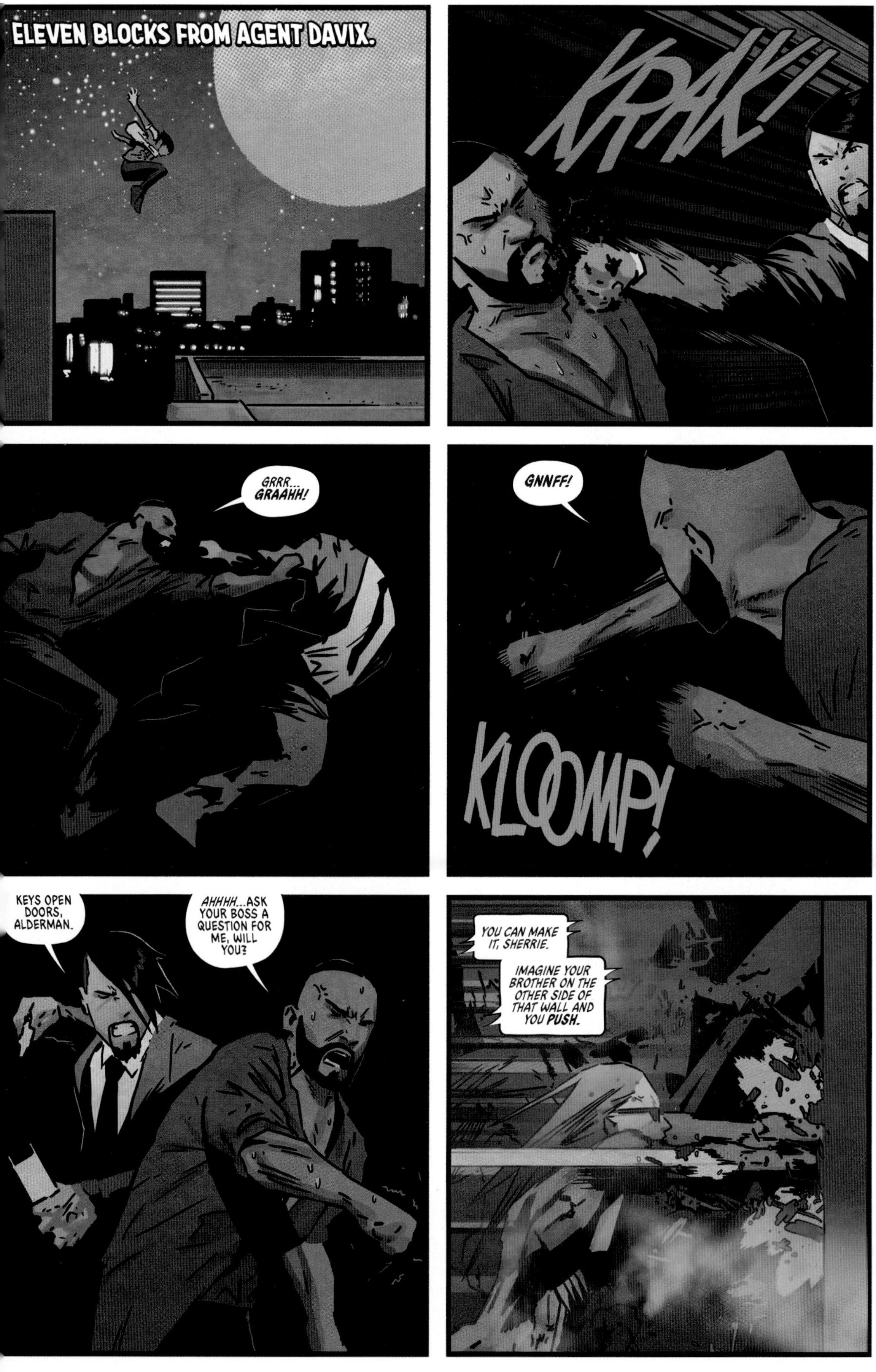
ELEVEN BLOCKS FROM AGENT DAVIX.
KRAK!
GRRR... GRAAHH!
GNNFF!
KLOOMP!
KEYS OPEN DOORS, ALDERMAN.
AHHHH...ASK YOUR BOSS A QUESTION FOR ME, WILL YOU?
YOU CAN MAKE IT, SHERRIE.
IMAGINE YOUR BROTHER ON THE OTHER SIDE OF THAT WALL AND YOU PUSH.

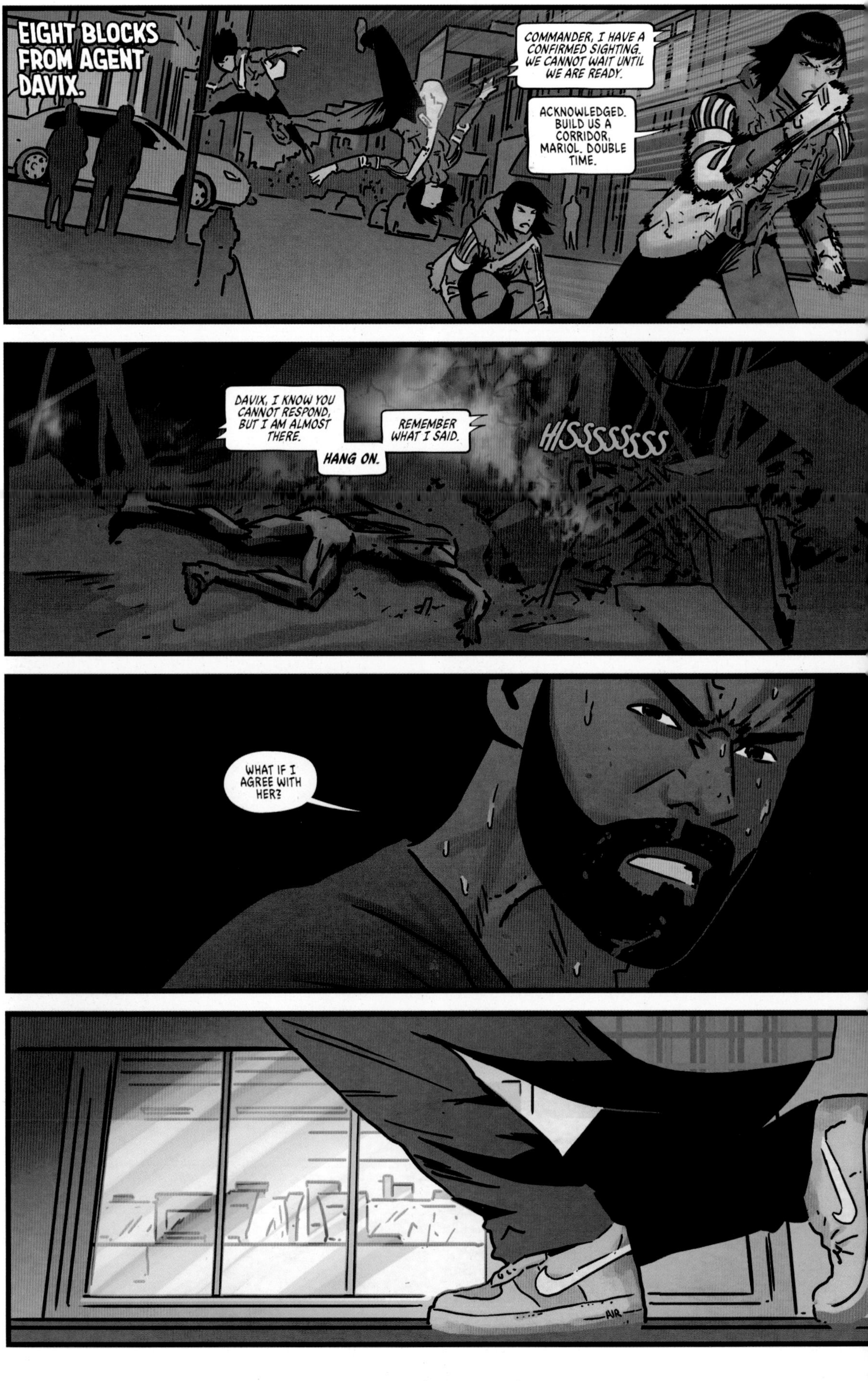
EIGHT BLOCKS FROM AGENT DAVIX.
COMMANDER, I HAVE A CONFIRMED SIGHTING. WE CANNOT WAIT UNTIL WE ARE READY.
ACKNOWLEDGED. BUILD US A CORRIDOR, MARIOL. DOUBLE TIME.
DAVIX, I KNOW YOU CANNOT RESPOND, BUT I AM ALMOST THERE.
HANG ON.
REMEMBER WHAT I SAID.
HISSSSSSSS
WHAT IF I AGREE WITH HER?

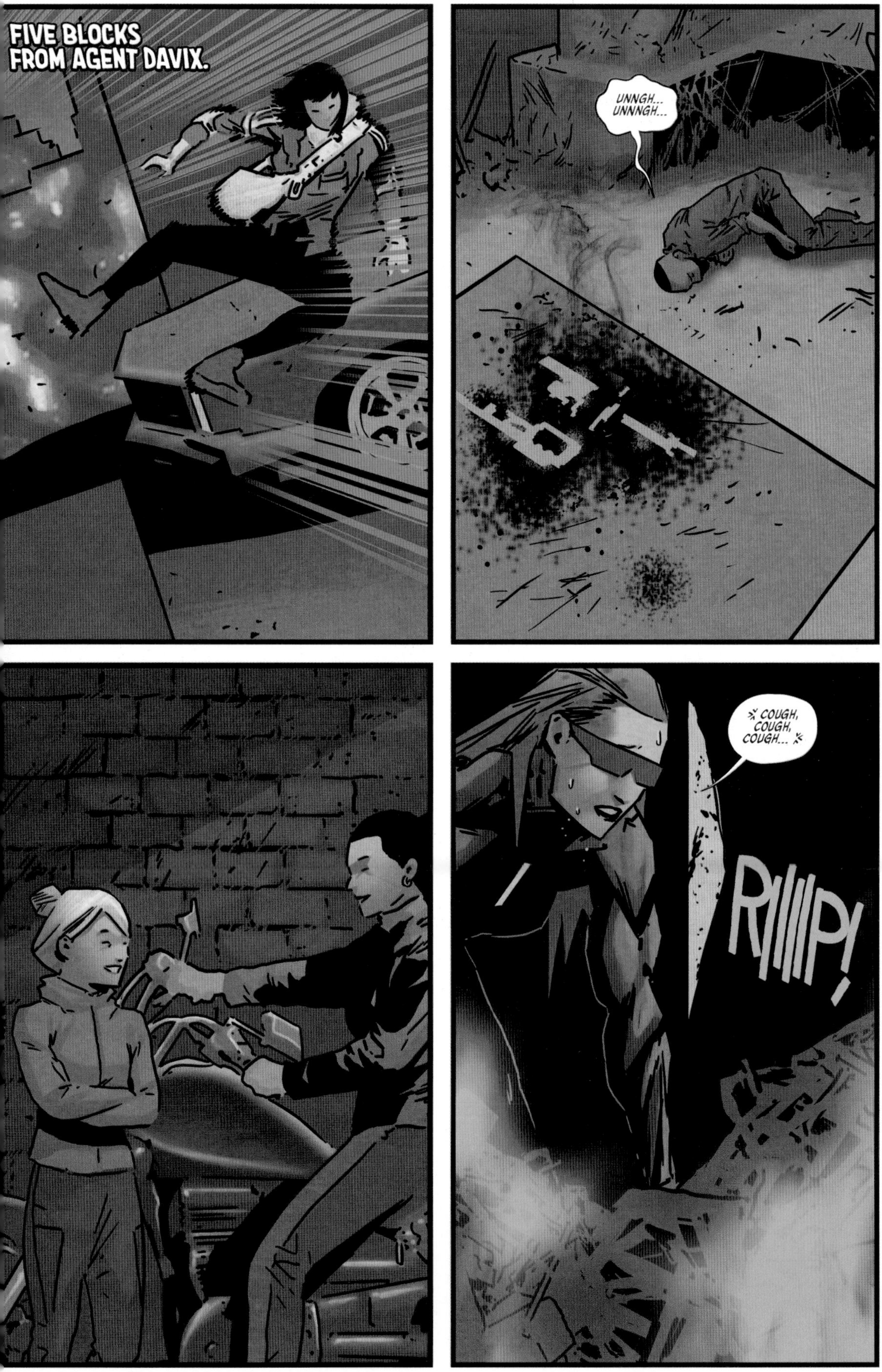
FIVE BLOCKS FROM AGENT DAVIX.
UNNGH... UNNNGH...
COUGH, COUGH, COUGH...
RIIIIP!

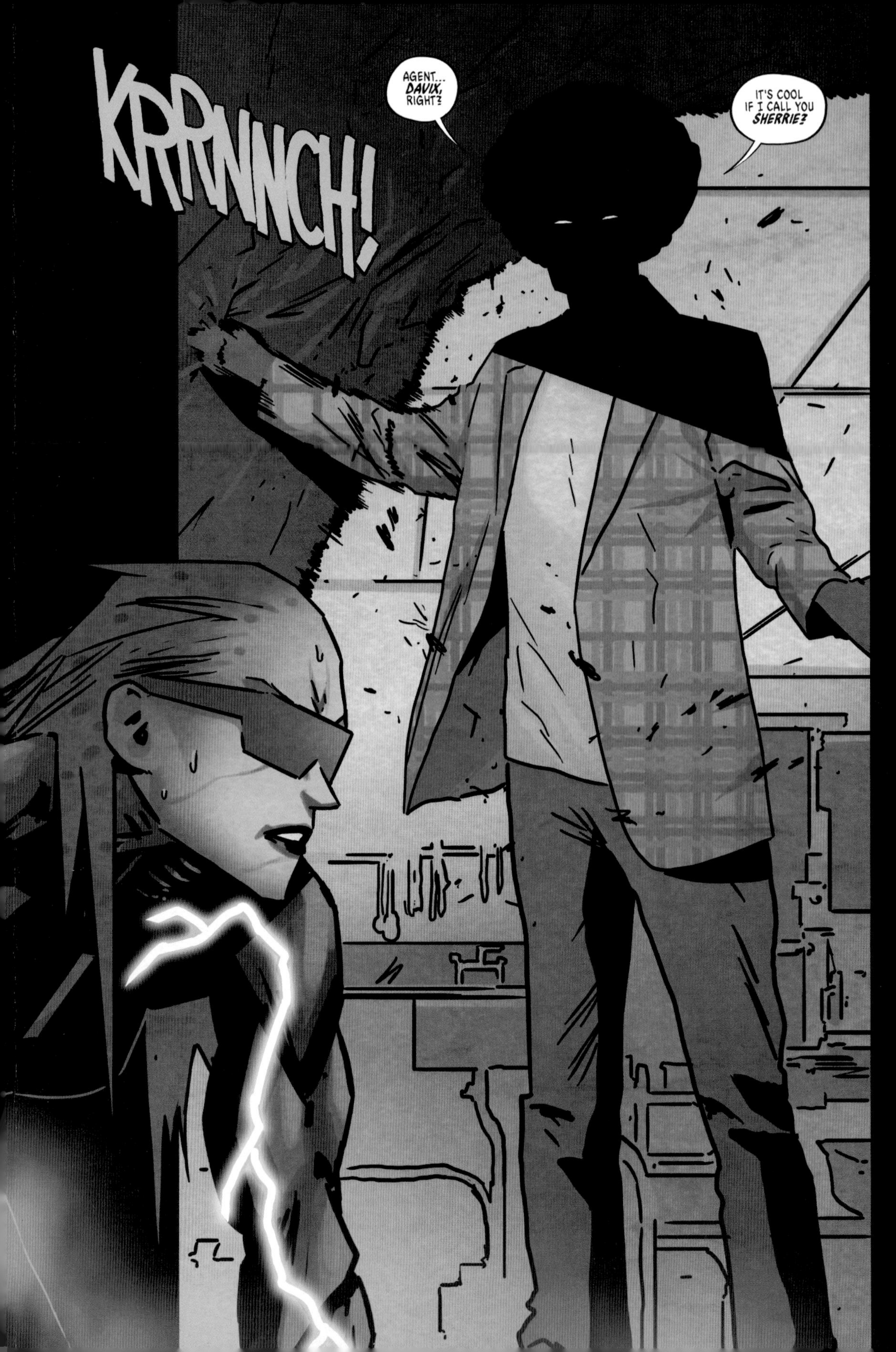

KRRNNCH!
AGENT... DAVIX, RIGHT?
IT'S COOL IF I CALL YOU SHERRIE?

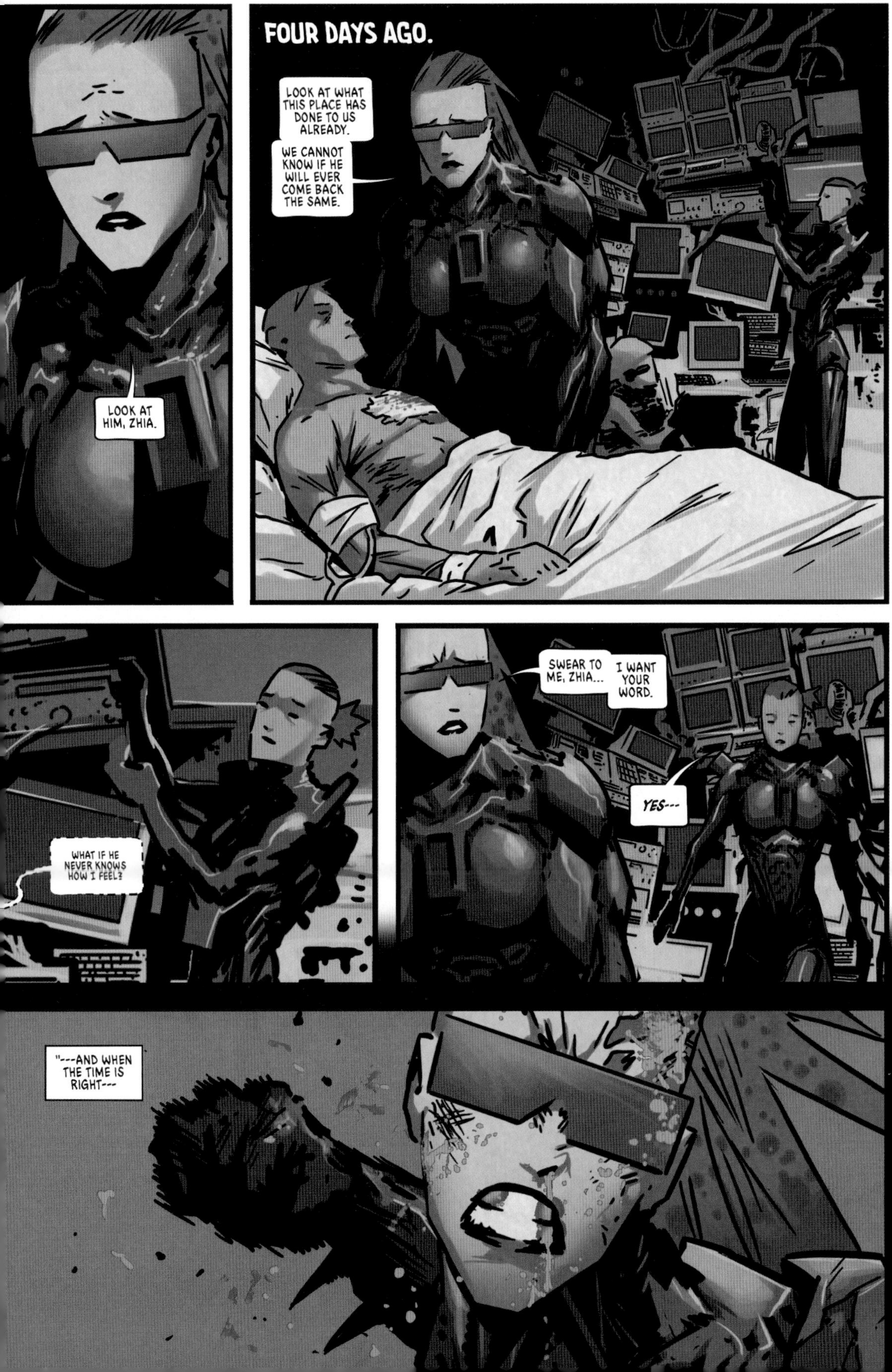
FOUR DAYS AGO.
LOOK AT HIM, ZHIA.
LOOK AT WHAT THIS PLACE HAS DONE TO US ALREADY.
WE CANNOT KNOW IF HE WILL EVER COME BACK THE SAME.
WHAT IF HE NEVER KNOWS HOW I FEEL?
SWEAR TO ME, ZHIA...
I WANT YOUR WORD.
YES---
"---AND WHEN THE TIME IS RIGHT---

NOW.

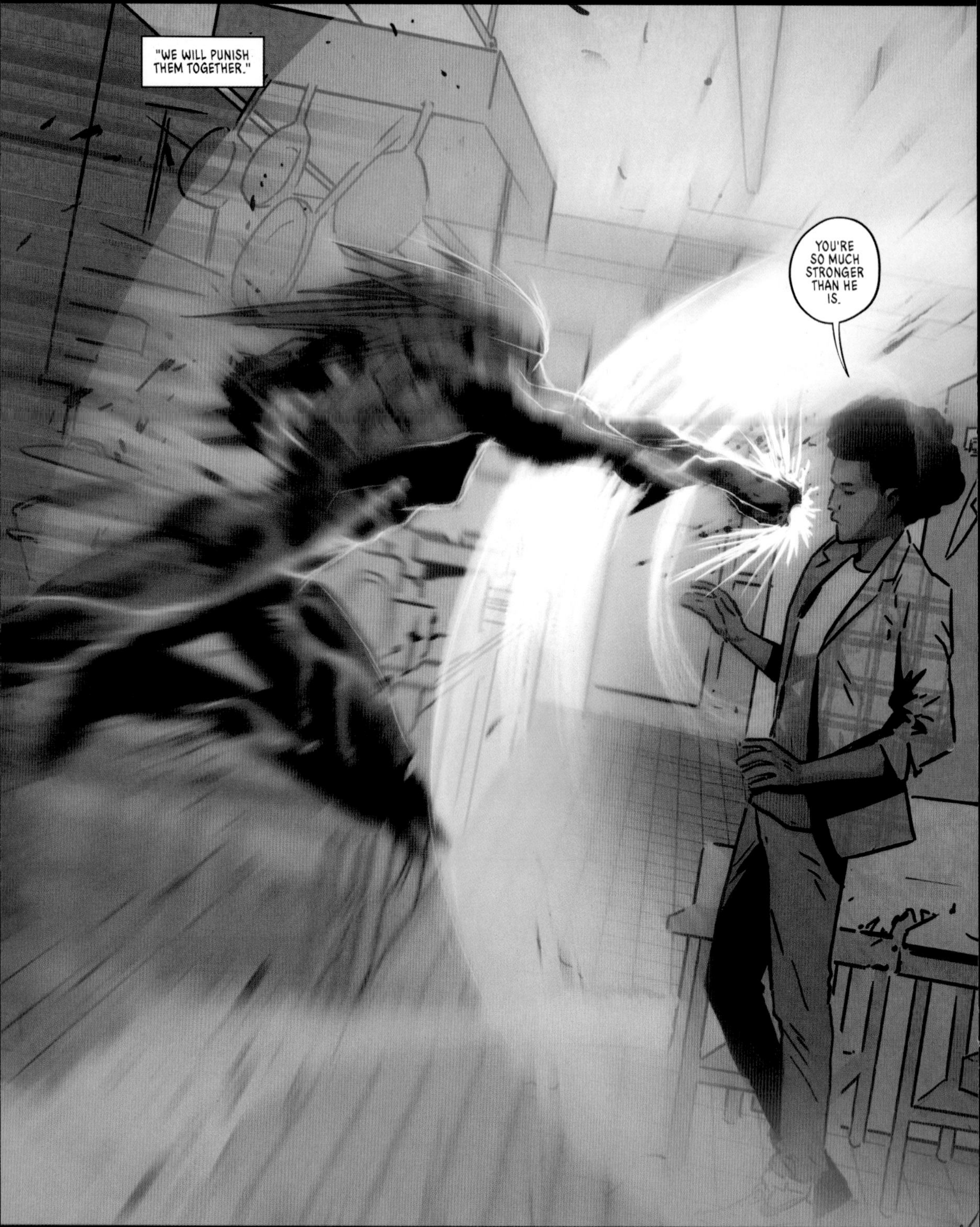
"WE WILL PUNISH THEM TOGETHER."
YOU'RE SO MUCH STRONGER THAN HE IS.

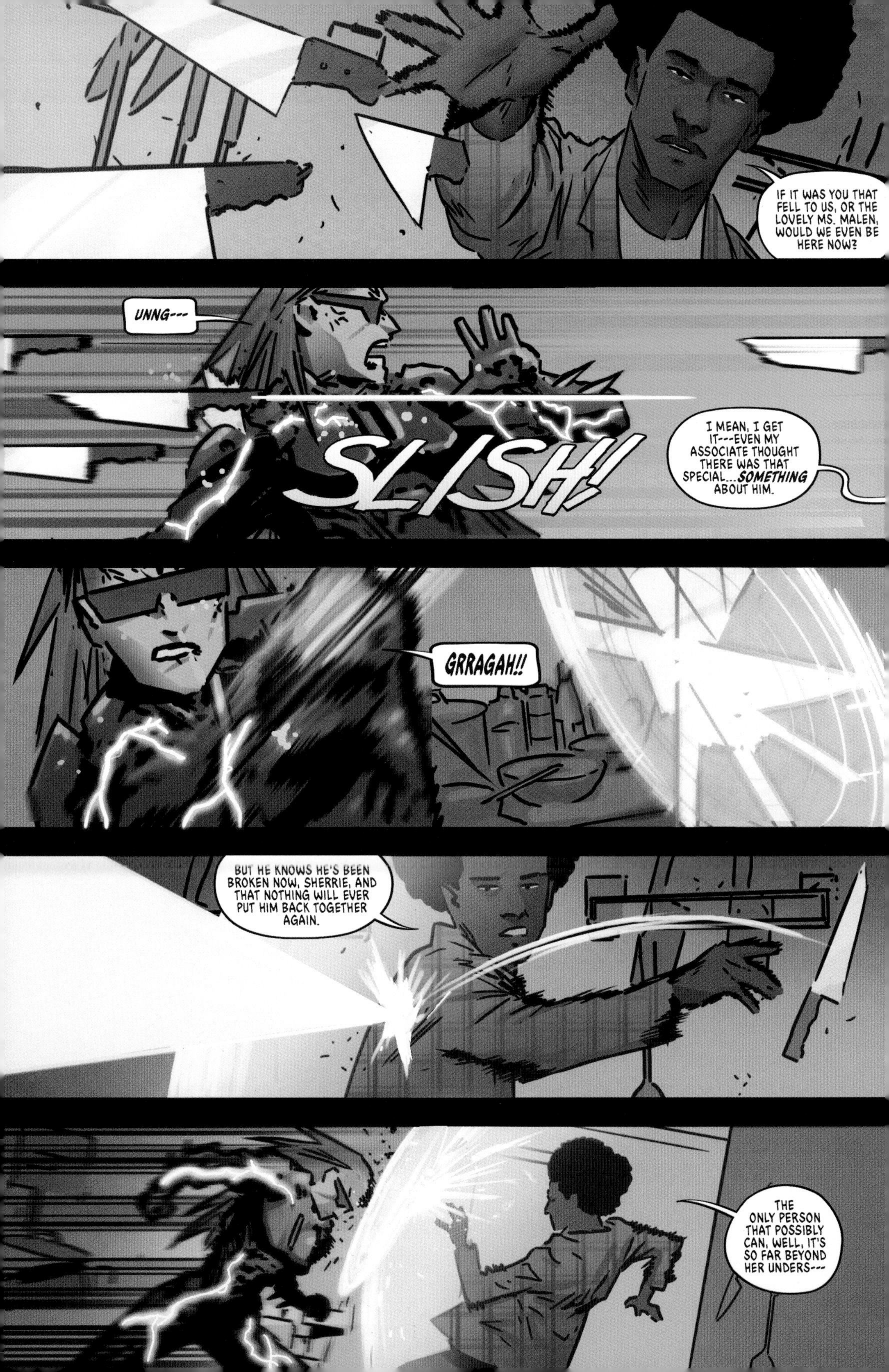
IF IT WAS YOU THAT FELL TO US, OR THE LOVELY MS. MALEN, WOULD WE EVEN BE HERE NOW?
UNNG---
SLISH!
I MEAN, I GET IT---EVEN MY ASSOCIATE THOUGHT THERE WAS THAT SPECIAL...SOMETHING ABOUT HIM.
GRRAGAH!!
BUT HE KNOWS HE'S BEEN BROKEN NOW, SHERRIE, AND THAT NOTHING WILL EVER PUT HIM BACK TOGETHER AGAIN.
THE ONLY PERSON THAT POSSIBLY CAN, WELL, IT'S SO FAR BEYOND HER UNDERS---

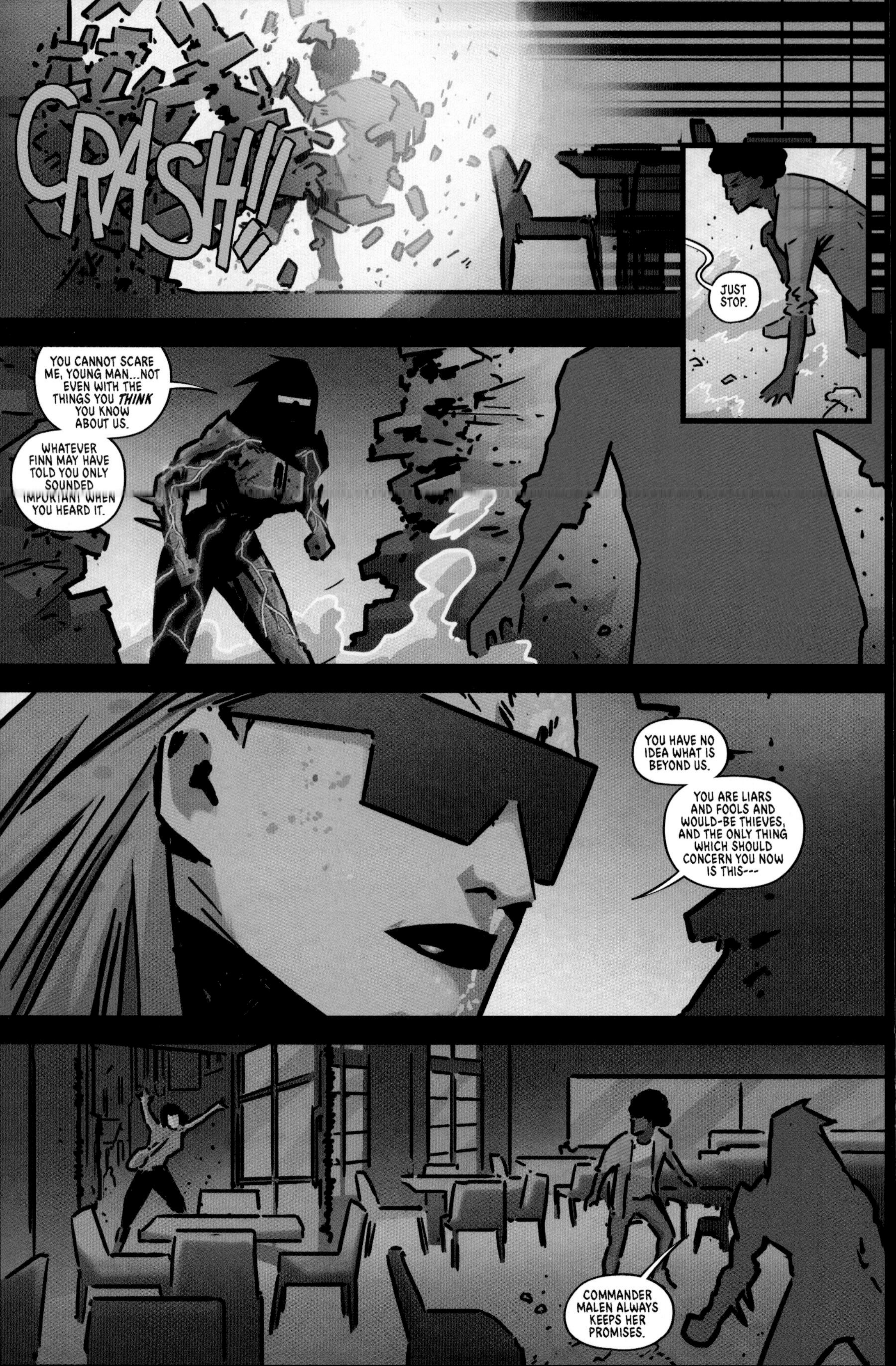
CRASH!!
JUST STOP.
YOU CANNOT SCARE ME, YOUNG MAN...NOT EVEN WITH THE THINGS YOU *THINK* YOU KNOW ABOUT US.
WHATEVER FINN MAY HAVE TOLD YOU ONLY SOUNDED IMPORTANT WHEN YOU HEARD IT.
YOU HAVE NO IDEA WHAT IS BEYOND US.
YOU ARE LIARS AND FOOLS AND WOULD-BE THIEVES, AND THE ONLY THING WHICH SHOULD CONCERN YOU NOW IS THIS---
COMMANDER MALEN ALWAYS KEEPS HER PROMISES.

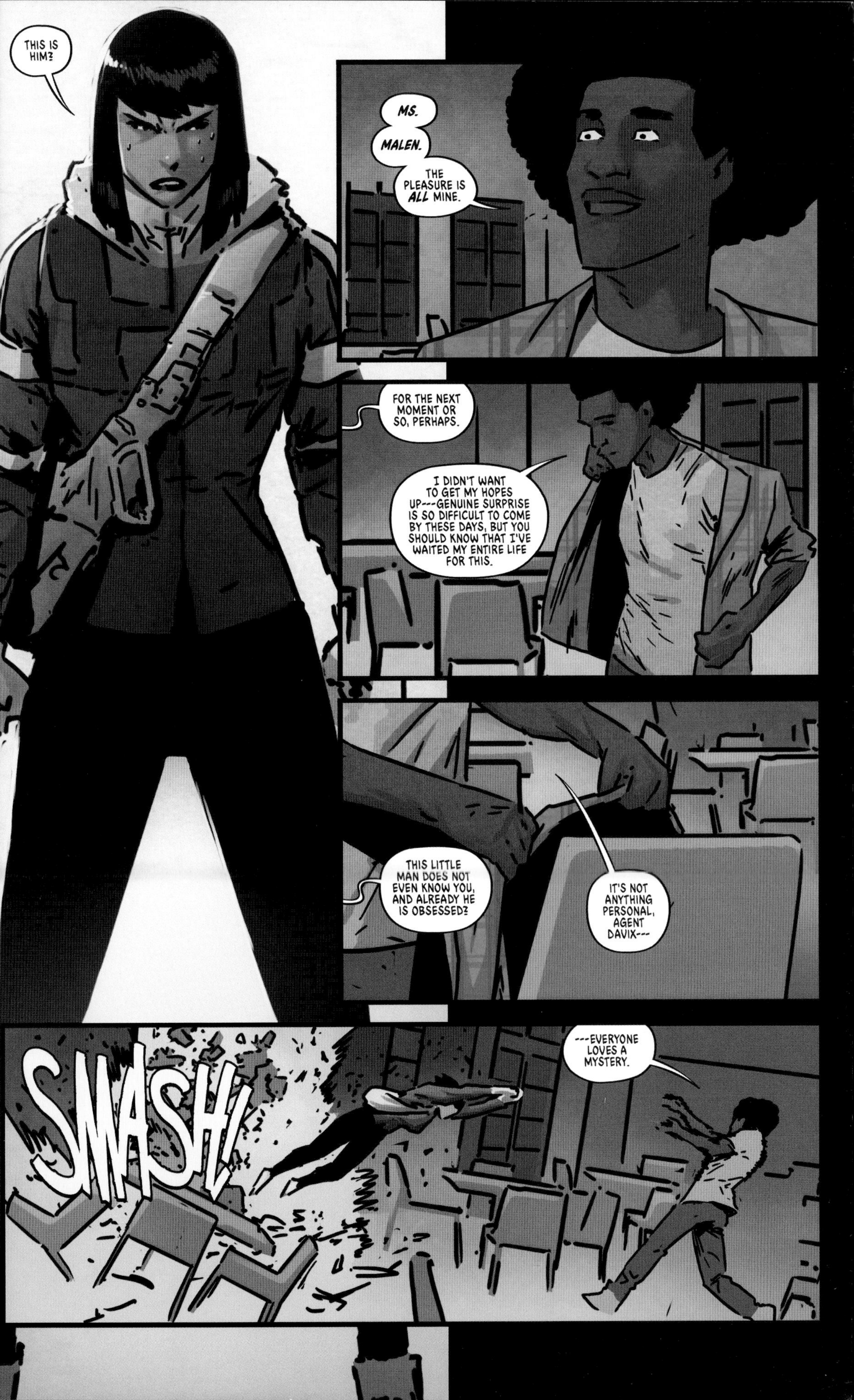
THIS IS HIM?
MS.
MALEN.
THE PLEASURE IS ALL MINE.
FOR THE NEXT MOMENT OR SO, PERHAPS.
I DIDN'T WANT TO GET MY HOPES UP---GENUINE SURPRISE IS SO DIFFICULT TO COME BY THESE DAYS, BUT YOU SHOULD KNOW THAT I'VE WAITED MY ENTIRE LIFE FOR THIS.
THIS LITTLE MAN DOES NOT EVEN KNOW YOU, AND ALREADY HE IS OBSESSED?
IT'S NOT ANYTHING PERSONAL, AGENT DAVIX---
SMASH!
---EVERYONE LOVES A MYSTERY.

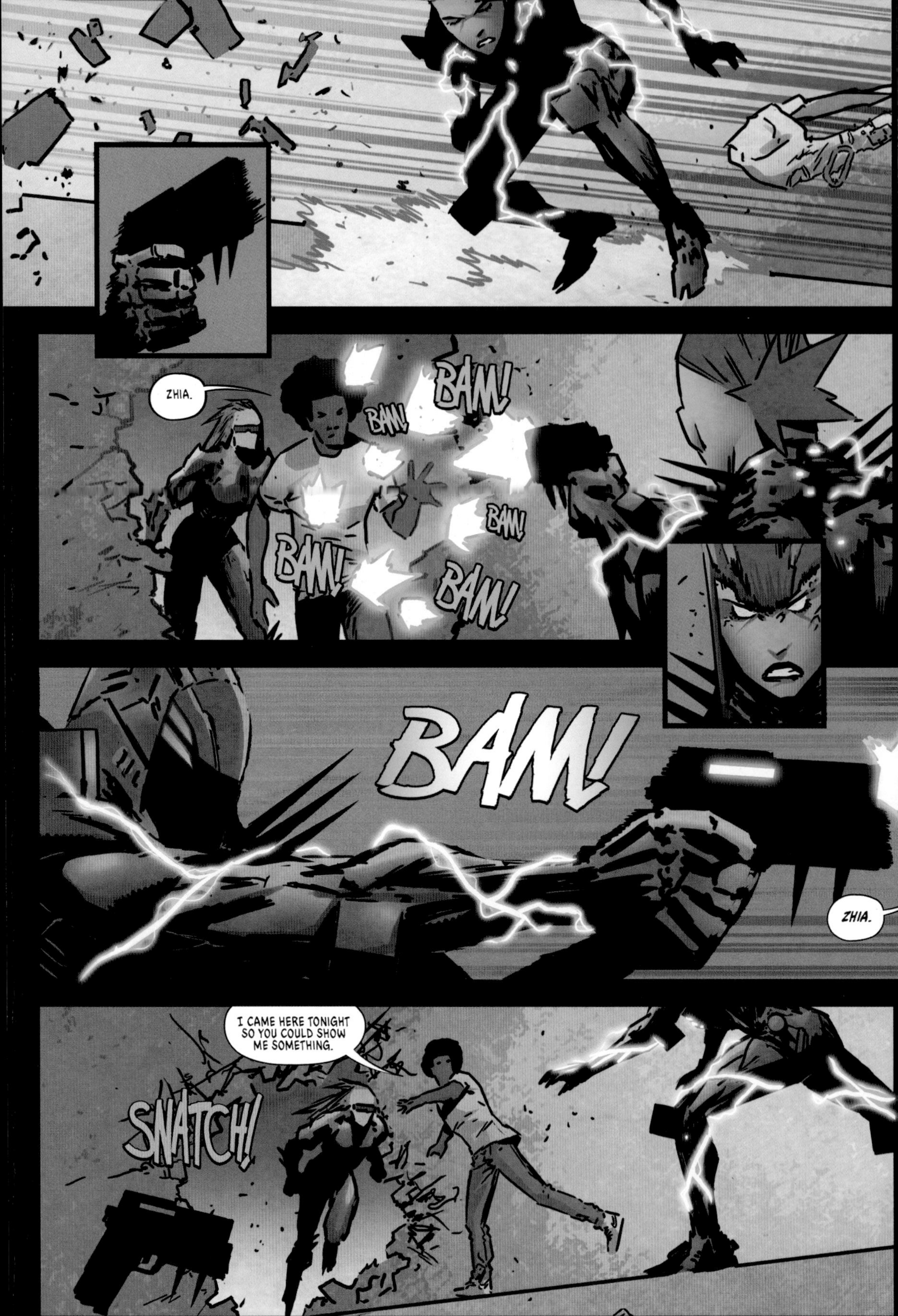
ZHIA.
BAM!
BAM!
BAM!
BAM!
BAM!
BAM!
ZHIA.
I CAME HERE TONIGHT SO YOU COULD SHOW ME SOMETHING.
SNATCH!

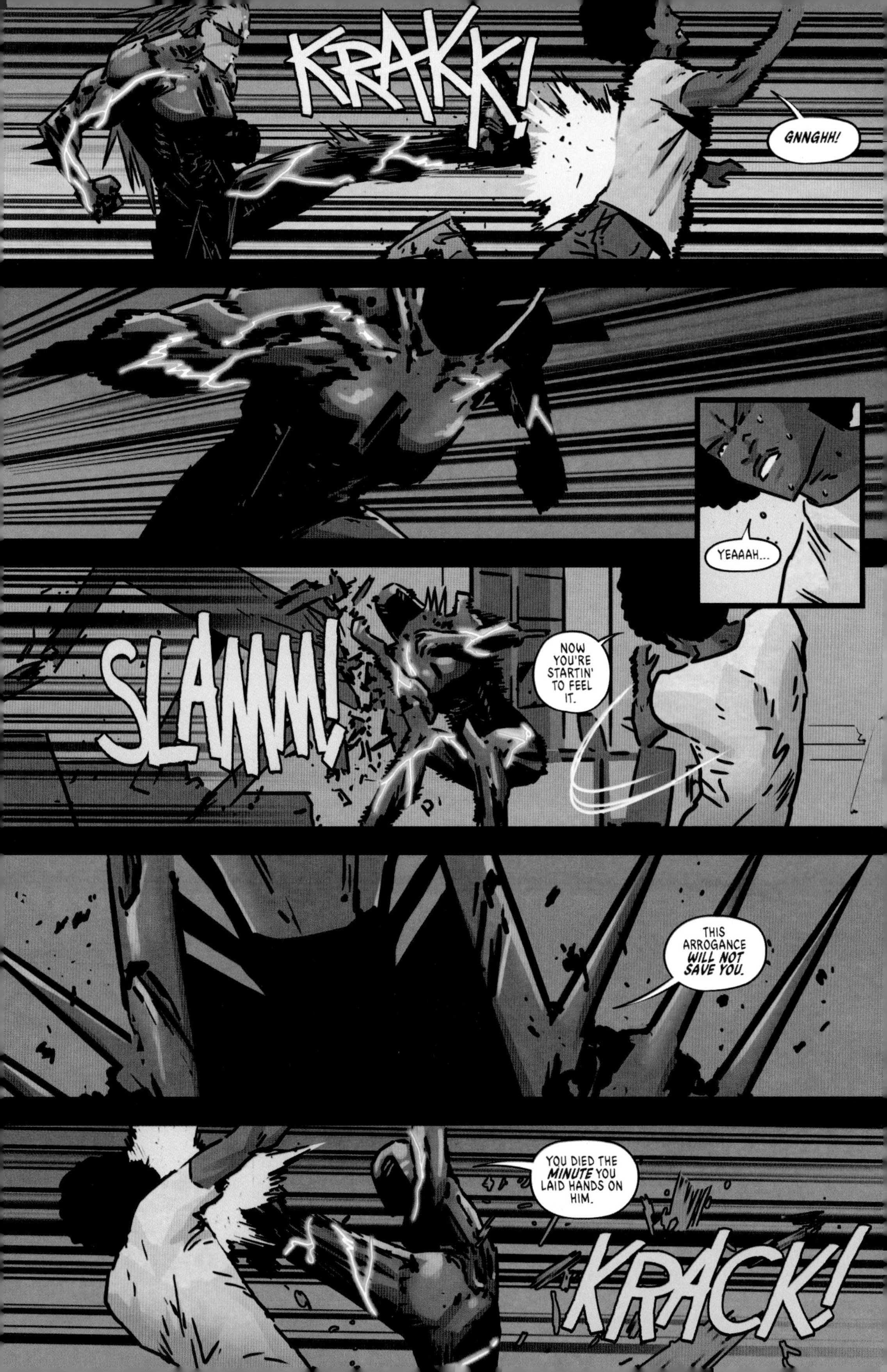
KRAKK!
GNNGHH!
YEAAAH...
SLAMM!
NOW YOU'RE STARTIN' TO FEEL IT.
THIS ARROGANCE ***WILL NOT SAVE YOU.***
YOU DIED THE ***MINUTE*** YOU LAID HANDS ON HIM.
KRACK!

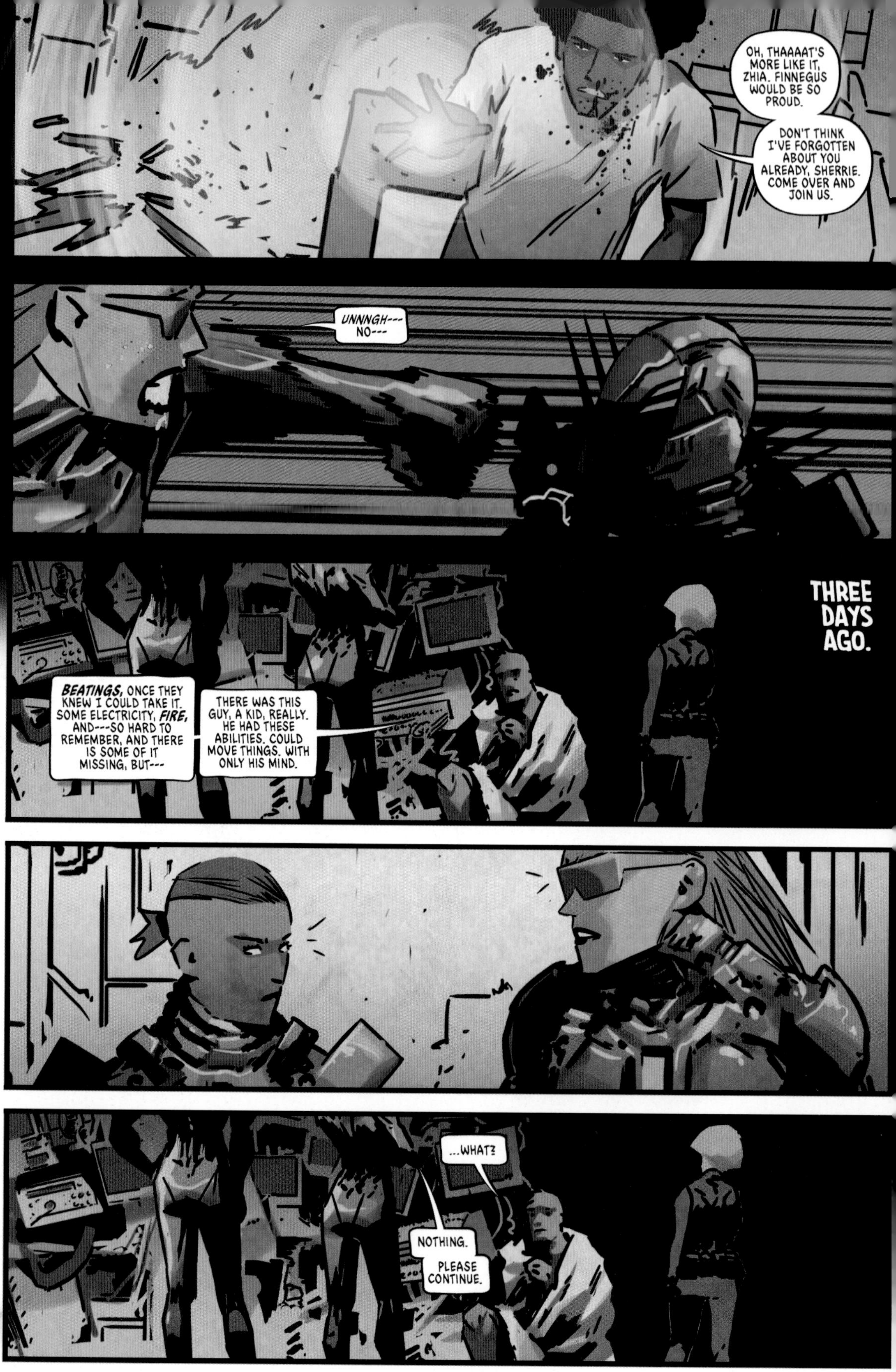
OH, THAAAAT'S MORE LIKE IT, ZHIA. FINNEGUS WOULD BE SO PROUD.
DON'T THINK I'VE FORGOTTEN ABOUT YOU ALREADY, SHERRIE. COME OVER AND JOIN US.
UNNNGH--- NO---
THREE DAYS AGO.
BEATINGS, ONCE THEY KNEW I COULD TAKE IT. SOME ELECTRICITY, FIRE, AND---SO HARD TO REMEMBER, AND THERE IS SOME OF IT MISSING, BUT---
THERE WAS THIS GUY, A KID, REALLY. HE HAD THESE ABILITIES. COULD MOVE THINGS. WITH ONLY HIS MIND.
...WHAT?
NOTHING.
PLEASE CONTINUE.

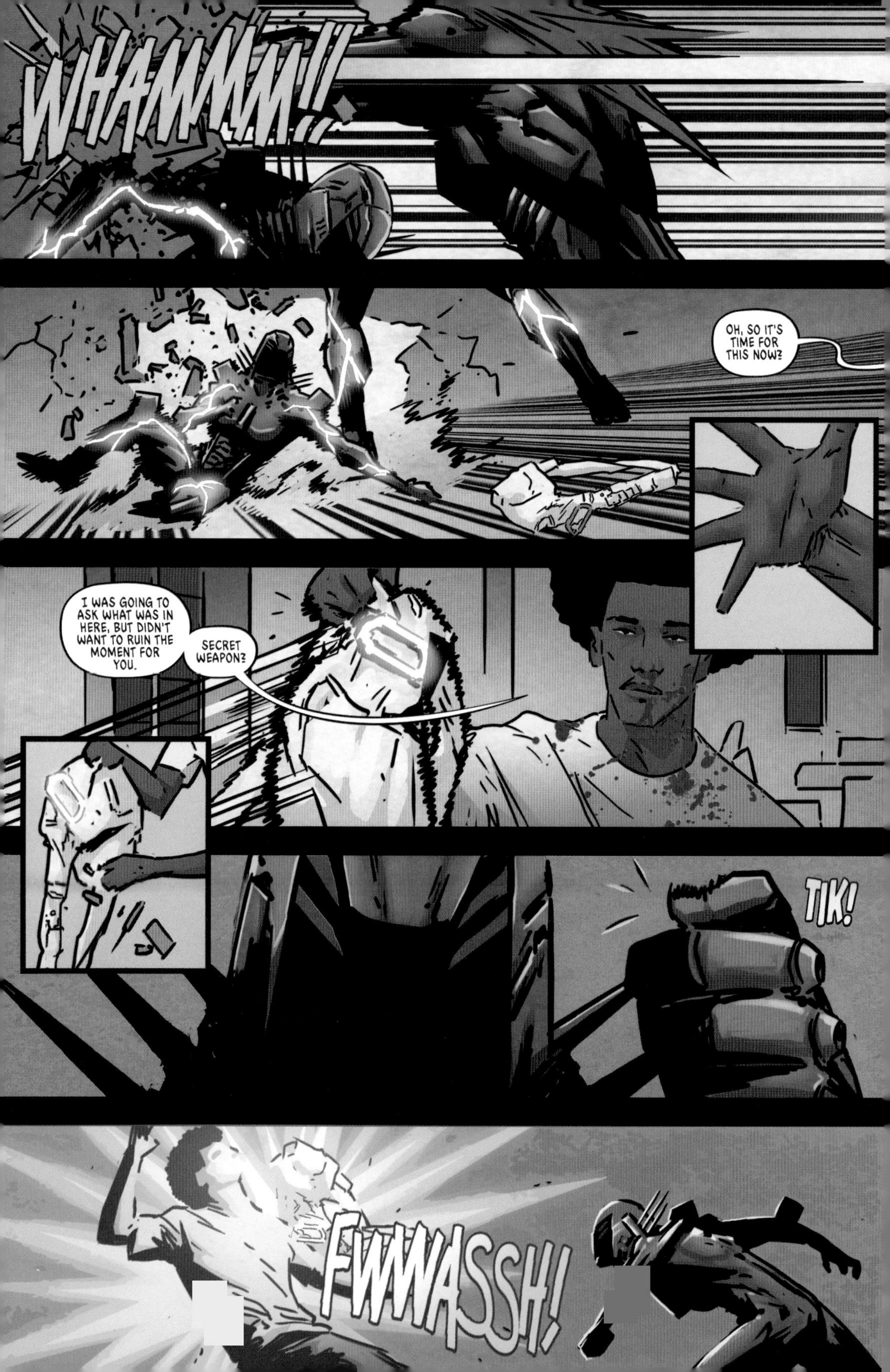
WHAMMM!!
OH, SO IT'S TIME FOR THIS NOW?
I WAS GOING TO ASK WHAT WAS IN HERE, BUT DIDN'T WANT TO RUIN THE MOMENT FOR YOU.
SECRET WEAPON?
TIK!
FWWASSH!

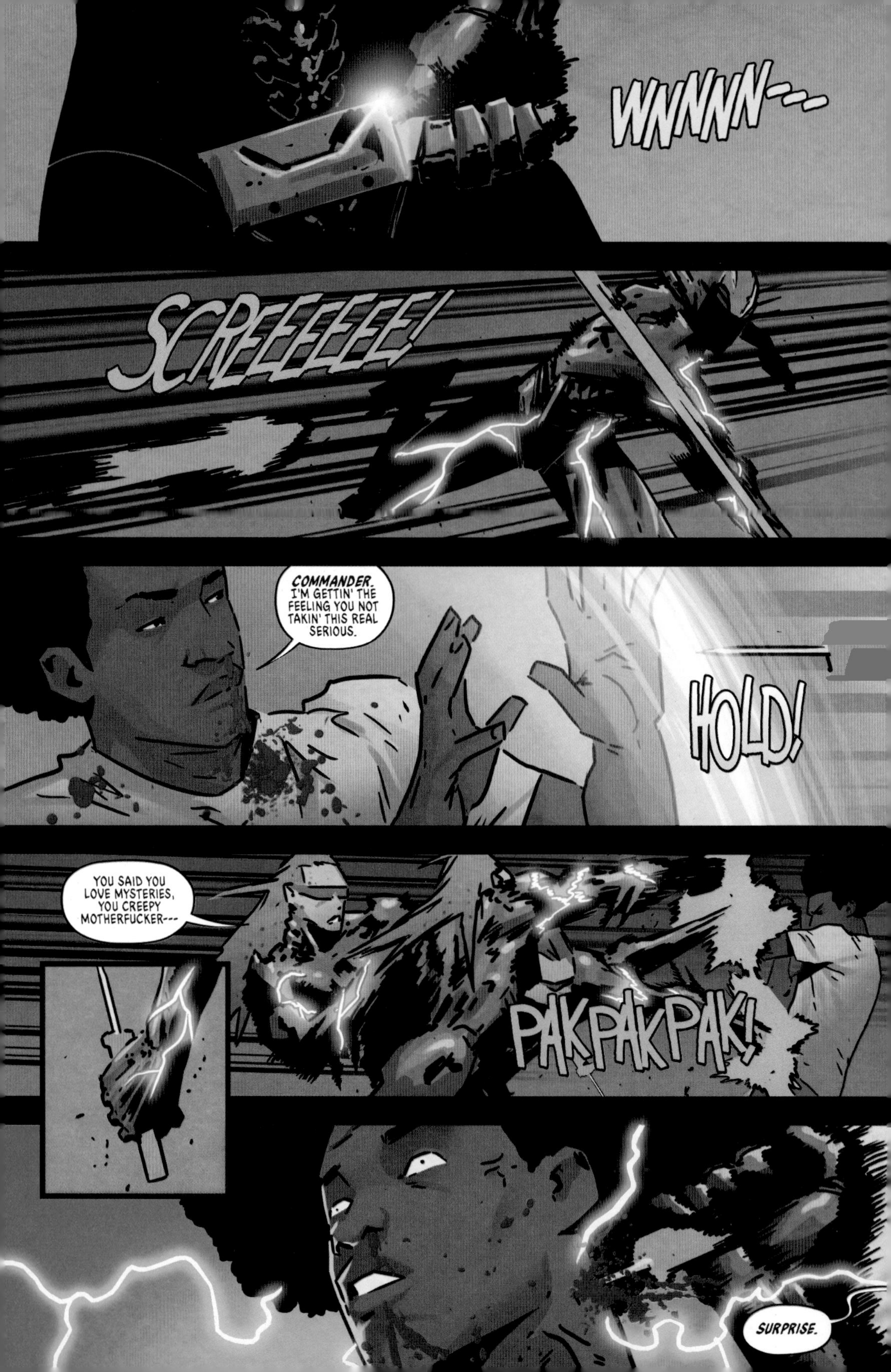
WNNNN---
SCREEEEEEE!
COMMANDER. I'M GETTIN' THE FEELING YOU NOT TAKIN' THIS REAL SERIOUS.
HOLD!
YOU SAID YOU LOVE MYSTERIES, YOU CREEPY MOTHERFUCKER---
PAKPAKPAK!
SURPRISE.

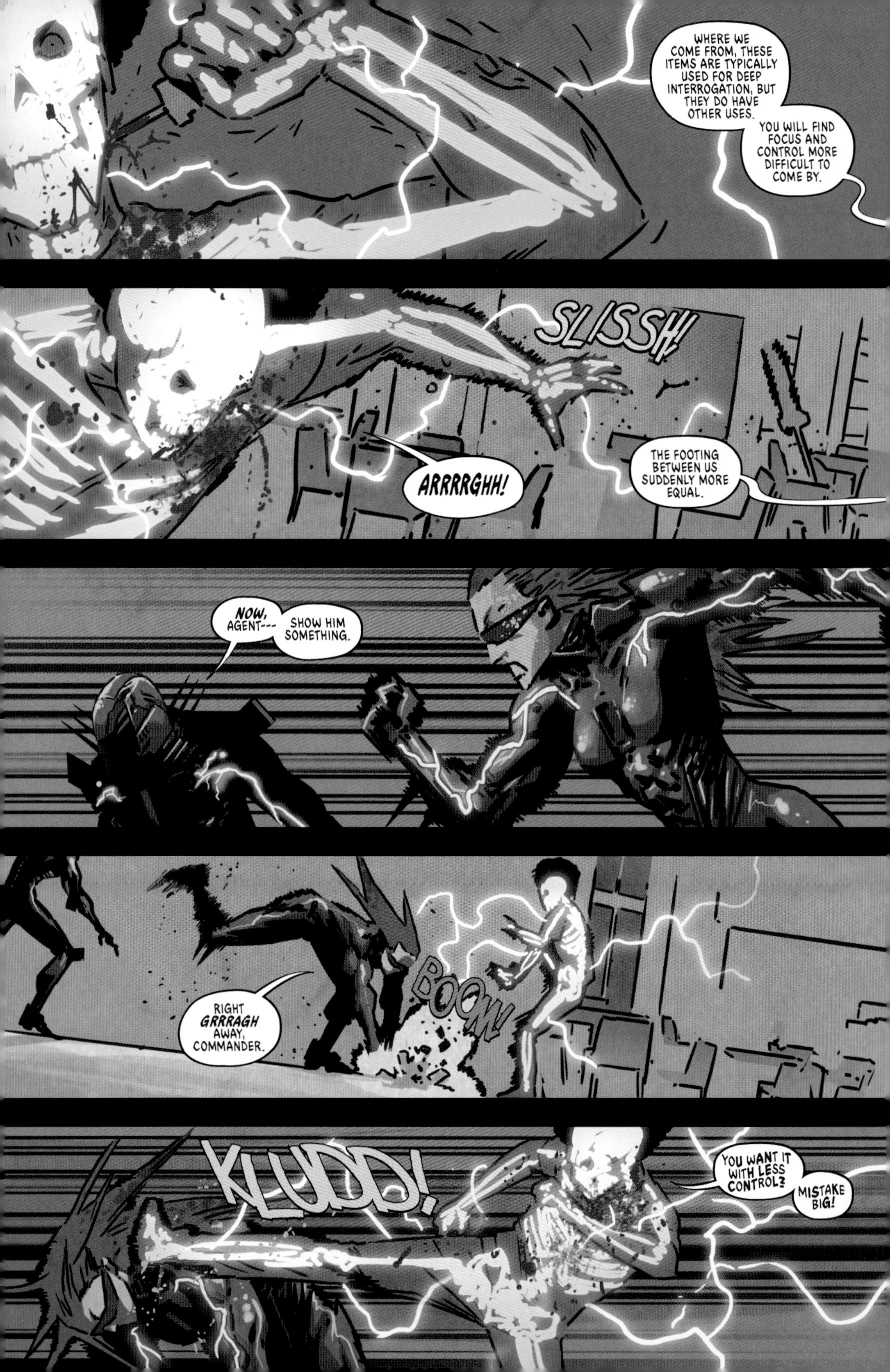
WHERE WE COME FROM, THESE ITEMS ARE TYPICALLY USED FOR DEEP INTERROGATION, BUT THEY DO HAVE OTHER USES.
YOU WILL FIND FOCUS AND CONTROL MORE DIFFICULT TO COME BY.
SLISSH!
ARRRRGHH!
THE FOOTING BETWEEN US SUDDENLY MORE EQUAL.
NOW, AGENT---
SHOW HIM SOMETHING.
RIGHT GRRRAGH AWAY, COMMANDER.
BOOM!
KLUDD!
YOU WANT IT WITH LESS CONTROL?
MISTAKE BIG!

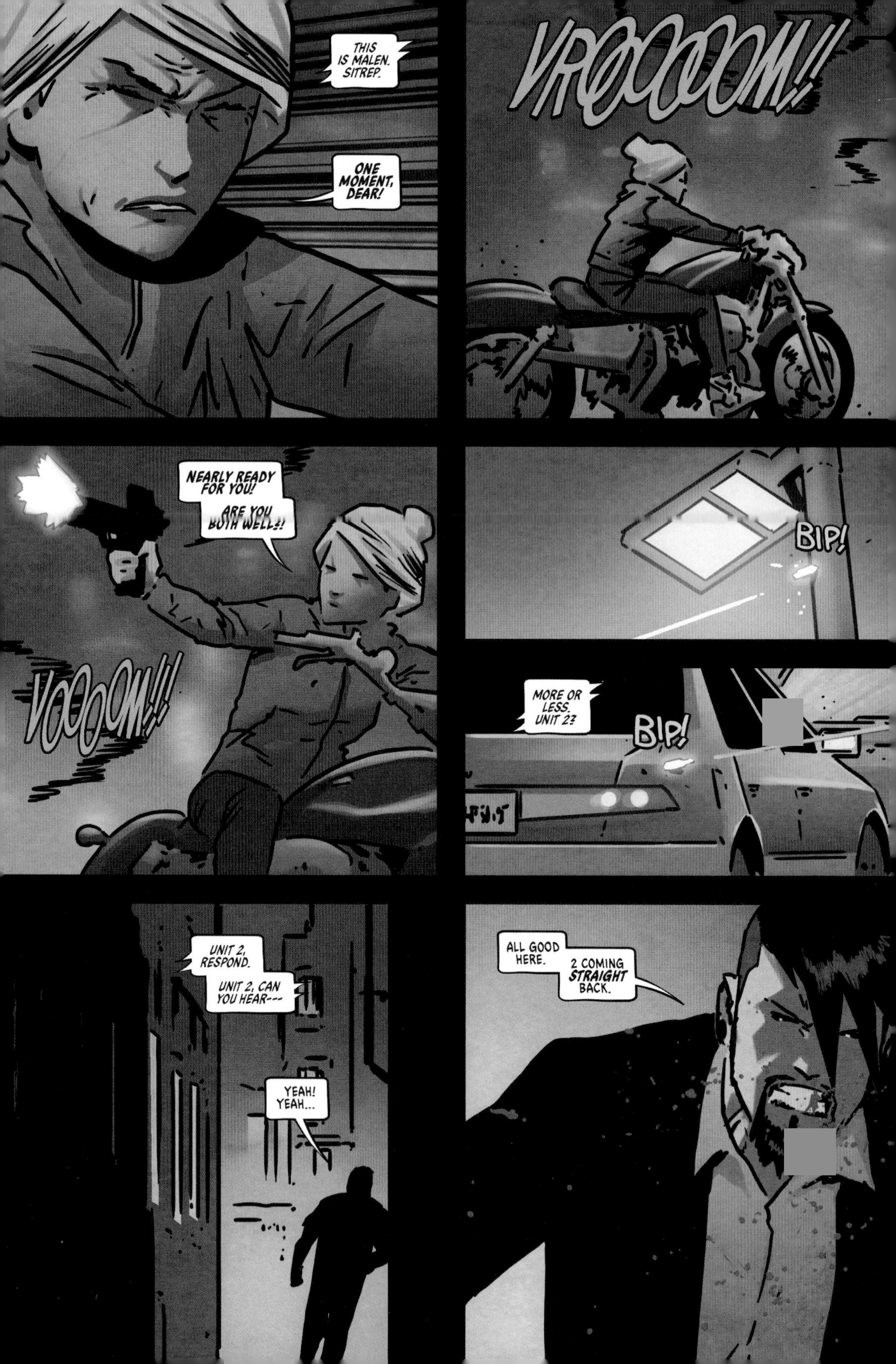
THIS IS MALEN. SITREP.
ONE MOMENT, DEAR!
VROOOOOM!!
NEARLY READY FOR YOU!
ARE YOU BOTH WELL?!
VOOOOM!!
BIP!
MORE OR LESS. UNIT 2?
BIP!
UNIT 2, RESPOND.
UNIT 2, CAN YOU HEAR---
YEAH! YEAH...
ALL GOOD HERE.
2 COMING STRAIGHT BACK.

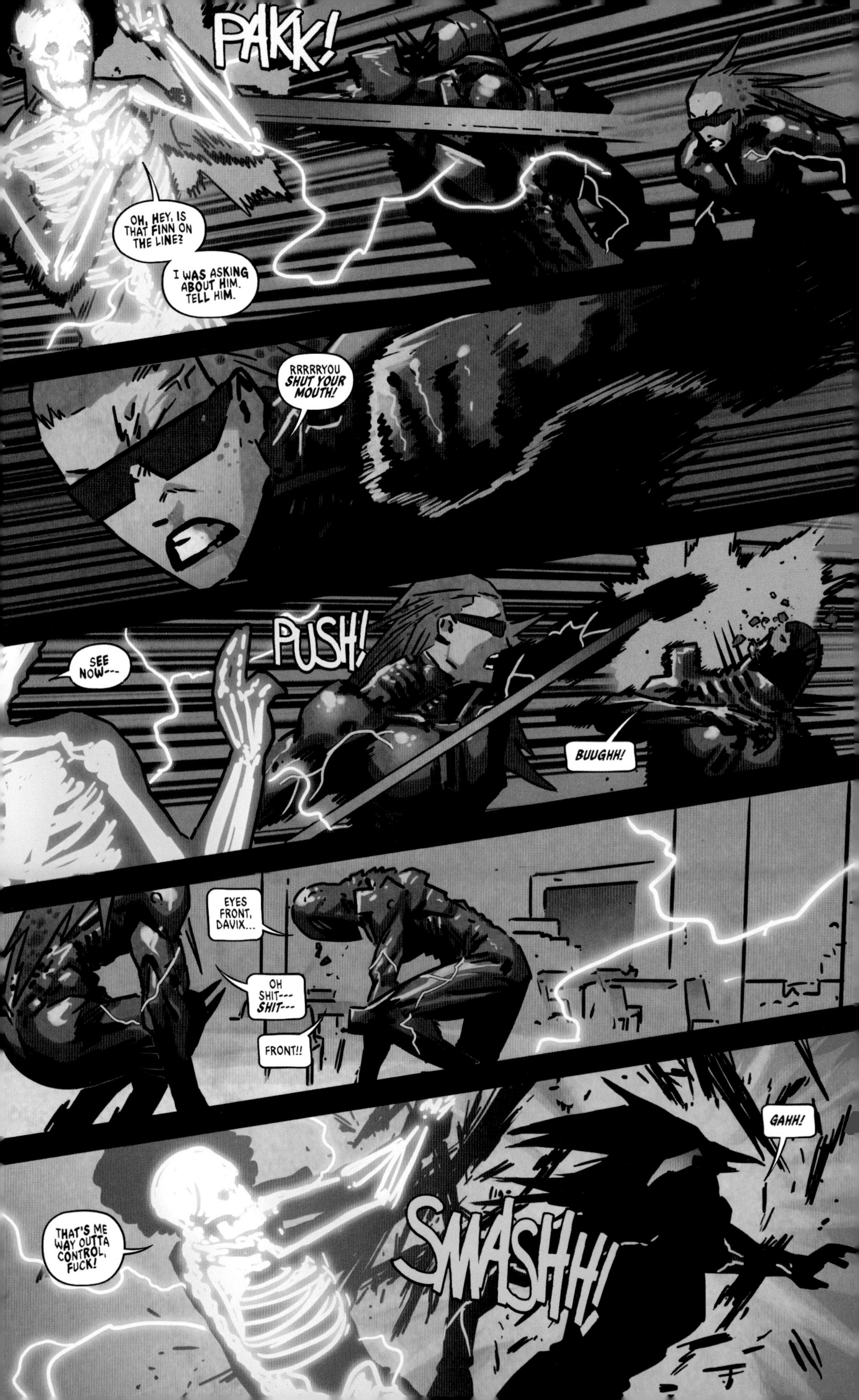
PAKK!
OH, HEY, IS THAT FINN ON THE LINE?
I WAS ASKING ABOUT HIM. TELL HIM.
RRRRRYOU SHUT YOUR MOUTH!
SEE NOW---
PUSH!
BUUGHH!
EYES FRONT, DAVIX...
OH SHIT--- SHIT---
FRONT!!
GAHH!
THAT'S ME WAY OUTTA CONTROL, FUCK!
SMASHH!

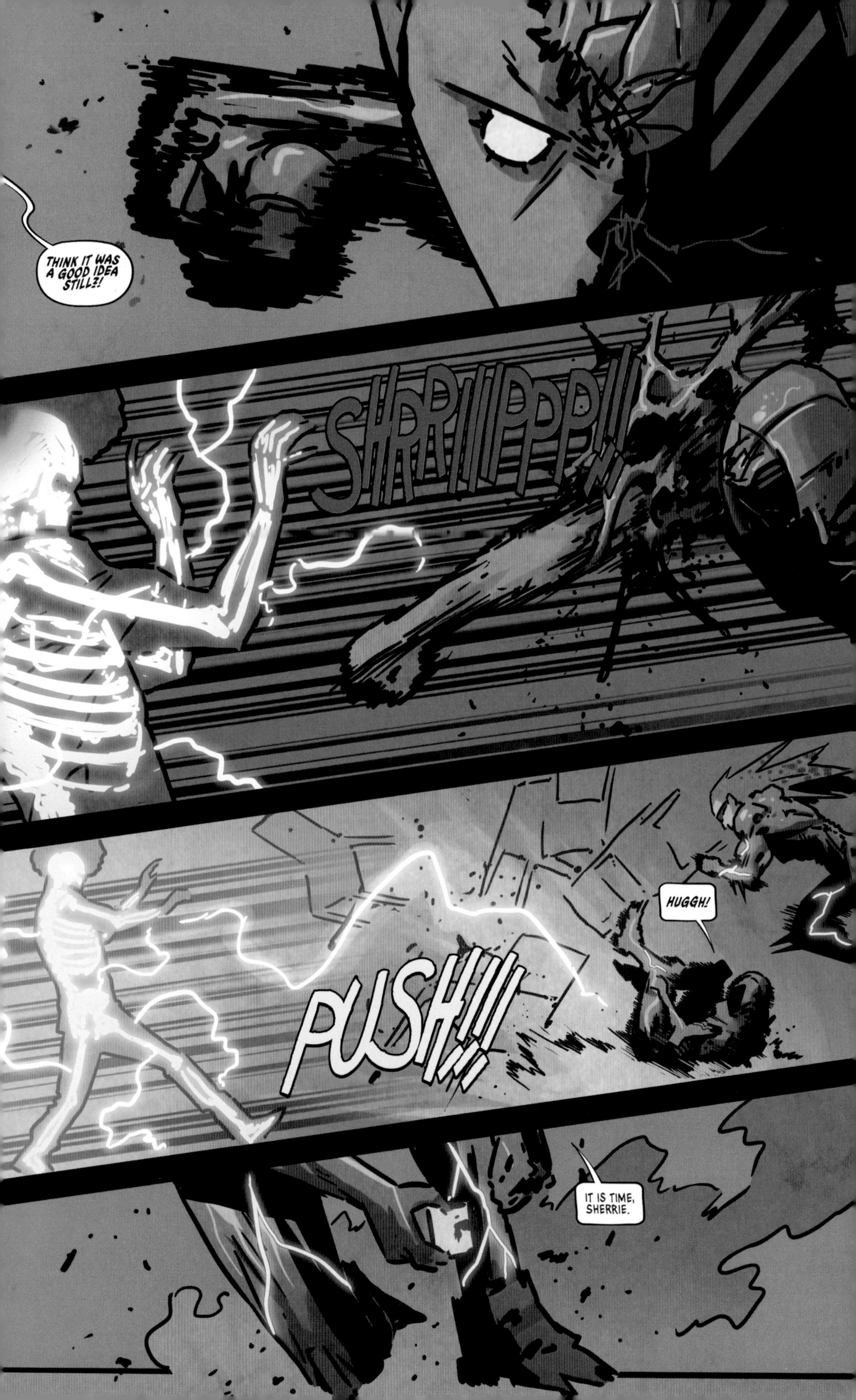
THINK IT WAS A GOOD IDEA STILL?!
SHRRIIIIPPPP!!!
HUGGH!
PUSH!!!
IT IS TIME, SHERRIE.

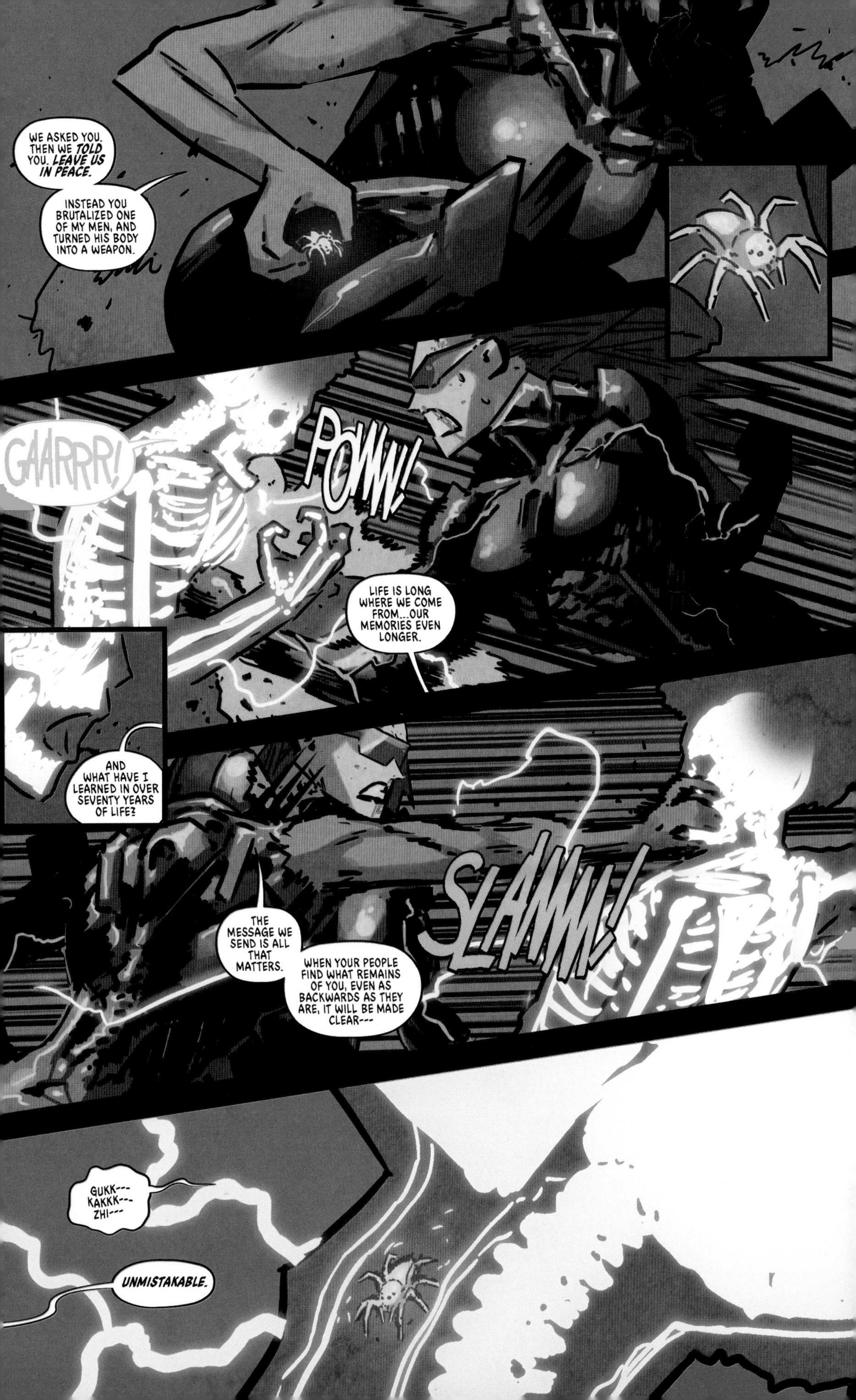
WE ASKED YOU. THEN WE *TOLD* YOU. ***LEAVE US IN PEACE.***
INSTEAD YOU BRUTALIZED ONE OF MY MEN, AND TURNED HIS BODY INTO A WEAPON.
GAARRR!
POWW!
LIFE IS LONG WHERE WE COME FROM...OUR MEMORIES EVEN LONGER.
AND WHAT HAVE I LEARNED IN OVER SEVENTY YEARS OF LIFE?
SLAMM!
THE MESSAGE WE SEND IS ALL THAT MATTERS.
WHEN YOUR PEOPLE FIND WHAT REMAINS OF YOU, EVEN AS BACKWARDS AS THEY ARE, IT WILL BE MADE CLEAR---
GUKK--- KAKKK--- ZHI---
UNMISTAKABLE.

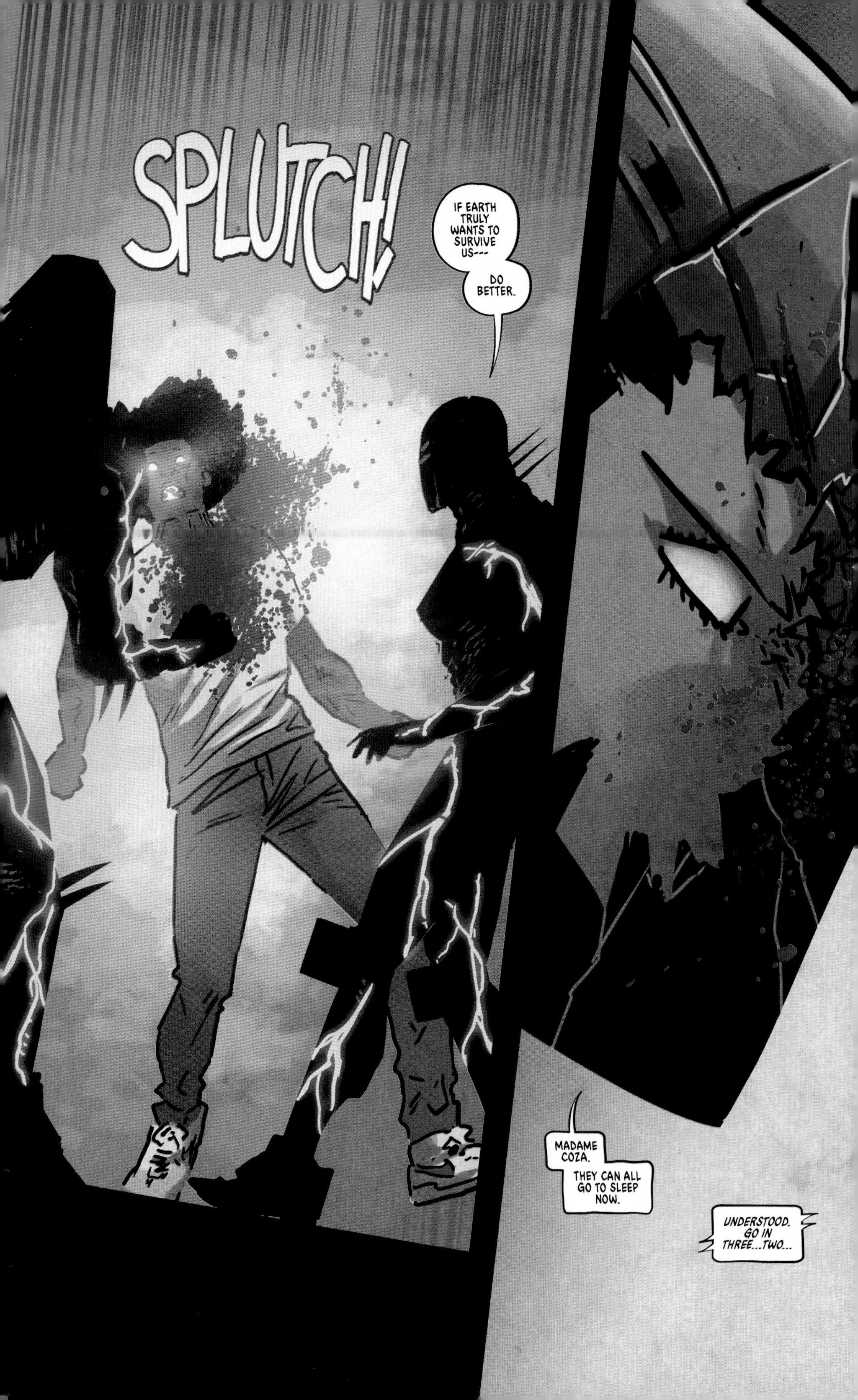
SPLUTCH!
IF EARTH TRULY WANTS TO SURVIVE US---
DO BETTER.
MADAME COZA.
THEY CAN ALL GO TO SLEEP NOW.
UNDERSTOOD. GO IN THREE...TWO...

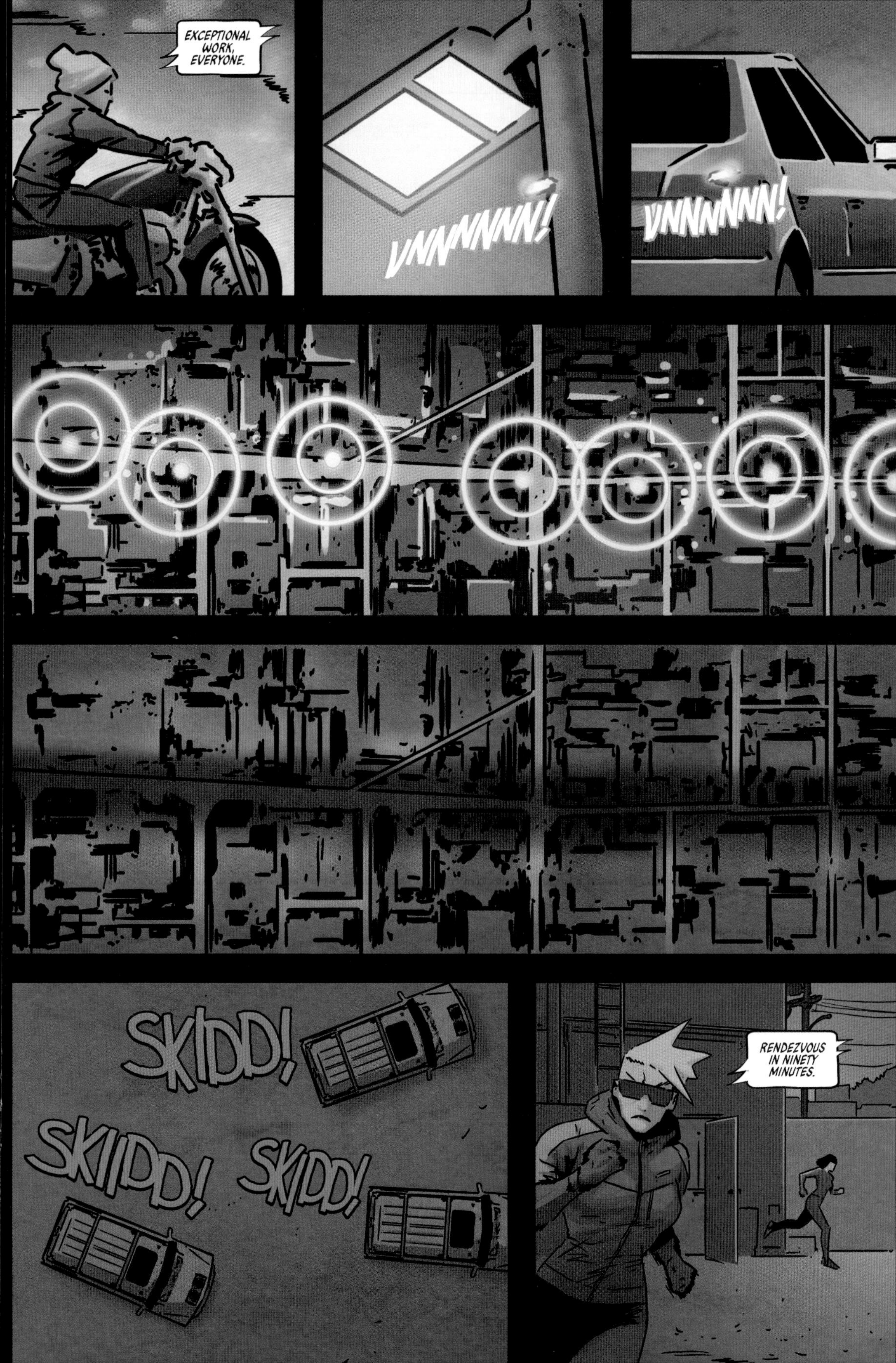
EXCEPTIONAL WORK, EVERYONE.
VNNNNNN!
VNNNNNN!
SKIDD!
SKIDD!
SKIDD!
RENDEZVOUS IN NINETY MINUTES.

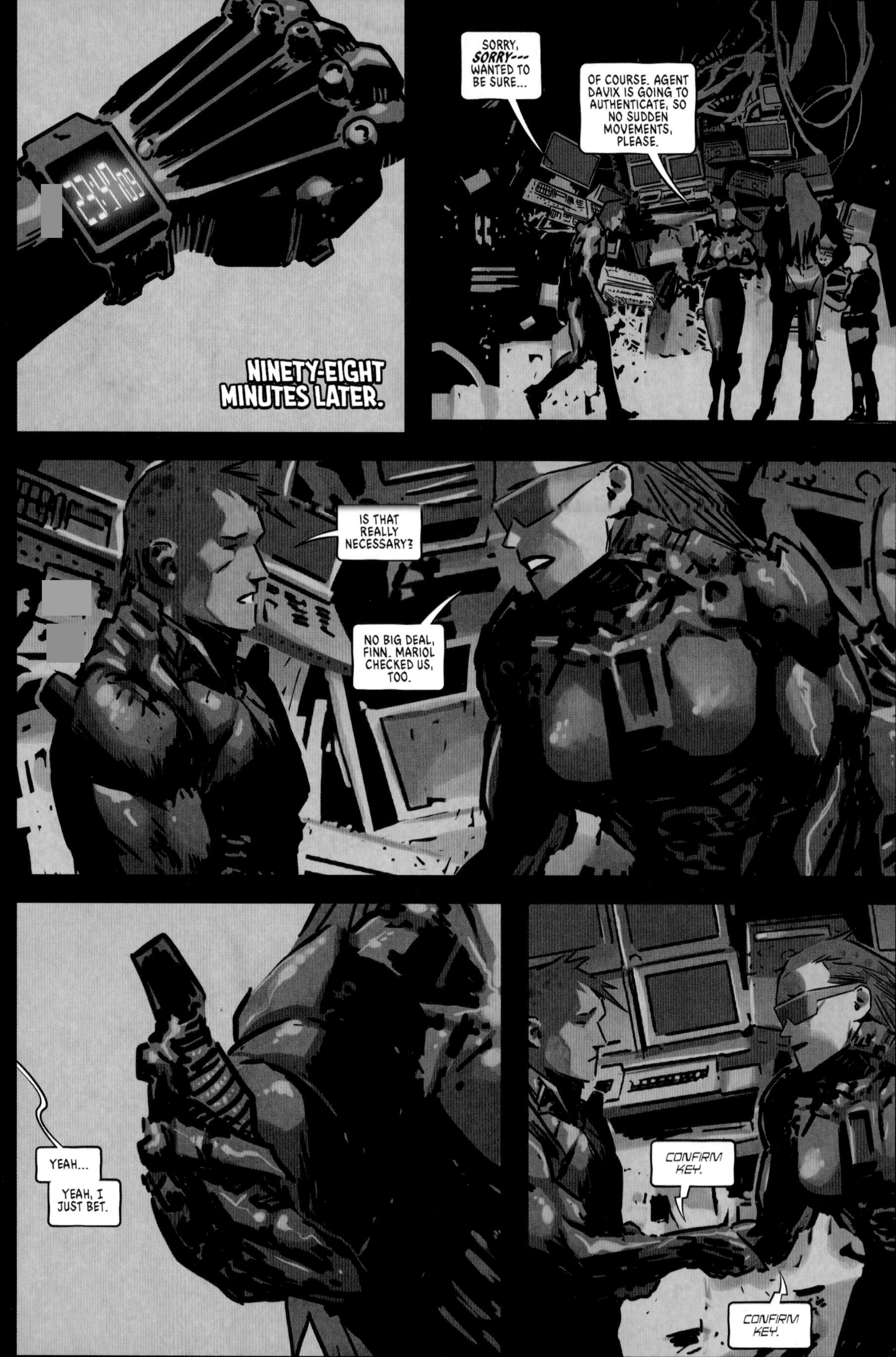
NINETY-EIGHT MINUTES LATER.
SORRY, SORRY--- WANTED TO BE SURE...
OF COURSE. AGENT DAVIX IS GOING TO AUTHENTICATE, SO NO SUDDEN MOVEMENTS, PLEASE.
IS THAT REALLY NECESSARY?
NO BIG DEAL, FINN. MARIOL CHECKED US, TOO.
YEAH...
YEAH, I JUST BET.
CONFIRM KEY.
CONFIRM KEY.

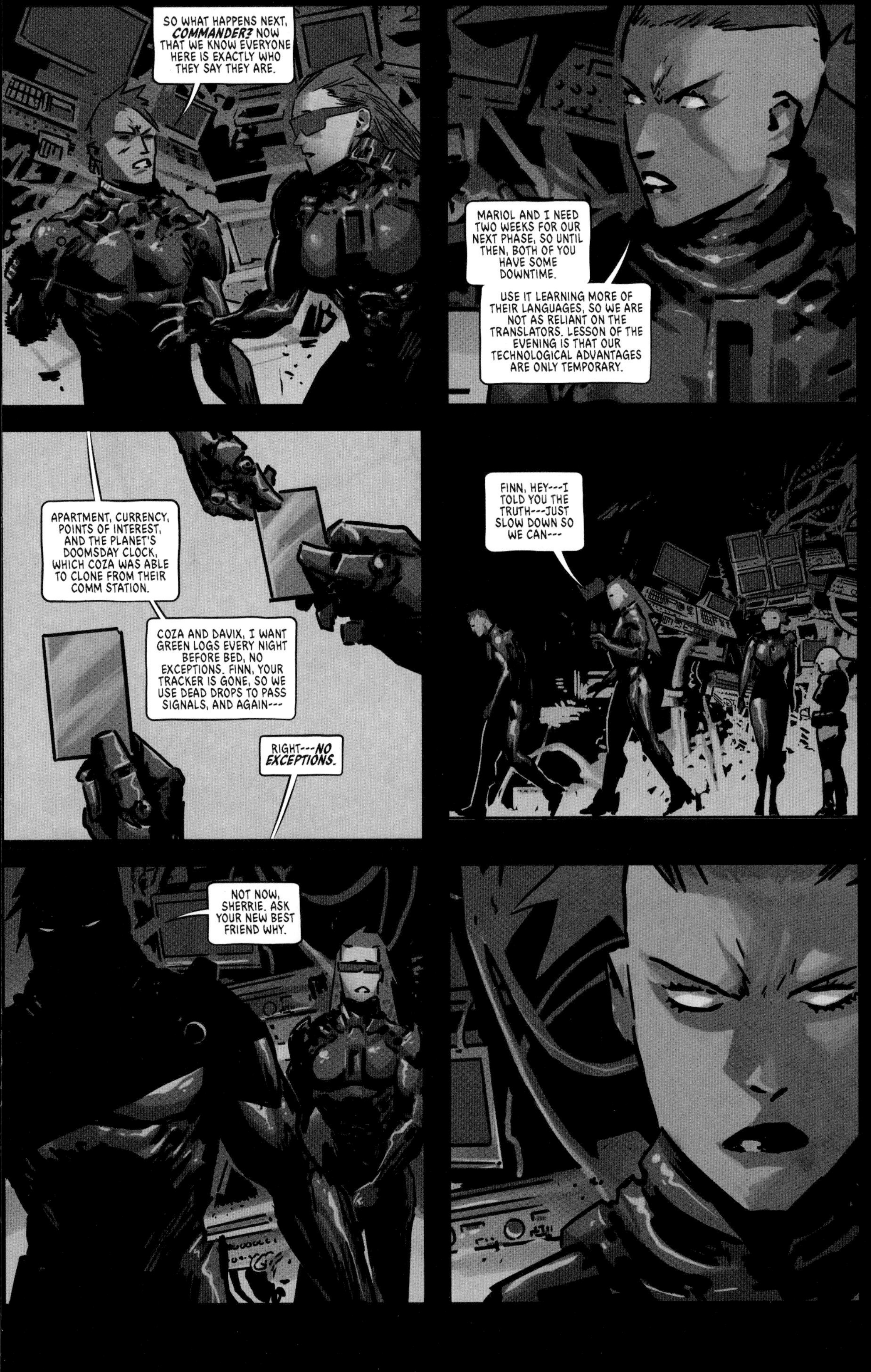

SO WHAT HAPPENS NEXT, COMMANDER? NOW THAT WE KNOW EVERYONE HERE IS EXACTLY WHO THEY SAY THEY ARE.
MARIOL AND I NEED TWO WEEKS FOR OUR NEXT PHASE, SO UNTIL THEN, BOTH OF YOU HAVE SOME DOWNTIME.
USE IT LEARNING MORE OF THEIR LANGUAGES, SO WE ARE NOT AS RELIANT ON THE TRANSLATORS. LESSON OF THE EVENING IS THAT OUR TECHNOLOGICAL ADVANTAGES ARE ONLY TEMPORARY.
APARTMENT, CURRENCY, POINTS OF INTEREST, AND THE PLANET'S DOOMSDAY CLOCK, WHICH COZA WAS ABLE TO CLONE FROM THEIR COMM STATION.
COZA AND DAVIX, I WANT GREEN LOGS EVERY NIGHT BEFORE BED, NO EXCEPTIONS. FINN, YOUR TRACKER IS GONE, SO WE USE DEAD DROPS TO PASS SIGNALS, AND AGAIN---
RIGHT---NO EXCEPTIONS.
FINN, HEY---I TOLD YOU THE TRUTH---JUST SLOW DOWN SO WE CAN---
NOT NOW, SHERRIE. ASK YOUR NEW BEST FRIEND WHY.

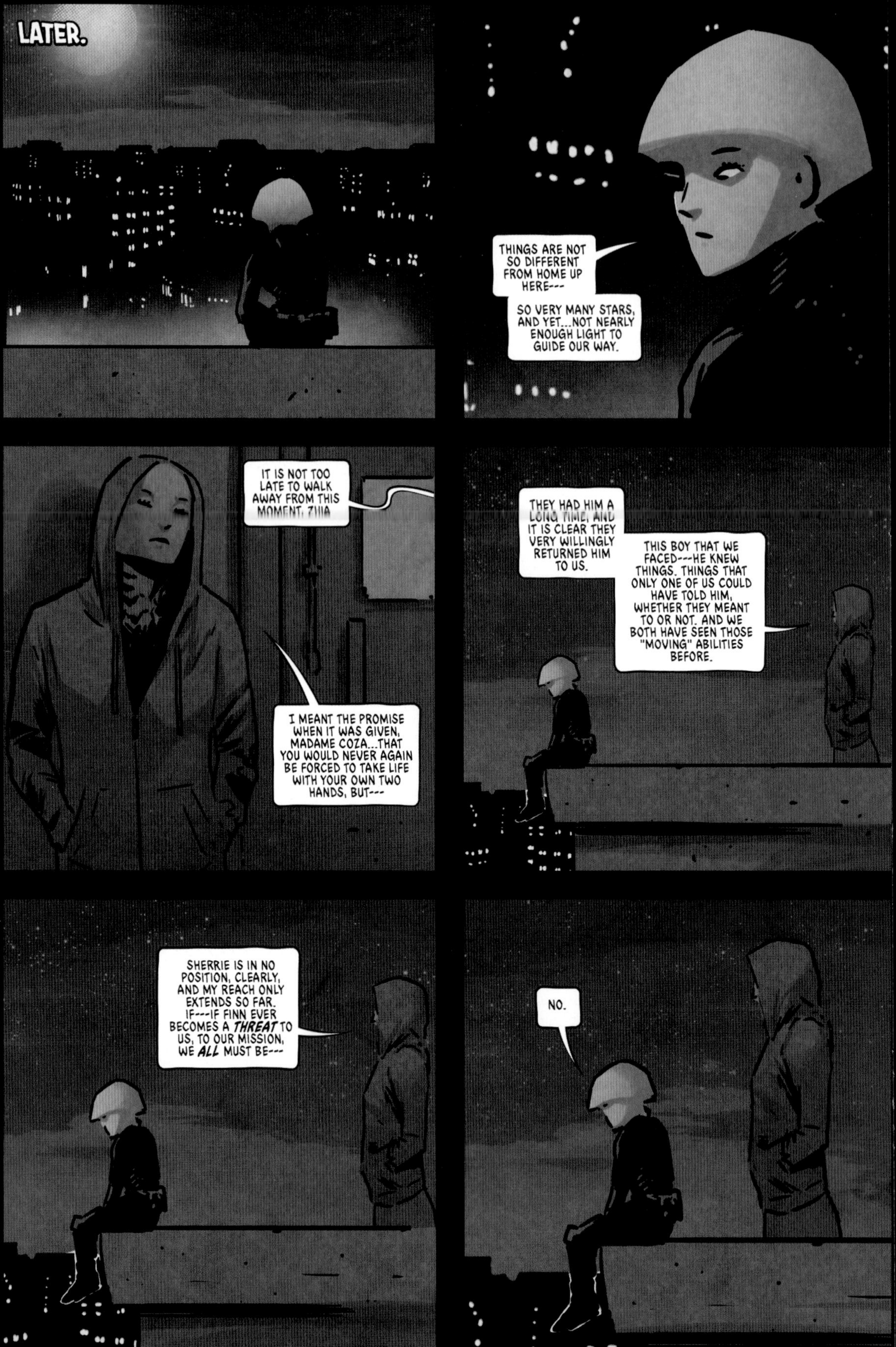
LATER.
THINGS ARE NOT SO DIFFERENT FROM HOME UP HERE---
SO VERY MANY STARS, AND YET...NOT NEARLY ENOUGH LIGHT TO GUIDE OUR WAY.
IT IS NOT TOO LATE TO WALK AWAY FROM THIS MOMENT, ZUA
I MEANT THE PROMISE WHEN IT WAS GIVEN, MADAME COZA...THAT YOU WOULD NEVER AGAIN BE FORCED TO TAKE LIFE WITH YOUR OWN TWO HANDS, BUT---
THEY HAD HIM A LONG TIME, AND IT IS CLEAR THEY VERY WILLINGLY RETURNED HIM TO US.
THIS BOY THAT WE FACED---HE KNEW THINGS. THINGS THAT ONLY ONE OF US COULD HAVE TOLD HIM, WHETHER THEY MEANT TO OR NOT. AND WE BOTH HAVE SEEN THOSE "MOVING" ABILITIES BEFORE.
SHERRIE IS IN NO POSITION, CLEARLY, AND MY REACH ONLY EXTENDS SO FAR. IF---IF FINN EVER BECOMES A THREAT TO US, TO OUR MISSION, WE ALL MUST BE---
NO.

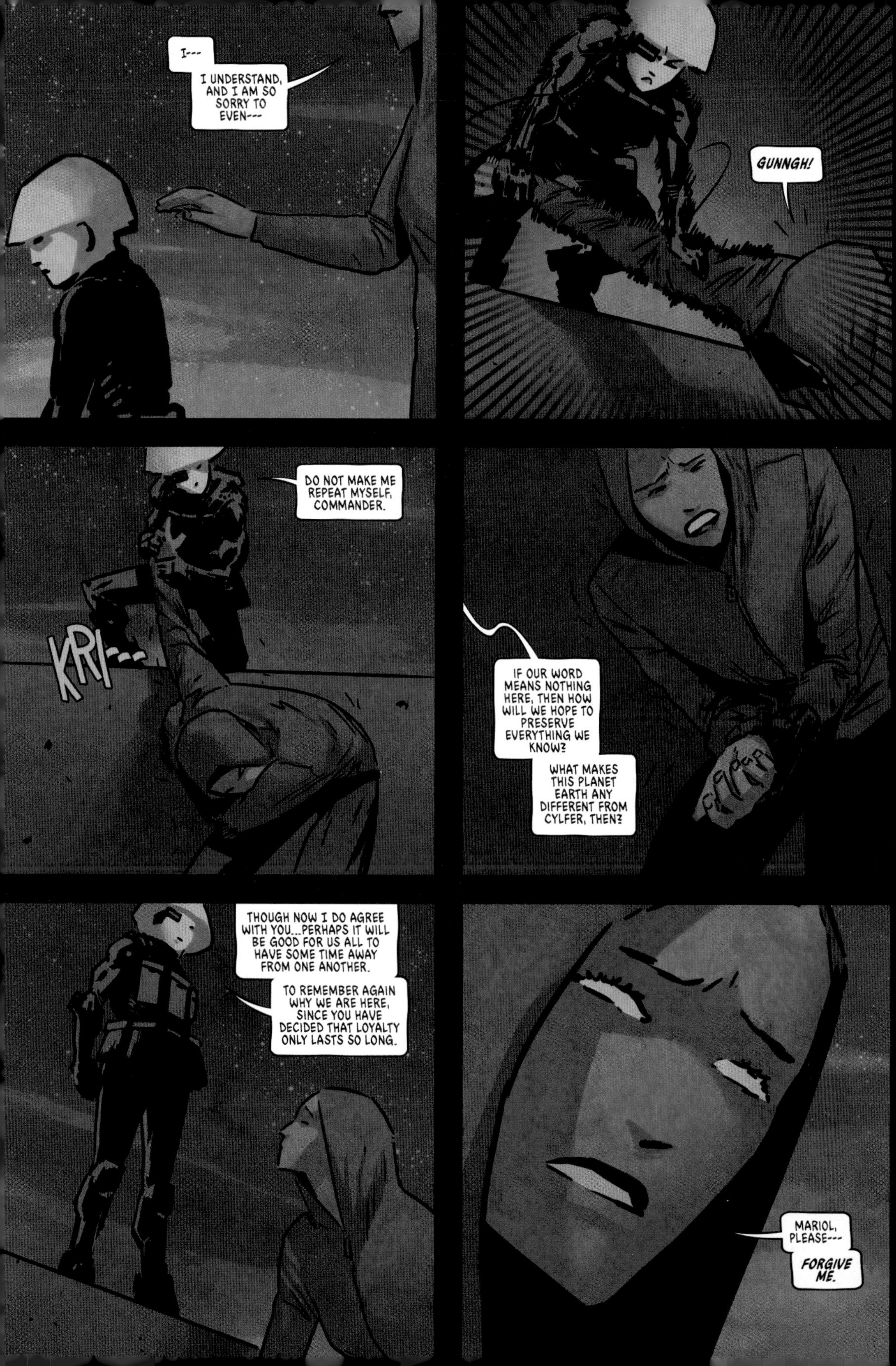
I---
I UNDERSTAND, AND I AM SO SORRY TO EVEN---
GUNNGH!
DO NOT MAKE ME REPEAT MYSELF, COMMANDER.
KRI---
IF OUR WORD MEANS NOTHING HERE, THEN HOW WILL WE HOPE TO PRESERVE EVERYTHING WE KNOW?
WHAT MAKES THIS PLANET EARTH ANY DIFFERENT FROM CYLFER, THEN?
THOUGH NOW I DO AGREE WITH YOU...PERHAPS IT WILL BE GOOD FOR US ALL TO HAVE SOME TIME AWAY FROM ONE ANOTHER.
TO REMEMBER AGAIN WHY WE ARE HERE, SINCE YOU HAVE DECIDED THAT LOYALTY ONLY LASTS SO LONG.
MARIOL, PLEASE---
FORGIVE ME.

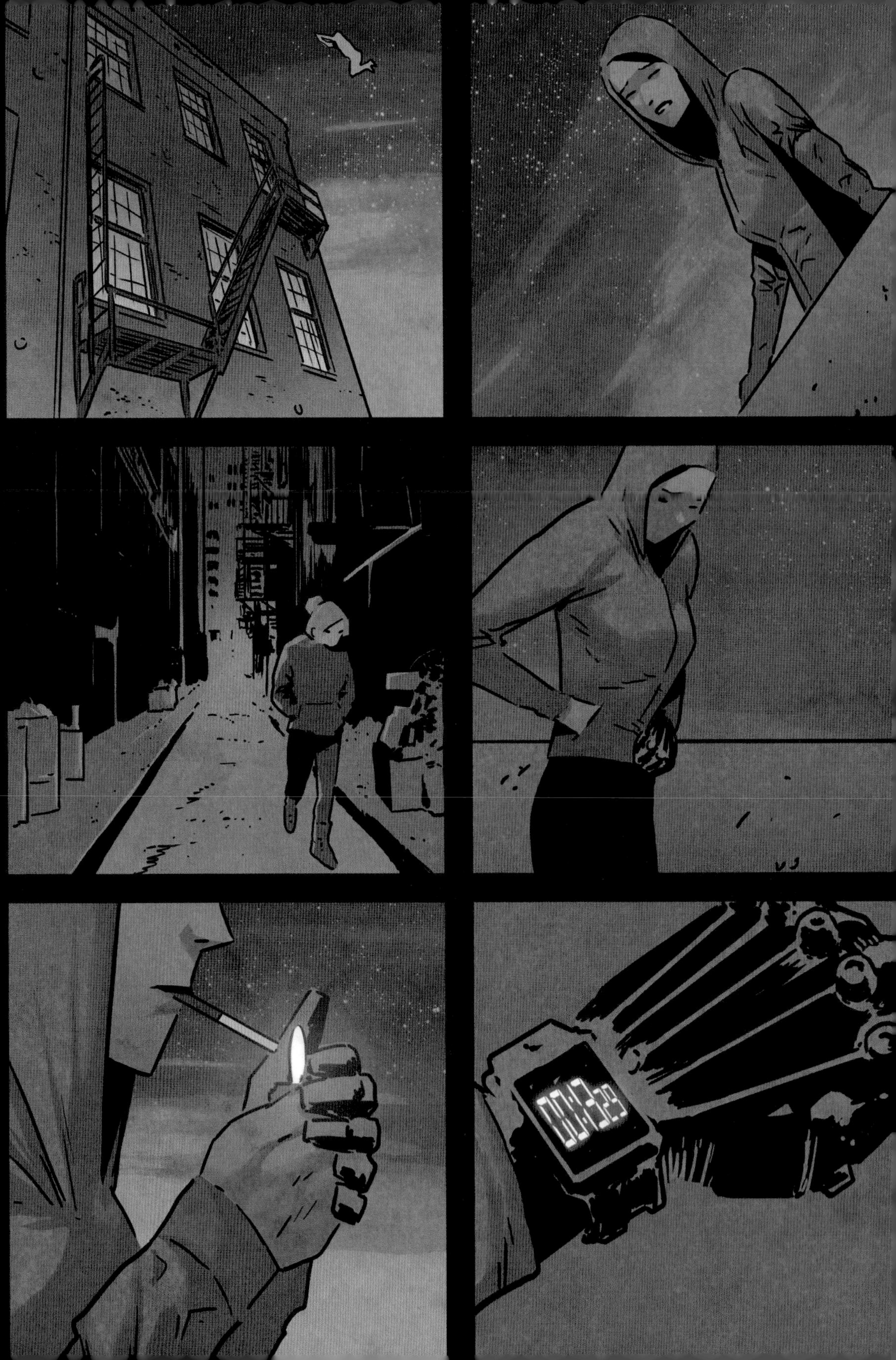

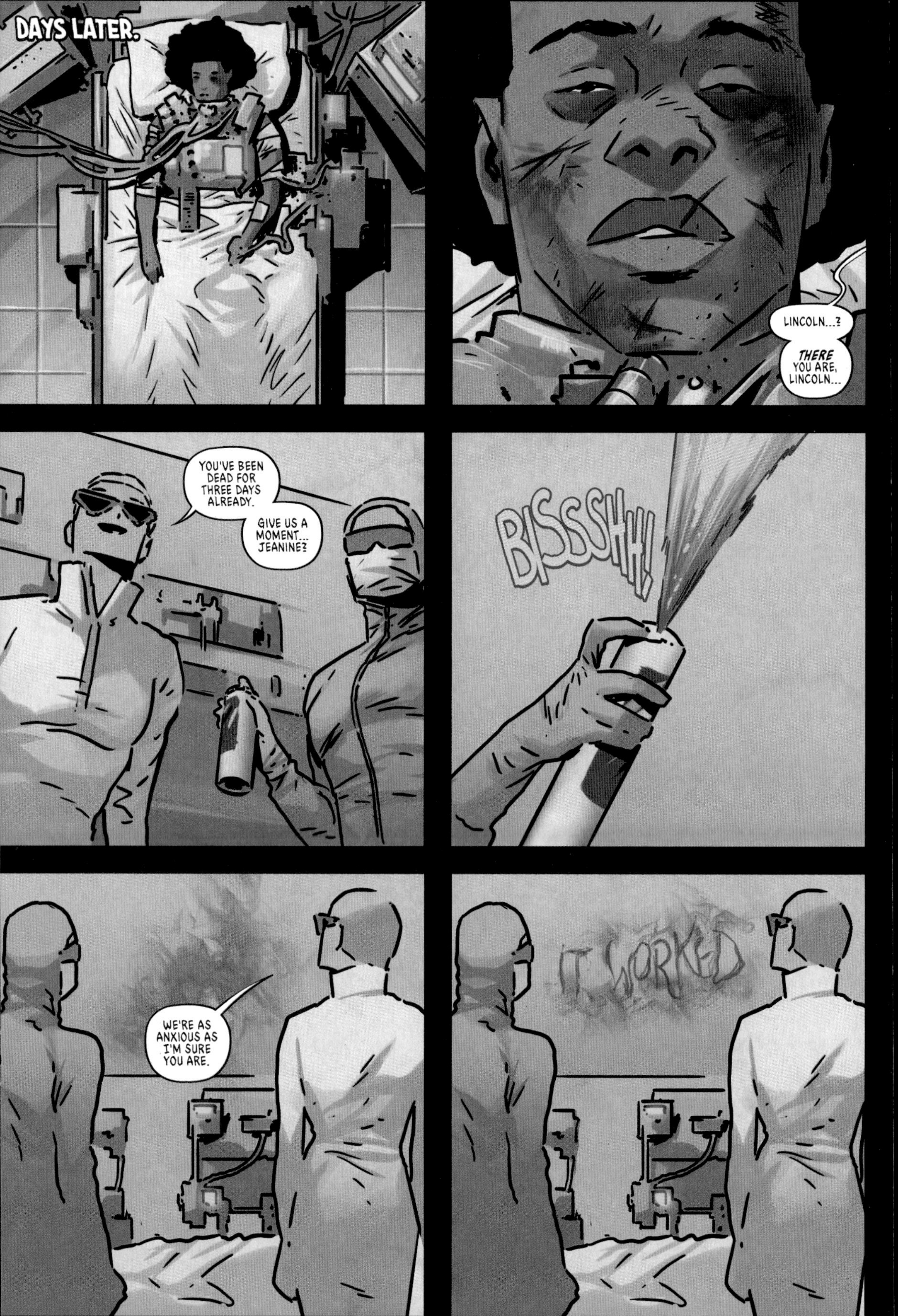
DAYS LATER.
LINCOLN...?
THERE YOU ARE, LINCOLN...
YOU'VE BEEN DEAD FOR THREE DAYS ALREADY.
GIVE US A MOMENT... JEANINE?
BISSSHH!
WE'RE AS ANXIOUS AS I'M SURE YOU ARE.
IT WORKED

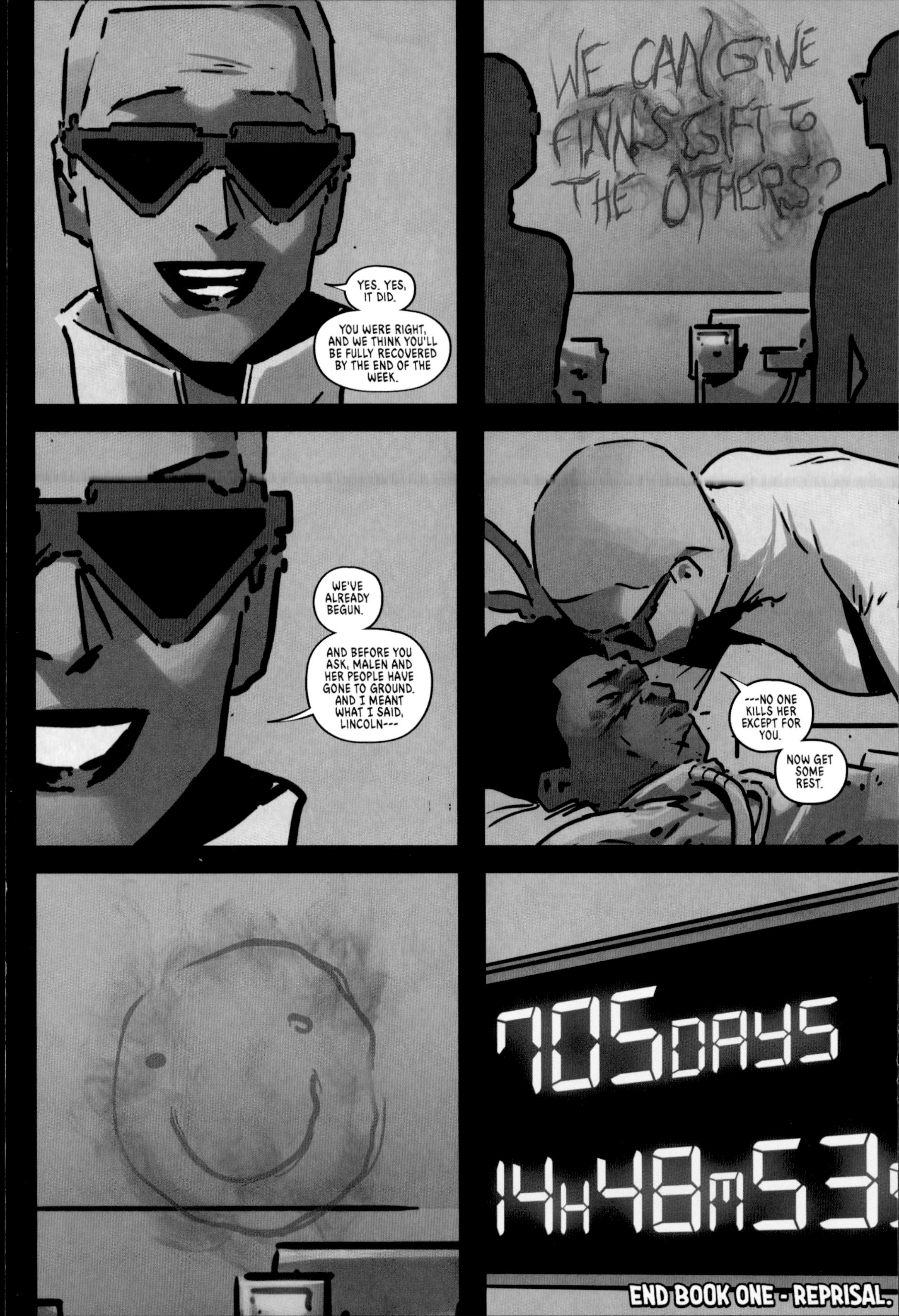
YES. YES, IT DID.
YOU WERE RIGHT, AND WE THINK YOU'LL BE FULLY RECOVERED BY THE END OF THE WEEK.
WE CAN GIVE FINN'S GIFT TO THE OTHERS?
WE'VE ALREADY BEGUN.
AND BEFORE YOU ASK, MALEN AND HER PEOPLE HAVE GONE TO GROUND. AND I MEANT WHAT I SAID, LINCOLN---
---NO ONE KILLS HER EXCEPT FOR YOU.
NOW GET SOME REST.
705 DAYS
14H 48M 53
END BOOK ONE - REPRISAL.

TO BE CONTINUED...

ENSURE

NOT A ONE

OF THEM

EVER AGAIN

LEAVES

THIS

PLANET.

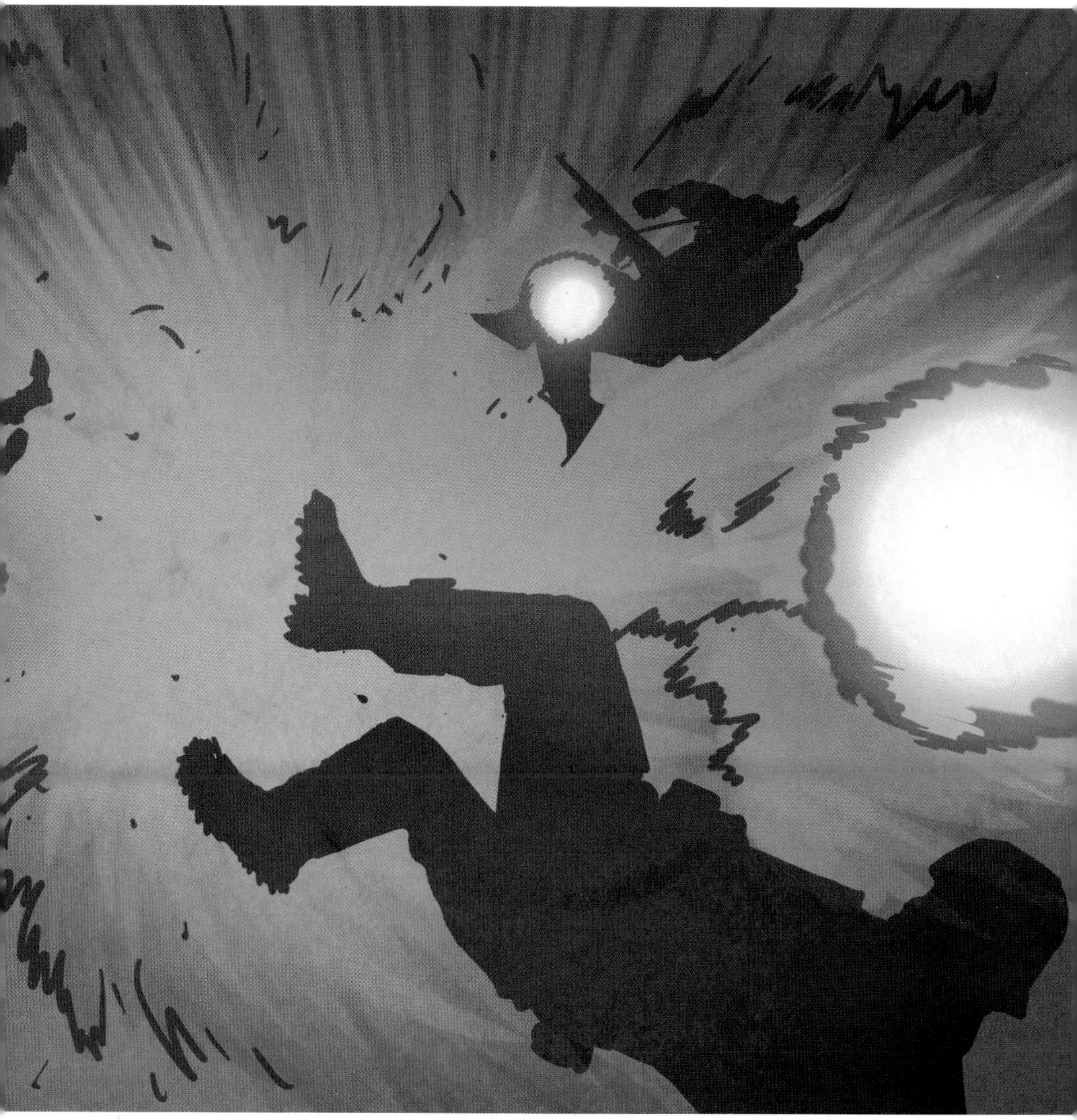

FOR MORE TALES FROM ROBERT KIRKMAN AND SKYBOUND

VOLUME 3: THIS LITTLE LIGHT
BY KIRKMAN & AZACETA
OUTCAST

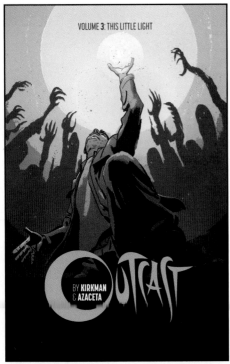

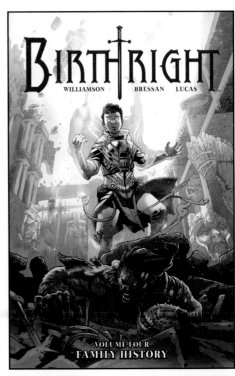

VOL. 1: A DARKNESS SURROUNDS HIM TP
ISBN: 978-1-63215-053-0
$9.99

VOL. 2: A VAST AND UNENDING RUIN TP
ISBN: 978-1-63215-448-4
$14.99

VOL. 3: THIS LITTLE LIGHT TP
ISBN: 978-1-63215-693-8
$14.99

BIRTHRIGHT
WILLIAMSON BRESSAN LUCAS
VOLUME FOUR
FAMILY HISTORY

VOL. 1: HOMECOMING TP
ISBN: 978-1-63215-231-2
$9.99

VOL. 2: CALL TO ADVENTURE TP
ISBN: 978-1-63215-446-0
$12.99

VOL. 3: ALLIES AND ENEMIES TP
ISBN: 978-1-63215-683-9
$12.99

VOL. 4: FAMILY HISTORY TP
ISBN: 978-1-63215-871-0
$12.99

CLONE
VOLUME 4
FOURTH GENERATION

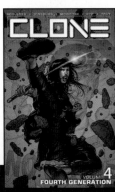

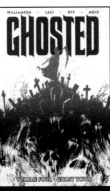

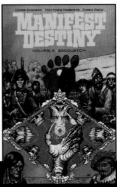

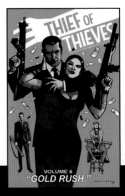

VOL. 1: FIRST GENERATION TP
ISBN: 978-1-60706-683-5
$12.99

VOL. 2: SECOND GENERATION TP
ISBN: 978-1-60706-830-3
$12.99

VOL. 3: THIRD GENERATION TP
ISBN: 978-1-60706-939-3
$12.99

VOL. 4: FOURTH GENERATION TP
ISBN: 978-1-63215-036-3
$12.99

GHOSTED
VOLUME FOUR • GHOST TOWN

VOL. 1: HAUNTED HEIST TP
ISBN: 978-1-60706-836-5
$9.99

VOL. 2: BOOKS OF THE DEAD TP
ISBN: 978-1-63215-046-2
$12.99

VOL. 3: DEATH WISH TP
ISBN: 978-1-63215-051-6
$12.99

VOL. 4: GHOST TOWN TP
ISBN: 978-1-63215-317-3
$12.99

MANIFEST DESTINY
VOLUME 4 SASQUATCH

VOL. 1: FLORA & FAUNA TP
ISBN: 978-1-60706-982-9
$9.99

VOL. 2: AMPHIBIA & INSECTA TP
ISBN: 978-1-63215-052-3
$14.99

VOL. 3: CHIROPTERA & CARNIFORMAVES TP
ISBN: 978-1-63215-397-5
$14.99

VOL. 4: SASQUATCH TP
ISBN: 978-1-63215-890-1
$14.99

THIEF OF THIEVES
VOLUME 6
"GOLD RUSH."

VOL. 1: "I QUIT."
ISBN: 978-1-60706-592-0
$14.99

VOL. 2: "HELP ME."
ISBN: 978-1-60706-676-7
$14.99

VOL. 3: "VENICE."
ISBN: 978-1-60706-844-0
$14.99

VOL. 4: "THE HIT LIST."
ISBN: 978-1-63215-037-0
$14.99

VOL. 5: "TAKE ME."
ISBN: 978-1-63215-401-9
$14.99

VOL. 6: "GOLD RUSH."
ISBN: 978-1-53430-037-8
$14.99